Shan Hai Jing

The Book of Mountains and Seas

Book One - Shan Jing

山經

Book of Mountains

Translated with Notes by

Eric Serejski

Innovations and Information, Inc. Frederick, MD

The information in this book is given in good faith. However, the translators and the publishers cannot be held responsible for any error or omission. Nor can they be held in any way responsible for treatment given on the basis of information contained in this book. The publishers make this information available to English language readers for scholarly and research purposes only.

The publishers do not advocate nor endorse self-medication by laypersons. Chinese medicine is a professional medicine. Laypersons interested in availing themselves of the treatments described in this book should seek out a qualified professional practitioner of Chinese medicine.

http://www.iandi.cc

ISBN 978-0-9797824-0-4

"Thirty years ago, before I meditated, I saw mountains as mountains and water as water. When I arrived at a more intimate knowledge, I came to the point where I saw that mountains are not mountains, and waters are not waters. But now, having seen and attained enlightenment in a restful place, "mountains are truly mountains and water is truly water." Qingyuan Weixin 青原惟信. Xu Chuandeng lu 續傳燈錄 (*Continued records of lamp transmissions*).

Table of Contents

Introduction vii

1. 南山經 – Book of the Southern Mountains 9
   Mountain Range 1 11
   Mountain Range 2 15
   Mountain Range 3 19

2. 西山經 – Book of the Western Mountains 23
   Mountain Range 1 - Huá 華 25
   Mountain Range 2 31
   Mountain Range 3 35
   Mountain Range 4 43

3. 北山經 – Book of the Northern Mountains 49
   Mountain Range 1 51
   Mountain Range 2 58
   Mountain Range 3 62

4. 東山經 - Book of the Eastern Mountains 73
   Mountain Range 1 75
   Mountain Range 2 78
   Mountain Range 3 82
   Mountain Range 4 84

5. 中山經 - Book of the Central Mountains 87
   Mountain Range 1 - Bó 薄山 89
   Mountain Range 2 - Jǐ 煇山 93
   Mountain Range 3 - Bèi 賁山 95
   Mountain Range 4 - Lí 釐山 98
   Mountain Range 5 - Bó 薄山 101
   Mountain Range 6 - Gǎodǐ 縞羝山 105
   Mountain Range 7 - Kǔ 苦山 109
   Mountain Range 8 - Jīng 荊山 115
   Mountain Range 9 - Mín 岷山 120
   Mountain Range 10 - Shǒuyáng 首陽之山 125
   Mountain Range 11 - Jīng 荊 127
   Mountain Range 12 - Dòngtíng 洞庭山 137

General Summary 141
Annexes 145
   Deities 147
   Disease and Remedies 153
   Fauna 159
   Flora 188
   Minerals 208
   Geography 216
   The Problem of Distances 250
   References 252

Introduction

The *Shan hai jing* or "Book of Mountains and Seas" is probably one of the most ancient if not the most ancient book of all geographies of the world. The *Shan hai jing* seems to be as ancient as the Zhōu Dynasty 周朝 (1134 BC to 256 BC) and probably precedes it. It is suggested as a descriptive relationship of maps carved on nine vases belonging to Yǔ the Great 大禹 (2224 B.C.). Yǔ the Great had them manufactured after completion of the works allowing the drainage of the waters from the Flood that occurred at the time of the reign of Emperor Shùn 舜 (2278 B.C.).

The title of the *Shan hai jing* first appeared in the *Shǐ jì* 史記 (Records of the Historian, 123: 3179) of Sī Mǎqiān 司馬遷 (145- 86 BC).

The *Shan hai jing* is structured into eighteen fascicles (*juǎn* 卷) and has remained generally unaltered since the Yuan Dynasty 元朝 (1271–1368). The only commentary to be compiled before the Ming Dynasty 明朝 (1368–1644) was that of Guō Pú 郭璞 (276-324) which is considered to be the standard one.

The eighteen chapters of the *Shan hai jing* may be divided into five groups:

1. Chapters 1-5: "*Wǔ cáng shān jīng*" 五臧山經 - Five treasures: The classic of mountains later referred to by its abbreviated title, Shān jīng (山經) or "The Classic of the Mountains."
2. Chapters 6-9: "*Hǎi wài jīng*" 海外經 - Classic of regions beyond the seas.
3. Chapters 10-13: "*Hǎi nèi jīng*" 海內經 - Classic of regions within the seas.
4. Chapters 14-17: "*Dà huāng jīng*" 大荒經 - Classic of great wilderness.
5. Chapter 18: "*Hǎi wài jīng*" 海內經 - Classic of regions within the seas.

Chapters 1 through 5 of the *Shan hai jing* tell of the sacred mountains of the central region and the surrounding regions in the four cardinal points (south, west, north, and east), Chapters 6 through 9 describe foreign peoples and lands in the regions beyond the seas (to the south, west, north, and east). Chapters 10 through 13 deal with foreign peoples and places to the cardinal points beyond the central lands. Chapters 14 through 17 depict those at the edge of ancient Chinese civilization. Finally, Chapter 18 consists of one essay which coordinates and integrates the preceding four divisions and their respective topical elements into one interconnected conclusion.

Shan Hai Jing - Books of Mountains

This translation is that of the *Five Treasures*, or *Classic of the Mountains,* referred to in the text as SJ. The remaining chapters (6 to 18) are referred to globally as HJ (*Hǎi jīng*). The *Classic of the Mountains* alone contains a considerable amount of ethnographic data describing the social customs and rituals of the early Eastern Zhōu Dynasty and in particular those traditions of the state of Chu (楚). It refers to no less than 61 deities, 88 diseases, 307 animals and animal hybrids, 183 plants and plants hybrids, 82 minerals, and 846 geographical structures.

The entire work was presumably written as an explanation of a map which has long since been lost, describing the mountains, rivers, material culture, folk medicine, and other aspects. The annexes list and provide preliminary information on some of these. The purpose of this volume is to provide a core translation, among those already existing, that could be used in further study and evaluate the meaning of its content.

1. 南山經 – Book of the Southern Mountains

Mountain Range 1

1. Mount Què 鵲山

2. Mount Què 鵲山

The first mountain of the Book of Southern Mountains is called Què. Its head is the Zhāoyáo which overlooks the Western Lake. There are lots of laurel trees, and lots of gold and jade. There are plants there that look like Chinese chives[1] and have blue-green flowers. Their name is zhùyú. Their consumption stops hunger. There is also a tree there with dark veins and splendid flowers[2]. This tree looks like the paper mulberry tree. Its name is mígǔ.
Carrying it prevents getting lost[3]. There is an animal there that resembles a spider monkey with white ears. It can bend over and walk[4]. Its name is xīngxīng. Its consumption facilitates running.
The river Lìjī springs from this mount, goes west, and pours in the sea. It contains many plants called yùpèi. As pendant waist ornament, they protect from abdominal lumps.

3. Mount Tángtíng 堂庭山

Three hundred li[5] further east is found Mount Tángtíng. It harbors many yǎn trees, many white apes, water jade and yellow gold.[6]

---

[1] 韭 jiǔ. The *Erya* says: There are many of these plants on Mt Huò 霍山. The Huòshān is a high peak in the Hunan province, also called Heaven Pillar (天柱 Tiān zhù).

[2] 四照 sìzhào, the "four brilliances". In other words, they are shiny. Since the flowers of this tree are red, they glisten on the ground (Guopu). The expression sìzhào means to spread radiance in all directions.

[3] 不迷 bù mí. Lit. "not mistaken". This meaning is explained in the *Peiwen Yunfu* as "to loose one's tracks and being unable to orient oneself" (迷行失路，不知南北) and in Hexagram 62 of the *Yijing* 易经.

[4] 伏行人走. This expression suggests the quadrupedal or bipedal locomotion displayed by orangutans.

[5] A lǐ (里) is a unit of linear measurement equivalent to approximately one-third of an English mile.

[6] The *Shuowen* states: "There are metals of five colors: the yellow one (gold) is the superior one."

4. **Mount Yuányì** 猨翼山

Three hundred and eighty li further east is found Mount Yuányì. It harbors many rare animals. Its water also contains many rare fishes, lots of white jade, lots of venomous reptiles, lots of rare snakes and lots of rare trees. Its top cannot be reached.

5. **Mount Chǒuyáng** 杻阳山

Three-hundred sixty li further east is Mount Chǒuyáng. There is a lot of deep-colored gold in the south and lots of white metal in the north. There are animals there resembling horses. Their head is white, the pattern of their skin like that of a tiger, and their tail is scarlet. Their sound resembles human singing. Their name is lùshǔ. As pendant waist ornament, it is suitable for the posterity.
The river guài springs from this mount. It goes east and pours into the Xiànyì. It contains many xuánguī that resemble turtles but have the head of a bird and the tail of a snake. Their name is xuánguī. Their call is like the sound of wood breaking. As pendant waist ornament, they cure ear loss. They may also cure callus.

6. **Mount Dì** 柢山

Three-hundred li further east is Mount Dì, from which spring many waterways. This mountain has no vegetation. There are fishes there that look like a bull and live in the highlands. They have a serpent tail with wings. Their feathers are below their flanks.[7] Their call is that of the liúniú. Their name is lù. They die during the winter and are born in the summer. Its consumption prevents swellings.

7. **Mount Chányuán** 擅爰之山

Four hundred li further east is found Mount Chányuán. There is lots of water but no vegetation. Its top cannot be reached. There is an animal there that looks like the raccoon dog and has a mane. Its name is lèi. It is hermaphrodite. Its consumption cures jealousy.

8. **Mount Jī** 基山

Three hundred li further east is found Mount Jī. Its southern side has lots of jade and its northern side lots of extraordinary trees.[8] There, there is goat-

---

[7] 魼 qū is the original character but Guopu and Hao Yixing suggest its homophone 胠 qū (flank).
[8] This passage is mentioned in the *Taiping Yulan* section 5.

like animal having nine tails, four ears, and its eyes on the back. Its name is bóyí. As pendant waist ornament, it protects against fear.

There is also a bird on Mount Jī that resembles the rooster and has three heads, six eyes, six feet and three wings. Its name is chǎngfù. Its consumption decreases having to lie down.

9. Mount Qīngqiū 青丘山

Three hundred li further east is found Mount Qīngqiū. Its southern side has lots of jade and its northern side lots of ultramarine.

There is a beast there that looks like a fox with nine tails. It sounds like a young child. It can devour a man. Its consumption protects against evil energies.

There is a bird there that looks like a kind of turtledove that sounds like men calling. Its name is guànguàn. As pendant waist ornament, it protects against confusion. The river Yīngshuǐ originates from this mountain, flows southwards, and pours into the marsh Jíyì. This river contains lots of chìrú. They have the body of a fish and the face of a human. Their sounds resemble that of the mandarin duck.[9] Its consumption prevents scabies.

10. Mount Jīwěi 箕尾山

Three hundred fifty li further east is found Mount Jīwěi. Its extremity extends to the eastern sea. There are lots of sandstones. The river Fāng originates there, flows southwards, and pours into the river Yù. It contains lots of jade.

11. Summary and Rituals

In summery, the system of mount Què, from Zhāoyáo to Mount Jīwěi, presents a set of ten mountains spreading across two thousands nine hundred fifty lis.

Its divinities all have a bird body and a dragon head. The ceremonies conducted in their temples [consist of]: fur[10], one ritual jade zhāng[11] blade,

---

[9] 鴛鴦 yāngyuān. Symbol of affectionate couple and conjugal fidelity. It is said that the male never leave its female and that, if separated, they immediately die.

[10] 毛 máo. Hair. This word means hair, wool or feather. The choice of the sacrificial animal depends on the fur features (i.e. color). In these rituals, the animals consist of pig, chicken, cow, or sheep. In this context, it probably means that a specific color is chosen according to the ritual used.

[11] 璋 zhāng. This is probably the ritual jade blade. The red ones (赤璋) were used in the worship of the South. They had straight, toothed, sloped or scalloped cutting edges likely to butcher sacrificial animals. See also 壁 bì.

jade burial,[12] glutinous rice and raw unhusked rice for ritual porridge, one ritual bì[13] jade, rice paddy, and white coarse grass for the mats.

---

[12] 玉瘗 yùyí. This may suggest the annual earth sacrifice to the divinity.

[13] 壁 bì. Round flat piece of jade with a whole in the center. One of the six ritual jades (六礼) or six ceremonial jades (六瑞) described in the Zhōulǐ 周礼 (Rites of Zhou), chapter Offices of Spring.

Mountain Range 2

1. Mount Jǔ 柜山

The main mountain on Section Two of the Southern mounts is called Jǔ in the west. It is adjacent to Liúhuáng in the west, faces Zhūpí in the north and Chángyòu in the east.

The river Yīng originates there, flows southwest, and pours into the river Chì. It contains lots of white jade and lots of thin red sand. There is a beast there that looks like a piglet. This animal has cock spurs and a bark-like sound. Its name is lílì. Its apparition in a county is a sign of major public works.

There is a bird there that looks like the sparrow hawk, with human extremities and a quail-like sound.[14] Its name, deriving from its call, is zhū. Its apparition in a county is a sign of numerous administrative layoffs.

2. Mount Chángyòu 長右山

Four hundred fifty li south-east, is found Mount Chángyòu. It has no vegetation but lots of water. There is a beast there that looks like a spider monkey with four ears. Its name, deriving from its call, is Chángyòu. Its apparition in a county is a sign of floods.

3. Mount Yáoguāng 堯光之山

Three hundred forty li further east is found Mount Yáoguāng. Its northern slope produces numerous jade and its southern one numerous gold. There is a beast there that looks like a man with whiskers of pigs. It lives in caves and hibernates in winter. Its name is huáhuái. Its sound is like that of wood breaking. Its apparition in a county is a sign of major local disturbances.

4. Mount Yǔ 羽山

Three hundred fifty li further east is found Mount Yǔ. There are many rivers below and it rains frequently above. There is no vegetation. There are many venomous reptiles.

---

[14] 痹 here pronounced bēi. According to the *Erya*, it is the female quail.

5. Mount Qúfù 瞿父山

Three hundred seventy li further east is found Mount Qúfù. It has no vegetation but lots of gold and jade.

6. Mount Jùyú 句餘山

Four hundred li further east is found Mount Jùyú. It has no vegetation but lots of gold and jade.

7. Mount Fúyù 浮玉山

Five hundred li further east is found Mount Fúyù. It faces Jùqū in the north and Zhūpí in the east. There is a beast there that looks like a tiger and has an oxtail. It has a bark-like sound. Its name is zhì. It eats humans.
The river Tiáo springs from the northern side, flows north, and pours into the [lake] Jùqū. It has lots of Chinese herrings.

8. Mount Chéng 成山

Five hundred li further east is found Mount Chéng. It has four sides and three altars. Its top has lots of gold and jade. Its basis has lots of ultramarine.
The river zhuō springs from it, flows south[15] and pours into lake Hūsháo. It contains lots of yellow gold.

9. Mount Guìjì 會稽山

Five hundred li further east is found Mount Guìjì. It has four sides. Its top has lots of gold and jade; its basis, lots of banded-white red agates. The river Sháo spings from it, flows south, and pours into the Jué.

10. Mount Yí 夷山

Five hundred li further east is found Mount Yí. There is no vegetation but lots of sandstones.. The river Jué springs from it, flows south, and pours into the Lìètú.

---

[15] In one version of the Shanhai jing, it states "flows west."

11. Mount Púgōu 僕勾之山

Five hundred li further east is found Mount Púgōu. Its top has lots of gold and jade; its basis, lots of vegetation. It has no birds, no animals, and no water.

12. Mount Xiányīn 咸陰山

Five hundred li further east is found Mount Xiányīn. It has neither vegetation nor water.

13. Mount Xún 洵山

Four hundred li further east is found Mount Xún. In the north, there are lots of gold and in the south lots of jade. There is a beast there that looks like a goat, has no mouth and cannot be killed.[16] Its name is yánghuàn.
The river Xún springs from this mount, flows south, and pours into the marshes of È. It contains lots of purple snails.

14. Mount Hūshuò 虖勺之山

Four hundred li further east is found Mount Hūshuò. Its top has lots of catalpas and náns. Its basis has lots of thorn bushes and qǐ. The river Pāng springs from it, flows east, and pours into the sea.

15. Mount Qūwú 區吳之山

Five hundred li further east is found Mount Qūwú. There is no vegetation but lots of stones. The river Lù springs from it and pours into the river Pāng.

16. Mount Lùwú 鹿吳之山

Five hundred li further east is found Mount Lùwú Its top has no vegetation but lots of gold and stones.
The river Zégèng springs from it, flows south, and pours into the river Pāng. River Zégèng has lots of animal called gǔdiāo. They look like vultures and have a horn. They sound resembles that of babies. They eat humans.

17. Mount Qīwú 漆吳之山

Five hundred li east is found Mount Qīwú. There is no vegetation and not jade, but lots of bó stones. It is located on the eastern seashore, and looks

---

[16] Figure of speech alluding to the fact that it cannot die even if it does not eat.

at Mount Qiū. This mount alternates between being shiny or shady according to the steps of the sun.

18. Summary and Rituals

In summery, the second book of the Southern Mounts, from mount Jǔ to mount Qīwú includes a total of seventeen mountains spreading over 7200 lis. Their divinities all have a dragon body and a bird head. In their temple, animals are offered. One ritual bì jade is used and then buried. Glutinous rice is used as sacrificial rice.

Mountain Range 3

1. Mount Tiānyú 天虞之山

The main mount of the third section of the Book of the Southern Mountains is called Mt Tiānyú. Its basis has lots of water. It cannot be climbed.

2. Mount Dǎoguò 禱過之山

Five hundred li east is found Mount Dǎoguò. Its top has lots of gold and jade. Its basis has lots of rhinoceros, sì one-horned bovines and elephants. There is a bird there that resembles the night heron, has a white head, three legs, and a human face. Its name, derived from its call, is qúrú.
The river Yín springs from this mount, flows south, and pours into the sea. River Yín harbors tiger flood-dragons. They have a fish-like body and a snake-like tail. Their sounds resemble that of the mandarin duck. Its consumption prevents swellings and is acceptable for hemorrhoids.

3. Mount Dānxué 丹穴之山

Five hundred li further east is found Mount Dānxué. Its top has lots of gold and jade.
The river Dān springs from it, flows south, and pours into the Bóhǎi sea.
There is a bird there that resembles the chicken, has five variegated colors[17] and patterns. Its name is [phoenix] fènghuáng. The patterns on its head are called "virtue-dé", those of his wings "justice-yì", those of its back "ceremony-lǐ", those of its chest "benevolence-rén", and those of its belly "faith-xìn." When feeding, it sings and dances. Its apparition is a sign of peace everywhere under Heaven.[18]

4. Mount Fāshuǎng 發爽之山

Five hundred li further east is found Mount Fāshuǎng. It has no vegetation but lots of water and lots of white apes.
The river Fàn springs from it, flows south, and pours into the Bóhǎi sea.

---

[17] 五采 wǔcǎi. It is difficult to differentiate this term from 五彩 wǔcǎi, the five colors. See *Da Cidian*.
[18] See HJ 13.21, Mountains within the Seas, 鸞鳥鳳鳥.

5. Mount Máo 旄山

Four hundred li further east is found the tail of Mount Máo. In its south, there is a valley called Yùyí. It contains many strange birds. The wind kǎifēng comes from it.

6. Mount Fēi 非山

Four hundred li further east is found the head of Mount Fēi. Its top has lots of gold and jade but no water. Its basis has many Pallas pit vipers and insects.

7. Mount Yángjiā 陽夾之山

Five hundred li further east is found Mount Yángjiā. It has no vegetation but lots of water.

8. Mount Guànxiāng 灌湘之山

Five hundred li further east is found Mount Guànxiāng. Its top has many trees but no grass. It harbors many remarkable birds but no beasts.

9. Mount Jī 雞山

Five hundred li further east is found Mount Jī. Its top has lots of gold and its basis lots of red ochre.
The river Hēi springs from it, and pours in the south into the sea. This river has lots of anchovy fishes. They resemble Crucian carps and have pig hair.[19] They sound like a piglet. Their apparition is a sign of general draught.

10. Mount Lìngqiū 令丘之山

Four hundred li further east is found Mount Lìngqiū. There is no vegetation but lots of fire. In the south there is a valley called Zhōnggǔ. The wind tiáofēng comes from it.
There is a bird there that resembles the owl, has a human face, four eyes, and ears. Its name, derived from its call, is Yú. Its apparition is a sign of general draught.

---

[19] The *Guangyun* and the *Taiping Yulan* 35 says pig tail 尾 instead (Guopu and Annotation).

11. Mount Lúnzhě 侖者之山

Three hundred seventy li further east is found Mount Lúnzhě. Its top has lots of gold and jade. Its basis has lots of ultramarine. There are trees there that resemble the paper mulberry tree,[20] and have red grain. Their sap is like lacquer, and they taste like sweet cakes.[21]. Its consumption soothes hunger and is not bad for fatigue from labors. Its name is báigāo. It is used to dye jade.

12. Mount Yúgǎo 禺稿之山

Five hundred eighty li further east is found Mount Yúgǎo. It harbors numerous legendary animals and numerous big snakes.

13. Mount Nányú 南禺之山

Five hundred eighty li further east is found Mount Nányú. Its top has lots of gold and jade. Its basis has lots of water. There are grottos there where water flows out and immediately back in. In summertime, waters flow out; in wintertime they are obstructed.
The river Zuǒ springs from it, flows south-east, and pours into the sea.
There are some fènghuáng phoenix and some phoenix-like birds yuānchú.

14. Summary and Rituals

In summary, from mount Tiānyú, head of the third section of the Southern mountains, to mount Nányú, there is a total of 14 mountains, spreading over 6530 lis.
The divinities of these mountains have a dragon body and a human face. All their temples use a white dog for worship.[22] The food offered to them is glutinous rice.

The records[23] of the Southern mountains describe altogether forty mountains, large and small, covering 16,380 lis.

---

[20] 穀 gǔ. Millet. It should be 榖 gǔ, paper mulberry tree, according to the annotation.

[21] 飴 yí. Sweet cake

[22] Guopu: "祈 qí, a prayer for request." 祈 qí suggests the notion of pouring blood in a sacrificial utensil in order to use the energy contained within it.

[23] 志 zhì. Annals, records; weigh, measure. Because of this term, which appears posterior to the text, it is suggested that this sentence is actually not part of the original text. See HJ 1 [notes].

2. 西山經 – Book of the Western Mountains

The nine celestial virtues. 天之九德 huàiyú.

(1) 宽仁而又严肃，Benevolent and yet solemn,
(2) 柔和而又坚定，Yielding and yet firm,
(3) 谨厚而又干练，Sincerely magnanimous and yet capable and experienced,
(4) 有为而又谦敬，Promising and yet humbly respectful,
(5) 和顺而又果敢，Amiable and soothing and yet courageous and resolute,
(6) 正直而又温良，Upright and yet gentle and kindheartedness,
(7) 简率而又清廉，Simple to lead and yet honest and upright,
(8) 刚劲而又踏实，Vigorous and yet dependable,
(9) 强直而又行义。Unyielding and yet upholding justice.

Answer of Gao Yao 皋陶 to Yu 禹 (Shang Shu. Yu Shu - Counsels of Gao Yao)

Mountain Range 1 - Huá 華

1. Mount Qiánlái 錢來之山

The first mountain of the mountains Huá of the Book of the Western Mountains is called Mt Qiánlái. Its top has lots of pine trees and its base lots of wash stones.

There is an animal there that looks like a goat and has a horse tail. Its name is xián goat. Its suet treats chap skin of the xī kind.

2. Mount Sōngguǒ 松果之山

Forty-five li west is found Mount Sōngguǒ. The river Huò springs from it, flows north, and pours into the Wèi. This river contains lots of copper. There is a bird there called tōngqú. It looks like a mountain pheasant, has a black body and red legs. It treats chap skin of the bào kind.

3. Mount Tàihuá 太華之山

Sixty li further west is found Mount Tàihuá. It is sharply shaped and has four slopes. It is five thousand rèn tall and ten lǐ wide.[24] It has no birds or animals. [However] there are snakes there. Their name is féiyí. They have six feet and four wings. Their apparition is a sign of great drought everywhere.

4. Mount Xiǎohuá 小華之山

Eighty li further west is found Mount Xiǎohuá. Its trees include many thorn bushes and wolfberry shrubs. Its beasts include many heavy cows. The northern side of this mountain includes lots of chime stones, and its southern side lots of agate. Its birds include lots of red pheasants. They have the property to protect against fire. Its herbs include aromatic lichens that resemble the fairy fern and grow on stones or anchor to trees. The consumption of these plants heals heart pain.

5. Mount Fúyú 符禺之山

Eighty li further west is found Mount Fúyú. Its southern side has lots of copper; its northern one lots of iron.

---

[24] 仞 rèn. A measure of eight feet, or 40,000 Chinese feet.

On the top, there are trees called wénjīng.[25] Their fruits resemble those of the jujube tree. They are used for ear loss. There are lots of tufts of plants that resemble winter sunflower plants. Their flowers are red; their fruits are yellow and resemble the tongue of a newborn. Their consumption prevents indecisiveness.

The river Fúyú springs from this mountain, flows north, and pours into the Wèi. The animals of this mountain include the cōnglóng. It resembles goats and has red horse's mane. Its birds include many kingfisher-like birds with red beaks. Raising them protects against fire.

6. Mount Shícuì 石脆之山

Sixty li further west is found Mount Shícuì. Among its trees, there are lots of "cedar palm"-like trees. Among its grasses, there are lots of tufts of plants resembling Chinese chives, with white flowers and black seeds. Its consumption treats scabies.

On the southern slope, there are lots of yǔfú jade; on the northern slope, lots of copper.

The river Guàn springs from this mountain, flows north, and pours into river Yú. The flow of Guàn is ochre. Spreading [this liquid] on oxen and horses protect them from diseases.

7. Mount Yīng 英山

Seventy li further west is found Mount Yīng. Its top has lots of wild cherry trees. Its northern side abounds in iron and its southern side in deep-colored gold. The river Yú springs from it, flows north, and pours in the river Zhāo. This river has lots of fishes called bàng. They resemble soft-shelled turtles and bleat like goats.

Its southern side has lots of arrow-like bamboos and lots of heavy cows and xiányáng. There are birds on this mountain that are like quails and have a yellow body and a red beak. Their name is féiyí. Their consumption cures pestilence and may also kill worms.

8. Mount Zhú 竹山

Fifty-two li further west is found Mount Zhú. Its top has many tall qiáomù trees. Its northern side abounds in iron. There is a grass there called huángguàn. It resembles the tree of Heaven. Its leaves are like that of hemp. Its flowers are white and its fruits red-crimson. It is purple. Soaked in water, they cure itching and edema.

---

[25] 文莖 wénjīng Striated stem.

The river Zhú springs from it, flows north, and pours into the Wèi. On the northern side, there are lots of arrow bamboos and azure jade. The river Dān springs from there, flows southeast, and pours into the river Luò. Its bed abounds in water jade and in salamanders. It contains an animal that looks like a young pig. It has hair is white, long like ancient hair pins and has black extremities. Its name is háozhì.

9. Mount Fú 浮山

One hundred and twenty li further west is found Mount Fú. It has lots of pàn trees. Their leaves resemble those of the hedge thorn but without its affect[26]. Wood-living insects are there.

There is a grass there called xūn. It has hemp leaves, a squared stem, red flowers and black fruits. It smells like the stems and leaves of chuanxiong. As pendant waist ornament, it protects from pestilence.

10. Mount Yúcì 羭次之山

Seventy li further west is found Mount Yúcì. The river Qī strangely springs from it, flows north, and pours into river Wèi. Its top has lots of thorny oak shrubs. Its base has lots of arrow bamboos. Its northern side abounds in red copper and its southern one in yīngyuán jade.

There is an animal on this mountain that resembles a spider monkey and has long arms which are good for throwing. Its name is xiāo. There is a bird on this mountain that resembles the owl, has a human face and a single foot. Its name is tuóféi. It can be seen during winter and it hides during summer. As pendant waist ornament, it [its feathers] removes the fear of thunder.

11. Mount Shí 時山

One-hundred fifty li further west is found Mount Shí. There is no vegetation. The river Zhú springs from it, flows north, and pours into the Wèi. It has lots of water jade.

---

[26] 傷 shāng. Wound, injury. Guopu and Kean suggest that "without wounding" would mean without horns since the hedge could inflict wounds with its thorns. However, the hedge thorn has poisonous fruits and reactions to thorn pricks have been reported. It could be that the pàn tree is similar to the hedge thorn without its poisonous aspect.

12. Mount Nán 南山

One-hundred seventy li further west is found Mount Nán. Its top has lots of cinnabar. The river Dān springs from it, flows north, and pours into the Wèi. Its animals include lots of měngbào leopards, and its birds lots of cuckoos.

13. Mount Dàshí 時之山

One-hundred eighty li further west is found Mount Dàshí. Its top has lots of paper mulberry trees and oaks, its basis lots of wild cherry trees. In the north there are lots of silver and in the south lots of white jade. The river Qiàn rises there, flows north, and pours into the Wèi. The river Qīng also rises there, flows south, and pours into the river Hàn.

14. Mount Bōzhǒng 嶓冢之山

Three-hundred twenty li further west is found Mount Bōzhǒng. The river Hàn rises there, flows southeast, and pours into the Miǎn. The river Xiao originates there, flows north, and pours into the river Tāng.
Its top abounds in peach-branch bamboos. Animals include lots of xīsì one-horned bovines, common bears and brown bears. Birds include lots of white pheasants and red pheasants.
There is a grass there whose leaves are like that of the huì orchid. Its roots are like that of balloon flower. It has black flowers and no fruits. Its name is gǔróng. Its consumption causes infertility.

15. Mount Tiāndì 天帝之山

Three-hundred fifty li further west is found Mount Tiāndì. Its tip has lots of "cedar palm"-like trees and its basis lots of coarse grass and huì orchids. There is an animal there that resembles a dog and is called xībiān. Those covering themselves with its skin are protected against evil energies. There is a bird there that resembles the quail, has black patterns and red feathers on its neck. Its name is lì. Its consumption cures hemorrhoids.
There is a grass there whose shape resembles that of winter sunflower plants. It smells like míwú and is called dùhéng. It has the property to render horses tireless when running. Its consumption cures goiter.

16. Mount Gāotú 皋塗之山

Three-hundred eighty li further southwest is found Mount Gāotú. The river Sé springs from it, flows west, and pours into the river Zhūzī. The river Tú also springs from it, flows south, and pours into the river Jíhuò. The south abounds in cinnabar and the north in silver and yellow gold. The top has lots of laurel trees. There is also a white stone called yù. It is used to poison rats.

There is a plant there whose shape is that of the Chinese lovage. Its leaves are like that of the winter sunflower; they are red on the back. Its name is wútiáo. It is used to poison rats.

There is an animal there that resembles the deer, has a white tail, the [back] legs of a horse, the [front legs] of human, and four horns. Its name is juérú.

There is a bird there that resembles the sparrow hawk and has human feet. Its name is shùsī. Its consumption cures goiter.

17. Mount Huáng 黃山

One-hundred eighty li further west is found Mount Huáng. It has no vegetations except arrow bamboos.

The river Pàn springs from it, flows west, and pours into the river Chì. This river contains lots of jade.

There is an animal there that resembles the bull, is greenish and has wide eyes. Its name is mǐn.

There is also a bird there that resembles the owl, has green feather and a red beak. It has a human tongue and can speak. Its name is yīngmóu.

18. Mount Cuì 翠山

Two-hundred li further west is found Mount Cuì. Its top has lots of "cedar palm"-like trees and its basis lots of arrow bamboos. In the south, there are lots of yellow gold and jade and in the north lots of yaks or yaks, líng goats, and musk deers.

Its birds include lots of leï. Their shape is that of the magpie. They are red and black, have two heads and four feet. They protect against fire.

19. Mount Guī 騩山

Two-hundred fifty li further west is found Mount Guī. It forms a barrier with the western lake. There is no vegetation but lots of jade.

The river Qī rises there, flows west, and pours into the lake. It contains lots of multicolor rocks, yellow gold and cinnabar.

20. Summary and Rituals

In summary, from Mount Qiánlái, located in the head of the first section of the Western Mountains to Mount Guī is found a total of nineteen mounts spreading over 2957 li.

As graves[27] of the Huá complex, the ritual of the divinities is the Sacrifice to Heaven.[28] Yú is the god of these mountains. In the sacrificed made to him, torches are used. A 100-days ritual[29] is rendered to him including 100 sacrificial victims. The object to burry consists of one hundred pieces of fine jade. The libation[30] wine consists of warm wine in one hundred wine vessels.[31] The ornaments[32] of its temple consist of one hundred suspended squared jade guī[33] and one hundred rounded jade bì.[34]

There are seventeen other additional mountains. Their ceremonies use the single-color fur,[35] and a whole goat. The torches are made of medicinal herbs that have not yet been burned.[36] White and simple mats are chosen.

---

[27] The sleeping places of the supernatural beings (Guopu).

[28] 太牢 tàiláo. Sacrifice to Heaven. This means the use of large animals such as bulls, goats, or boars. These sacrifices are known as the "three sacrifices" or sān-shēng 三牲 (bull, goat and boar). See also *Qingshigao – Lizhi Yi*. This passage seems to have inspired several passages of the *Xiashang Yeshi*, section 3.

[29] 齋 zhāi. Vegetarian religious diet, fast, purification.

[30] 湯 tāng. Hot/boiling water; hot springs; soup, broth; decoction.

[31] 樽 zūn. Ancient wine vessel.

[32] 嬰 yīng. Infant. It may be the ancient small-mouthed earthen jar called yú 盂 (Guopu). Kean thinks that the term has a special connection with jade worships to divinities.

[33] 珪 guī. The jade tablet. This is an old variant of 圭 guī. It is a jade tablet with a square base and a pointed top used in rituals.

[34] 璧 bì. Round flat piece of jade with a circular hole in the middle.

[35] 牷 quán. Single-color fur. Cow or ox of one color, perfect.

[36] For details, see *Shishu* 詩疏 and *Zhouli* 周禮.

Mountain Range 2

1. Mount Qián 鈐山

The main mountain of the second section of the Book of Western Mounts is called Mt Qián. Its tip has lots of copper and its basis lots of jade. This mountain's trees include lots of wild cherry trees.

2. Mount Tàimào 泰冒

Two hundred li west is found Mount Tàimào. In the south, there are lots of gold and in the north lots of iron. The river Yù springs from there, flows east, and pours into the Yellow River. Yù has lots of striated jade and lots of white water snakes.

3. Mount Shùlì 數歷之山

One hundred seventy li further west is found Mount Shùlì. Its tip has lots of yellow gold and its basis lots of silver. Its trees include lots of wild cherry trees and its birds lots of parrots.
The river Chu springs from it, flows south, and pours in the Wèi. The river Chu has lots of white pearls.

4. Mount Gāoshān 高山

Fifty li further northwest is found Mount Gāoshān. Its tip has lots of silver and its basis lots of blue-green gems and realgar.   Its trees include lots of Lady Palm and its grasses lots of zhú bamboos.
The river Jīng springs from it, flows east, and pours into the Wèi. Jīng has lots of chime stones and blue-green gems.

5. Mounts Nǚchuáng 女床之山

Three hundred li southwest is found Mount Nǚchuáng. In the south there are lots of red copper and in the north lots of graphite.
Its animals include lots of tigers, leopards and xīsì one-horned bovines. There are birds there resembling long-tailed pheasants, and having multicolor feathers. Their name is luánniǎo. Their apparition is a sign of peace in the empire.

6. **Mount Lóngshǒu** 龍首之山

Two hundred li further west is found Mount Lóngshǒu. In the south there are lots of yellow gold; in the north, lots of iron. The river Tiáo springs from it, flows southeast, and pours into the river Jīng. It has lots of beautiful jade.

7. **Mount Lùtái** 鹿臺之山

Two hundred li further west is found Mount Lùtái. Its tips has lots of white jade, it basis lots of silver. Its animals include lots of heavy cows, xián goats and badgers.
There are birds there that look like roosters and have a human face. Their name, derived from their call, is fúxī. Their apparition indicates the presence of soldiers.

8. **Mount Niǎowēi** 鳥危之山

Two hundred li southwest is found Mount Niǎowēi. In the south, there are lots of chime stones and in the north lots of sandalwood and paper mulberry. This mountain contains lots of nǚchuáng.
The river Niǎowēi springs from it, flows west, and pours in the river Chì. It contains lots or red sand.

9. **Mount Xiǎocì** 小次之山

Four hundred li further west is located Mount Xiǎocì. Its top has lots of white jade and its basis lots of red copper. Its animals include some resembling apes with a hoary had and bare feet. Their name is zhūyàn. Their apparition is a sign of great rise of troops.

10. **Mount Dàcì** 大次之山

Three hundred li further west is located Mount Dàcì. In the south is found a lot of loess, in the north lots of blue-green stones. Its animals include lots of heavy cows and líng goats.

11. **Mount Xūnwú** 薰吳之山

Four hundred li further west is located Mount Xūnwú. It has no vegetation but lots of gold and jade.

12. Mount Zhìyáng 厎陽之山

Four hundred li further west is located Mount Zhìyáng. Its trees include lots of China cypress, of Phoebe nanmu and of camphor trees. Its animals include lots of rhinoceros, sì one-horned bovines, tigers, panthers and heavy cows.

13. Mount Zhòngshòu 眾獸之山

Two hundred fifty li further west is located Mount Zhòngshòu. Its tip has lots of agate, and its basis lots of mulberry trees and yellow gold. Its animals include lots of xīsì one-horned bovines.

14. Mount Huángrén 皇人之山

Five hundred li further west is located Mount Huángrén. Its tip has lots of gold and jade, its basis lots of [green jade and] realgar.
The river Huáng springs from this mountain, flows west, and pours into river Chì. It contains lots of thin red sand.

15. Mount Zhōnghuáng 中皇之山

Three hundred li further west is located Mount Zhōnghuáng. Its tip has lots of yellow gold and its basis lots of huì orchids and birchleaf trees.

16. Mount Xīhuáng 西皇之山

Three hundred fifty li further west is located Mount Xīhuáng. In the south there are lots of gold and in the north lots of iron. Its animals include lots of Père David's deers, deers and heavy cows.

17. Mount Lái 萊山

Three hundred fifty li further west is located Mount Lái. Its trees include lots of sandalwood and paper mulberry and its birds the man-eater luóluo.

18. Summary and Rituals

In summary, from mount Qián, located in the head of the section of the Western Mounts to Mount Lái, there are seventeen mountains spreading over 4140 li.

Ten of their divinities have a human head and a horse body. Seven other divinities have a human head, a bull body, four feet and a single arm. They use a stick to walk. They are the gods of the flying animals. Their rituals require the fur of sacrificial lambs and pigs[37] and white coarse grass sitting mats. For the ten ancestral divinities,[38] the feathers of a rooster are chosen. [For prayers] use the utensil called qián,[39] but do not present ritual porridge. Offer multicolor [feathers].

---

[37] 少牢 shǎoláo. Sacrificial lamb and pigs Ritual. Literally, it means small sacrifice. The *Yili*, § 17, contains a detailed description of the shǎoláo ritual.

[38] 輩神 bèishén. This term remains unclear: bèi suggests a category, and means "lifelong."

[39] 鈐 qián. Unclear sentence. It could be the name of a sacrificial utensil for which not much is known (Guopu). This term is also the name of the mountain in 2.2.1: Mt Qián 鈐山.

Mountain Range 3

1. Mount Chóngwú 崇吾之山

Mount Chóngwú is the head of the third western mountain range. It is located south of the Yellow River.[40] In the north, if faces Mount Zhǒngsuì; in the southern marsh Yáoyao; in the west Mound Bóshòu of Emperor Wang and in the east the Abyss Yān.

There are trees there [tree of Mt Chóngwú] that have round leaves, white calyx; red flowers with black veins, and trifoliate orange-like fruits. Their consumption enhances fertility.

There are animals there that resemble the spider monkey, with arms spotted like leopards and tigers.[41] These arms have great throwing strength. Their name is jǔfù.

There are birds there that are like wild ducks but have a single wing and a single eye. They can fly by helping one another. Their name is mánmán. Their apparition is a sign of general floods.

2. Mount Chángshā 長沙之山

Three hundred li northwest is found Mount Chángshā. The river Zǐ springs from it, flows north, and pours into the river Yōu. It has no vegetation but lots of realgar.

3. Mount Bùzhōu 不周之山

Three hundred seventy li further northwest is found Mount Bùzhōu. In the north it faces Mount Zhūpí. It neighbors Mount Yuèchóng. In the east it faces the marsh Yōu. The Yellow river[42] runs underground there and its source is tumultuous.

It has delicious fruits whose pits are like those of the peaches. The leaves resemble those of the jujube tree, and the flowers are yellow with a red calyx. Their consumption prevents fatigue.

---

[40] This actually means that the starting point of the third itinerary of western mountains is to the south of the Yellow River.

[41] 豹虎. According to a comment, the term 豹虎 "leopards and tigers" should be 豹尾 "leopards' tail".

[42] Although an underground river can hardly be located, this reference is coherent with the location of Chóngwú to the south of the Yellow River, as Chóngwú is found to the east of Bùzhōu.

4. Mount Mì 崒山

Four hundred twenty li further northwest is found Mount Mì. Its tip has lots of dān trees. They have round leaves, red trunk, yellow flowers and red fruits tasting like sweets cakes.[43] Their consumption prevents hunger.

The river Dān springs from it, flows west, and pours into the marsh Jì. It has lots of white jade exudates and its spring is very turbulent.[44] Emperor Huangdi fed from them and used them during entertainments. This spring also produces black jade. When this liquid jade flows out, it waters the dān trees. These trees live five-hundred years; they have five pristine colors, and five aromatic fragrant flavors. Huangdi took the thriving jade from Mount Mì and seeded the south of Mount Zhōng.

The jǐn jade is the best one: it is strong and fine like millet, and has a moist and shiny glister. Five colors manifest within it and gather softness to strength. For the divinities of heaven and earth, it is a meal and an offering item. The wise ones carry it to conjurer bad luck.

Mount Mì and Mount Zhōng are separated by four-hundred sixty li.[45] This area is filled with marshes and has lots of marvelous birds, legendary animals, and rare fishes. All of them are equally extraordinary.

5. Mount Zhōng 鍾山

Four hundred twenty li further northwest is found Mount Zhōng. Its child is called Gǔ. It has a human face and a dragon body. With the help of Qīnpī, it killed Bǎojiāng on the southern slope of Mount Kūnlún. Then, the emperor[46] killed Qīnpī on the eastern slope of Mount Zhōng, on a cliff called Yáo.[47] Afterwards, Qīnpī changed into the big osprey È. This bird resembles a vulture.[48] It has dark spots, a white head, a red beak and tiger claws. Its call is like that of the morning swan. Its apparition is a sign of major military operations.

Then it changed and became a jùn bird. It looks like a sparrow hawk, with red legs, a straight beak, yellow spots and a white head. Its call is like that of the swan. Its apparition is a sign of great local dryness.

---

[43] 飴 yí. Malt sugar, sweet; or sweet cakes.

[44] 沸沸湯湯 fèifèi shāngshāng. This expression reminds the poetic style of the *Shijing*.

[45] The distance is four hundred twenty li according to SH 2.3.5.

[46] The emperor is identified as Huangdi 黃帝 in the notes of HJ 6.1 by cross-references with this chapter.

[47] 瑤[王改山]崖. The cliff 崖 of yáo 瑤. The term 王改山 is unexplained by annotators or translators.

[48] 雕 diāo. Raptor or vulture.

6. Mount Tàiqì 泰器之山

One hundred eighty li further west is found Mount Tàiqì. The river Guān springs from it, flows west, and pours into the Liúshā.[49] It has many flying fishes that resemble the carp [hybrid of Mt Tàiqì]. They have a fish body and bird wings, with dark green streaks, a white head and a red mouth. They continuously go toward the western sea and travel to the eastern sea. They fly at night. Their call is like that of the luánjī bird. They taste sweet and sour. Their consumption renders someone crazy. Their apparition is a sign of great abundance in the world.

7. Mount Huáijiāng 槐江之山

Three hundred twenty li further west is found Mount Huáijiāng. The river Qiūshí springs from it, flows north, and pours into the river Yōu. It has lots of luǒmǔ conches.

Its top has lots of green realgar, hidden pearl-like stones, yellow gold and jade. Its southern side has lots of thin red sand. Its northern side has lots of speckled yellow gold and silver.[50] Truly, it is the garden of peace[51] of the Emperor Di. The divinity called Yīngzhāo manages it. It has the body of a horse, a human face, tiger spots and bird wings. It crosses the four seas.[52] Its call resembles the liú.[53]

In the south it faces Mount Kūnlún. It has a glistening beauty[54] and its aspects have endless varieties.[55] In the west, it faces the marsh Dà where Hòujì dove. It contains lots of jade. In the north, there are many regenerating yáo trees.

In the north, it faces Mount Zhūpí.. The divinity Huáiguǐ lílún lives there. It is a residence of sparrow hawks. In the east it faces the [Northern] four-layered mount Héng. The qióng divinities live there, each at one layer. There is the river yáo.[56] It has a shiny limpidity.[57]

---

[49] 流沙 liúshā. Moving sand.

[50] 采黃金銀 cǎi huángjīnyín. Speckled yellow gold and silver. This expression could be understood as "multicolored or striated gold and silver" or "gold and silver are taken out of the mines."

[51] 平圃 píngpǔ. Garden of peace. This term refers to 玄圃 xuánpǔ, the mythical garden in the Kunlun Mountains (Guopu). In the *Mu tianzi zhuan* and the *Huainanzi* (4. Zhuixing), it is cited as xiànpǔ 县圃, a residence for the divinities.

[52] 四海 sìhǎi. Lit. The four seas. Allegorically, the world.

[53] 榴 liú. Unclear sound (Guopu). It may be 抽 chōu, a lash, a whip.

[54] 熊熊 xióngxióng. Glistening beauty. Lit. flaming, blazing, raging.

[55] 魂魂 húnhún. Endless varieties.

[56] 淫水 yín (pronounced yáo). It may refer to flooding waters (洪水 hóngshuǐ). It is about the waters cascading down from the top of the mountain.

[57] 洛洛 luòluò. Describes the water glide.

There are celestial divinities there that have the shape of a bull with eight feet, two heads and a horse tail. Their call is like the bóhuáng. Their apparition is a sign of local war.

8. Mound Kūnlún 昆侖之丘

Four hundred li southwest is found is found Mound Kūnlún. This is truly the only lower capital of the Emperor. The divinity Lùwú keeps it. This divinity has the body of a tiger with nine tails, a human head and tiger claws. It manages the nine parts of heaven and the seasonal rhythms of the ancient wall garden of the Emperor Di.

There are animals there that have the shape of a goat and four horns. Their name is tǔlóu. They eat humans.

There are birds there that resemble bees or wasps that are as big as mandarin duck. Their name is qīnyuán. When they sting animals or birds, they kill them. When they sting trees,[58] they make them wither.

There are birds called chúnniǎo. They manage the one-hundred items of Emperor Di.

There are trees there that resemble birchleaf trees. They have yellow flowers and red fruits that taste like plums and have no pits. Their name is shātáng. They resist water. Their consumption prevents drowning.

There are plants there called píncǎo. They resemble winter sunflowers and taste like onions. Their consumption prevents fatigue from labors.

The Hé river rises there, flows south, and pours into Wúdá. The river Chì rises there, flows southeast and pours into the Fàntiān. The river Yáng rises there, flows southwest, and pours into the Chǒutú. The river Hēi rises there, flows west and irrigates Mount Dàyú. There are many extraordinary birds and animals.[59]

9. Mount Lèyóu 樂游之山

Three hundred seventy li further west is found Mount Lèyóu. The river Táo rises there, flows west, and pours into the march Jì. It has lots of white jade and in the middle lots of huái fishes. They have the shape of snakes with four legs and feed from fishes.

---

[58] The edition with Guopu's comments has the character water shuǐ instead of tree.

[59] According to Guopu, these are categories of nine-heads beasts and six heads birds. The Comment calls them nine-heads illuminated beasts and six heads tree birds and refers to HJ 1.

10. Mounts Liúshā 流沙 and Guǒmǔ 蠃母

Four hundred[60] li west, by water means, are found quicksands[61] and two hundred li from it is Mount Guǒmǔ. The divinity chángchéng manages this place of the nine celestial virtues.[62] Its divinity has a human shape and a leopard tail.

The tip of this mountain has lots of jade and its base lots of lapis-lazuli. It has no rivers.

11. Mount Yù 玉山

Three hundred fifty li further west is found Mount Yù. This is where The Queen Mother of the West lives. The Queen Mother of the West has a human shape with a leopard tail. She has tiger teeth and powerful roar. She is disheveled and carries a hoopoe-like crown. She governs the celestial plagues and the five destructive influences.[63]

There are animals there that resemble dogs,[64] have leopard spots, and bull-like horns. Their name is jiǎo. Their call is like that of a dog's bark. Their apparition is a sign of great calamities.

There are birds there that have a shape like that of long-tailed pheasants and are red. Their name is xìngyù. They feed from fishes and their call resembles that of the deer. Their apparition is a sign of floods in the countries.

12. Mound Xuānyuán 軒轅之丘

Four hundred eighty li further west is found Mound Xuānyuán. It has no vegetation. The river Xún springs from it, flows south, and pours into the River Hēi. River Xún has lots of thin red sand and lots of realgar.

---

[60] According to the annotation, the distance should be 200 li and not 400.

[61] 流沙 liúshā (2.3.10). Quicksand, sediment.

[62] 天之九德 huàiyú. The nine celestial virtues.

[63] 天之厲 tiān zhī lì. Celestial plagues and five destructive influences. The celestial plagues and 五殘 wǔcán, the five destructive influences. Cán refers to injury (radicals of "broken bones" and "two spears"). Lì and Wǔcán are also names of stars. Wǔcán is found in the *Shiji*, chapter 27 where it is described as rising up from the east, ruling over the east, having the shape of the planet mercury, and being distant from earth by six zhàng units. These two terms together suggest that Xīwángmǔ rules over major epidemics and disasters or celestial punishments.

[64] According to another edition, they are like of the goat.

13. Mount Jīshí 積石之山

Three hundred li further west is found Mount Jīshí. Its base has a stone gate: the river Hé goes through it and flows west. There is nothing on this mountain.

14. Mount Chángliú 長留之山

Two hundred li further west is found Mount Chángliú. It is the residence of the divinity White Lord, or Shǎohào.
All the animals of this mount have spotted tails.[65] All its birds have spotted heads.[66] It also has lots of spotted jade.[67] This mount is truly the only palace of this divinity of the class of mountain ghosts. This divinity manages the turn over of the scenery.

15. Mount Zhāngé 章莪之山

Two hundred eighty li further west is found Mount Zhāngé. It has no vegetation but lots of green jasper and green jade. This is a place of extraordinary things.
There are beasts there that are like red leopards[68] with five tails and one horn. Their call is similar to the [noise] of stones hitting one another. Their name is zhēng.
There are birds there that resemble cranes, with one foot, red spots, green body and white beak. Their name, derived from their call, is bìfāng. Their apparition is a sign of strange fires in the city.

16. Mount Yīn 陰山

Three hundred li further west is found Mount Yīn. The river Zhuóyù springs from it, flows south, and pours into the marsh Fān. It has lots of spotted clams.
There are beasts there that are like fox[69] and have a white head. Their name is Heavenly Hound Tiāngǒu. Their call is like liúliú. They are used to avoid bad luck.

---

[65] Guopu: according to another edition, it should be "long tails."
[66] See Guopu's notice: long instead of spotted.
[67] Long instead of spotted.
[68] 赤豹 chì bào: Fur is red with leopard black stripes. The *Shī* (Dà Yǎ - Hán Yì) says: "to offer its leopard (貔 pí) skin, red leopard (豹 bào) and yellow bear (羆 pí)." About the fur, "red fur and black stripes, this is the chì bào."
[69] Guopu suggests that it may be 豹 bào, leopard; panther.

17. Mount Fúyāng 符惕之山

Two hundred li west is found Mount Fúyāng. Its tip has lots of "cedar palm"-like trees; its base lots of gold and jade. The divinity Jiāngyí lives there. This mountain has strange rains, and is a place where winds and clouds originate.[70]

18. Mount Sānwēi 三危之山

Two hundred twenty li further west is found Mount Sānwēi. Its harbors the three Blue Birds Qīngniǎo. This mountain has a perimeter of one hundred li. There are beasts on its top. They have the shape of a bull, a white body[71] and four horns. Their porcupine-like fur is like a short rain cape made of reed. Their name is àoyē. They eat humans.
There are birds there. They have one head and three bodies and resemble the luò vulture. Their name is chī.

19. Mount Guī 騩山

One hundred ninety li further west is found Mount Guī. Its top has lots of jade and no stones. The divinity Qítóng lives there. The sound of his voice is constant like that of a bell and chime stone instrument.[72] The base of this mountain is pilled up with snakes.

20. Mount Tiān 天山

Three hundred fifty li further west is found Mount Tiān. It has lots of gold, and there are green [jade] and realgar.
The river Yīng originates from this mountain, flows southwest, and pours into the valley Tāng.
There is a divinity there. It has the shape of a yellow bag and is red like bright fire.[73] It has six legs and for wings. It is Húndūn. It has neither face nor eyes. It knows singing and dancing. Truly, it is the Emperor Dì Hóng.

---

[70] See *Liji* Chapter 20 – Rules about sacrifices: "As the mountains, forests, rives, valleys, hills can produce clouds, wind and rain, and present strange things, it is said that they are ruled by divinities."
[71] The Guangyun states "white head" instead of "white body." (Hao Yixing)
[72] 鍾磬 zhōng qìng. Name of an ancient musical instrument, the ancestor of the long zither 長琴. See *Zhouli*, Chunguan, Small Official, *Bowu Zhi*, scroll 4, and the famous poet Du Fu (or Gong Bu) in his *Cao tang shi hua*, scroll 1. See also HJ 11.12.
[73] Guopu clarifies that the body color is yellow and that "red like fire" is to be understood "bare naked."

21. Mount Yŏu 泑山

Two hundred ninety li further west is found Mount Yŏu. The divinity Rùshōu lives there. Its top has lots of yīngduǎn jade. Its south has lots of jǐnyú jade and its north lots of green [jade] and realgar. In the west it faces the setting of the sun whose shape is circular. The divinity Hóngguāng is in charge of it.

22. Mount Yìwàng 翼望

One hundred li west by water means, is found Mount Yìwàng. It has no vegetation but lots of gold and jade. There is an animal there that resembles the fox, has one eye and three tails. Its name is huān. Its call is as forceful as one hundred sounds. It can be used against bad luck. Also, as a medicine, it protects against jaundice.
There is a bird there that resembles a crow, has three heads and six tails and is good at laughing. Its name is yīyú. As a medicine, it protects from nightmares. Also, it can be used against bad luck.

23. Summary and Rituals

In summery, from Mount Chóngwú, located in the head of the third section of the Western mountains, to Mount Yìwàng, there are together twenty-three mountains covering 6744 li.

The divinities of these mountains all have a goat body and a human face. In the ceremonies of their temples, auspicious jade is used and buried.[74] The sacrificial food consists of millet[75] and rice.

---

[74] 吉 jí. Lucky, auspicious. Here it refers to the adequate color of jade.
[75] 稷 jì. Refers today to the harvest god. Archaic term referring to edible crop grains, known today as 谷子 gǔzi, millet or unhusked rice.

Mountain Range 4

1. Mount Yīn 陰山

The mountain found in the head of the fourth section of the Book of Western Mountains is called Mount Yīn. Its top has lots of paper mulberry[76] and no stones. Its grasses include lots of water mallows and sedges. The river Yīn rises there, flows west, and pours into the Luò.

2. Mount Láo 勞山

Fifty li north is found Mount Láo. It contains lots of gromwells. The river Ruò rises there, flows west, and pours into the river Luò.

3. Mount Bàfù 罷父之山

Fifty li west is found Mount Bàfù. The river Ěr rises there, flows west, and pours into the river Luò. It contains lots of purple stones and blue-green stones.

4. Mount Shēn 申山

One-hundred seventy li north is found Mount Shēn. Its tip has lots of paper mulberry and oak trees. Its basis has lots of wild cherry trees. Its southern side has lots of gold and jade. The river Qū rises there, flows east, and pours into the Yellow River.

5. Mount Niǎo 鳥山

Two-hundred li north is found Mount Niǎo. Its tip has lots of mulberry trees and its basis lots of paper mulberry trees. Its northern side has lots of iron and its southern side lots of jade. The river Rǔ rises there, flows east, and pours into the Yellow River.

---

[76] 穀 gǔ. cereal; grain. According to the Commentary, it should be 榖 gǔ, paper mulberry. See SJ 1.1.

6. **Mount Shàngshēn** 上申之山

One-hundred twenty li further north is found Mount Shàngshēn. Its tip has no vegetations but lots of big protruding rocks. Its basis has lots of hazel and arrow trees.
Its animals include lots of white deers. Its birds include lots of dānghù. Their shape resembles that of pheasants and they fly assisted by their rictal bristles.[77] Their consumption prevents blepharospams.
The river Tang springs from this mountain, flows east, and pours into the Yellow River.

7. **Mount Zhūcì** 諸次之山

One-hundred eighty li further north is found Mount Zhūcì.
The river Zhūcì rises there, flows east, and pours into the Yellow River.
This mountain has lots of trees but no grasses. It has neither animals nor birds, but crowds of snakes.

8. **Mount Hào** 號山

One-hundred eighty li further north is found Mount Hào. Its trees include lots of varnish and Lady Palm trees. Its grasses include lots of angelica, white angelica and Ligusticum. There are also lots of dié stones.
The river Duān rises there, flows east, and pours into the Yellow River.

9. **Mount Yú** 盂山

Two-hundred twenty li further north is found Mount Yú. Its northern side has lots of iron and its southern side lots of copper.
Its animals include lots of white wolves and white tigers. Its birds include lots of white pheasants and white kingfishers.
The river Shēng rises there, flows east, and pours into the Yellow River.

10. **Mount Báiyū** 白於之山

Two-hundred fifty li further west is found Mount Báiyū. Its tip has lots of pine and cypress trees. Its basis has lots of lì oaks and white sandalwood.
Its animals include lots of heavy cows and xiányáng goats. Its birds include lots of owls.

---

[77] 髯 rán. Side whiskers. Some birds have rictal bristles, term chosen here rather than neck feathers.

The river Luò springs from its southern slope, flows east, and pours into the Wei. The river Jiā springs from its northern slope, flows east, and pours into the river Shēng.

11. Mount Shēnshǒu 申首之山

Three-hundred li northwest is found Mount Shēnshǒu. It has no vegetations. In winter and summer, it has snow.
The river Shēn originates on its top and runs underground on its lower slopes. There are lots of white jade.

12. Mount Jīnggǔ 涇谷之山

Fifty-five li further west is found Mount Jīnggǔ.
The river Jīng rises there, flows southeast, and pours into the river Wèi. There are lots of white metal and white jade.

13. Mount Gāng 剛山

One-hundred twenty li further west is found Mount Gāng. It has lots of varnish trees and lots of agate. The river Gāng rises there, flows north, and pours into the river Wèi.
There are lots of mountains demons. They have a human face, an animal body, a single foot and a single hand. Their voice is like an animal groan.[78]

14. Mount Zhìgāng 至剛

Two-hundred li further west is found Mount Zhìgāng. The river Luò rises there, flows north, and pours into the Yellow River. It contains lots of mánmán which have a rat body and a soft-shelled turtle head. Their call resembles the dog's bark.

15. Mount Yīngdī 英鞮之山

Three-hundred fifty li further west is found Mount Yīngdī. Its tip has lots of varnish trees and its basis lots of gold and jade. Animals and birds are entirely white.
The river Yuān rises there, flows north, and pours into the língyáng marsh. There are lots of rǎnyí fishes. They have a fish body, a snake head, six legs

---

[78] 欽 qīn. Respect, admire. This is a phonetic loan for 吟 yín, pointing to groan, or animal cry, according to Guopu.

and eyes like the ears of a horse. Its consumption protects against nightmares. It can be used again evil spells.

16. Mount Zhōngqū 中曲之山

Three-hundred li further west is found Mount Zhōngqū. Its southern side has lots of jade and its northern side lots of realgar, white jade and gold.
There are animals there that have the shape of a horse with a white body, a black tail, a single horn, tiger teeth and tiger claws. Their call resembles that of the drum sound. Their name is bó. They eat tigers and leopards. They can be used to push military forces away.
There are trees there that resemble birchleaf trees, their leaves are round, and their fruits red and big as the quince fruit. Their name is guīmù. Their consumption gives lots of strength.

17. Mount Guī 邽山

Two-hundred sixty li further west is found Mount Guī. Its tip has animals resembling bulls and having the spines of a hedgehog.[79] Their name is qióngqí. Their call is like that of the howl of a dog. They eat humans.
The river Méng rises there, flows south, and pours into the river Yáng. This river has lots of yellow huángbèi, and guǒyú fishes that have fish bodies and bird wings. Their call is like that of the mandarin duck. Their apparition is a sign of floods in villages.

18. Mount Niǎoshǔ Tóngxué 鳥鼠同穴之山

Two-hundred twenty li further west is found Mount Niǎoshǔ Tóngxué. Its tip has lots of white tiger and white jade.
The river Wèi rises there, flows east, and pours into the Yellow River. This river contains lots of sāo fishes whose form resembles that of the huso sturgeon. When they are agitated,[80] it is a sign of big battle in the area.
The river Kǎn springs from its occidental side, flows west, and pours into the river Hàn.
There are lots of rúpí fishes. Their shape is like that of a decoction pot,[81] their head like that of a bird, they have fins and a fish tail. Their call resembles the sound of a chime stone. They produce pearls.

---

[79] 蝟 wèi.
[80] Or "where they move."
[81] 銚 diào. Pot (for boiling water, herbs). This is a small utensil with a handle and a steam mouth.

19. Mount Yānzī 崦嵫之山

Three-hundred sixty li southwest is found Mount Yānzī. Its tip has lots or dān trees. Their leaves are like that of the paper mulberry. Their fruits are large like those of gourds, with crimson calyx and black veins. Their consumption prevents fatigue. They are also used to prevent fires.
Its southern side has lots of turtles and the northern one lots of jade.
The river Tiáo rises there, flows west, and pours into the Hǎi. It contains lots of grindstones and sharpening whetstones.
There are animals there that have the body of a horse and wings of a bird, a human face and the tail of a snake. They like to grasp people. Their name is Shúhú.
There are birds there that resemble owls (owl-like bird), have a human face, a macaque body, and the tail of a dog. Their name is derived from their call. Their apparition is a sign of great drought in the locality.

20. Summary and Rituals

In summary, from Mount Yīn, located in the head of the fourth section of the Western Mountains to Mount Yānzī is found a total of nineteen mountains, spreading over 3680 li.

These mountains divinity temples all use a white chicken as offering for the ritual. The sacrificial porridge consists of rice paddy. White coarse grass is used to make the mats.

The Book of the Western Mountains includes a total of seventy-seven mountains, spreading over 17, 517 li.

3. 北山經 – Book of the Northern Mountains

Mountain Range 1

1. Mount Dānhú 單狐之山

The first mount of the Book of Northern Mount is called Mount Dānhú. It has many alder trees. Its top is covered with huácǎo flowering plants.
The river Fēng springs there, flows west, and pours into the river Yōu. River Fēng abounds in císhí amethysts and in aragonites.

2. Mount Qiúrú 求如之山

Two hundred fifty li further north is found Mount Qiúrú. Its top has lots of copper and its base lots of jade. It has no vegetation. The river Huá springs there, flows west, and pours into the river Zhūpí. This river abounds in ray-finned fishes. They have the shape of an eel, with a red back. Their call is like the lute sound.[82] Their consumption cures warts. This river also contains many water horses. They resemble a horse with spotted legs[83] and an ox tail. Their call resembles the shout.

3. Mount Dài 帶山

Three hundred li further north is found Mount Dài. Its tip has lots of jade and its basis lots of blue-green gems. There are beasts there that look like horses and have a very hard[84] and striated horn. Their name is huānshū. They can be used to protect against fire. There are birds there that resemble the crow. They are multicolor with red spots. Their name is yīyú. They are hermaphrodite. Their consumption protects against deep-rooted ulcers.
The river Péng exit from this mountain, flows west, and pours into the river Bìhú. It contains many white sharpbelly fishes. They have a chicken shape, red feathers, three tails, six feet, and four eyes.[85] Their call resembles that of the magpie. Their consumption removes worries.

Mount Qiáomíng 譙明山

Four hundred li further north is found Mount Qiáomíng. The river Qiáo springs there, flows west, and pours into the Yellow River. This river

---

[82] 梧 wú. Chinese parasol tree. Its delicate wood is used to make the soundboard of the guqín musical instrument.
[83] 臂 bì. Arm. Refers to the front legs (Hao Yixing).
[84] Hard as a sharpening stone and striated.
[85] According to the annotation, it should be four eyes 目 and not four heads 首.

contains lots of héluó fishes. They have one head and ten bodies. Their call resembles the dog's bark. Their consumption cures ulcers.

There are animals there that resemble porcupine and have long fine reddish hair. Their call is like liúliú.[86] Their name is mènghuái. They protect against bad luck. This mountain has no vegetation but lots of green [jade and] realgar.

4. Mount Zhuōguāng 涿光之山

Three hundred fifty li further north is found Mount Zhuōguāng. The river Xiāo goes out of this mountain, flows west, and pours into the Yellow River. It contains lots of xíxí. They resemble the magpie, have ten wings, and scales at the feathers' extremities. Their call is like that of the magpie. They protect against fire. Their consumption prevents soreness.

Its tip has lots of pine and cedar trees and its base palm trees. Its animals include lots of líng goats, its birds lots of fān.

5. Mount Guó 虢山

Three hundred eighty li further north is found Mount Guó. Its top has lots of varnish trees, its base lots of tung and zelkowa trees. Its south abounds in jade and its north in iron.

The river Yī springs from this mountain, flows west, and pours into the Yellow River.

Its animals include lots of camels. Its birds include lots of yù. They resemble rats with bird wings, and their call is like that of the goat. They protect against wars.

6. Mount Guó - Extremity 虢山之尾

Four hundred li further north is found the extremity of Mount Guó. Its top has lots of jade but no stones.

The river Yú springs there, flows west, and pours into the Yellow River. This river has lots of spotted cowries.

7. Mount Dānxūn 丹熏之山

Two hundred li further north is found Mount Dānxūn. Its top has lots of trees of heaven and cypresses. Its grasses include lots of Chinese chives and Chinese onions. It also has lots of red ochre stones.

The river Xūn springs there, flows west, and pours into the river Táng.

---

[86] 榴榴 liúliú. This appears to be an onomatopoetic sound of well-pulley drawn water (辘轳抽水).

There is an animal there that resembles a rat and has the head of a hare and a Père David's Deer body.[87] Its call is like the roar or howl of a dog. If flies by means of its whiskers.[88] Its name is ěrshǔ. Its consumption prevents abdominal distention. In addition, it can be used against the hundred poisons.

8. Mount Shízhě 石者之山

Two hundred eighty li further north is found Mount Shízhě. Its top has no vegetation but lots of green jasper and green jade.
The river Cǐ springs from this mountain, flows west, and pours into the Yellow River.
There are animals there that resemble the leopard, have a spotted forehead and a white body. Their name, derived from their call, is mèngjí. They love lying down.[89]

9. Mount Biānchūn 邊春之山

One hundred ten li further north is found Mount Biānchūn. It has lots of scallions, sunflowers, Chinese chives, peach trees and plum trees.
The river Gāng springs there, flows west, and pours into the marsh Yōu.
There are animals there that look like spider monkeys and have a spotted body. They often laugh. When they see human beings, they lie down.[90]
Their name, derived from their call, is yōué.

10. Mount Mánlián 蔓聯之山

Two hundred li further north is found Mount Mánlián. Its top has no vegetation.
There are animals there that look like monkeys, have a mane, an oxtail, spotted arms, and horse's hoofs. When they see human beings, they start shouting. Their name, derived from their call, is zúzǐ.
There are birds there that are gregarious and fly in flocks. Their feather is like that of the female pheasant. Their name, derived from their call, is jiāo.
Their consumption cures wind conditions.

---

[87] The *Chuxue Ji* says ears (míěr 耳) instead of body.
[88] Two versions exist: tail wěi 尾 or beard rán 髯.
[89] Lying down or hiding prostrate.
[90] This means that they fake sleeping (Hao Yixing).

11. Mount Dānzhāng 單張之山

One hundred eighty li further north is found Mount Dānzhāng. Its top has no vegetation.
There are animals there that are like leopards with a long tail, a human head, cow ears, and a single eye. Their name is zhūjiān. They often shout. When they walk, they hold their tail in their mouth; when they rest, they hold it curled.
There are birds there that are like pheasants with a mottled head, white wings and yellow feet. Their name is báiyè. Their consumption stops throat pain and can also cure madness.
The river Lì goes out of this mountain, flows south, and pours into the river Gàng.

12. Mount Guàntí 潘侯之山 灌題之山

Three hundred twenty li further north is found Mount Guàntí. Its top has lots of trees of Heaven and zhè thorny trees; its basis lots of quicksand and whetstones. It includes bull-like animals with a white tail and a call similar to the human voice. Their name is nàfù. It includes pheasant-like birds with a human face. When they see someone, they start jumping. Their name, derived from their call, is sǔsī.
The river Jiànghán springs from this mountain, flows west, and pours into the marsh Yōu. Its bed contains lots of lodestones.

13. Mount Pānhóu 潘侯山

Two hundred li further north is found Mount Pānhóu. Its top has lots of pine and cypress trees; its base lots of hazel and arrow trees. The southern side has lots of jade and the northern side lots of iron.
It includes bull-like animals that have a fur renewing itself by successive shedding at the four seasons. Their name is yak.
The river Biān springs from this mountain, flows south, and pours into Marsh Lì.

14. Mount Xiǎoxián 小咸之山

Two hundred thirty li further north is found Mount Xiǎoxián. It has no vegetation. Winter and Summer it has snow.

15. Mount Dàxián 大咸之山

Two hundred eighty li further north is found Mount Dàxián. It has no vegetation but its base has lots of jade. This mountain has four sides that cannot be climbed.
It has snakes called chángshé. They have pig-like bristles. Their call is like the drumming of a watchman clapper.

16. Mount Dūnhōng 敦薨之山

Three hundred twenty li further north is found Mount Dūnhōng. Its top has lots of "cedar palm"-like trees and its base lots of gromwells.
The river Dūnhōng exits from this mountain, flows west, and pours into the marsh Yōu. It originates from the northeast angle of Mount Kūnlún. It is truly where the source of this river is. It contains lots of red salmons.
Its animals include sì one-horned bovines and yaks and its birds lots of turtledoves.

17. Mount Shǎoxián 少咸之山

Two hundred li further north is found Mount Shǎoxián. It has no vegetation. It has lots of blue-green gems. It includes bull-like animals. They have a red body,[91] a human face and horse feet. Their name is zháyǔ. Their call is like that of a small child. They devour humans.
The river Dūn springs from this mountain, flows east, and pours into the river Yànmén. Its bed includes lots of péipéi fishes. Their consumption kills people.

18. Mount Yùfǎ 獄法之山

Two hundred li further north is found Mount Yùfǎ. The river Huáizé springs there, flows northeast and pours into the marsh Tài. This river contains lots of zǎo fishes. Their shape is like that of carps but they have chicken legs. Their consumption protects against warts.
It includes a dog-like creature. It has a human face and great throwing strength. When it sees humans, it starts laughing. Its name is shānhún. It walks like the wind.[92] Its apparition is a sign of strong wind in the world.

19. Mount Běiyuè 北嶽之山

Two hundred[93] li further north is found Mount Běiyuè. It has lots of knotty trees and hardwood trees.

---

[91] 赤身 chìshēn. Either red body, or bare body (hairless).
[92] Or as fast as an arrow.

It includes bull-like animals. They have four horns, human eyes, and pig ears. Their name is zhūhuái. Their call is like that of the wild goose. They eat humans.
The river Zhūhuái springs there, flows west, and pours into the river Xiāo. It has lots of fishes looking like the grouper (grouper-like fish). They have a fish body and a dog head. Their consumption cures mania.

20. Mount Húnxī 渾夕之山

One hundred eighty li further north is found Mount Húnxī. It has no vegetation but lots of copper and jade.
The river Xiāo springs there, flows northwest, and pours into the sea. It contains a snake that has one head and two bodies. Its name is féiyí. Its apparition is a sign of great drought in the country.

21. Mount Běidān 北單之山

Fifty li further north is found Mount Běidān. It has no vegetation but lots of scallions and Chinese chives.

22. Mount Píchā 羆差之山

One hundred li further north is found Mount Píchā. It has no vegetation but lots of horses.

23. Mount Běixiān 北鮮之山

One hundred eighty li further north is found Mount Běixiān. It has lots of horses.
The river xiān springs there, flows northwest, and pours into the river Túwú.

24. Mount Dī 隄山

One-hundred seventy li further north is found Mount Dī. It has lots of horses. It [also] includes an animal that resemble the leopard and has a spotted head. Its name is yāo.
The river Dī springs from this mountain, flows east, and pours into the marsh Tài. This rive has lots of dragons and tortoises.

---

[93] The annotation suggests it was originally "one hundred."

25. Summary and Rituals

In summary, from Mount Dānhú, mentioned in the beginning of the first section of the Book of Northern Mountains to Mount Dī, there are twenty-five mountains spreading over 5490 lis.

The divinities of these mountains all have a human face and a snake body. The victims for the sacrificial rituals include the burial of rooster and pig having one specific feather and fur. The lucky jade to be buried consists of one squared jade guī. Sacrificial rice is not used. The people living north of these mountains do not eat cooked food.

Mountain Range 2

1. Mount Guǎncén 管涔之山

The first mountain of the second section of the Book of Northern Mountains is located east of the Yellow River. Its head is adjacent to the river Fén.[94] It is called Mount Guǎncén.
Its top has no trees but lots of grass; its base has lots of jade.
The river Fén springs there, flows west, and pours into the Yellow River.

2. Mount Shǎoyáng 少陽之山

Two hundred fifty li further north[95] is found Mount Shǎoyáng. Its top has lots of jade and its base lots or red silver. The river Suān springs there, flows east, and pours into the river Fén. The bed of river Suān has lots of red ochre.

3. Mount Xiànyōng 縣雍之山

Fifty li further north is found Mount Xiànyōng. Its top has lots of jade and its base lots of copper. Its animals include lots of black rams and elks. Its birds include lots of white long-tailed mountain pheasants and white pheasants.
The river Jìn springs there, flows southeast, and pours into the river Fén. It has lots of Chinese herrings that resemble the white sharpbelly. Their scales[96] are red and their call resembles a shout. Their consumption cures disturbed body smell.

4. Mount Húqí 狐岐之山

Two hundreds li further north is found Mount Húqí. It has no vegetation but lots of blue-green gems. The river Shèng springs there, flows northeast, and pours into the river Fén. The bed of this river has lots of azure jade.

---

[94] It neighbors the lower waterways of the river Fén (Guopu).
[95] North. The original has west but the structure of the text, Guopu citing the *Zangjing* and Wukian's Transcript of the SHJ, mentions that it should be north and not west.
[96] 麟 lín is the original character but it should be 鱗 lín, scale.

5. Mount Báishā 白沙山

Three hundred fifty li further north is found Mount Báishā. It has a wide perimeter[97] covering three hundred lis and consists mainly of desert land. It has no vegetation, no birds and no animals. The river Wěi springs from its top and runs underground at its base. There are lots of white jade.

6. Mount Ěrshì 爾是之山

Four hundreds li further north is found Mount Ěrshì. It has neither vegetation, nor river.

7. Mount Kuáng 狂山

Three hundred eight li further north is found Mount Kuáng. It has no vegetation. On this mountain, there is snow all year round. The river Kuáng springs there, flows west, and pours into the river Fú. Its bed has lots of beautiful jade.

8. Mount Zhūyú 諸餘之山

Three hundred eight li further north is found Mount Zhūyú. Its top abounds in copper and jade; its base has lots of pine and cypress trees. The river Zhūyú springs there, flows east, and pours into the river Máo.

9. Mount Dūntóu 敦頭之山

Three hundred fifty li still further north is found Mount Dūntóu. Its top has lots of gold and jade but no vegetation.
The river Máo exits from this mountain, flows east, and pours into the marsh Yīn. It has lots of bómǎ unicorns. They have an ox tail, a white body and a single horn. Their call is like a shout.[98]

10. Mount Gōuwú 鉤吾之山

Three hundred fifty li further north is found Mount Gōuwú. Its tip abounds in jade and its basis in copper.
It has animals with a goat body, a human face, eyes on their armpits, tiger teeth and human nails. Their call resembles that of an infant. Their name is páoxiāo. They eat human.

---

[97] 員 yuán. Archaic meaning of circle.
[98] 呼 hū. Shout. It may be a homophone of the call of this animal.

11. Mount Běixáo 北嚣之山

Three hundreds li further north is found Mount Běixáo. It has no rocks. In the south there are lots of blue-green stones and in the north lots of jade.
It has animals that resemble tigers, have a white body, a dog head, a horse tail and pig hairs. Their name is dúgǔ. The birds of this mountain resemble crows and have a human face. Their name is bànmào. They fly at night and hide during the day. Their consumption protects against sunstrokes.
The river Cén exits from this mountain, flows east, and pours its waters into the marsh Qióng.

12. Mount Liángqú 梁渠之山

Three hundred fifty li further north is found Mount Liángqú. It has no vegetation but lots of gold and jade.
The river Xiū springs there, flows east, and pours into the Yànmén.
Its animals include lots of jūjì. They resemble hedgehogs and have red hair. Their call is like that of small pigs. It has birds that resemble the kuāfù. They have four wings, one eye, and a dog tail. Their name is xiāo. Their call is like that of the magpie. Their consumption cures intestinal diseases. It is also a method to stop diarrhea.

13. Mount Gūguàn 姑灌之山

Four hundred li further north is found Mount Gūguàn. It has no vegetation. On this mountain, there is snow all year round.

14. Mount Húguàn 湖灌之山

Three hundred eighty li further north is found Mount Húguàn. In the south there are lots of jade and in the north lots of blue-green stones. There are also lots of horses.
The river Húguàn exits from this mountain, flows east, and pours into the sea. It has lots of eels.
On Mount Húguàn grows a tree that has leaves like that of the willow with red veins.

15. Mount Huán 洹山

Five hundreds li north across water, and three hundred li across moving sands is found Mount Huán. The tip of this mount has lots of gold and jade. The triple mulberry grows there. It is a tree without branches reaching a height of eight hundreds Chinese feet. All kinds of fruit trees also grow there. Its base has lots of strange snakes.

16. Mount Dūntí 敦題之山

Three hundreds li further north is found Mount Dūntí. It has no vegetation but lots of gold and jade. It props against the Northern sea.

17. Summary and Rituals

In summary, from Mount Guǎncén, mentioned in the beginning of the second section of the Book of the Northern Mountains, to Mount Dūntí, there are seventeen[99] mountains covering 5690 lis.
The divinities of these mountains all have a snake body and a human face. In their sacrifices, the fur and feather of one rooster and swine are used and buried. The ritual items consist of a squared jade tablet and a round jade tablet. They are thrown. Ritual rice is not used.

---

[99] The text says "seventeen" even though there are only "sixteen" mountains in this section. In the note of SJ 3.3.33, Hao Yixing points to this discrepancy and associates it with the redundancy between the name Mt Kōngsāng found both in SJ 3.3.33 and in SJ 4.2.1.

Mountain Range 3

1. Mount Tàihàng 太行之山

The first mountain of the third section of the Book of the Northern Mountains is called Tàihàng. Its head is called Guī.
Its tip has lots of gold and jade, its base lots of blue-green stones.
It has an animal that resembles a líng goat, has four horns, a horse tail and rooster's spurs. Its name, derived from its call, is huī. It is good at twirling and dancing.
It has a bird that resembles the magpie, has a white body, a red tail and six legs. Its name, derived from its call, is bēn. It is easily frightened.

2. Mount Lónghóu 龍侯之山

Two hundreds li further northeast is found Mount Lónghóu. It has no vegetation but lots of gold and jade.
The river Juéjué exits from this mountain, flows east, and pours into the Yellow River. Its bed has lots of salamanders that resemble the Giant Salamander (Giant Salamander-like reptile). They have four legs, and a call like the sound of an infant. Their consumption protects against insanity.

3. Mount Mǎchéng 馬成之山

Two hundreds li further northeast is found Mount Mǎchéng. Its tip has lots of aragonite. On the northern side, there are lots of gold and jade.
It harbors animals resembling white dogs with black head. When they meet humans, they fly away. Their name is tiānmǎ. Their name derives from their call.
It has a bird that resembles a crow, has a white head, a green body, and yellow legs. Its name, derived from its call, is qūjū. Its consumption prevents hunger and it addresses amnesia.

4. Mount Xián 咸山

Seventy li further northeast is found Mount Xián. Its tip abounds in jade and its base in copper.
It has lots of pine and cypress trees, and its grass include lots of gromwells.

The river Tiáojiān exits from this mountain, flows southwest, and pours into the marsh Cháng. It has lots of qìsuān, reaching potency after three years. Its consumption addresses epidemic diseases.

5. Mount Tiānchí 天池之山

Two hundreds li further north is found Mount Tiānchí.   Its tip has no vegetation but lots of aragonites. It has animals that resemble the hare and have a rat head. They glide by means of something on their back. Their name is fēishǔ.
The river Shéng exits from this mountain and disappears at its base. Its bed has lots of loess.

6. Mount Yáng 陽山

Three hundreds li further east is found Mount Yáng. Its tip has lots of jade and its base lots of gold and copper.
It has ox-like animals. They have a red tail and a dewlap on the neck that looks like a dipper. Their name, derived from their call, is lǐnghú. Their consumption prevents mania.
It has birds that resemble female pheasants and display the five colors. They are hermaphrodite animals. Their name, derived from their call, is xiàngshé.
The river Liú exits from this mountain, flows south, and pours into the Yellow River. Its bed contains lots of xiànfù fishes. This fish is like the Crucian carp; it has a fish head and a swine body. Its consumption prevents vomiting.

7. Mount Bēnwén 賁聞之山

Three hundred fifty li further east is found Mount Bēnwén. Its tip has lots of green jade and its base lots of loess, and lots of alum stones.

8. Mount Wángwū 王屋之山

One hundred li further north is found Mount Wángwū. It is filled with rocks.
The river Niǎn springs there, flows northwest, and pours into the marsh Tài.

9. Mount Jiāo 教山

Three hundreds li further northeast is found Mount Jiāo. Its tip has lots of jade and no rocks.

The river Jiāo springs there, flows west, and pours into the Yellow River. This river is dry in the winter and flows in the summer. This is why it is called a river which can dry up.[100]
In the middle of it is found a double mountain spreading over three hundreds steps. It is called Mount Fāwán. Its tip has gold and jade.

10. Mount Jǐng 景山

Three hundreds li further south is found Mount Jǐng. In the south it faces marsh Yánfàn[101] and in the north marsh Shǎo[102]. Its tip has lots of grass, mountain potatoes. Among its grasses, there are lots of red peppers.
On its northern side there are lots of hematite and on the southern one lots of jade.
It has a bird with the shape of a snake, four wings, six eyes and three feet. Its name, derived from their call, is suānyǔ. Its apparition is a sign of terror in the country.[103]

11. Mount Mèngmén 孟門之山

Three hundred twenty li further southeast is found Mount Mèngmén. Its tip has lots of blue jade and gold and its basis lots of loess.

12. Mount Píng 平山

Three hundred twenty li further southeast is found Mount Píng.
The river Píng exits from its top and disappears at its base. There are lots of beautiful jade.

13. Mount Jīng 京山

Two hundreds[104] li further east is found Mount Jīng. It has beautiful jade, lots of varnish trees and lots of bamboos. Its northern side has red copper and its southern side black whetstones.
The river Gāo exits from this mountain, flows south, and pours into the Yellow River.

---

[100] 乾河 gān hé, a dry river.
[101] 鹽販之澤 yánfàn zhī zé. According to Guopu, marsh Yánfàn (鹽販之澤) is the salt pond (鹽池 Yánchí) of Xièxiàn (解縣) in Shanxi. Xièxiàn is the place where Chi You was beheaded by the men of Huangdi. The salt lake nearby (probably Yánchí) has a water of reddish color, tinted, people say, by Chi You's blood.
[102] 少澤 Shǎo zé.
[103] Another text says that "its consumption prevents drunkenness."
[104] Kean suggests that it is actually three hundreds and not two hundreds.

14. Mount Chóngwěi 虫尾之山

Two hundreds[105] li further east is found Mount Chóngwěi. Its tip has lots of gold and jade and its base lots of bamboos and lots of blue-green gems.
The river Dān exits from this mountain, flows south, and pours into the Yellow River. The river Bó also exits from it, flows southeast and pours into the marsh Huáng.

15. Mount Péngpí 彭毗之山

Three hundreds li further east is found Mount Péngpí. It tips has no vegetation but lots of gold and jade. Its base has lots of water(s).
The river Zǎolín springs there, flows southeast and pours into the Yellow River. The river Féi also exits from this mountain, flows south, and pours into river Chuáng. There are lots of féiyí snakes.

16. Mount Xiǎohóu 小侯之山

One hundred eighty li further east is located Mount Xiǎohóu. The river Míngzhāng springs there, flows south, and pours into the marsh Huang.
It has birds that are like crows with white spots. Their name is gūxī. Their consumption prevents obscuring of the vision.

17. Mount Tàitóu 泰頭之山

Three hundred seventy li further east is found Mount Tàitóu.
The river Gòng springs there, flows south, and pours its water into the Hūchí.
Its tip has lots of gold and jade and its basis lots of arrow bamboos.

18. Mount Xuānyuán 軒轅之山

Two hundreds li further northeast is found Mount Xuānyuán. Its tip has lots of copper and its basis lots of bamboo.
It has birds that look like white-headed owls. Their name, derived from their call, is Huángniǎo. Their consumption prevents jealousy.

19. Mount Yèlì 謁戾之山

Two hundreds li further north is found Mount Yèlì. Its tip has lots of pine and cypress, and there is gold and jade.

---

[105] The annotation suggests that it is actually three hundreds and not two hundreds.

The river Qìn springs there, flows south, and pours into the Yellow River.
In the east is found a forest called Dānlín.
The river Dānlín springs there, flows south, and pours into the Yellow River.
The river Yīnghóu [also] springs there, flows north, and pours into the river Fàn.

20. Mount Jǔrù 沮洳之山

Three hundreds li east is found Mount Jǔrù. It has no vegetation but it has gold and jade.
The river Qí exits from it, flows south, and pours into the Yellow River.

21. Mount Shénqūn 神囷之山

Three hundreds li further north is found Mount Shénqūn. Its tip has aragonites and its basis white snakes and winged insects.
The river Huáng springs there, flows east, and pours into the Huán.
The river Fǔ also springs there, flows east, and pours into the river Oū.

22. Mount Fājiū 發鳩之山

Two hundreds li further north is found Mount Fājiū. Its top has lots of silkworm thorn trees.
It has a bird that look like a crow, and has a spotted head, a white beak and red feet. Its name, derived from its call, is Jīngwèi. This bird is the young girl of emperor Yándì, called Nǔwá. Swimming in the Dōnghǎi sea, Nǔwá drowned and did not return. Then, she changed into Jīngwèi.[106]
Ceaselessly she put into her mouth wood and stones from the western mountains and builds up a nest with them[107] in the eastern sea.
The river Zhāng exits from this mountain, flows east, and pours into the Yellow River.

23. Mount Shǎo 少山

One hundred twenty li further northeast is found Mount Shǎo. Its tip has lots of gold and jade and its base lots of copper.
The river Qīngzhāng springs there and flows east in the river Zhuózhāng.

---

[106] Or rather into the jīngwèi bird, mentioned in the same chapter.
[107] 堙 yīn. Build up, stop up, block. The etymological idea here seems to be important since it is about the work of a bird: From 土 (tǔ) 'earth' and 亜 yīn 'masonry'. Etymologically the same word as 亜. "西 picture of a bird's nest built up with 土 earth, mud" Karlgren.

24. Mount Xī 錫山

Two hundreds li further east is found Mount Xī. Its tip has lots of jade, and its basis lots of whetstones. The river Niúshǒu exits from this mountain, flows east, and pours into the river Fǔ.

25. Mount Jǐng 景山

Two hundreds li further north is found Mount Jǐng, where beautiful jade is found.
The river Jǐng springs there, flows east, and pours into the sea marshes.

26. Mount Tíshǒu 題首山

One hundred li further north is found Mount Tíshǒu. It has jade, lots of rocks and no waterways.

27. Mount Xiù 繡山

One hundred li further north is found Mount Xiù. Its tip has jade and blue-green gems.
Its trees include lots of xún, and its grasses lots of peony and Ligusticum.
The river Wěi exits from this mountain, flows east, and pours into the Yellow River. Its bed has lots of catfishes and mǐn frogs.

28. Mount Sōng 松山

One hundred twenty li further north is found Mount Sōng. The river Yáng exits from this mountain, flows northeast, and pours into the Yellow River.

29. Mount Dūnyǔ 敦與之山

One hundred twenty li further north is found Mount Dūnyǔ. Its tip has no vegetation but lots of jade and gold.
The river Suǒ springs from the southern slope of this mountain, flows east, and pours into the river Tàilù. The river Dǐ springs from the northern slope, flows east, and pours into the river Péng. The river Huái also springs from it, flows east, and pours into the marsh Chí.

30. Mount Zhè 柘山

One hundred seventy li further north is found Mount Zhè. Its southern side has gold and jade and its northern one iron.

The river Lìjù springs there, flows north, and pours into the river Wěi.

31. Mount Wéilóng 維龍之山

Three hundred li further north is found Mount Wéilóng. Its tip has blue-green stones and jade. In the south there is gold and in the north iron.
The river Féi springs there, goes east and flows into the marsh Gāo. It has lots of lěi stones.
The river Chǎngtiě also springs there, flows north, and pours into the marsh Dà.

32. Mount Báimǎ 白馬之山

One hundred eighty li further north is found Mount Báimǎ. In the south there are lots of jadeite and in the north lots of iron and lots of red copper.
The river Mùmǎ springs there, flows northeast, and pours into the Hūtuó.

33. Mount Kōngsāng 空桑之山

Two hundred li further north is found Mount Kōngsāng. It has no vegetation. Winter and summer there is snow. The river Kōngsāng springs there, flows east, and pours into the Hūtuó.

34. Mount Tàixì 泰戲之山

Three hundred li further north is found Mount Tàixì. It has no vegetation but lots of gold and jade.
It has animals that resemble goats and have one horn. They [also] have one eye located behind the ear. Their name, derived from their call, is dōngdōng. The river Hūtuó originates there, flow east and pour into the river Lóu. The river Yènǔ originates from the southern side of this mountain, flows south, and pours into the river Qìn.

35. Mount Shí 石山

Three hundred li further north is found Mount Shí. It has lots of hidden gold and jade.
The river Huòhuò springs there, flows east, and pours into the spring Hū. The river Xiānyú also originates there, flows south, and pours into the Hūtuó.

36. Mount Tóngróng 童戎之山

Two hundred li further north is found Mount Tóngróng.

The river Gāotú springs there, flows east, and pours into the river Lǚyè.

37. Mount Gāoshì 高是之山

Three hundreds li further north is found Mount Gāoshì.
The river Zī springs there, flows south, and pours into the Hūtuó. Its trees include lots of Lady Palm, its grasses lots of tufts of plants. The river Kòu springs there, flows east, and pours into the Yellow River.

38. Mount Lù 陸山

Three hundred li further north is found Mount Lù. It has lots of beautiful jade. The river Jiāng exits from this mountain, flows east, and pours into the Yellow River.

39. Mounts Qí 沂山 and Yàn 燕山

Two hundred li further north is found Mount Qí.
The river Pán springs there, flows east, and pours into the Yellow River.
One hundred twenty li north is found Mount Yàn. It has lots of ornamental stones.
The river Yàn exits from this mountain, flows east, and pours into the Yellow River.

40. Mount Ráo 饒山

In addition, going through five hundreds li in the northern mountains and five hundreds li across waters, is found Mount Ráo. I It has no vegetation but lots of green jasper and green jade.
Its animals include lots of camels and its birds lots of striped head owlets.
The river Lìguó springs there, flows east, and ends in the Yellow River. Its bed includes shī fishes. Their consumption kills

41. Mount Gān 乾山

Four hundreds li further north is found Mount Gān. It has no vegetation. In the south there are lots of gold and jade; in the north lots of iron and no water.
It has animals that resemble the bull and have three legs. Their name, derived from their call, is huán.

42. Mount Lún 倫山

Five hundred li further north is found Mount Lún.
The river Lún springs there, flows east, and pours into the Yellow River.
It has some animals that look like Père David's Deers. Their hindquarter is above the tail. Their name is pí.

43. Mount Jiéshí 碣石之山

Five hundreds li further north is Mount Jiéshí.
The river Shéng exits from this mountain, flows east, and pours into the Yellow River. Its bed has lots of púyí fishes.
The tip has lots of jade and the base lots of blue-green gems.

44. Mount Yànmén 鴈門之山

Five hundreds li further north by waters is found Mount Yànmén. It has no vegetation.

45. Mount Dìdōu 帝都之山

Four hundreds li further north by waters is found the marsh Tài. In the middle of it is found Mount Dìdōu. It spreads over one hundred lis. There is no vegetation but there are lots of jade and gold.

46. Mount Chúnyú Wúféng 錞于毋逢之山

Five hundred li further north is found Mount Chúnyú Wúféng. It faces Mount Jīhào. An impetuous wind is found there. In the west it faces Mount Yōudū. The river Yù springs there. It has large snakes with a red head and a white body. They call is like that of cows. Their apparition is a sign of major drought in the surroundings.

47. Summary and Rituals

In summary, from Mount Tàixíng, located in the beginning of the third section of the northern mountains to Mount Chúnyú Wúféng, there are altogether forty-six mountains[108] spreading over 12,350 lis.

---

[108] Other texts count 47 mountains (see SJ 3.3.39). This would differ with the final note.

Among the divinities of these mountains, twenty have a horse body and human face. In their ancestral temples, aquatic plants and aromatic plants are used and buried.[109]
Fourteen other divinities have a pig body and wear jade. In their rituals, jade is used but not buried.
Finally, ten other divinities[110] have a pig body, eight legs and a serpent tail. In their rituals, round jade tablets are buried.
Altogether, there are forty-four divinities for which glutinous rice is used in their ancestral temples. These ceremonies do not use fire for cooking.[111]

Note: The book of the northern mountains contains eighty-seven mountains covering 23,230 li.

---

[109] The ancient ancestral temples all used jade objects as main items for burial ceremonies. There are no records of using and burying aquatic and aromatic plants aside from this passage. There is probably a corruption of the characters used here, or a missing passage.
[110] Hao Yixing mentions that there are 44 divinities for 46 mountains. He concludes that some of these divinities were linked to several mountains.
[111] The Northern mountains people ate raw food (Annotation). The same observation was made in the end of the first section of the Northern mountains (See SJ 3.1.25).

4. 東山經 - Book of the Eastern Mountains

Mountain Range 1

1. Mount Sǔzhǔ 橾蟊[矛改朱]之山

The initial mountain of the first eastern mountains range is called Mount Sǔzhǔ. In the north, it is adjacent to Mount Gānnmèi.
The river Shí springs there, flows northeast, and pours into the sea.[112] It has lots of doctor fishes. They look like colored cattle. Their call is like that of the pig.

2. Mount Lěi 矗山

Three hundred li further south is found Mount Lěi. Its tip has lots of jade, its base lots of gold.
The river Hú springs there, flows east, and pours its waters into the river shí. It has lots of tadpoles.

3. Mount Xúnzhuàng 枸狀之山

Three hundreds li further south is found Mount Xúnzhuàng. Its tip has lots of gold and jade and its basis lots of blue-green gem stones.
There are animals there resembling dogs and having six legs. Their name, derived from their call, is cóngcóng.
There are birds there resembling chicken covered with rat's hair.[113] Their name is zīshǔ. Their apparition in a locality, it is a sign of major draught.
The river zhǐ springs there, flows north, and pours into the river Hú. Its bed has lots of needlefishes. They look like the sharpbelly fish, their mouth is armed with a needle. Eating them protects against epidemic diseases.

4. Mount Bóqì 勃齊之山

Three hundreds li further south is found Mount Bóqì. It has neither vegetation nor waterways.

---

[112] This sea appears to be the present-day Bay of Láizhōu 莱州湾, in the south of Bó Sea 渤海.
[113] According to Hao Yixing, hair 毛 should be understood as tail 尾.

5. Mount Fāntiáo 番條之山

Three hundreds li further south is found Mount Fāntiáo. It has no vegetation but lots of sand.
The river Jiǎn springs there, flows north, and pours into the sea. Its bed has lots of yellow-cheek carps.

6. Mount Gūér 姑兒之山

Four hundreds li further south is found Mount Gūér. Its tip has lots of varnish trees, and its basis lots of mulberry trees and silkworm thorny trees.
The river Gūér springs there, flows north, and pours into the sea. It has lots of yellow-cheek carps.

7. Mount Gāoshì 高氏之山

Four hundreds li further south is found Mount Gāoshì. Its tip has lots of jade and its basis lots of thorn stones.
The river Zhūshéng springs there, flows east, and pours into the zé. It has lots of gold and jade.

8. Mount Yuè 嶽山

Three hundreds li further south is found Mount Yuè. Its tip has lots of mulberry trees and its basis lots of trees of heaven.
The river Luò springs there, flows east, and pours into the zé. It has lots of gold and jade.

9. Mount Chái 犲山

Three hundred li further south is found Mount Chái. Its tip has no vegetation. Its basis has lots of water which contains lots of kānxǔ fishes.
There are animals that look like the kuāfù (kuāfù-like animal) and have pig's hair. Their call is like a shout. Their apparition is a sign of severe floods in the Empire.

10. Mount Dú 獨山

Three hundreds li further south is found Mount Dú. Its tip has lots of gold and jade and its base lots of beautiful stones.
The river Mòtú springs there, flows east, and pours into the Miǎn. It has lots of tiáoróng that look like yellow snakes with fish fins.[114] Their movements are

---

[114] 魚翼 yùyì. Lit. fishes' wings. Archaic expression pointing to the pectoral fins.

accompanied by glistens.[115] Their apparition is a sign of great drought in a locality.

11. Mount Tài 泰山

Three hundreds li further south is found Mount Tài. Its tip has lots of jade and its basis lots of gold.
There are animals there resembling young pigs with pearls. Their name, derived from their call, is tōngtōng.
The river huán springs there, flows east, and pours into the Jiāng. Its bed has lots of water jade.

12. Mount Zhú 竹山

Three hundred li further south is found Mount Zhú. It has a sharp slope into the Jiāng.[116] It has no vegetation but lots of green jasper and green jade.
The river Jī springs there, flows southeast, and pours into the river Qǔtán. Its bed has lots of purple snails.

13. Summary and Rituals

In summary, from the leading Mount Sǔzhǔ to Mount Zhú, the first eastern mountains range include twelve mountains spreading over three thousands and six hundred lis.

The divinities of these mountains all have a human body and a dragon head. The rituals in the ancestral temples call for the fur of a specific dog for the invocation. For the ér, use a fish.[117]

---

[115] 有光 yǒuguāng. Glazed, bright.

[116] 江 Jiāng. Elsewhere it is said on the shore side. See previous note on 江 jiāng in SJ 4.1.11.

[117] [耳申] ér. Blood unction made during prayers. It may mean a kind of religious soaking. This may be 衈 èr, the blood of a sacrificial fowl which was sprinkled on the doors and vessels. It is also written as 祈珥 qíěr, and 刉珥 jīěr. The *Zhouli* (Spring 春官 – 肆师) says: At the appropriate time of the seasons, the rituals offers to the divinities are made and the ěr prayers done. In addition, the *Zhouli* (Autumn 秋官– 士师) says, "during the 刉珥 (jīěr), conduct a dog sacrifice." Zheng Xuan 郑玄注 says, "in the case of dispute over ceremony, use a sacrifice, the hair of one said 刉 (jī), the feather of one said 衈 (ěr)."

Mountain Range 2

1. Mount Kōngsāng 空桑之山

The first mountain of the second eastern mountains range is called Mount Kōngsāng. In the north it overlooks the river Shí, in the east it looks at Jǔwú, in the south it looks at Shālíng and in the west is looks at the marsh Mǐn.
There are animals there resembling the bull and having tiger stripes. Their call is like an animal groan. Their name, derived from their call, is línglíng. Their apparition is a sign of floods in the empire.

2. Mount Cáoxī 曹夕之山

Six hundreds li further south is found Mount Cáoxī. Its base has lots of paper mulberry trees but it has no waterways. It has lots of birds and animals.

3. Mount Yìgāo 嶧皋之山

Four hundreds li further southwest is found Mount Yìgāo. Its tip has lots of gold and jade. Its base has lots of chalky soil. The river Yìgāo springs there, flows east, and pours into the river Jīrǔ. It contains lots of bivalve mollusks.

4. Mount Gé - Extremity 葛山之尾

Five hundreds li further south across water and three hundred li across desert is found the extremity of Mount Gé. It has no vegetation but lots of grindstones and sharpening whetstones.

5. Mount Gé - Head 葛山之首

Three hundred eighty li further south is found the head of Mount Gé. It has no vegetation.
The river Lǐ springs there, flows east, and pours into the marsh Yú. Its bed has lots of zhūbiē fishes that looks like lungs.[118]   They have eyes and six feet that have pearl-like structures. The taste of their flesh is sour and sweet. Their consumption protects against epidemic diseases.

---

[118] 胏 zǐ (pronounced fèi). An ancient term that corresponds to 肺 fèi, the lungs.

6. Mount Yú'é 餘峨之山

Three hundreds eighty li further south is found Mount Yú'é. Its tip has lots of catalpas and náns and its base lots of thorn bushes and wolfberry shrubs jīngqǐ.
The river Záyú springs in this mountain, flows east, and pours into the Yellow River. There are animals there resembling hares, and having a bird beak, owl eyes and snake tail. When they see humans, they pretend to be dead. Their name, derived from their call, is qiúyú. Their apparition is a sign of locust invasion (in the cultivated fields).

7. Mount Dùfù 杜父之山

Three hundreds li further south is found Mount Dùfù. It has no vegetation but lots of water.

8. Mount Gěng 耿山

Three hundreds li further south is found Mount Gěng. It has no vegetation but lots of shuǐbì amethysts and lots of big snakes.
There are animals there resembling foxes with fish fins. Their name, derived from their call, is zhūrú. Their apparition is a sign of dread in the country.

9. Mount Lúqí 盧其之山

Three hundreds li further south is found Mount Lúqí. It has no vegetation but lots of sand and stones.
The river Shā springs from this mountain, flows south, and pours into the river Cén. It has lots of teals. They look like mandarin ducks but have human feet. Their name derives from their call. Their apparition is a sign of major achievements in the country.

10. Mount Gūyè 姑射之山

Three hundreds eighty li further south is found Mount Gūyè. It has no vegetation but lots of waters.

11. Mount Gūyè - North 北姑射之山

Three hundreds li further south across water and one hundreds li across the desert is found the northern Mount Gūyè. It has no vegetation but lots of rocks.

12. Mount Gūyè - South 南姑射之山

Three hundreds li further south is found the southern Mount Gūyè. It has no vegetation but lots of water.

13. Mount Bì 碧山

Three hundreds li further south is found Mount Bì. It has no vegetation but lots of big snakes, lots of blue-green stones and lots of water jade.

14. Mount Gōushì 緱氏之山

Five hundreds li further south is found Mount Gōushì. It has no vegetation but lots of gold and lots of jade. The river Yuán springs there, flows east, and pours into the marsh Shā.

15. Mount Gūféng 姑逢之山

Three hundreds li further south is found Mount Gūféng. It has no vegetation but lots of gold and jade.
There is an animal there resembling a fox with wings. Its call is like that of the swan goose. Its name is bìbì. Its apparition is a sign of major drought in the Empire.

16. Mount Fúlí 凫麗之山

Five hundreds li further south is found Mount Fúlí. Its tip has lots of gold and jade and its base lots of thorn stones.
There is an animal there resembling a fox and has nine tails and nine heads. It has tiger paws. Its name is lóngzhí. Its call is like the wail of the newborn. It eats humans.

17. Mount Zhēn [石垔]山

Five hundreds li further south is found Mount Zhēn. In the south it neighbors the river Yīn and in the north it faces Húzé.
There are animals there that have the shape of a horse, sheep eyes,[119] four horns and a bull tail. Their call is like that of the bark of a dog. Their name is yōuyōu. Their apparition is a sign of deception.
There are birds there that look like wild ducks and have a rat tail. They are experts in climbing trees. Their name is xiégōu. Their apparition is a sign of numerous epidemics in the country.

---

[119] The *Zangjing Ben* says sheep head and not sheep eyes (Hao Yixing).

18. Summary and Rituals

In summary, from the leading Mount Kōngsāng to Mount Zhēn, the second mountains range includes seventeen mountains spreading over 6,640 lis.

The divinities of these mountains all have an animal body and a human face. They carry antlers on their head. Their ancestral temples require: one chicken of a specific feather type for the invocations. The utensils of the temple include a bì jade for burial.

Mountain Range 3

1. Mount Shīhú 尸胡之山

The first mountain of the third eastern mountains range is called Mount Shīhú. In the north it faces Mount Xiāng. Its top has lots of gold and jade and its base lots of knotty trees.
There are animals there that look like Père David's Deers and have fish eyes. Their name, derived from their call, is wānhú.

2. Mount Qí 岐山

Eight hundreds li further south across water is found Mount Qí. Its trees include lots of peach and prune trees and its animals, lots of tigers.

3. Mount Zhūgōu 諸鉤之山

Five hundreds li further south across water is found Mount Zhūgōu. It has no vegetation but lots of sand and rocks. Its area is one hundreds li. There are lots of Garra pingi fishes.

4. Mount Zhōngfù 中父之山

Seven hundreds li further south across water is found Mount Zhōngfù. It has no vegetation but lots of sand.

5. Mount Húshè 胡射之山

One thousand li further east across water is found Mount Húshè. It has no vegetation but lots of sand and rocks.

6. Mount Mèngzǐ 孟子之山

Seven hundreds li further south across water is found Mount Mèngzǐ. Its trees include lots of catalpa and Tung, and lots of peach and prune trees. Its grasses include jūnpú seaweeds. Its animals include lots of David's deers.
The area covered by this mountain is one hundred li.
There is a river that springs from its top. It is called Bìyáng. Its bed has lots of sturgeons.

7. Mount Qǐzhǒng 跂踵之山

Five hundreds li further south across water and five hundreds li across a sand desert is found Mount Qǐzhǒng. Its area covers two hundred lis. There is no vegetation but there are big snakes. Its top has lots of jade.

There is a water area there covering forty li. It is always gushing. It is called marsh Shēn. It has lots of large turtles with variegated carapaces.

There are also fishes that look like a carp. They have six feet and a bird tail. Their name, derived from their call, is fish háhá.

8. Mount Mǔyú 踇隅之山

Nine hundreds li further south across water is found Mount Mǔyú. Its tip has no vegetation but there is lots of gold, jade and lots of hematite.

There are animals there resembling bulls and having a horse tail. Their name, derived from their call, is jīngjīng.

9. Mount Wúgāo 無皋之山

Five hundreds li further south across water and three hundred li further across a sand desert is found Mount Wúgāo. In the south it faces the sea Yòu and in the east the Fǔmù. It has no vegetation and has lots of winds. The area of this mountain covers one hundred lis.

10. Summary and Rituals

In summery, the third eastern mountains range, from the leading Mount Shīhú to Mount Wúgāo, includes nine mountains, covering 6,900 lis.

The deities of these mountains all have a human body and ram's horns. Their sacrifice animals consist in a ram, and the sacrificial grain, broomcorn millet. Their appearance causes wind, rain and waters disasters.

Mountain Range 4

1. Mount Běiháo 北號之山

The first mountain of the fourth eastern mountains range is called Mt Běihào. It overlooks the northern sea.
There is a tree there resembling the poplar tree [poplar-like tree],[120] with red flowers and jujube-like fruits but without pit. The taste of this fruit is sweet and sour. Its consumption protects against fever.
The river Shí springs there, flows northeast, and pours into the sea.
There is an animal there that has the shape of a wolf, with a red head and rat eyes. Its grunt is similar to the one of a young pig. Its name is géjū. It eats humans.
There is a bird there that resembles the chicken, has a white head, rat feet and tiger paws. Its name is qíqiāo. It also eats humans.

2. Mount Máo 旄山

Three hundred li further south is found Mount Máo. It has no vegetation.
The river Cāngtǐ springs there, flows west, and pours into the river Zhǎn. It has lots of bighead carps that resemble the carp but have a bigger head. Their consumption prevents warts.

3. Mount Dōngshǐ 東始之山

Three hundreds li further south is found Mount Dōngshǐ. Its top has lots of azure jade.
There is a tree there that resembles the poplar and has red veins. Its sap is like blood and it has no fruits. Its name is qǐ. The sap of this tree is used to scrub horses.[121]
The river Cǐ exits from this mountain, goes northwest, and pours into the sea. Its bed has lots of beautiful cowries and lots of sea stars that look like Crucian carps. They have a single head and ten bodies. Their fragrance is like that of the sea moss ogonori. Their consumption prevents passing gas.

---

[120] The text does not gives its name. In the appendix on plants I refer to it as the Poplar-like tree of Mt Běihào.
[121] Guopu: it is used to scrub the horse's fur and enhance the beauty of its luster.

4. Mount Nǚzhēng 女烝之山

Three hundred li further southeast is found Mount Nǚzhēng. Its top has no vegetation. The river Shígāo springs there, flows west, and pours into the river Gé. Its bed has lots of carp-like fishes that look like huso sturgeons and have a single eye. Their call is like that of someone vomiting. Their apparition is a sign of great drought in the empire.[122]

5. Mount Qīn 欽山

Two hundred li further southeast is found Mount Qīn. It has lots of gold and jade but no rocks.
The river Shī exits from this mountain, flows north, and pours into the marsh Gāo. It has lots of bighead carps and striped cowries.
There are animals there that look like small pigs and have tusks. Their name, derived from their call, is dàngkāng. Their apparition is a sign of great abundance in the empire.

6. Mount Zǐtóng 子桐之山

Two hundred li further southeast is found Mount Zǐtóng. The river Zǐtóng springs from it, flows west, and pours into the marsh Yúrú. It contains many huái fishes. They are like fishes and have birds' wings. Their movements are accompanied by glistens. Their call is like that of the mandarin duck. Their apparition is a sign of great drought on earth.

7. Mount Shàn 剡山

Two hundred li further northeast is found Mount Shàn. It has lots of gold and jade.
There is an animal there that looks like a pig and has a human face, a yellow body and a red tail.[123] Its name is héyǔ. Its call is like that of the newborn. It eats humans, insects and snakes. Its apparition is a sign of great floods in the world.

8. Mount Tài 太山

Two hundreds li further east is found Mount Tài. Its top has lots of gold and jade and it has zhēnmù glossy privets.
There is an animal there that looks like a bull and has a white head. It has one eye and a snake tail. Its name is fěi. When it goes into water, it dries it

---

[122] The *Chuxue ji* § 13 cites this passage with a mild variation: 見則天下反 jiàn, zé tiānxià, fǎn, or "their apparition is a sign of insurrection in the empire."
[123] 赤 chì. Red or bare.

up. When it goes into grass, it kills it. Its apparition is a sign of great epidemics.
The river Gōu springs in this mountain, flows on the northern side and pours into the river Láo. It has lots of bighead carps.

9. Summary

In summary, the fourth eastern mountain range, from Mount Běihào, the first one, to Mount Tài, includes eight mountains spreading over 1,720 lis.[124]

The book of the Eastern Mountains includes a total of forty-six mountains spreading over 18,860 lis.

---

[124] This section does not include a paragraph on divinities, suggesting that the text is incomplete.

5. 中山經 - Book of the Central Mountains

Mountain Range 1 - Bó 薄山

1. **Mount Gānzǎo** 甘棗之山

Mount Gānzǎo is the head of Mt Bó, the first central mountains range.
The river Gòng springs there, flows west, and pours into the Yellow River.
Its top has lots of red apricot trees. Its base has plants whose stem resembles that of the sunflower, and whose leaves resemble that of the apricot tree. Their flowers are yellow and their fruits pod-like. Their name is tuò. They prevent sight loss.
There are animals there that resemble huìshǔ with stripes. Their name is nài. Their consumption cures goiter.

2. **Mount Lì'ér** 歷兒之山

Twenty li further east is found Mount Lì'ér.
Its top has lots of Ring-cup oak trees and lots of lìmù trees whose trunk is squared, its leaves round, the flowers yellow and fury, and the fruit like that of the chinaberry. As a medicine, it prevents forgetfulness.

3. **Mount Qúzhū** 渠豬之山

Fifteen li further east is found Mount Qúzhū. Its tip has lots of bamboos.
The river Qúzhū springs there, flows south, and pours into the Yellow River.
Its bed contains lots of háo fishes. They resemble sturgeons, and have red mouth and tail and red wings. They are used against white ringworms.

4. **Mount Cōnglóng** 蔥聾之山

Thirty-five li further east Is found Mount Cōnglóng   It has lots of big valleys.
There, there are lots of white, green and yellow porcelain soils.[125]

5. **Mount Wō** 湊山

Fifteen li further east is found Mount Wō. Its top has lots of red copper and its southern side lots of iron.

---

[125] 黃堊 huáng'è. Of various colors (Hao Yixing).

6. Mount Tuōhù 脫扈之山

Seventy li further east is found Mount Tuōhù. There is a plant there whose leaves resemble that of the sunflower. Its flowers are red and its pod fruits resemble those of the palm tree. It is called zhíchǔ. It can be used to prevent melancholia. Its consumption prevents nightmares.

7. Mount Jīnxīng 金星之山

Twenty li east is found Mount Jīnxīng. It has lots of tiānyīng fossils whose form is like that of a dragon bone. It is a remedy against carbuncles.

8. Mount Tàiwēi 泰威之山

Seventy li further east is seen Mount Tàiwēi. In the middle of it is a valley called Xiāogǔ. This valley contains lots of iron.

9. Mount Jiānggǔ 橿谷之山

Fifteen li further east is found Mount Jiānggǔ. It contains lots of red copper.

10. Mount Wúlín 吳林之山

One hundred twenty li further east is found Mt Wúlín. It has lots of White Patrinia plants.

11. Mount Niúshǒu 牛首之山

Thirty li further north is found Mount Niúshǒu. There is a plant there called Devil grass. Its leaves are like those of the sunflower; it has a red stem, and ears like standing [rice] grains. As a medicine, it protects from sadness.
The river Lao springs there, flows west, and pours into the river Jué. It contains lots of flying fishes that resemble Crucian carps. Their consumption protects against hemorrhoids.

12. Mount Huò 霍山

Forty li further north is found Mound Huò. Its trees include lots of paper mulberry. There are animals there that look like foxes, and have a white tail and a mane. Their name is fěifěi. Their consumption prevents sadness.

13. Mount Hégǔ 合谷之山

Fifty-two li further north is found Mount Hégǔ. There are lots of asparagus.

14. Mount Yīn 陰山

Thirty-five li further north is found Mount Yīn. It has lots of whetstones and aragonites.
The river Shǎo exits from this mountain. It contains lots of diāotáng trees. The leaves of this tree are like those of the elm but squared. Its fruits are like red beans.[126] Their consumption cures ear loss.

15. Mount Gǔdèng 鼓鐙之山

Four hundreds li further northeast is found Mount Gǔdèng. It has lots of red copper.
There is a plant there called róngcǎo. Its leaves are like that of the willow and its roots like chicken eggs. Its consumption protects against wind conditions.

16. Summary and Rituals

In summary, from Mount Gānzǎo, the head of the Bó mounts, to Mount Gǔdèng, there are a total of fifteen mountains covering 6670 li.[127]
The sacred burial mound is on Mount Lì'ér.[128]

---

[126] Guopu suggests that bean should be understood as soybean.

[127] This may be an inexact estimation.

[128] 歷兒冢也. The structure of this sentence comes back regularly in the SHJ and appears to stand by itself. The literal translation is, the *tumulus* (冢 zhǒng) is *Lì'ér* (歷兒). 冢 zhǒng means something elevated, an artificial mound; a monticule covered by tombs, a cemetery. According to the *Kangxi zidian*, zhǒng means the top of a mountain (山頂) and a small elevation of soil for the cult of local divinities (封土爲社). This meaning is used in the *Shijing*, in the dàyǎ section where "then a soil monticule was elevated (乃立冢土). The height of the major sanctuaries is higher, and in this case the words zhǒng tǔ 冢土 are used. The *Yu pian* says therefore that zhǒng means a "major sanctuary." It also says that this character expresses the "dwelling of the divinities; elevated tombs" (鬼神舍也, 高墳也). Guopu also interprets zhǒng as "dwelling of the mountains divinities" (冢爲山神靈之. 舍). The Erya states that "the hilltop is called zhǒng (山頂, 冢)." In other words, mountains tops were used for the ceremonies of the cult of the sacred Mountains." Now most sections of the Book of the Central Mountains mention a special mountain for the cult of the local divinities. Here the sentence identifies Mt Lì'ér. In final, this repetitive sentence is a key to the location of the sacrificial structure for each mountain range.

The ceremonies of the ancestral temples consist of the following: Fur, utensils of the Sacrifice to Heaven, hanging[129] usage of the auspicious jade. For the other thirteen mountains the ritual animal consists of a sheep with one specific fur color. . The hanging ornaments consist in the variegated jade[130] used for offering and buried. No porridge is used. The variegated jade consists of assembled tablets. These tablets are squared below and sharp pointed above. Their central part is carved and adorned with gold.

---

[129] 縣 xiàn. Archaic meaning of xiàn. According to Guopu, it is the name of a mountain sacrificial utensil, defined in the *Erya*.

[130] 桑封 "mulberry wood tablet" are the original characters but this is a confusion that occurred and the term is actually referring to jade tablet 藻玉. In addition, the notes on the sacrificial places at each section show examples of stone tables that usually were offered to the Earth divinities, and that were buried during the religious ceremonies. Here, it would be the only mention of a wood tablet.

Mountain Range 2 - Jǐ 煇山

1. Mount Huīzhū 煇諸

Mount Huīzhū is the head of Mount Jǐ, the second central mountains range. Its top has lots of mulberry trees.
Its animals include lots of black rams and elks. Its birds include lots of fighting birds.

2. Mount Fāshì 發視之山

Two hundreds li further southwest is found Mount Fāshì. Its top has lots of gold and jade. Its base has lots of grindstones and sharpening whetstones. The river Jíyú springs there, flows west, and pours into the river Yī.

3. Mount Háo 豪山

Three hundreds li further west is found Mount Háo. Its top has lots of gold and jade but no vegetation.

4. Mount Xiān 鮮山

Three hundreds li further west is found Mount Xiān. It has lots of gold and jade but no vegetation.
The river Xiān springs there, flows north, and pours into the river Yī. Its bed has lots of singing snakes. They look like ordinary snakes but have four wings. Their call is like the sound of chime stones. Their apparition is a sign of great drought in the locality.

5. Mount Yáng 陽山

Three hundreds li further west is found Mount Yáng. It has lots of rocks and no vegetation. The river Yáng springs there, flows north, and pours into the river Yī. This river contains lots of huà snakes that have a human face, a jackal body, bird wings, and the motion of a snake. Their call resembles powerful shouts. Their apparition is a sign of major floods in the locality.

6. Mount Kūnwú 昆吾之山

Two hundreds li further west is found Mount Kūnwú. Its top has lot of red copper. There are animals there that resemble pigs and have a horn. Their call is like a howl.[131] Their name is lóngchí. Their consumption protects against nightmares.

7. Mount Jiān 蔍山

One hundred and twenty li further west is found Mount Jiān. The river Jiān springs there, flows north, and pours into the river Yī. The top abounds in gold and jade, and the base in [green jade and] realgar. There is a tree there that looks like the birchleaf, and has red leaves. Its name is Chinese silvergrass. It can be used to poison fishes.

8. Mount Dúsū 獨蘇之山

One hundred fifty li further west is found Mount Dúsū. Its top has no vegetation but lots of waters.

9. Mount Mánqú 蔓渠之山

Two hundreds li further west is found Mount Mánqú. Its top has lots of gold and jade and its base lots of arrow bamboos.
The river Yī exits from it, flows east, and pours into the Luò.
There are animals there called mǎfù. They have a human face and a tiger body. Their call is like that of infants. They eat humans.

10. Summary and Rituals

In summary, in the section relative to the head of the mountains Jǐ, from Mount Huīzhū to Mount Mánqú, there are altogether nine mountains spreading over 1670 li.

The divinities of these mountains all have a human face and a bird body. The rituals of their ancestral temples require: An animal of a specific fur. One auspicious jade is used and then thrown. Sacrificial rice is not used.

---

[131] 號 háo. Howl (of humans or wind).

Mountain Range 3 - Bèi 賁山

1. Mount Aóan 敖岸

Mount Aóan is the head of Mount Bèi, the third central mountains range.
In the south, there are lots of agate and in the north lots of hematite and yellow gold.   The divinities of the pond Xūn live there.   Beautiful jade constantly goes out of it.
In the north, it faces the forest Hé that consists of qiàn madder plant and purpleblow maple.
There are animals there that look like white deers and have four horns.   Their name is fūzhū.   Their apparition is a sign of major floods in the area.

2. Mount Qīngyào 青要之山

Ten li further east is found Mount Qīngyào.   This is in fact the secret[132] residence of the Emperor.[133]   In the north, it faces the meanderings of the Yellow River. It has lots of wild geese. In the south, it faces the islet of Tián. This is where the father of [Emperor] Yǔ underwent metamorphosis.
There are lots of snails and clams.
The divinity Wǔluó governs there. It has a human face, with leopard stripes, a small waist,[134] white teeth[135] and pierced ears for ear pendants.[136] Its voice is like the sound or resonating jade.
This mountain is also suitable for the Woman.[137]

---

[132] 密 mì: 隱密, secret and 深邃, profound, abstruse, deep and far.

[133] Huangdi's secret palace. The expression 實惟帝 comes four times in the SJ, twice about Huangdi's palaces (SJ 2.3.8 and 5.3.2), once about his garden (SJ 2.3.7) and once about his river (SJ 2.3.20).

[134] 要 yào. Small waist.

[135] Or white head (Guopu).

[136] 鐻 jù. Drumstick. In this context it may be an unknown expression. It probably refers to ear pendants.

[137] The identification remains undone and several aspects can be considered. (1) The sentence "是山也，宜女子" may be a general reference to women, where the mountain may be suitable for fertility. (2) The term "woman" may refer to the mountain divinity Green Girl Qīngnǚ or 青女. She is a divinity of the white frost and of snow (乃王女主霜雪者). It would be the one mentioned in the *Huainanzi*, and referred to by the words 青要玉女 qīngyào yùnǚ, the "jade woman of the Qīngyào [mount]". (3) The term 宜 yí could either be a proper name whose signification in this context has been lost or it could refer to an archaic meaning pertain to rituals as its etymology suggests an altar under a roof (see also the etymology of mi seen above where there

The river Zhěn exits from this mountain, flows north, and pours into the Yellow River.

There are birds there called yăo. They are like wild ducks but have a blue-green body, bright-red eyes and a red tail. Their consumption brings suitable children.

There is also a plant there that resembles the White Patrinia plant. Its stem is squared, its flowers yellow, its fruits red and its root like the găo plant. Its name is xúncăo. It has the property to bring beauty back.

3. **Mount Guī** 騩山

Ten li further east is found Mount Guī. Its tip has beautiful jujube trees. On the northern side, it contains agate.

The river Zhènghuí exits from this mountain, flows north, and pours into the Yellow River. Its bed has lots of flying fishes that resemble piglets with red stripes. As pendant waist ornament, it protects from the fear of thunder. It can be used to keep aggression away.[138]

4. **Mount Yísū** 宜蘇之山

Forty li further east is found Mount Yísū. Its tip has lots of gold and jade and its base lots of Hemp-leaved chaste trees.

The river Yōngyōng exits from this mountain, flows north, and pours into the Yellow River. It has lots of yellow cowries.

5. **Mount Hé** 和山

Twenty li further east is found Mount Hé. Its tip has no vegetation but lots of green jasper and green jade.

This is actually where the nine tributaries of the Yellow River are found. This mountain has five folds. The nine rivers exit from there and then reunite, flow north, and pour into the Yellow River. Their beds have lots of green jade.

The auspicious divinity Tàiféng governs this region. It has a human body and a tiger tail.[139] It loves residing in the south of the Bèi mounts. When it

---

is a mountain under a roof). (4) Finally, this "Woman" could be related to the divinity wŭluó, which is introduced right before.

[138] The *Yiwen Leiju* section 2 explains about this section that "flying fish are like piglets, red stripes and no feathers; their consumption keeps soldiers away, and defies thunder." SJ 5.1.11 describes also describes a flying fish. It is similar except for (1) the indications and (2) the body cover, Guopu cites the *Taiping Yulan* section 44 where this creature has no scales. Note that I have translated 可以禦兵 "keeping soldiers away" as "keeping aggression away."

[139] Guopu notes that it may be a sparrow tail (雀尾).

comes and goes, it produces a light. The divinity Tàiféng moves the energies of Heaven and Earth.

6. Summary and Rituals

In summary, from the head of mountains Bèi, from Mt Aóan to Mt Hé, there is a total of five mountains spreading over 440 li.

In the ancestral temples of Tàiféng, Xūnchí and Wǔluó, one ram is sacrificed. The ornaments use auspicious jade. To it, a lucky jade tablet is added. For two of these divinities, a rooster is used and buried. The sacrificial grain uses glutinous rice.

Mountain Range 4 - Lí 犛山

1. Mount Lùtí 鹿蹄之山

Mount Lùtí is the head of Mt Lí, the fourth central mountain range. Its top has lots of jade and its base lots of gold.
The river Gān exits from this mountain, flows north, and pours into the Luò. It has lots of líng stones.

2. Mount Fúzhū 扶豬之山

Fifty li west is found Mount Fúzhū. Its top has lots of ruǎn stones. There is an animal there that looks like a raccoon dog with a human head.[140] Its name is yín.
The river Guó exits from this mountain, flows north, and pours into the Luò. Its bed has lots of ruǎn stones.

3. Mount Lí 犛山

One-hundred twenty li further west is found Mount Lí. In the south there are lots of jade and in the north lots of madders.
There are animals there that look like bull but have a blue-green body. Their call resembles that of infants. They eat humans. Their name is xīqú.
The river Yōngyōng exits from this mountain, flows south, and pours into the river Yī. It contains animals named jié. They look like growling dogs and have scales. Their fur is like pig bristles.[141]

4. Mount Jīwěi 箕尾之山

Two hundreds li further west is found Mount Jīwěi. It has lots of paper mulberry trees and lots of tú stones. Its top has lots of agate.

5. Mount Bǐng 柄山

Two-hundred and fifty li further west is found Mount Bǐng. Its top has lots of jade and its base lots of copper.
The river Tāodiāo exits from this mountain, flows north, and pours into the Luò.

---

[140] Sometimes written rénmù 人目 or "human eyes". It is probably incorrect.
[141] Between the scales are found bristles.

There are lots of xián goats. There is a tree there resembling the tree of heaven. Its leaves are like those of the tung tree and its fruits are pods. It is called bá. It can poison fishes.

6. Mount Báibiān 白邊之山

Two hundreds li further west is found Mount Báibiān. Its top has lots of gold and jade and its base lots of [green jade and] realgar.

7. Mount Xióng'ěr 熊耳之山

Two hundreds li further west is found Mount Xióng'ěr. Its top has lots of varnish trees and its basis lots of Lady Palm trees.
The river Fúháo exits from this mountain, flows west, and pours into the Luò. Its bed has lots of water jade and lots of salamanders.
There is a plant there that resembles the wild basil and has red flowers. Its name is tíngníng. It can poison fishes.

8. Mount Mǔ 牡山

Three hundreds li further west is found Mount Mǔ. Its top has lots of aragonites and its base lots of arrow bamboos and arrow-like bamboos.
Its animals include lots heavy cows and xián goats. Its birds include lots of red pheasants.

9. Mount Huānjǔ 讙舉之山

Three-hundred fifty li further west is found Mount Huānjǔ.
The river Luò exits from this mountain, flows northeast, and pours into the river Xuánhù. There are lots of tigers there.

These two mountains[142] are located at the confluent of the river Luò [and of the river Xuánhù].

10. Summary and Rituals

In summary, in the section where the head is Mount Lí, from Mount Lùtí to Mount Xuánhù, there are nine mountains spreading over 1670 li.
The divinities of these mountains all have a human face and an animal body.
Their sacrificial temples require the feather of one white chicken. Blood ritual

---

[142] This is about Mounts Huānjǔ and Xuánhù, lined up at the level of the confluent of the river Luo. The notes of the *Shuijing* on the section about river Luo state that "river Xuánhù originates at Mt Xuánhù."

prayers are made but sacrificial porridge is not used. Multicolor garments are wrapped to the victim.

Mountain Range 5 - Bó 薄山

1. Mount Gǒuchuáng 苟床

Mt Gǒuchuáng is the head of the mountain range Bó, the fifth central mountain range. It has no vegetation but lots of strange stones.

2. Mount Shǒu 首山

Three hundreds li east is found Mount Shǒu. Its northern side has lots of paper mulberry trees and oak trees. Its herbs include lots of mountain thistles and of Lilac daphne shrubs.
Its southern side includes lots of agate, and its trees lots of pagoda trees.
In the north there is a valley called Jī. It has lots of dì birds looking like owls. They have three eyes and they have ears. Their call is like that of the deer.[143] Their consumption protects from lingering dampness.

3. Mount Xiànzhuó 縣斸之山

Three hundreds further li east is found Mount Xiànzhuó. There is no vegetation but lots of aragonites.

4. Mount Cōnglóng 蔥聾之山

Three hundreds li further east is found Mount Cōnglóng. It has no vegetation but lots of stones having lower quality than jade.

5. Mount Tiáogǔ 條谷之山

Five hundreds li northeast is found Mount Tiáogǔ. Its trees include lots of pagoda and tung trees. Its grasses include lots of peonies and the large tuber plants méndōng.

6. Mount Chāo 超山

Ten li further north is found Mount Chāo. Its northern side has lots of azure jade and its southern side has a well filled with water in winter and dry in summer.[144]

---

[143] 錄 lù (鹿 lù). Deer. It should be the pig, according to the *Yu pian*.

7. **Mount Chénghóu** 成侯之山

Five hundreds li further east is found Mount Chénghóu. Its tip has lots of [chūn trees that are] large trees resembling the tree of heaven and its grasses include lots of jiāo medicinal plants.

8. **Mount Zhāogē** 朝歌之山

Five hundreds li further east is found Mount zhāogē. Its valley has lots of beautiful loess.

9. **Mount Huái** 槐山

Five hundreds li further east is found Mount Huái. Its valley has lots of gold and tin.

10. **Mount Lì** 歷山

Ten li further east is found Mount Lì. Its trees include lots of pagoda trees. In the south there are lots of jade.

11. **Mount Shī** 尸山

Ten li further east is found Mount Shī. It has lots of azure jade.
Its animals include lots of red deers.
The river Shī exits from this mountain, flows south, and pours into the river Luò. It has lots of beautiful jade.

12. **Mount Liángyú** 良餘之山

Ten li further east is found Mount Liángyú. Its top has lots of paper mulberry and Mongolian oaks, but no rocks.
The river Yú exits from this mountain on its northern slope, goes north, and pours into the Yellow River.
The river Rǔ exits from this mountain on its southern slope, flows southeast, and pours into the river Luò.

---

[144] A well is a man-made.

13. Mount Gǔwěi 蠱尾之山

Ten li further southeast is found Mount Gǔwěi. It has lots of whetstones and red copper.
The river Lóngyú exits from this mountain, flows southeast, and pours into the Luò.

14. Mount Shēng 升山

Twenty li further northeast is found Mount Shēng. Its trees include lots of paper mulberry, Mongolian oak, and knotty trees. Its grasses include lots of mountain potatoes, huì orchids, and lots of kòutuō.
The river Huángsuān exits from this mountain, flows north, and pours into the Yellow River. It has lots of beautiful gems.

15. Mount Yángxū 陽虛之山

Twelve li further east is found Mount Yángxū. It has lots of gold. It neighbors the river Xuánhù.[145]

16. Summary and Rituals

In summary, the mountain range Bó, from the head Mt Gǒuchuáng to Mt Yángxū, includes sixteen mountains spreading over 2982 li.

The burial mound is on Mount Shēng. The ceremonies of the ancestral temple consist of the Sacrifices to Heaven together with ornamental auspicious jade.
The divinities of Mt shǒu require gluttonous rice, a black sacrificial animal, the instruments of the Sacrifices to Heaven, and rice wine.[146] The General Dance[147] is accompanied by a drum. Finally, one bì jade tablet is used for ornament.
The river Shī is the celestial communication portal.[148] It uses large sacrificial victims consisting in one black dog on top, one hen below, and one ewe.

---

[145] 玄扈 xuánhù. Guopu mentions that the Hé map 河圖 says that Cāngjié on the behalf of the Emperor, in his journey to the South, climbed Mt Yángxū and saw the confluence of Xuánhù and the Luo.
[146] 糵釀 nièniàng. Lit. "yeast wine"; here "rice wine" 糵米 (Hao Yixing).
[147] 干儛 gànwǔ. An antique martial dance, using a tree-stem. This was the dance called 萬儛 wànwǔ, the Ten Thousands dance or General Dance. Wan became the specific name of this dance. It is said that emperor Yu used ten thousands men to master the flood waters, thus the name wàn (ten thousands). See also SJ 5.9.17.
[148] This is the path used by the divinities to ascend to the Heavens.

The throat of the ewe is slit and the blood offered.[149] Multicolor auspicious jade is used as ornament. Then, the divinity is asked to participate in the celebration.[150]

---

[149] 刏一牝羊，獻血 Cutting the ewe, blood offering: Guopu says that "using blood sacrifice, 刏 as cutting." 刏 was originally written as [气刀] and pronounced jī. This was the ritual during which cattle and sheep were sacrificed by "cutting their vital energy" out and offering it through the blood obtained.

[150] Rituals of special sacrifices consist in offering cooked food and expressing the wish and follow the expression "尸答拜, 執奠, 祝饗" dead body salutation, hold in hands and give offerings to the dead, express good wish (celebrate) and provide with food (entertain)."

104

Mountain Range 6 - Gǎodī 縞羝山

1. **Mount Píngféng** 平逢之山

Mount Píngféng is the head of Mt Gǎodī, the sixth central mountain range. In the south it faces the basin formed by rivers Yī and Luò, and in the east Mount Gǔchéng. It has neither vegetation nor waters but lots of sand and stones.

There is a divinity there that has a human body and two heads. Its name is jiāochóng. It is the master of stinging insects. Truly, this is where a honeybee nest is found.

Its ancestral temple requires one rooster. Bad influences are averted by prayers and the rooster must not be killed.

2. **Mount Gǎodī** 縞羝之山

Ten li west is found Mount Gǎodī. There is no vegetation but there are lots of gold and jade.

3. **Mount Guī** 廆山

Ten li further west is found Mount Guī. Its northern side has lots of agate. In its west is the valley Guàn where are lots of willows and paper mulberries. In these trees are birds looking like pheasants; they have a long tail, their [feathers] are crimson red, and their beak green. Their name, derived from their call, is língyào. As pendant waist ornament, they protect against nightmares.

The river jiāoshāng exits on the southern side of this mountain, flows south, and pours into the Luò.

The river Yúsuí exits on the northern side, flows north, and pours into the river Gǔ.

4. **Mount Zhānzhū** 瞻諸之山

Thirty li further west is found Mount Zhānzhū. In the south there are lots of gold and in the north lots of aragonites.

The river Xiè springs there, flows southwest, and pours into the river Luò.

The river Shǎo exits from the northern side, flows east, and pours into the river Gǔ.

5. Mount Lóuzhuō 娄涿之山

Thirty li further west is found Mount Lóuzhuō. It has no vegetation but lots of gold and jade.
The river Zhān exits from the south of this mountain, flows east, and pours into the Luò.
The river Bēi exits from the north, flows north, and pours into the river Gǔ. It includes lots of purple stones and aragonites.

6. Mount Báishí 白石之山

Forty li further west is found Mount Báishí. The river Huì exits from its south, flows south, and pours into the Luò. It has lots of water jade.
The river Jiàn comes from the north of this mountain, flows northwest, and pours into the river Gǔ. Its bed has lots of mí stones and lúdān.

7. Mount Gǔ 榖山

Fifty li further west is found Mount Gǔ. Its top has lots of paper mulberry trees and its base lots of common mulberry trees.
The river Shuǎng exits from this mountain, flows northwest, and pours into the river Gǔ. Its bed has lots of dark-green stones.

8. Mount Mì 密山

Seventy-two li further west is found Mount Mì. Its south has lots of jade and its north lots of iron.
The river Háo exits from this mountain, flows south, and pours into the Luò. This river has lots of xuánguī with a bird head and a soft-shelled turtle tail. Their call is like the noise of shattering wood.
This mountain has no vegetation.

9. Mount Chángshí 長石之山

One hundred li further west is found Mount Chángshí. It has no vegetation but lots of gold and jade.
In the west is found the valley called Gòng. It has lots of bamboos. The river Gòng exits from it, flows southwest, and pours into the Luò. Its bed has lots of sounding stones.

10. Mount Fù 傅山

One hundred and forty li further west is found Mount Fù. It has no vegetation but lots of green jasper and green jade.

The river Yànrǎn exits from the south of this mountain, flows south, and pours into the Luò. It has lots of salamanders. In the west is found the forest called Fánzhǒng.

The river Gǔ exits from it, flows east, and pours into the Luò. Its bed has lots of yān jade.

11. Mount Tuó 橐山

Fifty li further west is found Mount Tuó. It has lots of trees of heaven and salt trees.

The southern part has lots of gold and jade, the northern part lots of iron, and there is lots of artemisia.

The river Tuó exits from this mountain, flows north, and pours into the Yellow River. Its bed has lots of xiūbì fishes. They have the shape of the mǐn frog, with a white mouth. Their call is like that of the sparrow hawk. Their consumption protects from white ringworms.

12. Mount Chángzhēng 常烝之山

Ninety li further west is found Mount Chángzhēng. It has no vegetation but lots of loess.

The river Qiáo springs there, flows northeast, and pours into the Yellow River. It has lots of azure jade.

The river Zī also exits from it, flows north, and pours into the Yellow River.

13. Mount Kuāfù 夸父之山

Ninety li further west is found Mount Kuāfù. It has lots of cedar palm-like trees and arrow bamboos. Its animals include lots of heavy cows, xián goats, and its birds include lots of pheasants.

The southern side has lots of jade and the northern one lots of iron.

In the north is found the forest Táolín. It spreads over 300 li. Numerous horses live in it.

The river Hú exits from this mountain, flows north, and pours into the Yellow River. It contains lots of yān jade.

14. Mount Yánghuá 陽華之山

Ninety li west is found Mount Yánghuá. In the south are found lots of gold and jade and in the north lots of [green jade and] realgar. Its plants include lots of mountain potatoes and lots of kǔxīn. The shape of the kǔxīn resembles that of the yellow catalpa and it has fruits like gourds that taste sweet and sour. Their consumptions protects against fever.

The river Yang exits from this mountain, flows southwest, and pours into the
Luò. It has lots of salamanders.
The river Mén also exits from it, flows northeast, and pours into the Yellow
River. It has lots of black whetstones.
The river Jígū springs in the north, flows east, and pours into the river Mén.
On top are found lots of copper.
The river Mén arrives at the Yellow River and, at 790 li, enters into the river
Luò.[151]

15. Summary and Rituals

In summary, from the initial Mount Píngféng to Mount Yánghuá, the sixth
central mountain range Gǎodī includes fourteen mountains spreading over
790 li.

The high mountain peak is in the center.[152] The sacrifices are conducted
there on the sixth month [of the year]. If all methods for the ancestral
temples occur on the high mountain peak, then the empire benefits from
peace.

---

[151] In the Song edition, the character 至 (arrive) is used instead of 出 (emerge). This
sentence is illogical in several aspects; (1) with the term "emerge" since the river
already emerges from Mt Yánghuá, which is why I use the term arrive; (2) the rest of
the sentence remains unclear.
[152] This grammatical construction may allude to the way sacrifices were made by the
Emperor from the central Sacred Mountains to cover all four others, around Eastern
Zhou times (770-256 B.C.)

Mountain Range 7 - Kǔ 苦山

1. Mount Xiūyú 休與

The head of the seventh central mountains range Kǔ is called Mt Xiūyú. Its top has stones called board game of Emperor Tái,[153] or dìtái stones.[154] Molted and multicolored, they look like quail eggs.

These dìtái stones are used during the prayers addressed to the one hundred divinities. As pendant waist ornament, they protect against evil energies.

There is a plant there that looks like the yarrow plant, has red leaves and a vigorous growth. Its name is sùtiáo. It is suitable to make arrow stems.

2. Mount Gǔzhōng 鼓鍾之山

Three hundreds li east is found Mount Gǔzhōng. This is where Emperor Tái offers wine libations[155] to the one hundreds divinities.

There is a plant there whose stem is squared, its flowers yellow, its leaves round and triple. It is called yānsuān. It is used to cure poisonings.

The tip of this mountain has lots of grindstones and its base lots of and sharpening whetstones.

3. Mount Gūyáo 姑媱之山

Two hundreds li further east is found Mount Gūyáo. This is where the Emperor's daughter died. Her name is Nǚshī. She metamorphosed into a morning glory. Its foliage is dense, its flowers yellow, its fruits like those of the cuscuta. As pendant waist ornament, it is pleasant to men.

---

[153] 帝臺 dìtái. Dìtái (Sovereign Platform) is, according to Guopu, the name of an immortal human. This term also seem to refer to as Gate of the Emperor's palace. Both terms as sparsely found in the literature.

[154] 帝臺之棋 dìtái zhī qí. 棋 qí appears to be an ancient board game. Some have suggest that it is also called 博棋 bóqí, for which also very little is known. This is also true for the board games called 博 bó and 六博 liùbó. Liùbó was immensely popular during the Han Dynasty (202 BCE–220 CE). However, after the Han Dynasty it rapidly declined in popularity, possibly due to the rise in popularity of the game of Go, and it eventually became almost totally forgotten. Knowledge of the game has increased in recent years with archeological discoveries. With regard to the construction 帝臺之棋, it has parallels in SJ 5.7.2 (帝臺之所) and SJ 5.7.16 (帝臺之漿).

[155] The offering of the wine in a cup may have given the name to this mountain, Mt "Drum and Cup."

4. Mount Kǔ 苦山

Twenty li further east is found Mount Kǔ. It has animals called shāngāo. Their shape is like that of the piglet. They are red like fire and good at cursing at people.
Its tip has a tree called huángjí. Its flowers are yellow and its leaves round. Its fruits are like those of an orchid. As pendant waist ornament, it prevents having children.[156] There is also a plant there that has round leaves and no stem. Its flowers are red and it has no fruits. It is called wútiáo. As pendant waist ornament, it protects from goiter.

5. Mount Dǔ 堵山

Twenty-seven li further east is found Mount Dǔ. The Divinity Tiānyú resides there. There are lots of strange winds and rains.
Its top has a tree called tiānbiān. Its trunk is squared and resembles that of the winter sunflower. As pendant waist ornament, it protects from throat constriction.

6. Mount Fànggāo 放皋之山

Fifty-two li further east is found Mount Fànggāo. The river Míng springs there, flows south, and pours into the river Yī. Its bed has lots of azure jade.
There is a tree there whose leaves are like that of the pagoda tree. It has yellow flowers and no fruits. Its name is mēngmù. As pendant waist ornament, it protects against confusion.
There is an animal there that look like a bee. Its tail is forked and its tongue reversed.[157] It is good at shouting. It is called wénwén.

7. Mount Dàkǔ 大𦼫之山

Fifty-seven li further east is found Mount Dàkǔ. It has lots of agate and míyù stones. There is a plant there whose leaves are like of the elm, its stem is squared, and it has blue green thorns.[158] It is called niúshāng. Its roots have blue green patterns. As pendant waist ornament, it protects from fainting. It can be used to resist against soldiers.
The river Kuáng springs in the south, flows southwest, and pours into the river Yī. Its bed has lots of three-footed turtles. Their consumption prevents major diseases. It is also pretty good against swellings.

---

[156] 服之不字.

[157] 反 fǎn. Turned over, upside down, inside out.

[158] The SHJ uses the term 傷 shāng, which in its context means 刺 cì thorn.

8. Mount Bànshí 半石之山

Seventy li further east is found Mount Bànshí. Its top has a plant that blossoms as soon as it is born. It is more than ten feet high, it has red leaves and red flowers, and although it has flowers it gives no fruits. It is called jiāróng. As pendant waist ornament, it protects from the fear of thunder.[159]

The river Láirú exits from this mountain in the south, flows west, and pours into the river Yī. Its bed contains lots of lún fishes with black spots that look like Crucian carps. Their consumption prevents sleeping.

The river Hé emerges from the northern side, flows north, and pours into the Luò. It has lots of stargazer fishes. They look like the mandarin fish and live in water eddies. They have blue green spots and a red tail. Their consumption prevents furuncles. They can be used against worm abscess.

9. Mount Shàoshì 少室之山

Fifty li further east is found Mount Shàoshì. It has lots of various plants and trees fitted for granary.[160]

Its top has a tree called dìxiū. Its leaves are like that of the poplar tree. Its branches present [clusters] of five ramifications.[161] It has yellow flowers and black fruits.[162] As pendant waist ornament, it protects from anger. The top of this mountain has lots of jade[163] and its base lots of iron.

The river Xiū springs there, flows north, and pours into the Luò. Its bed contains lots of salamanders having the shape of the zhòuwěi (zhòuwěi -like salamander). They have long spurs, and their legs are white and tucked in.[164] Their consumption prevents insanity. They can be used to resist against soldiers.

---

[159] 不霆 bùtíng. The word fear is absent in the original text. However the *Beitang Shuchao* (Scroll 152) and the *Taiping Yulan* (Scroll 13), citing this chapter, uses 畏 wèi fear, dread:不畏霆

[160] 百草木成囷. According to Hao Yixing, it may be a metaphorical language suggesting the abundance of the vegetation's growth.

[161] 五衢 wǔqú. Five roads or thoroughfares.

[162] In the *Yiwen Leiju* (Scroll 88), the passage referring to this chapter states "black leaves."

[163] According to Guopu, on this mountain top there is also white jade ointment (玉膏 yùgāo). Its consumption leads to immediate immortality. However, the top cannot be reached by common people.

[164] According to Hao Yixing, this alludes to the toes looking at one another.

10. Mount Tàishì 泰室之山

Thirty li further east is found Mount Tàishì. Its top has a tree whose leaves are like that of the pear tree, with red veins. Its name is yūmù. As pendant waist ornament, it prevents female infertility.
There is a plant there that looks like the thistle. Its flowers are white and its fruits black and lustrous like those of the mountain grape plant. Its name is morning glory. As pendant waist ornament, it protects against inability to see. The top of this mountain has lots of beautiful stones.

11. Mount Jiǎng 講山

Thirty li further north, is found Mount Jiǎng. Its top has lots of jade, silkworm thorny trees and cypress trees. There is a tree there called dìwū. Its leaves are shaped like those of the pepper tree, with hooked thorns[165] and red fruits. It is used to protect against ominous events.

12. Mount Yīngliáng 嬰梁之山

Thirty li further north is found Mount Yīngliáng. Its top has lots of azure jade, echoing stones and black stones.

13. Mount Fúxī 浮戲之山

Thirty li further east is found Mount Fúxī. There is a tree there whose leaves are shaped like those of the tree of heaven and whose fruits are red. It is called kàngmù. Its consumption protects against evil energies.
The river Sì springs there, flows north, and pours into the Yellow River.
In the east is found a valley [containing snakes], whose name therefore is valley Shé. On top of it are found lots of small wild ginger plants.

14. Mount Shǎoxíng 少陘之山

Forty li further east is found Mount Shǎoxíng. There is a plant there called gāngcǎo. It has leaves shaped like those of the sunflower, a red stem, white flowers and fruits like those of the mountain grape plant. Its consumption prevents stupidity.
The river qìnán exits from this mountain, flows north, and pours into the river Yì.

---

[165] 傷 shāng. Wound, injury, but in the context of this passage, a thorn, a needle (according to the SHJ).

15. Mount Tài 太山

Ten li further southeast is found Mount Tài. There is a plant there called lí. Its leaves are like those of the bush clover, and its flowers are red. It can be used against subcutaneous ulcers.
The river Tài emerges from its southern side, flows southeast, and pours into the river Yì.
The river Chéng emerges from its northern side, flows northeast, and pours into the river Yì.

16. Mount Mò 末山

Twenty li further east is found Mount Mò. Its top has lots of deep-colored gold.
The river Mò springs there, flows north, and pours into the river Yì.

17. Mount Yì 役山

Twenty-five li further east is found Mount Yì. Its top has lots of white metal and iron.
The river Yì springs there, flows north, and pours into the Yellow River.

18. Mount Mǐn 敏山

Thirty-five li further east is found Mount Mǐn. There is a tree on its top that has the shape of the chaste tree. It gives white flowers and red fruits. Its name is jìbǎi. As pendant waist ornament, it protects from cold.
Its southern slope has lots of agate.

19. Mount Dàguī 大騩之山

Thirty li further east is found Mount Dàguī. Its northern part produces lots of iron, of beautiful jade, and of green loess. There is a plant there that looks like the yarrow. It has a fur, blue-green flowers and white fruits. Its name is hěn. As pendant waist ornament, it prevents premature death. It is also used to heal bowel diseases.

20. Summary and Rituals

In summary, from the initial Mount Xiūyǔ to Mount Dàguī, the mountain range Kǔ includes nineteen mountains spreading over 1184 li.
The sixteen divinities of these mountains all have a pig body and a human head. Their ancestral temples require: the animal of perfectly even color fur

is a dedicated sheep or lamb.[166] The ornament consists of one striated jade that is buried.

On the mounts Kǔ, Shǎoshì, and Tàishì are found sacred tumuli. Their ancestral temples use the ritual instruments for the Great Sacrifice, and the ornaments consist in auspicious jade. The divinities of these tumuli all have a human body and three heads. The others belong to [the class of] pig body and human head.

---

[166] 羊羞 yángxiū. The sacrificial sheep preparations.

Mountain Range 8 - Jīng 荆山

1. Mount Jǐng 景山

The head of the mounts Jǐng, in the eighth section of the Central Mountains is called Mount Jǐng. Its top has lots of gold and jade. Its trees include lots of chestnut-leaved oak and sandalwood trees.

The river Jū exits from this mountain, flows southeast, and pours into the Jiāng. Its bed has lots of thin red sand and lots of spotted fishes.

2. Mount Jīng 荆山 (II)

One hundred li northeast is found [the actual] Mount Jīng. In the north there are lots of iron and in the south lots of red metal.

In the interior, there are lots of long hair bulls, leopards and tigers.

Its trees include lots of pine and cypress trees. Its grasses include lots of bamboos, tangerines and pomelos.

The river Zhāng springs there, flows southeast, and pours into the Jū. Its bed contains lots of yellow gold and lots of perches.

The animals of this mountain include lots of black rams and elks.

3. Mount Jiāo 驕山

One hundred fifty li further northeast is found Mount Jiāo. Its top has lots of gold, and its base lots of ultramarine.

Its trees include lots of pine and cypress trees, and lots of peach-branch bamboos.

This is the dwelling of the divinity Tuówéi. It has a human face, ram's horns, and tiger's claws. Its habit is to wander in the depth of the rivers Jū and Zhāng. When it comes and goes, a light occurs.

4. Mount Nǔjǐ 女几之山

One-hundred twenty li further northeast is found Mount Nǔjǐ. Its tip has lots of jade and its base lots of yellow gold.

Its animals include lots of leopards and tigers, and lots of black rams and elks, red deers and Muntjac deers. Its birds include lots of white Reeves's pheasants, long-tailed mountain pheasants and poison-feathered zhèn birds.

5. Mount Yízhū 宜諸之山

Two hundreds li further northeast is found Mount Yízhū. Its top has lots of gold and jade and its base lots of ultramarine.
The river Guǐ springs there, flows south, and pours into the Zhāng. Its bed includes lots of white jade.

6. Mount Lún 綸山

Three hundred fifty li further northeast is found Mount Lún. Its trees include lots of catalpas and náns, lots of táozhī bamboos, lots of hawthorns, chestnuts, tangerines, and pomelos.
Its animals mostly include lots of black rams, duster-tail deers, líng goats, and chuò.

7. Mount Lùguì 陸[危邑]之山

Two hundreds li further east is found Mount Lùguì.
Its top has lots of agate, and its base lots of loess. Its trees include lots of wild cherry trees.

8. Mount Guāng 光山

One hundred thirty li further east is found Mount Guāng. Its top has lots of blue-green stones, and its base lots of waters.[167]
The divinity Jìmēng lives in this mountain. It has a human body and a dragon head. It walks ceaselessly in the abyss Zhāng. Its apparition is a sign of windstorms and torrential rains.

9. Mount Qí 岐山

One hundred fifty li further east is found Mount Qí. In the south there are lots of red metal and in the north lots of white alabaster. The top abounds in gold and jade and the base in ultramarine. Its trees include lots of trees of Heaven.
The divinity Shètuó resides in this mountain. It has a human body, a squared head and three feet.

---

[167] 多木 duōmù (lots of trees) are the original characters. It should be corrected to 多水 duō.

10. Mount Tóng 銅山

One hundred thirty li further east is found Mount Tóng. Its top has lots of gold, silver and iron. Its trees include lots of paper mulberry, Mongolia oaks, hawthorns, chestnut, tangerines, and pomelos. Its beasts include lots of leopards.

11. Mount Měi 美山

One hundred li further northeast is found Mount Měi. Its beasts include lots of sì one-horned bovines, black rams and duster-tail deers, pigs and deers. Its top has lots of gold and its base lots of ultramarine.

12. Mount Dàyáo 大堯之山

One hundred li further northeast is found Mount Dàyáo. Its trees include lots of pine and cypress trees, Chinese catalpa, mulberry and alder trees. Its grasses include lots of bamboos.
Its animals include numerous leopards, tigers, líng goats, and chuò hares.

13. Mount Líng 靈山

Three hundreds li further northeast is found Mount Líng. Its top has lots of gold and jade and its base lots of ultramarine.
Its trees include lots of peach trees, prune trees, black thorns, and apricot trees.

14. Mount Lóng 龍山

Seventy li further northeast is found Mount Lóng. Its tip has lots of parasite plants.
The tip abounds in blue-green stones and the base in red tin
Its grasses include lots of peach-branch bamboos.

15. Mount Héng 衡山

Fifty li further southeast is found Mount Héng. Its top has quantities of parasite plants, paper mulberry trees and Mongolian oaks. There are also lots of yellow and white loess.

16. Mount Shí 石山

Seventy li further southeast is found Mount Shí. Its tip has lots of gold and its base lots of ultramarine and parasite plants.

17. Mount Ruò 若山

One hundred-twenty li further south is found Mount Ruò. Its top has lots of agate, red ochre and guī stones. It also has lots of parasite plants and silkworm thorny trees.

18. Mount Zhì 巇山

One hundred-twenty li further southeast is found Mount Zhì. It has lots of beautiful stones and lots of silkworm thorny trees.

19. Mount Yù 玉山

One hundred-fifty li further southeast is found Mount Yù. Its top has lots of gold and jade. Its base abounds in blue-green stones and iron. Its trees include lots of cypress trees.

20. Mount Huān 灌山

Seventy li further southeast is found Mount Huān. Its trees include lots of sandal trees and its minerals, lots of guī stones and white tin.
The river Yù emerges from the top of this mountain and runs underground on its base. It contains lots of grindstones and sharpening whetstones.

21. Mount Rénjǔ 仁舉之山

One hundred-fifty li further northeast is found Mount Rénjǔ. Its trees include lots of paper mulberry trees and Mongolian oaks. In the south there are lots of red metal and in the north lots of hematite.

22. Mount Shīměi 師每之山

Fifty li further east is found Mount Shīměi. In the south there are lots of grindstones and sharpening whetstones and in the north lots of ultramarine. Its trees include lots of cypress, sandal trees, and thorny silkworm oaks. Its grasses include lots of bamboos.

23. Mount Qíngǔ 琴鼓之山

Two hundreds li further southeast is found Mount Qíngǔ. It has lots of paper mulberry trees, Mongolian oaks, pepper trees, and thorny silkworm oaks.
Its top has lots of white alabasters and its base lots of wash stones. Its animals include lots of pigs, deers, and white rhinoceros. Its birds include lots of poison-feathered birds.

24. Summary and Rituals

In summary, the mountain range Jīng, from its head Mount Jǐng to Mount Qíngǔ, includes twenty-three mountains spreading over 2890 li.
All the divinities of these mountains have a bird body and a human face. Their ancestral temples use the following: One rooster buried during the prayer, an embellished burial guī jade tablet,[168] and glutinous rice as ritual grain.
The sacred burial mound is on Mount Jiāo. Its ancestral temple uses the following: tasty wine, small sacrifice with prayer and burial,[169] and a bì jade adorned with fur.

---

[168] 藻圭 zǎoguī. Literally, a jade tablet with aquatic plants. However, the term zǎo has the extended meaning of "embellished" or "adorned."
[169] 少牢祈瘞 shǎoláo qíyì.

Mountain Range 9 - Mín 岷山

1. Mount Nǔjǐ 女几山

Mount Nǔjī is the head of the mounts Mín, the ninth mountain range of the Central Mountains. Its top has lots of rocks and alunite. Its trees include lots of wild cherry trees. Its grasses include lots of wild chrysanthemums and zhú.

The river Luò exits from this mountain, flows east, and pours into the Jiāng. It contains lots of realgar.

It has lots of tigers and leopards.

2. Mount Mín 岷山

Three hundreds li further northeast is found Mount Mín.

The river Jiāng springs there, flows northeast, and pours into the sea. Its bed has lots of good turtles and large water lizards.

Its top has lots of gold and jade and its base lots of white alabasters.

Its trees include lots of plum and birchleaf pear trees. Its animals include lots of rhinoceroses and elephants, and lots of kuí bulls. Its birds include lots of white pheasants and red pheasants.

3. Mount Lái 崍山

One hundred forty li further northeast is found Mount Lái. The river Jiāng emerges from it, flows east, and pours into the river Yangtze. In the south there are lots of yellow gold and in the north lots of Père David's deers and duster-tail deers.

Its trees include lots of sandal trees and thorny silkworm oaks. Its grasses include lots of Chinese onions and Chinese chives, Dahurian angelica, and kòutuō.

4. Mount Jū 崌山

One hundred fifty li further east is found Mount Jū. The river Jiāng exits from this mountain, flows east, and pours into the Yangtze. Its bed has lots of strange snakes and lots of zhì fishes.

Its trees include lots of qiū and red apricot trees, and lots of black thorns and Chinese catalpas.

Its animals include lots of kuí, bulls, xù goats, chuò, and xīsì one-horned bovines. There are also birds that look like owls, have a red body and a white head. Their name is qièzhī. They can be used to protect against fire.

5. Mount Gāoliáng 高梁之山

Three hundreds li further east is found Mount Gāoliáng. Its top abounds in loess and its base in grindstones and sharpening whetstones. Its trees include lots of peach-branch bamboos. There is a plant there that has the shape of the sunflower, has red flowers, and pod fruits. It is used to make horses run fast.

6. Mount Shé 蛇山

Four hundreds li further east is found Mount Shé. Its top abounds in yellow gold and its base in loess.
Its trees include lots of xún and xiàngzhāng. Its grasses include lots of jiāróng and small wild ginger plants.
There is an animal there that resembles a fox, has a white tail and long ears. Its name is yǐláng. Its apparition is a sign of turmoil in the country.

7. Mount Gé 鬲山

Five hundreds li further east is found Mount Gé. Its south abounds in gold and its north in white alabaster.
The river Púhōng springs there, flows east, and pours into the Jiāng. Its bed includes lots of white jade.
Its animals include lots of rhinoceros, elephants, common bears, brown bears, gibbons and long-tailed monkeys.

8. Mount Yúyáng 隅陽之山

Three hundreds li further northeast is found Mount Yúyáng. Its top has lots of gold and jade; its base lots of ultramarine.
Its trees include lots of Chinese catalpa and mulberry trees; its grasses lots of gromwells.
The river Xú exits from this mountain, flows east, and pours into the river Jiāng. Its bed is filled with thin red sand.

9. **Mount Qí** 岐山

Two-hundred and fifty li further east is found Mount Qí. Its top has lots of white metal and its base lots of iron. Its trees include lots of black thorns, Chinese catalpa, red apricot trees and qiū trees.
The river Jiǎn exits from this mountain, flows southeast, and pours its waters in the river Jiāng.

10. **Mount Gōumí** 勾欄之山

Three hundreds li further east is found Mount Gōumí. Its top has lots of jade and its base lots of yellow gold.
Its trees include lots of green oaks and silkworm thorny trees. Its grasses include lots of Chinese peony.

11. **Mount Fēngyǔ** 風雨之山

One hundred fifty li further east is found Mount Fēngyǔ. Its top has lots of white metal and its base lots of graphite. Its trees include lots of zōushàn trees and poplar trees.
The river xuānyú exits from this mountain, flows east, and pours into the river Jiāng. It has lots of [river] snakes.
Mount Fēngyǔ's animals include lots of black rams and David's deers, duster-tail deers, leopards and tigers. Its birds include lots of white pheasants.

12. **Mount Yù** 玉山

Two hundreds li further northeast is found Mount Yù. In the south are lots of copper and in the north lots of red metal.
Its trees include lots of camphor trees, red apricot trees and qiū trees.
Its animals include lots of pigs, deers, líng goats, and chuò. Its birds include lots of poison-feathered birds.

13. **Mount Xióng** 熊山

One hundred fifty li further east is found Mount Xióng. There is a grotto there called Xióng Grotto.
There is an immortal in permanence there. This grotto opens in the summer and closes in the winter.[170] When it opens in the winter, there will be wars.

---

[170] Some editions have the wrong inversion 夏啟而東閉 (open during summer and closed in the east). The *Taiping Yulan* (Scroll 54) says about this section that it opens in the winter and closes in the summer.

The top of this mountain has lots of white jade and its base lots of white metal.

Its trees include lots of trees of heaven and willows. Its grasses include lots of kòutuō.

14. Mount Guī 騩山

One hundred forty li further east is found Mount Guī. Its south has lots of beautiful jade and red metal and its north lots of iron.

Its trees include lots of táozhī bamboos and wolfberry shrubs.[171]

15. Mount Gé 葛山

Two hundreds li further east is found Mount Gé. Its tip has lots of red metal and its base lots of jiān rocks.

Its trees include lots of hawthorn, chestnut, orange, grapefruit, qiū trees and red apricot trees.

Its beasts include lots of líng goats and chuò. Its grasses include lots of jiāróng.

16. Mount Jiǎchāo 賈超之山

One hundred seventy li further east is found Mount Jiǎchāo. Its southern slopes have lots of yellow loess and its northern one lots of red ochre.

Its trees include lots of hawthorn, chestnut, orange and grapefruit trees. Its grasses include lots of rush grasses.

17. Summary and Rituals

In summary, the mountain range Mín, from its head Mt Nǔjī to Mt Jiǎchāo, includes sixteen mountains, spreading over 3500 li.

The divinities of these mountains all have a horse body and a dragon head. Their ritual temples require: single fur, one rooster that is buried. The ritual grain is the glutinous rice.

The sacred burial grounds are on mounts Wón, Gōumi, Fēngyǔ and Guī. Their ritual temples require: Libation wine, small sacrificial ritual, and one auspicious jade adorned with fur.

On Mount Xióng there is a seat.[172] Its ritual temple requires: Libation wine, major sacrificial ritual, and one bì jade adorned with fur. Do the General

---

[171] 荊芭 jīngqǐ. Hao Yixing mentions that the original 芭 bā should be 芑 qǐ (See SJ 1.2.14 and SJ 4.4.3).

[172] 席 xí. It seems that it is a kind of mat, on which feasts were prepared in honor of the divinities.

Dance[173] and use the weapons to avert misfortune away.[174] For the prayer, the coiffure of the dancers is adorned with beautiful jade.[175]

---

[173] One version has the term 干儛 gànwǔ, General Dance (see SJ 5.5.15). Another version has the term 十艀 gānzhì, the martial spear-shield dance.

[174] 禳 xí. To hold a ceremony to ward of calamities or avert misfortune away.

[175] According to Wangfu, ask auspicious blessing through the sacrificial use of the beautiful jade (璆玉 qiúyù), the one who dance uses the official costume. The *Erya* defines 璆 qiú as 琳 lín, a variety of jade. According to Guopu, it is a synonym of fine jade (美玉 měiyù). The meaning of the sentence is "to avert misfortune by prayers during the spear dance, and wearing the costume and holding the jade item.

Mountain Range 10 - Shǒuyáng 首陽之山

1. Mount Shǒuyáng 首陽之山

Mount Shǒuyáng forms the head of the mounts included in the tenth section of the Central Mountains. Its top has lots of gold and jade, but no vegetation.

2. Mount Hǔwěi 虎尾之山

Fifty li further west is found Mount Hǔwěi. Its trees include lots of pepper and zelkowa trees. It also has lots of fēng stones. In the south are found lots of red metal and in the north lots of iron.

3. Mount Fánkuì 繁續之山

Fifty li further southwest is found Mount Fánkuì. Its trees include lots of qiū and red apricot trees. Its grasses include lots of zhīgōu bamboos.

4. Mount Yǒngshí 勇石之山

Twenty li further southwest is found Mount Yǒngshí. It has no vegetation but lots of white metal and lots of waters.

5. Mount Fùzhōu 復州之山

Twenty li further west is found Mount Fùzhōu. It has lots of sandal trees. In the south are found lots of yellow gold. There is a bird there that looks like an owl, has one foot and a pig tail. Its name is qǐzhǒng.[176] Its apparition is a sign of major epidemics in the country.

6. Mount Chǔ 楮山

Thirty li further west is found Mount Chǔ. It has lots of parasite plants, pepper, zelkowa, and silkworm thorn trees. It also has lots of loess.

---

[176] 跂踵 qǐzhǒng. The *Taiping Yulan* Section 742, mentioning this passage, says pig fur instead of pig tail, and 企踵 qǐzhǒng instead of 跂踵 qǐzhǒng. It is also the name of a country (see HJ 3.14).

7. Mount Yòuyuán 又原之山

Twenty li further west is found Mount Yòuyuán. In the south are found lots of ultramarine and in the north lots of iron. Its birds include lots of mynas.

8. Mount Zhuō 涿山

Fifty li further west is found Mount Zhuō. Its trees include lots of paper mulberry, Mongolia oaks, and wild prune trees. The south abounds in agate.

9. Mount Bǐng 丙山

Seventy li further east is found Mount Bǐng. Its trees include lots of catalpa and sandals, as well as lots of shěnniǔ red apricot-like trees.

10. Summary and Rituals

In summary, the mountain range Shǒuyáng, from its head Mt Shǒu to Mt Bǐng, includes nine mountains, spreading over 267 li.

The divinities of the mountains all have a dragon body and a human face. Their ancestral temples require: a single fur/feather type [consisting of] one rooster which is buried. The sacrificial rice consists of quintessential five kinds of cereals.[177]
There is a sacred burial mound on Mount Dǔ. It requires the small sacrifice utensils, and the libation wine. One adorned bì jade is used and buried. The chief resides on Mount Guī. Its ancestral temple requires: libation wine and the great sacrifice. It requires two persons who make the incantations and the prayers.[178] The ornamentation consists of one bì jade.

---

[177] The five kinds of sacrificial grains consist of broomcorn millet (黍), non-glutinous broomcorn millet (稷), sorghum millet (粱), growing rice (稻), and wheat (麦).

[178] 巫祝 wūzhù. This term represent two individuals: (1) 巫 wū, the shaman; the person conducting the rituals, generally a female shaman (女巫 nǔwū); and (2) 祝 zhù, the officer administering the sacrifices, generally the male shaman (男巫 nánwū).

Mountain Range 11 - Jīng 荆

1. Mount Yìwàng 翼望山

Mount Yìwàng is the head of the mounts Jīng, the eleventh mountain range of the Central Mountains.[179]
The river Zhuān exits from this mountain, flows east, and pours into the Jǐ.
The river Kuàng also exits from it, flows southeast, and pours into the Hàn [river]. Its bed includes lots of flood dragons. Its top has lot of pine and cypress trees and its base lots of varnish and catalpa trees. The south abounds in red metal and the north in alabaster.

2. Mount Cháogē 朝歌之山

One hundred fifty li further northeast is found Mount Cháogē. The river Wǔ exits from this mountain, flows southeast, and pours into the Xíng.
Its bed abounds in salamanders. The top of this mountain abounds in catalpa and nanmu trees. Its animals include lots of líng goats and David's deers.
There is a grass there called Japanese star anise. It is used to poison fishes.

3. Mount Dìqūn 帝囷之山

Two hundreds li further southeast is found Mount Dìqūn. Its southern side has lots of agate and its northern one lots of iron.
The river Dìqūn originates on top of this mountain and runs underground in its base. There are lots of singing snakes.

4. Mount Shì 视山

Fifty li further southeast is found Mount Shì. Its tip has lots of Chinese chives.
There is a well there called Tiānjǐng. In summertime it has water and in wintertime it is dry.
The top of this mountain has lots of mulberry trees, lots of beautiful loess, and lots of gold and jade.

---

[179] SJ 5.11 appears to have been modified compared to the original text, where the mountains were changed to conform to the logic of the text. Many redundancies occur between SJ 2 and SJ 5.11. Unless excavation of an old SHJ version occurs, there may be no way to rectify these degradations.

5. **Mount Qián** 前山

Two hundreds li further southeast is found Mount Qián. Its trees include lots of oak-like trees and cypresses.
In the south are found lots of gold and in the north lots of hematite.

6. **Mount Fēng** 豐山

Three hundreds li further southeast is found Mount Fēng. There is an animal there whose shape is like that of an ape. Its eyes and mouth are red, its body yellow. Its name is yōnghé. Its apparition is a sign of terrible events in the country.
The divinity Gēngfù lives in this mountain. It roams ceaselessly in the Qīnglíng abyss. When it comes and goes, a light occurs. Its apparition is a sign of spoilage or defeat in the country.
There are nine bells[180] there that announce the frost.
On top of Mount Fēng are found lots of gold, its base has lots of paper mulberry trees, Mongolian oaks, wild prune trees and ring-cup oaks.

7. **Mount Tùchuáng** 兔床之山

Eight hundreds li further northeast is found Mount Tùchuáng. Its south has lots of iron. Its trees include lots of zhū chestnut oaks. Its grasses include lots of jīgǔ. They have roots like a chicken egg. Their taste is sweet and sour. Their consumption is beneficial for people.

8. **Mount Pí** 皮山

Sixty li further east is found Mount Pí. It produces lots of loess and hematite. Its trees include lots of pine and cypress trees.

9. **Mount Yáobì** 瑤碧之山

Sixty li further east is found Mount Yáobì. Its top has lots of Chinese catalpa and Machilus nanmu trees.
In the north are found lots of ultramarine and in the south lots of white metal.
There is a bird there that looks like a pheasant and frequently eats cockroaches. Its name is zhèn.

---

[180] 鐘 náo. Archaic term referring to a musical instrument hung upside down to produce a clearer sound when struck. The character overlays the reference of bell and time (clock).

10. Mount Zhīlí 支離之山

Forty li further east is found Mount Zhīlí.
The river Jǐ exits from this mountain, flows south, and pours into the Hàn.
There is a bird there whose name, derived from its call, is yīngsháo. It looks like the magpie, its eyes and beak are red, its body is white, and its tail has the shape of a wine spoon.
There are also lots of heavy cows and xián goats.

11. Mount Zhìdiāo 袟[上竹下周]之山

Fifty li further northeast is found Mount Zhìdiāo. Its top has lots of pine, cypress, alder, and bǎi trees.

12. Mount Jǐnlǐ 堇理之山

One hundred li further northwest is found Mount Jǐnlǐ. Its top abounds in pine and cypress trees. There are also lots of beautiful catalpas. In the north are found lots of red ochre and gold.
Its animals include lots of leopards and tigers. There is a bird there that looks like the magpie. It has a green body and its beak, eyes and tail are white. Its name, derived from its call, is qīnggēng. It is used to protect against epidemics.

13. Mount Yīkū 依軲之山

Thirty li further southeast is found Mount Yīkū. Its top has lots of wild cherries and hawthorn trees.
There is an animal there that looks like a dog. It has tiger claws and a carapace. Its name is lìn. It loves to jump and hop.[181] Its consumption protects against wind conditions.

14. Mount Jígǔ 即谷之山

Thirty-five li further southeast is found Mount Jígǔ. It has lots of beautiful jade, black leopards, black rams and duster-tail deers, líng goats and chuò.
In the south are found lots of alabaster and in the north lots of ultramarine.

---

[181] 駃[分/牛] yángfén. These two characters express the notion of jumping, leaping, and hoping together as the shaking motion of the horse under leather strap over its neck.

15. Mount Jī 雞山

Forty li further southeast is found Mount Jī. Its top has lots of beautiful catalpa and mulberry trees. There are also lots of Chinese chives.

16. Mount Gāoqián 高前之山

Fifty li further southeast is found Mount Gāoqián. There is water on its top that is very cold, still and clear. It is the syrup of Emperor Tái.[182] Drinking from it protects from heart pain. The top of this mountain has gold and its base hematite.

17. Mount Yóuxì 游戲之山

Thirty li further southeast is found Mount Yóuxì. It has lots of red apricot trees, ring-cup oaks, and paper mulberry trees. It also has lots of jade and fēng stones.

18. Mount Cóng 從山

Thirty-five li further southeast is found Mount Cóng. Its top has lot of pine and cypress trees. Its base has lots of bamboos.
The river Cóng emerges on top and runs underground below. Its bed has quantities of three-footed soft-shelled turtles with a forked tail. Their consumption prevents insanity.

19. Mount Yīngzhēn 嬰[石豐]之山

Thirty li further southeast is found Mount Yīngzhēn. Its top has lots of pines and cypress trees and its base lots of catalpa and varnish trees.

20. Mount Bì 畢山

Thirty li further southeast is found Mount Bì. The river Dìyuàn exits from this mountain, flows northeast, and pours into the Qín. Its bed has lots of water jade and flood dragons. The tip of this mountain abounds in agate.

---

[182] 帝臺之漿 dìtái zhī jiāng. "Syrup of Emperor Tái." 漿 jiāng: syrup; starch. The *Yiwen Leiju* (Scroll 8) and the *Taiping Yulan* (Scroll 59) citing this chapter, have the character water 水. In SJ 5.7.1, there is the board game of Emperor Tái. There is here an association with Emperor Tái and the prayer to the 100 divinities. On Mt Gǔzhōng (SJ 5.7.2) Emperor Tái offers wine libations to the 100 divinities.

21. Mount Lèmǎ 樂馬之山

Twenty li further southeast is found Mount Lèmǎ. There is an animal there whose shape is that of the hedgehog and is red like cinnabar fire. Its name is lì. Its apparition is a sign of major epidemics in the country.

22. Mount Jiān 葳山

Twenty-five li further southeast is found Mount Jiān. The river Qín exits from this mountain, flows southwest, and pours into the river Rǔ Its bed has lots of salamanders, flood dragons and jiá.

23. Mount Yīng 嬰山

Forty li further east is found Mount Yīng. Its base has lots of ultramarine and its top lots of gold and jade.

24. Mount Hǔshǒu 虎首之山

Thirty li further east is found Mount Hǔshǒu. It has lots of hawthorn, diāo oaks and zelkowa trees.

25. Mount Yīnghóu 嬰侯之山

Twenty li further east is found Mount Yīnghóu. Its top has lots fēng stones and its base lots of red tin.

26. Mount Dàshú 大孰之山

Fifty li further east is found Mount Dàshú. The river Shā exits from this mountain, flows northeastern, and pours into the river Qín. It contains lots of loess.

27. Mount Bēi 卑山

Forty li further east is found Mount Bēi. Its tip has lots of peach, prune, hawthorn, and catalpa trees. It also has lots of runner beans.

28. Mount Yǐdì 倚帝之山

Thirty li further east is found Mount Yǐdì. Its top has lots of jade and its base lots of gold. There is an animal there resembling the fèi rat. It has white ears and nose. Its name is jūrú. Its apparition is a sign of major battles in the country.

29. Mount Ní 鯢山

Thirty li further east is found Mount Ní. The river Ní emerges from its top and runs underground in his base. This mountain has lots of beautiful loess. Its top has lots of gold and its base lots of ultramarine.

30. Mount Yǎ 雅山

Thirty li further east is found Mount Yǎ. The river Lǐ emerges from it, flows east, and pours into the river Qìn. It contains lots of large fishes. This mountain's top has lots of beautiful mulberry trees and its base lots of hawthorn trees. It also has lots of red metal.

31. Mount Xuān 宣山

Fifty-five li further east is found Mount Xuān.
The river Lún exits from this mountain, flows southeast, and pours into the river Qìn. Its bed has lots of flood dragons.
There is a mulberry tree on top of this mountain that measures 16.5 m in circumference. Its branches fork four times. The size of its leaves is 0.33 m. Its trunk has red streaks. Its flowers are yellow[183] and its stems blue-green. It is called dìnǔ zhī sāng,[184] the mulberry of the Emperor's daughter.

32. Mount Héng 衡山

Forty-five li further east is found Mount Héng. Its top has lots of ultramarine and mulberry trees. Its birds include lots of myna birds.

---

[183] The *Yiwen Leiju* (Scroll 88) states "blue-green" flowers, and the *Taiping Yulan* (Scroll 955) states blue-green "leaves."

[184] 帝女之桑 dìnǔ zhī sāng. The true meaning of this expression has not yet been found. According to Guopu it is "the silkworm keen, therefore the name mulberry tree." The *Taiping Yulan* (Scroll 921) cites this chapter differently: "The southern Red Emperor (Chìdì 赤帝) daughter learned the Way at Mt De (得仙), and resides on top of the mulberry trees of the southern slopes of Mt Yáng'è (陽崿山). Chìdì used fire to burn [the place], and the woman died. This is the origin of the name "mulberry of the Emperor's daughter."" Biyuan mentions that in the notes of the *Shuijing*, Mt (Xuān 宣) is now in the Henan, in the boundary of Mìyáng (泌陽) county, now unknown. The Mìyáng county belongs to the Nanyang prefecture, and therefore Mt Xuān is Mt È (崿山), and the mulberry of the daughter's emperor of Mt Xuān is the mulberry of the daughter's emperor of Mt È. Chìdì's woman residing in the mulberry trees was set on fire and died, therefore the name.

33. Mount Fēng 豐山

Forty li further east is found Mount Fēng. Its top has lots of fēng stones. Its trees have lots of mulberry trees and carambola trees. These last trees resemble the common peach tree but have a squared trunk. They can be used to heal skin swellings and ulcers.

34. Mount Yù 嫗山

Seventy li further east is found Mount Yù. Its top has lots of beautiful jade and its base lots of gold. Its plants include lots of jīgǔ.

35. Mount Xiān 鮮山

Thirty li further east is found Mount Xiān. Its trees include lots of qiū, red apricot and hawthorn trees. Its herbs include lots of large tuber plants. The south abounds in gold and the north in iron.
There is an animal there that resembles the Tibetan mastiff. Its mouth and eyes are red and its tail white. Its apparition is a sign of fire in the locality.[185] Its name is Yìjí.

36. Mount Zhāng 章山

Thirty li further east is found Mount Zhāng. The south abounds in gold and the north in beautiful stones.
The river Gāo exits from this mountain, flows east, and pours into the river Lǐ. Its bed has lots of friable stones.

37. Mount Dàzhī 大支之山

Twenty-five li further east is found Mount Dàzhī. In the south are lots of gold. Its trees include lots of paper mulberry trees and Mongolian oaks. There are no herbs.[186]

38. Mount Qūwú 區吳之山

Fifty li further east is found Mount Qūwú. Its trees include lots of hawthorns.

---

[185] According to Hao Yixing, the *Guangyun* mentions battles and not fire.
[186] The classical passage says erroneously no grass and no trees, which contradicts the previous statement. This was not supported in other texts and was therefore changed.

39. Mount Shēngxiōng 聲匈之山

Fifty li further east is found Mount Shēngxiōng. Its trees include lots of paper mulberry trees. This mountain also has lots of jade and its top has lots of fēng stones.

40. Mount Dàguī 大騩之山

Fifty li further east is found Mount Dàguī. The south includes lots of red metal and the north lots of whetstones.

41. Mount Zhǒngjiù 踵臼之山

Ten li further east is found Mount Zhǒngjiù. It has no vegetation.

42. Mount Lìshí 歷石之山

Seventy li further northeast is found Mount Lìshí. Its trees include lots of thorn bushes and wolfberry shrubs. In the south there are lots of yellow gold and in the north lots of whetstones.
There is an animal there that looks like the fox. It has a white head and tiger claws. Its name is liángqú. Its apparition is a sign of major battles in the country.

43. Mount Qiú 求山

One hundred li further southeast is found Mount Qiú. The river Qiú originates from its top and runs underground in its base. Its bed has lots of beautiful ocher.
The trees of this mountain include lots of hawthorns trees and small bamboos. In the south are lots of gold and in the north lots of iron.

44. Mount Chǒuyáng 丑陽之山

Two hundreds li further east is found Mount Chǒuyáng. Its top has lots of diāo oaks and zelkowa trees. There is a bird there that resembles the crow. Its feet are red. Its name is zhǐtú. It can be used to protect against fire.

45. Mount Ào 奧山

Three hundreds li further east is found Mount Ào. Its top has lots of cypress, wild prune trees and wild cherry trees. The south abounds in agate.
The river Ào exits from this mountain, flows east, and pours into the river Qìn.

46. Mount Fú 服山

Thirty-five li further east is found Mount Fú. Its trees include lots of hawthorns. Its top has lot of fēng stones and its base lots of red tin.

47. Mount Yǎo 杳山

Three hundred[187] li further east is found Mount Yǎo. Its top has lots of jiāróng cǎo grasses and lots of gold and jade.

48. Mount Jǐ 几山

Three hundred and fifty li further east is found Mount Jǐ. Its trees include lots of qiū, sandal, and red apricot trees. Its grasses include lots of proso millet. There is an animal there whose shape is like that of the pig. Its body is yellow, and its head and tail are white. Its name is wénlín. Its apparition is a sign of cyclones in the world.

49. Summary and Rituals

In summary, the mountain range Jīng, from its head Mount Yìwàng to Mount Jǐ, includes forty-eight mountains spreading over 3732 li.
The divinities of these mountains all have a pig body and a human head. Their ancestral temples require: a rooster with uniform feathers and a prayer.[188] The burial object is the guī jade tablet. The sacrificial rice consists of quintessential five kinds of cereals.
This is the dwelling of the Emperor of Mt Hé.[189] Its ancestral temple requires: The tools of the Sacrifice to Heaven, burial oblations, dǎomáo.[190] Use one bì jade and a cow without sacrificial tool.

---

[187] The original text has "one hundred li." This should be three hundred li, according to most editions (*Song, Wukuan, Maoyi, Wangfu, Wuren chen,* and *Biyuan jiao ben*). Birrell has one hundred and ten lis.

[188] 祈 qí. Pray, seek for. According to Hao Yixing, prayer should be (上幾下皿). See SJ 1.3.14

[189] Hao Yixing notes that the previous sections do not mention Mt Hé 禾山, and that it could be a degradation of Mt Qūn 困山 (SJ 5.11.3), or a transcription mistake of Mt Qiú 求山 (SJ 5.11.43).

On Mounts Dǔ and Yù are found sacred burial mounds. All require daocí.[191]
Use for oblation the fur of the Small Sacrifice ritual, and auspicious jade
adorned with fur.

---

[190] 倒毛 dǎomáo. According to Guopu, this is about sacrifices offered to the divinities
(薦羞 jiànxiū) instead of the burial sacrifices (牲薶 shēngmái).
[191] 倒祠 daocí. Ancestral temple of the dao type. According to Hao Yixing, it is also
called 倒毛 daomáo.

Mountain Range 12 - Dòngtíng 洞庭山

1. Mount Piānyù 篇遇山

Mount Piānyù is the head of the mounts Dòngtíng, the twelfth mountain range of the Central Mountains. It has no vegetation but lots of gold.

2. Mount Yún 雲山

Fifty li further southeast is found Mount Yún. It has no vegetation. [However] there is a poisonous Madake bamboo. If a person is pricked by it, he or she will die.

The top of this mountain has lots of gold, and its base lots of agate.[192]

3. Mount Guī 龜山

One hundred thirty li further southeast is found Mount Guī. Its trees include lots of paper mulberry, Mongolian oaks, diāo oaks, and zelkowa trees.

Its top has lots of yellow gold and its base lots of sulfur arsenic and fú bamboos.

4. Mount Bǐng 丙山

Seventy li further east is found Mount Bǐng. It abounds in Madake bamboos, yellow gold, copper and iron but has no trees.

5. Mount Fēngbó 風伯之山

Fifty li further southeast is found Mount Fēngbó. Its top has lots of gold and jade and its base lots of suān stones, aragonites and iron.

The most abundant trees of this mountain are willows, wild prune, sandalwood, and paper mulberry trees. In the east there is a forest called the Forest of Mǎngfú. It has lots of beautiful trees, birds and animals.

---

[192] In the mention of this passage, the *Chuxue Ji* (Scroll 28) describes plum trees on top of Mt Yún (乾腊 làqián which means plum 梅 méi according to Guopu). This information is absent here.

6. **Mount Fūfū** 夫夫之山

One hundred fifty li east is found Mount Fūfū. Its top abounds in yellow gold and its base in green [jade and] realgar.
Its trees include lots of mulberry and paper mulberry trees, and its grasses lots of bamboos and jīgǔ.
The divinity Yú'ér lives in this mountain. It has a human body and holds in its hands[193] two snakes. It usually roams in the Jiāng abyss. When it comes and goes, a light is produced.

7. **Mount Dòngtíng** 洞庭之山

One hundred-twenty li further southeast is found Mount Dòngtíng. Its top has lots of yellow gold and its base lots of silver and iron. It has lots of hawthorn, pear, tangerine and pomelo trees. It grasses include lots of white Patrinia, sea moss ogonori, peony, and Ligusticum.
The two daughters of the Emperor live there.[194] They usually roam in the Jiāng abyss. The wind of the rivers Lǐ and Yuán gather in the abyss of the rivers Xiāo and Xiāng. This is the region of the Nine Rivers.
When they come and go, whirlwinds and cloudbursts occur. There, there are numerous strange divinities that have a human shape and wear snakes.[195] They hold snakes in both their hands. There are also lots of strange birds.

8. **Mount Bào** 暴山

One hundred eighty li further southeast is found Mount Bào. Its trees include lots of Lady Palm, thorn bushes and wolfberry shrubs, bamboos, arrow-like bamboos, and tubular bamboos.
Its top has lots of gold and jade and its base lots of aragonites and iron.
Its animals include lots of David's deers, deers, and muntjacs, and [its birds] birds of prey.

9. **Mount Jígōng** 即公之山

Two hundreds li further southeast is found Mount Jígōng. Its top has lots of yellow gold and its base lots of agate.
Its trees include lots of willows, wild prune, sandalwood, and mulberry trees.
There is an animal there that is like a turtle, its body is white and its head red. Its name is Guǐ. It can be used to protect against fire.

---

[193] Holds in its hands or carries on its body. The original version has the character body 身.

[194] The two daughters of Emperor Yao, 湘夫人 Xiāng fūren, the Ladies of Xiāng.

[195] According to Hao Yixing, "this is about 載 (zài) carry, be loaded with, as well as 戴 (dài) wear; put on (of accessories)." Here, there is an idea of entanglement.

10. Mount Yáo 堯山

One hundred fifty-nine li further southeast is found Mount Yáo. In the north are found lots of yellow loess and in the south lots of yellow gold.
Its trees include lots of thorn bushes and wolfberry shrubs, willows, and sandalwoods. Its grasses include lots of mountain potatoes and mountains thistles.

11. Mount Jiāngfú 江浮之山

One hundred li further southeast is found Mount Jiāngfú. Its top has lots of silver, grindstones and sharpening whetstones but no vegetation. Its animals include lots of pigs and deers.

12. Mount Zhēnlíng 真陵之山

Two hundreds li further southeast[196] is found Mount Zhēnlíng. Its top has lots of yellow gold and its base lots of jade.
Its trees include lots of paper mulberry trees, oaks, willows and wild prune trees. Its herbs include lots of róngcǎo.

13. Mount Yángdì 陽帝之山

One hundred twenty li further southeast is found Mount Yángdì. It has lots of beautiful copper. Its trees include lots of ring-cup oak, wild prune, mountain mulberry, and paper mulberry trees.
Its animals include lots of líng goats and musk deers.

14. Mount Cháisāng 柴桑之山

Ninety li further south[197] is found Mount Cháisāng. Its top has lots of silver and its base lots of blue-green stones, líng stones, and red ocher.
Its trees include lots of willow, Chinese wolfberry shrub, paper mulberry, and mulberry trees.
This mountain includes lots of David's deers, white snakes and flying dragons.

---

[196] Southeast instead of east is suggested in the *Biyuan Jiao* edition.
[197] Southeast instead of east may be appropriate to comply with the general directions and the correction made for the mountains of 5.12.12 and 5.12.15.

15. Mount Róngyú 榮余之山

Two hundred thirty li further east[198] is found Mount Róngyú. Its top has lots of copper and its base lots of silver.
Its trees include lots of willows and Chinese wolfberry shrubs. Its insects include lots of strange snakes and strange insects.[199]

16. Summary and Rituals

In summary, the mountain range Dòngtíng, from its head Mount Piānyù to Mount Róngyú, includes fifteen mountains spreading over 2800 li.
The divinities of these mountains all have a bird body and a snake head. Their ancestral temples require a rooster of uniformed feather color and a young pig that is immolated.[200]
The ritual grain is the glutinous rice.
The burial mounds are found on the mounts Fūfū, Jígōng, Yáo and Yángdì. Their ritual temples have the victims exposed and then buried.[201] Libation wine is used for the prayers. The fur of victims is used, and the small sacrifice is accomplished, an auspicious jade adorned with fur or feather is used.

The ritual temples of the divinities of the mounts Dòngtíng and Róngyú require exposing the victims before burying them. Libation wine and Sacrifice to Heaven ritual temples. [Ritual objects include] fifteen ritual jade specters[202] and five multicolor painting ornaments.

---

[198] Southeast instead of east is suggested in the *Song* and *Maoyi* editions.

[199] In HJ 1.2, 蟲 chóng insect is considered 蛇 shé snake, and 蛇 shé is 魚 yú fish.

[200] 刉 jī. To put into peaces an animal for the sacrifice. According to Guopu, 刉 jī is also the name of the cutting thorn 割刺 gēcì.

[201] According to Guopu, "肂 sì means 陳 chén put on display; the sacrificial jade is displayed then buried."

[202] 圭璧 guībì. Guī is a burial object, a jade tablet as symbol of power. Bì is a round flat piece of jade with a hole in the center.

General Summary

In general summary, in the descriptions given above on the Central Mounts, there are one hundred ninety seven mountains spreading over 21,371 li. Altogether, the famous mountains of the Empire total 5370,[203] spreading over a total surface of 64,056 li.

Emperor Yu said:
"The famous mountains that I have crossed number 5370 and cover a surface of 64,056 li. They are called the "Five Treasuries."[204] As for the small mountains their number is such that it is not possible to count them.
Heaven and Earth, from east to west, measures 28,000 li, and from south to north 26,000 li. The mountains from where rivers emerge spread over of 8000 li. Those that receive rivers spread over 8000 li.[205] Those that contain copper number 467, those that contain iron number 3690.[206]
Those are, in the universe, the distribution of soil, trees and grains.[207] It is also where originate the spears and lances, the knifes and the pole-arms. Capable men can find more than what they need; incapable men cannot meet what they need.
Seventy-two main houses have made the fēng ritual on Mt Tài and the shàn ritual on the Liángfù.[208]
This is the number of all gain and losses.[209] This is what is called national expenditures.

---

[203] The *Hou Hanshu Junguo zhi*, in the notes about this chapter, says "5350."
[204] 五藏 wǔzāng. According to Hao Yixing, 藏 zāng is the archaic character for 藏 zāng treasury ; The *Hanshu* says that 'the Treasuries of all mountains and seas under heaven and earth, thus the name "five treasuries." Another interpretation assimilates 藏 zāng with 脏 zāng, the internal organs or Treasuries. In this way the five Mountain ranges assimilate with the five organs, Lung, Kidney, Liver, Heart and Spleen. The *Wu Zang Shan Jing* 五藏山經 is actually a synonym of the *Shan Jing*.
[205] These measures refer to the empire ruled by Yu of the Xia dynasty.
[206] The *Junguo zhi* says 3609 li.
[207] This sentence refers to soil, trees and grains that can be used for harvesting.
[208] The fēng ritual on Mt Tài (封于太山) is the sacrificial ritual to Heaven or 封 fēng. The shàn ritual on the Liángfù (禪于梁父) is the sacrificial ritual to Earth or 禪 shàn. The emperors built a flattening (bìjī 辟基) on top of the small mountain Liángfù located on the southern slope of Mt Tài to offer the annual sacrifice to earth (地的). These were rituals that could only be performed by the ruler of the state or empire, and were known collectively as fēngshàn 封禪. From Qin times until Song, they were performed ten times - five of which were by Emperor Wu of Western Han (Han Wudi 汉武帝) - at Mt Tài for the fēng ritual and Mt Liángfù (at Sùrán Peak (肅然山)) for the shàn ritual. Reference to the fēngshàn include the *Shiji*, where Sima Qian quotes a passage from a now-lost chapter of the *Guanzi* in which Guǎn zhòng (管仲, ?-645 BC) of the Qi state is quoted as saying that 72 ancient kings (from the time of sage-kings down to Western Zhou) had performed these rituals at Mt Tài and Mt Liángfù.
[209] Number here refers to the appropriate, auspicious, number.

In the five books pertaining to the five groups of mountains (forming the text above), there is a total of 15,503 characters. (Hao Yixing says that it is now 21,265).

Annexes

Deities

- **Báidì Shǎohào**. 白帝少昊. Ancient name for Emperor Di Huang 王帝. Shǎohào, also written 少皞, was the son of Huangdi 黄帝, of the Jīntiānshì clan 金天氏. He ruled by means of the virtues of metal (West and White in the systems of correspondences), thus his name "White Lord" Báidì 白帝. See also HJ 9.1. This divinity resides on Mount Chángliú and manages the turn over of the scenery (sunset and sundown cycles. See also SJ 2.3.21). 2.3.15.
- **Bǎojiāng**. 葆江. Mythological figure. Cited in 2.3.5.
- **Celestial divinities of Mt Huáijiāng**. Unnamed divinities that have the shape of a bull with eight feet, two heads and a horse tail. Their call is like the bóhuáng. Their apparition is a sign of local war. 2.3.7.
- **Chángchéng**. 長乘. Divinity managing Mount Guǒmǔ. It has a human shape and a leopard tail. It manages over the nine celestial virtues. 2.310.
- **Chin**. [鬼申]. A category of divinities (神 shén), or according to the *Yupian*, a mountain divinity.
- **Dì Hóng**. 帝鴻. Emperor Swan. Originally written 帝江 dì hóng, but 鴻 hóng should be 鴻 hóng. It resides on Mt Tiān. It has the shape of a yellow bag and is red like bright fire. It has six legs and for wings. It is Húndūn. It has neither face nor eyes. It knows singing and dancing. 2.3.20.
- **Divinities of the Mountains**
Central Range 2. Human face and a bird body.
Central Range 4. Human face and an animal body.
Central Range 7. Pig body and a human head.
Central Range 7. Sacred Tumuli of mounts Kǔ, Shǎoshì, and Tàishì. Human body and three heads.
Central Range 8. Bird body and a human face.
Central Range 9. Horse body and a dragon head.
Central Range 10. Dragon body and a human face.
Central Range 11. Pig body and a human head.
Central Range 12. Bird body and a snake head.
Eastern Range 1. Human body and a dragon head.
Eastern Range 2. Animal body and a human face.
Eastern Range 3. Human body and ram's horns.
Northern Range 1. Human face and a snake body.
Northern Range 2. Snake body and a human face.
Northern Range 3. Twenty have a horse body and human face, ten have a pig body, eight legs and a serpent tail.
Southern Range 1. Bird body and a dragon head.

Southern Range 2. Dragon body and a bird head.
Southern Range 3. Dragon body and a human face.
Western Range 2. Ten of their divinities have a human head and a horse body. Seven other divinities have a human head, a bull body, four feet and a single arm. They use a stick to walk. They are the gods of the flying animals.
Western Range 3. goat body and a human face.

- **Gēngfù**. 耕父. Divinity residing in Mt Fēng. It roams ceaselessly in the Qīnglíng abyss. When it comes and goes, a light occurs. This divinity is also mentioned in the *Hou Hanshu* (Liyi Rites) as a drought divinity (旱鬼 Hànguǐ). At the time of Guopu, there was still one of its temples in existence. 5.11.6.

- **Gǔ**. 鼓. This is the name of the child of the divinity of Mt Zhōng. "Child of a Mountain" refers to its divinity's child. In HJ 3.2 it is said that the divinity of Mt Zhōng is zhúyīn 燭陰 (or zhúlóng 燭龍), a creature with a human face and a snake body. Cited in 2.3.5.

- **Gǔn**. 鯀. Father of Yǔ the Great. He changed into a wild bear in the abyss of Yǔ 羽. According to another story, Gǔn was minister of public works under Emperor Yao (2297 B.C.) Since he could not control the flowing of the waters from the Flood, he was exiled to Mt Yu while his functions were given to his son, the future emperor Yǔ. This passage of the SHJ is thought to be apocryphal. 5.3.2.

- **Héshān dì**. 禾山帝. Emperor of Mt Hé. 5.11.49. Note that, according to Hao Yixing, Mt Hé 禾山, not mentioned in the SJ, could be a degradation of Mt Qūn 囷山 (SJ 5.11.3), or a transcription mistake of Mt Qiú 求山 (SJ 5.11.43).

- **Hóngguāng**. 紅光. Divinity, "red splendor." It manages Mt Yǒu. It could be a synonym of the divinity Rùshōu mentioned in the same chapter. 2.3.21.

- **Hòujì**. 后稷. One of the sons of the mythical emperor Dì Kù 帝嚳, Hòujì became the first ancestor of the Zhou house. He was minister of agriculture under the legendary Shun, and was known as "Lord of Millet." He was considered later as the God of fields and of Cultivators. For Hòujì, see SJ 2.3.7, SJ 5.5.9, HJ 6.5, HJ 6.6, HJ 11.8 Country of Xi Zhou, HJ 13.8, and HJ 13.37. 2.3.7.

- **Huáiguǐ lílún**. 槐鬼離侖. Divinity residing at Mt Huáijiāng. 2.3.7.

- **Húndūn**. 渾敦. In modern Written Chinese, húndūn "primordial chaos" is 混沌, but Chinese classic texts wrote it either 渾沌 (*Zhuangzi*, etc.) or 渾敦 (*Zuozhuan*). Hun "chaos; muddled; confused" is written either hùn 混 "abundantly flowing; turbid water; torrent; mix up/in; confuse; muddle through; drift along; thoughtless; senseless" or hún 渾 "sound of running water; muddy; muddled; turbid; concealed; confused; dull; stupid; unsophisticated; whole; all over". These two are interchangeable graphic variants readable as hùn 混 "muddy; dirty; filthy" and hún 渾 "nebulous;

stupid" (hundun 渾沌). Dun "dull; confused" is written either dùn 沌 "dull; confused; stupid" or dūn 敦 "thick; solid; generous; earnest; honest; sincere".. Húndūn is a worthless son of Huangdi, one of the mythical sìxiōng 四凶, four friends, banished by Shùn 舜 (*Zuozhuan*). See also HJ 9.14.

- **Jiāngyí**. 江疑. Divinity. It resides on Mount Fúyāng. 2.3.17.
- **Jiāochóng**. 驕蟲. Divinity of Mt Píngféng. It has a human body and two heads. It is the master of stinging insects. Its ancestral temple requires a live rooster. In the *Taiping Yulan*, 驕 jiāo is 嬌 jiāo. 5.6.1.
- **Jìmēng**. 計蒙. Divinity of Mt Guāng. It has a human body and a dragon head. It walks ceaselessly in the abyss Zhāng. Its apparition is a sign of windstorms and torrential rains. 5.8.8.
- **Kuí**. 魁. Mountain ghost. 2.3.15.
- **Lùwú**. 陸吾. Divinity, guardian of Mount Kūnlún. Also called 肩吾 jiānwú. According to Section *Within the Four Seas, Western Parts*, this deity belongs to the category of enlightened beasts (See HJ 6.12, 6.17). See also *Zhuangzi* (*Neipian - Dazong shi diliu*). 2.3.8.
- **Nine-heads illuminated beasts and six heads tree birds**. It refers to HJ 1. 2.3.8.
- **Nǔshī**. 女尸. Nǔshī, the daughter of the Emperor, died and metamorphosed into an iceplant (*Aptenia cordifolia*, lùcǎo 露草), with dense foliage, yellow flowers, and cuscuta-like fruits. When carrying it, it triggers love in men (服之媚于人). Nǔshī and the bird Jīngwèi 精卫 are one and the same, and are the daughter of Yándì 炎帝. It is said that ten suns appeared in the sky, Nǔshī invoked the rain for all people under heaven, so that they do not die, and she died under the sun. After her death, [as the Emperor's heart was full with sorrows, he asked 后羿 Hòuyì to shoot at the suns], she transformed into the morning glory yáocǎo 瑶草 (or 蘱草?). The Taiping Yulan (Scroll 299) says that the youngest daughter of the Emperor (Yándì) was called Yáojī 瑶姬. After dying, her spiritual beings became língmáng 灵芒, a marvelous herb of the cuscuta type. When carrying it, it triggers love in men" (令夫相愛 líng fū xiāngài). Later Yáojī was called the daughter of Mt Wu 巫山. In the anthology Gaotangfu, section Xiangyang qijiu ji, it is said that the daughter of Chìdì 赤帝 (the Southern Emperor (Yandi 炎帝)), called Yáojī 瑶姬, did not carry on and died, she was buried on the northern slope of Mt Wū, and was therefore called the girl of Mt Wū (巫山之女). King Huái of Chu (楚懷王說) traveled to Gāotáng 高唐, took a nap and dreamed about the divinity which made him happy. Due to his satisfaction, he had a temple build on the southern slope of Mt Wū and called it Cháoyún 朝雲. From then on, he received assistance every time he returned there. Another version of this tale goes like this. The youngest daughter of the Emperor named Yáojī did not carry and died. She was buried on

the platform of Mt Wū, and her essences jīng and hún 精魂 transformed into the mushroom língzhī (靈芝, *Glossy ganoderma*). It is said that she assisted Yu the Great in controlling the flood. See also notes on HJ 10 and on HJ 11. 5.7.3.

- **Nǚwá**. 女娃. This name, which resembles that of Nǚwā 女媧, does not occur in the ancients texts. In the *Peiwen Yunfu*, it occurs twice (Book ix, p. 64, and Book xxi, p. 222). The *Ruan Ji Qin Si Fu* says that "Nǚwá, dazzling with glory on the shore of the Eastern Sea, flew to the flooded western side" (女娃 耀榮于東海之濱而翩翻于洪西之旁). 3.3.22. The story in the SJ states that, swimming in the Dōnghǎi sea, Nǚwá drowned and did not return. Then, she changed into Jīngwèi. Ceaselessly she put into her mouth wood and stones from the western mountains and builds up a nest with them in the eastern sea. In the *Shu Yi Ji*, the story is slightly different. "The daughter of Yándì drowned in the Dōnghǎi Sea and changed into Jīngwèi. She mated with a petrel (or a sea swallow) and gave birth to children. The female child looked like Jīngwèi, and the male child like the sea swallow. Since Jīngwèi drowned in Dōnghǎi Sea in her previous state, it swore not to drink its water. Thus it was also called Oath Bird (誓鳥 shìniǎo), 坲禽 páoqín, and Willfull Bird (志鳥 zhìniǎo), as well as the Emperor' sparrow-Daughter." The first version became a popular story: "Jin Wei fills in the Eastern Sea" (精衛填海 jīng wèi tián hǎi).
- **Qīnpī**. 欽[丕鳥]. Mythological figure. The *Zhuangzi* (Dàzōng shī 大宗師) speaks of it as 堪坏 kānpī. Cited in 2.3.5.
- **Qióngguǐ**. 窮鬼. Qióng divinities residing at Mt Huáijiāng. 2.3.7.
- **Qítóng**. 耆童. It resides on Mount Guī. Also called 老童 Lǎotóng, supposetedly the son of Dìwáng 帝王. The sound of his voice is constant like that of a bell and chime stone instrument See also HJ 11.12. 2.3.19.
- **Rùshōu**. 蓐收. It resides on Mt Yǒu. See also the divinity Jīn, a divinity with a human head, tiger claws, white hair, holding a broadaxe, and in charge of the sunset. See also the divinity Hóngguāng, and HJ 2.21. 2.3.21.
- **Shānhún**. 山[犭軍]. Divinity of storms found on Mt Yùfǎ. It is dog-like creature with a human face and great throwing strength. When it sees humans, it starts laughing. It walks like the wind. Its apparition is a sign of strong wind in the world. 3.1.19.
- **Shénguì**. 神[光鬼]. The [光鬼] pertain to the family of mountain demons (魖魅 chīmèi). They have a human face, an animal body, a single foot and a single hand. Their voice is like an animal groan. See also the Wikipedia article on Chi (http://en.wikipedia.org/wiki/Chi_/mythology/), especially with regard to comparing the hornless dragon 螭 chī with 魖 chī. 2.4.13.
- **Shètuó**. 涉鼉. Divinity of Mt Qī. It has a human body, a squared head and three feet. 5.8.9.

- **Tàiféng**. 泰逢. Divinity governing over the region of Mt Hé. It has a human body and a tiger tail. It loves residing in the south of the Bèi mounts. When it comes and goes, it produces a light. The divinity Tàiféng moves the energies of Heaven and Earth. The *Yupian* suggests that féng expresses the name of a divinity. It controls the rain and in that way rules over the floods of the Yellow River. 5.3.5.

- **The divinities of pond Xūn**. Shén xūnchí or xūnchí shén. 神熏池. There are two of them: 泰逢 tàiféng, the main one, has a tiger tail, and 武羅 wǔluó who has a human face (see SJ 5.3.2 and SJ 5.3.5). Xūn 熏 means fog, and more specifically the fog rising up in the mountains. 5.3.1.

- **Tiānyú**. 天愚. Divinity of Mt Dǔ. 5.7.5.

- **Tuówéi**. 鼉圍. Divinity of Mt Jiāo. It has a human face, ram's horns, and tiger's claws. Its habit is to wander in the depth of the rivers Jū and Zhāng. When it comes and goes, a light occurs. In the notes of the SJ, according to Hao Yixing, the *Guangyun* does not mention the head of Tuówéi. The original comment of the text agrees with Hao Yixing. Guopu, in his comments on the HJ, states that it is short and small, with hairs. The *Song*, *Maoyi*, *Biye Jiao*, *Baizi Quanshu* editions, all specify the head. 5.8.3.

- **Wàngdì**. 望帝. Emperor Wang. This is also a compound name for cuckoo. 望帝 Wàngdì is also the name of 杜宇 Dùyǔ (cuckoo). Cited in 2.3.1.

- **Wǔluó**. 武羅. Divinity governing on Mt Qīngyào. It has a human face, with leopard stripes, a small waist, white teeth and pierced ears for ear pendants. Its voice is like the sound or resonating jade. 5.3.2.

- **Xiāng fūren**. 湘夫人. The two daughters of Emperor Yao, the Ladies of Xiāng (a river pouring into the Yangtze River). According to Guopu, they refer to (1) the two daughters of Emperor Tiān and (2) the divinity (or divinities) of river Chù 處江. Here, the young girls of Xiāng walk around and play in the bottom of the abyss of the river xiāng, where they command the wind and the waves to unite and generate extraordinary echoes. According to Wangfu; "It is about the two daughters of Emperor Yáo 堯 as well as the wives of Shùn 舜, called É'huáng 娥皇 and Nǚyīng 女英. The *Lienu Zhuan* of Liu Xiang states that "of the two daughters of Emperor Yao, the elder one was called É'huáng and the younger one Nǚyīng. Yao gave them in marriage to Shun. Once Shun became emperor, É'huáng became empress and Nǚyīng concubine. "According to the tradition, during 舜 Shùn's journey to the south, he collapsed and died in the wilderness of Cāngwú 蒼梧 (apparently in Hunan), the two imperial concubines hurried and cried, died in river Xiāng, thereupon becoming the spirits of Xiāng [river] (湘水之神 Xiāng shuǐshén), or the Ladies of Xiāng [river] (湘夫人 Xiāng fūren). They are mentioned in various works. The *Chi shi* stated that "Emperor Qin Shi Huangdi, navigating on the Xiāng, arrived to Mt Xiāng (a small island on river

Xiāng) where he was surprised by a storm. He then asked the learned man who was the divinity ruling over Xiāng and was answered that they are "the two daughters of Emperor Yao who became the spouses of Emperor Shun. When they died, they were buried in this location. After hearing this answer, the Emperor grew angry and gave the order to 300 soldiers to strip of all the trees of Mt Xiāng." They are also mentioned in the *Nine Songs* where Qū Yuán 屈原 composed Songs Four and Five to the deity of Xiāng River and in the *Cāngwú Lament* (蒼梧怨) in the *Xilutang Qintong* (Folio 12). See also HJ 7.21 and HJ 13.24.

- **Xīwángmǔ**. 西王母. The Queen Mother of the West. She resides on Mount Yù. She has a human shape with a leopard tail. She has tiger teeth and powerful roar. She is disheveled and carries a hoopoe-like crown. She governs the celestial plagues and the five destructive influences.
- **Yándì**. 炎帝. Considered by some to be 神農 Shénnóng, sovereign of the mythological period. His parents were Shàodiǎn 少典 and his wife Nǚdēng 女登 (or Fāngdēng 方登). She gave birth to him after seeing (or being touched by) a divine dragon. According to Sima Zhen, cited in the *Peiwen Yunfu* (Book 25, p. 227) Yándì had a human body and a cow head. He was raised on the banks of River Kiang 姜, whose name became that of his family. The tradition gives him numerous inventions, including the plow and agriculture, botany and medicine, the setup of markets where exchanges would occur during the day and was inactive at night (各得其所), and the development of the trigrams guà 卦. He first established his capital at Chén 陳, and then moved to Qūfù 曲阜. His reign lasted 120 years (Sima Zhen, *Sānhuáng běnjì*, in the preliminaries of the *Shǐjì* by Sima Zhen). The legend of Shénnóng belongs mainly to beliefs at place at the time of the writing of the SHJ. It is necessary to not confuse those with the reform mainly established by Confucius in the 6th century B.C. See also HJ 11.46 互人國. 3.3.22.
- **Yīngzhāo**. 英招. Divinity managing the Garden of peace. 2.3.7.
- **Yú**. 𦍩. Black ram. Divinity of the Mountain Range Huá (2.1). It was also the male goat and a mountain divinity under the Xia dynasty (see *Shuowen*). The concept of this divinity seems to come from the *Sanhai jing* as most dictionaries refer to the present passage. This Yú would particularly need to be linked to the Huá mountains and not to all Chinese mountains. Cited in 2.1.11.
- **Yú'ér**. 于兒. Divinity residing on Mt Fūfū. It has a human body and two snakes are held in its hands (or wrapped around its body). It usually roams in the Jiāng abyss. When it comes and goes, a light is produced. This divinity is found in the *Liezi* as 操蛇之神 Tàoshé zhī shén, the Divinity that holds snakes in its hands. 5.12.6.

Disease and Remedies

- **Amnesia**. 寓 yù. Yù is the original character but the annotations suggest it to be an erroneous character. Using homophonic search, it seems that it would indicate forgetfulness or the modern term amnesia, or maybe dementia. Another theory is that it refers to warts. Remedy: Qūjū bird (3.3.3).
- **Anger**. 怒 nù. Anger, rage. Remedy: Dìxiū tree (5.7.9).
- **Beneficial for people**. 利于人 lì yú rén. Benefit people. Remedy: Jīgǔ grass. (5.11.7).
- **Blepharospams**. 眴目 shùnmù. Dazzled eyes. This expression points to 瞬目 shùnmù, blinking (Guopu). Remedy: Dānghù bird. (2.4.6).
- Bring beauty back. 美人色 měirén sè. Beautiful person color, look, expression, charm. Remedy: Xúncǎo plant. (5.3.2).
- **Callus**. 底 dǐ. 底 dǐ (bottom) is the original character but the annotations suggest 胝 chī (callous) instead. Remedy: Xuánguī reptile (1.1.5).
- **Carbuncle**. 痤 cuó. Acne, carbuncle. The *Shuowen* defines it as small swelling from disease. See also Suwen (生桉通天论). The modern term indicates a swelling of the lymph node. Remedy: Tiānyīng fossil (5.1.7).
- **Cold**. 寒 hán. Cold. It creates resistance to cold 令人耐寒 (Guopu). Remedy: Jìbǎi tree (5.7.18).
- **Confusion**. 惑 huò. Confusion or delusion. Remedy: Guànguàn bird (1.1.9), Mēngmù tree. (5.7.7).
- **Crazy**. 狂 kuáng. Mania, insanity. Remedy: Hybrid of Mt Tàiqì (2.3.6).
- **Dampness, lingering**. 墊 diàn. Something grasping or lingering 執 over the 土 ground or earth, maybe a lingering dampness. The homophony diàn indicates conditions like 痁 chronic malaria, 癜 erythema, and anything pertaining to 沾 wetness, moist, or soak. Remedy: Dì bird (5.5.2).
- **Disease, animal**. 病 bìng. As an ointment, it protects oxen and horses from diseases. Remedy: Ochre water of the Guan river (2.1.6).
- **Disease, epidemic**. 疫疾 yìjí. Epidemic disease. This term is fairly rare compared to the other names referring to epidemic diseases, such as yìlì 疫癧, wēnyì 瘟疫 or yì 疫. (See Chén Yìguāng's article who does not mention the *Shan Hai Jing*). Remedy: Needlefish (4.1.3).
- **Disease, epidemic**. 癘 lì. Epidemic disease, or sore caused by varnish poisoning. This character is often used with 气, meaning 疠气 pestilent energy. Remedy: Qìsuān creature. (3.3.4), Zhūbiē fish (4.2.5).
- **Disease, epidemics**. 御疫 yùyí. Control, resist epidemics. Remedy: Qīnggēng animal. (5.11.12).

- **Disease, major**. 疾 jí. Disease; illness. Remedy: Three-footed turtle (5.7.7).
- **Disturbed body smell**. 驕 jiāo. According to Guopu, it should be understood as 騷臭 sāochòu, disturbed odor. Remedy: Chinese herring (3.2.3).
- **Drowning**. 溺 nì. Drowning, being addicted, urinate. The body becomes light. Or it could mean prevents excesses and indulgence. Remedy: Shātáng tree (2.3.8).
- **Ear loss**. 聾 lóng. Deafness, ear loss. Remedy: Xuánguī reptile (1.1.5), Wénjīng tree (2.1.5), Diāotáng tree (5.1.14).
- **Edema**. 胕 fú. As 浮肿 dropsy, edema. Remedy: Huángguàn tree (2.1.8).
- **Evil energies**. 蠱 gǔ. The most poisonous insects who survive after fighting each other. Name of Hexagram 18 (Corrupting). Also carries the meaning of intestinal parasite. In this context, the action needs to be considered in light of the meaning of the nine-tails fox, which has clear shamanistic associations. Remedy: Fox with nine tails (1.1.9), Dìtái stone (pendant) (5.7.1).
- **Evil spell**. 凶 xiōng. Inauspicious, ominous. Remedy: Rǎnyí fish (2.4.15).
- **Fainting**. 厥 jué. To faint, lose consciousness, an illness characterized by a counter-flow movement of energy. It may refer to a condition where the extremities turn dark during fainting; In other words, a sudden faint, a coma, with the hand and feet stiff and icy cold. Remedy: Niúshāng plant (5.7.7).
- **Fatigue**. 勞 láo. Labor. Remedy: Tree of Mt Bùzhōu (2.3.3), Píncǎo plant (2.3.8).
- **Fatigue**. 癉 dàn. Sickness from overwork, fever, a kind of malaria. Remedy: Dān tree (2.4.19).
- **Fear of thunder**. 畏雷 wèi léi. Fear or dread thunder or calamity. Remedy: Xiāo animal (2.1.10), Flying fish. (5.3.3).
- **Fertility**. 宜子孫 yí zǐsūn. Suitable [to bring forth] children and grandchildren. Remedy: Tree of Mt Chóngwú (2.3.1).
- **Fever**. 瘧 nüè. Fever, malaria. Remedy: Poplar-like tree (4.4.1), Kǔxīn plant. (5.6.14).
- **Forgetfulness**. 忘 wàng. Forgetfulness. Remedy: Ring-cup oak tree (5.1.2).
- **Furuncle**. 癰 yōng. Carbuncle, ulcer, abscess. Remedy: Stargazer fish (5.7.8).
- **GI, abdominal distension**. [月采] cǎi. This refers to 臌脹 gǔzhàng, swelling, tympanites, abdominal distension. Remedy: Ěrshǔ animal (3.1.8).
- **GI, abdominal lumps**. 瘕 jiǎ. Lump in abdomen. Guopu suggests intestinal worms. Remedy: Yùpèi plant (1.1.2).

- **GI, bowel disease**. 腹病 fùbìng. May [affect] diseases of the 腹 fù. 珂案：經文病，宋本作疾。. Remedy: Hěn plant. (5.7.19).
- **GI, diarrhea**. 衕 dòng. It may be diarrhea (腹瀉 fùxiè). Remedy: Kuāfù bird (3.1.12).
- **GI, intestinal disease**. 腹痛 fùtòng. Abdominal pain. Remedy: Kuāfù bird (3.1.12).
- **GI, passing gas**. [米費] pí. Flatulence, passing gas. Remedy: Sea star (4.4.3).
- **Goiter**. 癭 yǐng. Goiter; swelling on neck. Remedy: Dùhéng grass (2.1.15), Nài animal (5.1.1), Wútiáo plant. (5.7.4), Shùsī bird (2.1.16).
- **Heart pain**. 心痛 xīntòng. Feeling sorry or distressed; cardiac pain. Remedy: Aromatic lichen (2.1.4).
- **Hemorrhoids**. 痔 zhì. Hemorrhoids, piles. See also *Taiping Yulan* (scroll 743). Remedy: Tiger flood-dragons (1.3.2).
- **Hemorrhoids**. 痔衕 zhìdòng. Hemorrhoids. The term dòng is unclear in its association with zhì. Remedy: Flying fish (5.1.11).
- **Hunger**. 飢 jī. Hunger, starvation. Remedy: Dān tree (2.3.4), Báigāo tree (1.3.11).
- **Indecisiveness**. 惑 huò. Confusion or delusion. Remedy: Tufts of plants that resemble winter sunflower plants (2.1.5).
- **Infertility**. 人無子 rén wú zǐ. People not having offspring. Remedy: Gǔróng grass (2.1.14).
- **Infertility, female**. 妒 dù. Envy, jealousy. Rosny suggests considering the individual characters nǔshí 女石, sterility, instead of dù. Remedy: Yūmù (5.7.10).
- **Insanity**. 蠱疾 gǔjí. Insanity, derangement. SJ 3.3.2 states "salamanders that resemble the Giant Salamander... Their consumption prevents insanity (癡 chī) disease." Here, we have "their consumption prevents 蠱 gǔ (the legendary venomous insect) disease." Hao Yixing is unsure of the translation of the term in this context but suggests a same meaning as in SJ 3.3.2. Remedy: Zhòuwěi -like salamander (5.7.9), Three-footed soft-shelled turtles with a forked tail. (5.11.18).
- **Insanity**. 癡疾 chījí. Idiocy, insanity. SJ 5.7.9 says that "their consumption protects against 蠱疾 gǔjí, insanity or derangement." Remedy: Giant Salamander-like reptile (3.3.2).
- Itching. 疥 jiè. As 疥瘡 scabies. Remedy: Huángguàn tree (2.1.8).
- **Jaundice**. 癉 dān. Fever, a kind of malaria; dàn; sickness from overwork, hate. Remedy: Huān animal (2.3.22).
- Jealousy. 妒 dù. To envy, to be jealous of. Remedy: Lèi animal (1.1.7), Huángniǎo bird. (3.3.18).
- **Labors**. 勞 láo. Labor. Here, fatigue from labors. Hao Yixing suggests that it is a mistake and that the correct term is 憂 yōu, worry; grieve. Remedy: Báigāo tree (1.3.11).

- **Lie down**. 臥 wò. Lie down. Remedy: Chǎngfù bird (1.1.8).
- **Madness**. 癡 chì. Mental retardation (痴病 chī bìng and 疯癫病 fēng diān bìng). Remedy: Báiyè bird (3.1.12).
- **Mania**. 狂 kuáng. Mania; insanity. The original meaning is that of a dog gone mad. Remedy: Grouper-like fish (3.1.20), Lǐnghú animal (3.3.6).
- **Melancholia**. 瘋 shǔ. Sickness from grief; melancholy. Remedy: Zhíchǔ plant. (5.1.6).
- **Nightmare**. 厭 yàn. To detest, loathe, be disgusted with. Guopu suggests adding the term dreams, more congruent with the next indication. This expression replaces those of sections 2.4.15, 5.1.6, and 5.7.10. Remedy: Yīyú bird. (2.3.22).
- **Nightmare**. 眯 mī. Squint, getting something in the eye. The annotators suggest the term nightmare, more congruent with the next indication. Their logic rests on analysis of other texts. Mī may relate to the term dreadful nightmare 梦魇 mèngyǎn. Remedy: Zhíchǔ plant. (5.1.6), Rǎnyí fish (2.4.15), Lóngchí animal. (5.2.6), Língyào bird (5.6.3).
- **Pestilence**. 癘 lì. Pestilence. According to Guopu, it refers to epidemic diseases, and "evil wounds" according to some. It may be pronounced lài. Another opinion is that it refers to 癞病 làibìng, which is to say to 麻瘋 máfēng (insanity from syphilis?). Remedy: Féiyí bird (2.1.7), Xūn grass (2.1.9).
- **Poison, cure poisoning**. 毒 dú. Poison; toxin; narcotics; malicious; cruel. Remedy: Yānsuān plant. (5.7.2).
- **Poison, kills fish**. 毒魚 dú yú. Poison fish. Remedy: Japanese star anise (5.11.2), Chinese silvergrass. (5.2.7), Bá tree. (5.4.5), Tíngníng plant. (5.4.7).
- **Poison, kills people**. 殺人 shārén. Its consumption kills people. Remedy: Shī fish (3.3.40), Péipéi fish (3.1.18).
- **Poison, kills rat**. 毒鼠 dú shǔ. Poison rat. Remedy: Wútiáo plant (2.1.16).
- **Poison, the hundred poisons**. 百毒 bǎidú. The hundred poisons. Remedy: Ěrshǔ animal (3.1.8).
- **Protect against fire**. 禦火 yùhuǒ. Resist (ward off) fire, anger, temper, internal heat, or firearms. Remedy: Red pheasant (2.1.4), Kingfisher-like birds with red beaks (2.1.5), Leï bird (2.1.19), Dān tree (2.4.19), Huānshū animal (3.1.3), Xíxí bird. (3.1.5), Qièzhī bird (5.9.4), Zhǐtú bird (5.11.44), Guǐ reptile. (5.12.10).
- **Sadness**. 憂 yōu. Worry; sadness, grief. Remedy: Devil grass (5.1.11), Fěifěi animal (5.1.12).
- **Scabies**. 疥 jiè. Scabies. Remedy: Chìrú fish (1.1.9), Tufts of plants resembling Chinese Chives, with white flowers and black seeds. (2.1.6).
- **Skin, chap bào**. [月暴] bào. This is different from the term 腊 xī dried meat, used in SJ 2.1.1. Remedy: Tōngqú bird (2.1.2).

- **Skin, chap xī**. 腊 xī. Dried meat. Chapped or wrinkled ski. According to the *Shuowen*, this term was fixed in the Zhou calligraphy style from the ancient term 乾肉 gānròu (Hao yixing). Remedy: Xián (2.1.1).
- **Skin, swellings and ulcers**. 張 zhàng. Swelling, edema. Remedy: Carambola tree (5.11.3).
- **Sleep**. 睡 shuì. Sleep. According to Hao Yixing, the *Li Shan*'s notes, *Jiang's poetic collection* and the *Taiping Yulan* (Scroll 939) use the term 膧 zhǒng swelling instead of 睡 shuì sleep. Remedy: Lún fish (5.7.8.).
- **Soreness**. 癉 dàn (1) Sickness from overwork; (2) fever; a kind of malaria. Remedy: Xíxí bird. (3.1.5).
- **Strength**. 多力 duō lì. Multiplied strength, power or ability. Remedy: Guīmù tree (2.4.16).
- **Stupidity**. 愚 yú. Stupidity. Guopu suggests "or increases intelligence." Remedy: Gāngcǎo plant (5.7.14).
- **Sunstroke**. 暍 yē. Sunstroke or heatstroke. Remedy: Bànmào bird (3.1.11).
- **Swellings**. 膧 zhǒng. Swelling. Remedy: Three-footed turtle (5.7.7), Lù bird (1.1.6), Tiger flood-dragons (1.3.2).
- **Throat constriction**. [口壹] yē. Guopu explains this term as "eating without chocking." It is about food not being blocked up in the throat. Remedy: Tiānbiān tree. (5.7.5).
- **Throat pain**. 嗌痛 yìtòng. Throat pain. According to Guopu, it is about swallowing pain. Remedy: Báiyè bird (3.1.12).
- **Ulcer**. 癰 yōng. Carbuncle; ulcer; abscess. Remedy: Héluó fish (3.1.4).
- **Ulcer, subcutaneous**. 疽 jū. Subcutaneous or deep-rooted ulcer. Remedy: Yīyú bird (3.1.3), Lí plant. (5.7.15).
- **Vision, inability to see**. 昧 mèi. No sun; dark; obscure, muddled; hidden. Here, the term 昧 mèi would suggest the inability to see, to comprehend. However, it may be a mistake for 眯 mī (squint), or 眯 mī (get something in one's eye) in which case it would refer to not being afraid of dreaming. See SJ 2.4.15. Remedy: Morning glory (5.7.10).
- **Vision, obscuring of**. 瀸 jiào. In other words, mù jué (目爵) the darkness of the eyes. Remedy: Gūxī bird (3.3.16).
- **Vision, sight loss**. 瞢 méng. Dim sight. It also carries the meaning of a metaphorically unclear vision. Remedy: Tuò plant (5.1.1).
- **Vomiting**. 嘔 ǒu. To vomit. Or 嘔 òu, irritability, annoyance. Remedy: Xiànfù fish (3.3.6).
- **Wart**. 疣 yóu. Wart. The commentaries suggest 贅酱 zhuìjiàng for which I could not find a contemporary equivalent. Commentaries also suggest the term 肬 yóu, wart; tumor; goiter; papule. Remedy: Bighead carp (4.4.2), Ray-finned fish (3.1.2), Zǎo fish (3.1.19).
- **White ringworms**. 癬 xuǎn. White ringworm; tinea alba. Parasitic disease for which the Háo fish is used. Remedy: Háo fish (5.1.3), Xiūbì fish (5.6.11).

- **Wind conditions**. 風 fēng. Wind disease. It could be either external or internal wind. According to Guopu, it is about having no fear of the heavenly winds. Wangfu states that it may refer to the wind illness. Remedy: Lìn animal. (5.11.13), Jiāo bird. (3.1.11), Róngcǎo plant. (5.1.15).
- **Worm abscess**. 鞄 páo. To tan and soften leather. According to Guopu, 鞄 páo (pronounced lòu) is a form of carbuncle 癰 yōng with insects in the center. The *Huainanzi* says "[in the presence of] 雞頭 jītóu (gorgon plant *Euryale ferox*) there will be lòu." It may be the 瘑 lòu disease (not the present fistula), a condition described in the past as "sores (瘡 chuāng) appearing on top of the neck that are long lasting, suppurating, and filled with maggots (蛆虫 qūchóng)." Remedy: Stargazer fish (5.7.8).
- **Worms**. 蟲 chóng. Worm, insect. Remedy: Féiyí bird (2.1.7).
- **Worry**. 憂 yōu. Worry. Remedy: Sharpbelly fish (3.1.3).

Fauna

Animals

- **Ape**. Yuán 猿. This is a tall ape. Its lower mandible presents no bag, it has not tail and would include the orangutan, the gorilla, and the gibbon. Rosny: This type of monkey is also similar to the míhóu. It has broad shoulders, long legs and noticeable agility. Its fur is either yellow or black. It sound is whinny. Ref. 1.1.3.

- **Badger**. Háo 豪. Given as synonym of 貆豬 yuánzhū. Also described as a long white haired porcupine. See a similar animal in SJ 2.1.8. Ref. 2.2.7.

- **Bear, brown**. Pí 羆. This character appears with 熊 xióng (熊羆). It may be a compound word. Ref. 2.1.14.

- **Bear, common**. Xióng 熊. This character appears with 羆 pí (熊羆). It may be a compound word.

- **Bovine, one-horned sì**. Sì 兕. One-horned bovine animal (see also http://www.chinese-unicorn.com/qilin/book/contents/16-the-rhinoceros-in-ancient-china/). This character (1.3.2, 2.2.12, 3.1.17, 5.8.11) is thought of as an unknown wild bovine (Jean Lefeuvre, 1982) or the Sumatran rhinoceros (Ji Sun, 1982(8), 80). Guopu suggest that the character 兕 sì may be used as a connector. In later times both sì and xi were used to designate the rhinoceros. The earlier pictograph sì continued in use, but it was now joined by a new pictophonetic character xī. These were clearly two different characters, but phonetically similar (Lefeuvre, 1982, 25). Much later the sì was thought to be the "female," and the xi the "male" rhinoceros, but this distinction is not found in the oracle bone script (Sun, 1982(8), 81) and the usage of the characters is 兕犀. This passage of the *Shanhai jing* clearly differs (犀兕). Note that in the twentieth century a savage controversy erupted among scholars over the correct interpretation of these two characters. (See: Laufer, 1914; Bishop, 1933; Hopkins, 1939; and Jenyns, 1954–55.). Ref. 1.3.2, 2.2.12, 3.1.17, 5.8.11.

- **Bovine, one-horned xīsì**. Xīsì 犀兕. Cited in 2.1.14, 2.2.5, 2.2.13, 5.9.4. Depending on the punctuation, it can be understood as "犀兕" or as "犀、兕". It appears to differ from the rhinoceros. Ref. 2.1.14, 2.2.5, 2.2.13, 5.9.4.

- **Bull, long hair**. Líniú 犛牛. Long hair bull or "Yak bull". Long fur wild bull. According to Guopu, "This animal belongs to the category of yaks (旄牛). It is black and located in the southwest borders." The *Shuowen* specifies that is it the long fur bull of the southwest remote borders.

- **Camel**. Tuótuó 橐駝. This animal is adapted to go across moving sands and can go through 300 li in a day while carrying a weight of one thousand pounds. SJ 3.1.6 writes it tuótuó 橐駝 and SJ 3.3.40 tuóqín 橐錞. The annotation suggests that tuóqín was written camel tuótuó 橐駝 in the Song edition. Ref. 3.1.6.
- **Cattle, colored**. Líniú 犁牛. Colored cattle or draught ox. Its fur has black and yellow stripes like the fur of a tiger.
- **Cōnglóng**. Cōnglóng 蔥聾. It resembles goats and has red horse's mane. Hao Yixing identifies is as one kind of mountain sheep and reports that summer sheep have been seen with red horse's mane. Note that the mountain in SJ 51.4 has the same name. Ref. 2.1.5.
- **Dàngkāng**. Dàngkāng 當康. Animal that looks like small pigs and have tusks. Its name, derived from its call. Its apparition is a sign of great abundance in the empire. Ref. 4.4.5.
- **Deer**. Lù 鹿. Deers, including the white deer (白鹿 báilù). It may be a kind of Cervus cashmirianus. There may be a corruption of the character in 2.3.11 and 5.5.2 where it is written 錄 lù. Ref. 2.1.16, 2.2.16, 2.4.6, 5.3.1.
- **Deer, duster-tail**. Zhǔ 麈. Deer-like animal whose tail was used as a duster. Duster-tail deer. See also 麋 mí, the elk. These two characters are similar and may have been interchanged. Compare 閭麋 and 閭麈.
- **Deer, Muntjac**. Jǐ 麂. Muntjac or barking deer (Moschus chinensis), a small dear. This term used to refer both to a large deer and a small fallow deers. (1) The *Bencao* zhu describes it as "belonging to the roebuck family (large hornless river deers) but smaller, with bilateral tusks, fond of struggling. It has Muntjac eyes, thus its name." (2) The *Erya* describes this animal as big, with fluffy tail and dog legs. Guopu describes this animal as a roebuck called 獐 zhāng. It has fluffy hair and dog's legs. In modern dictionaries, 麂 jǐ also refers to the musk deer (*Moschus moschiferus*). In SJ 5.12.8 it is written 麢 (or [鹿/旨]) jǐ. Now, the commentaries state it is the Muntjac 麂 jǐ, also known as Barking Deer (*Muntiacus*), a small deer. Also written [鹿/旨].
- **Deer, musk**. Shè 麝. Siberian Musk Deer (*Moschus moschiferus*). The musk deer similar to the hornless river deer but smaller. It has short forelimbs, long hind legs long, small hoof, large ears, brown body hair, and no horns (both males and females). The male has musk glands and the secretion has medicinal properties.
- **Deer**, Père David's. Mílù 麋鹿. Depending on the punctuation, it can be understood as "麋鹿" or as "麋、鹿". 麋 mí points to the large and rare Père David's deer (*Elaphurus davidianus*) or 麋鹿 mílù. Its fur of this deer is light brown, its back compact and belly swallow, the male has horns that suggest the antler but is not. Its head is like that of a horse but it is not a horse, its body is like that of a donkey but it is not one. Its hoofs resemble those of a caw but it is not one. This is why it used to be

called the 四不像 sìbùxiàng or literally "four not resembling." See Wikipedia (http://en.wikipedia.org/wiki/Père David's Deer). It is to note that 麋 mí also suggests the elk. See 04.3.6, 05.12.8, 05.12.14. See also note on the black ram lǘ. Ref. 4.3.6, 5.12.8, 5.12.14.

- **Deer, red**. Jīng 麖. This appears to be the 馬鹿 mǎlù or red deer. According to Guopu, this is an animal that resembles the deer, but smaller and black. Hao Yixing, citing the *Erya*, states that it is about a large deer.

- **Dog, growling**. Nòuquǎn 獳犬. An infuriated mad dog. According to Rosny, the character 獳 presents a possible mistake in the left component 犭 which should be 魚. The character is then 鱬 rú, a fabulous animal having a fish body and a human face.

- **Dúgǔ**. Dúgǔ 獨[犬谷]. Animal that looks like a tiger, has a white body, a dog head, a horse tail and pig hairs.

- **Elephant**. Xiàng 象. The elephant lives in Tonkin (Dōngjīng 东京), ancient Chinese province of Yuènán 越南 on the China sea.

- **Elk**. Mí 麋. Elk or Père David's deer (*Elaphurus davidianus*). See SJ 3.2.3, 5.2.1, 5.8.2, 5.8.4, 5.9.11. See also note on the black ram lǘ. Ref. 3.2.3, 5.2.1, 5.8.2, 5.8.4, 5.9.11.

- **Fěifěi**. Fěifěi 胐胐. Animal that looks like foxes, and have a white tail and a mane. Its consumption prevents sadness.

- **Fēishǔ**. Fēishǔ 飛鼠. Resemble the hare and have a rat head. It glides by means of something on its back (SJ). Flying squirrel or bat. This is probably the endemic Groove-toothed flying squirrel or North Chinese flying squirrel (*Aeretes melanopterus*).

- **Fox**. Lí 貍. Old variant of 狸 lí fox. Ref. 1.1.7.

- **Géjū**. Géjū (Gédàn) 猲狙. Animal resembling a wolf, with a red head and rat eyes. Its grunt is similar to the one of a young pig. It eats humans. According to Hao Yixing, it should be 獦狙. A detailed analysis of the terms may suggest géjū. (1) 獦. 獦 xiē: 獦獢 - One kind of short mouth hunting dog; 獦 hè: Ancient word for frightened, threatened, intimidated; 獦 gé: 獦狙 - Huge, gigantic wolf; 獦 hài: Dog smell. (2) 狙. 狙 jū: A kind of monkey (maybe the míhóu monkey 獼猴, *Macacus tcheliensis*). Idea of waiting silently, of secret, of plot and trick, of sudden movement towards killing. See http://xh.5156edu.com/html3/6846.html.

- **Gibbon**. Yuán 猿. Originally meant the "Agile Gibbon, Black-handed Gibbon, *Hylobates agilis*" until the fourteenth century, and now generally means "ape, monkey". Ref. 5.9.7.

- **Goat, líng**. Língyáng 羚羊. Líng goat. Guopu, in his *Erya*'s comment, mentions that it is a big goat with round horns, comfortable in mountain terrains; in the *Shanhai Jing*'s comment, he mentions that it should be the character 麋 mí, the David's deer. The *Shuowen* mentions that is a big goat with small horns. Another version has 麢羊 língyáng, a big goat.

- **Goat, xián**. Xiányáng 羬羊. According to the *Erya*, six-foot tall goats are called 羬 xián. The country of the Dàyuè tribe (name of an ancient tribe having Caucasian features) contains a tall species of goats resembling a donkey and having a horse tail (Guopu). Kean suggests that Guopu's understanding of tall goats actually mean tall-tailed goats, with tails big enough to be eaten. See also HJ 1 (Mt Dí 狄山).

- **Háozhì**. Háozhì 豪彘. Piglet-like animal. Its fur is white, long like ancient hair pins and has black extremities. Háozhì, also known as 箭豬 jiànzhū "arrow pig" or porcupine. Its arrows are used to make needles to keep the hair style. Its skin is used for shoes. Its flesh is dangerous to eat. (See also *Bencao Gangmu*). Also called 豪豬 háozhū.

- **Hare**. Tú 菟. A thin hare. The key is the character grass above it. Rare character, met in some texts under its archaic form tù 兔 (rabbit, hare). Ref. 3.1.8, 4.2.6.

- **Hedgehog**. Wèi 彙. Archaic character for the hedgehog cìwèi 刺蝟. Guopu mentions that this animal resembles the rat and has red hairs like the spines of the hedgehog. Modern pronunciation: huì.

- **Héyǔ**. Héyǔ 合窳. Animal that looks like a pig and has a human face, a yellow body and a red tail. Its call is like that of the newborn. It eats humans, insects and snakes. Its apparition is a sign of great floods in the world.

- **Horse**. Mǎ 馬. In SJ 3.1.33, according to Guopu, it is the wild horse (野馬 yěmǎ). This would be the present Przewalski's horse (*Equus ferus przewalskii*) or takhi. It went extinct in China in the 1960thies and has been reintroduced successfully from European and North American zoos. This horse is considered the only remaining truly wild "horse" in the world. The *Taiping Yulan* (section 158), referring to 5.613, says that many breeds of horses originate there, like the red Huáliú 驊騮 and the swift Lù'ěr 騄耳, two of the fine steeds of the Zhou dynasty Emperor Mu 穆王 (1032-983 B.C.). (SJ 4.16.13).

- **Hound, Heavenly**. Tiāngǒu 天狗. This beast looks like red fox and have a white head. Its call is like liúliú. It is used to avoid bad luck. See also 16.35 Heavenly Dog, (天犬). Both names are also star names. See, among others, *Shiji*, Tian Guan Shu, *Sui Shu* – Sun Sheng Biography, Qinggu Yuanwu, *Autumn Mountain*, Poem 2.

- **Huáhuái**. Huáhuái 猾裹. This beast looks like a man with whiskers of pigs. It lives in caves and hibernates in winter. Its sound is like that of wood breaking. Its apparition in a county is a sign of major local disturbances.

- **Huānshū**. Huānshū [月蘿]疏. It looks like horses and have a very hard and striated horn. It can be used to protect against fire.

- **Huìshǔ**. Huìshǔ [虫犬]鼠. Squirrels??. Also written [虫/虫|犬]鼠 and [虽犬]鼠.

- **Jiá**. Jiá 頡. According to Guopu it is like a blue-green dog. Its fur is blue-green and some interpretations suggest the otter 水獺 shuǐtǎ.
- **Jiǎo**. Jiǎo 狡. This beast looks like a dog, or a goat (according to another edition). It has leopard spots, and bull-like horns. Its call is like that of a dog's bark. Its apparition is a sign of great calamities.
- **Jié**. Jié [犭頡]. River animal that looks like growling dogs and has scales. Its fur is like pig bristles. According to Guopu, it should pronounced jié. According to the *Hanyu dazi dian* and the *Hanyu daci dian*, it should be pronounced xié.
- **Jīngjīng**. Jīngjīng 精精. Animal resembling bulls and having a horse tail. Its name derives from its call.
- **Jǔfù**. Jǔfù 舉父. This beast looks like the spider monkey, with arms spotted like leopards and tigers and having great throwing strength.
- **Jūjì**. Jūjì (or Jìjū) 居暨. It resembles hedgehogs and has red hair. Its call is like that of small pigs (SJ). This animal resembles a red porcupine (*Kangxi zidian*).
- **Jūrú**. Jūrú 狙如. Animal resembling the fèi rat. It has white ears and nose. Its apparition is a sign of major battles in the country.
- **Kuāfù**. Kuāfù 夸父. Guopu suggests it could be the 舉父 jǔfù, the kind of rhesus monkey seen in SJ 2.3.1. See also SJ 3.2.12.
- **Kuāfù-like animal**. Unnamed in the SJ. This animal resembles the kuāfù and has pig's hair. Its call is like a shout. Its apparition is a sign of severe floods in the Empire.
- **Kuíniú**. Kuíniú 夔牛. According to Guopu, there are large and heavy cows in Mt Shǔ (蜀山) known as kuí cows or 魏 wèi according to the *Erya* (犩 wèi in the current version).
- **Lèi**. Lèi 類. This animal, called xiāng máo 香髦 by the natives, is found in the Yunnan province. It has two bodies (Yangshen). It looks like the raccoon dog and has a mane. It is hermaphrodite. Its consumption cures jealousy. It is possible that it could be identified with the common palm civet (*Paradoxurus hermaphrodites*) found in Southern China. The Latin name of this animal comes from its well-developed anal scent glands looking somewhat like testes. The text states that it is simultaneously female and male (自為牝牡). This is narrated in *Zhuangzi*: "the lèi is female and male and changes. This also occurs today with the animal huánzhū 狟豬." It is also narrated in the *Liezi*, section tianriu (天瑞): Yun said "there is an animal that self-fecundates and give birth to the lèi." *Zhuangzi* said "The lèi comes from male and female." The *Yiwu zhi* also says, "the animal called lí gathers in a same body both female and male organs (一體自為陰陽)". Finally, the *Bencao Gangmu* mentions that "the small Indian civet (língmāo 靈貓) originates from the mountains and valleys of the Southern sea 南海山谷; it has the shape of the li 狸 and it is hermaphrodite. Also written 沛 pèi (Guopu).

- **Leopard**. Bào 豹. Black leopard. The SJ locates it mainly in the western and central mountains (2.2.5, 2.3.1, 5.8.2, 5.8.4, 5.8.12, 5.9.1). It resembles the leopard and has a spotted head. According to Guopu, this is about the black leopard or panther, and black tigers have been noted in Mt Jīngzhōu (荊州山). Ref. 2.2.5, 2.3.1, 5.8.2, 5.8.4, 5.8.12, 5.9.1.

- **Leopard, měngbào**. Měngbào 猛豹. It is similar to a small panda with a light color and a lustrous fur. It can devour snakes and tear apart copper and iron. Guopu suggests that it is a leopard or tiger, while Hao yixing suggests the panther. Ref. 2.1.12.

- **Liángqú**. Liángqú 梁渠. Animal there that looks like the fox. It has a white head and tiger claws. Its apparition is a sign of major battles in the country.

- **Lìn**. Lìn 獜. Animal that looks like a dog. It has tiger claws and a carapace. It loves to jump and hop. Its consumption protects against wind. The character includes 犭 dog and the phonetic 粦 lín which, according to Karlgren is the "Ignis fatuus, will-o'-the-wisp -- 米 is a corruption of the 炎 of the seal; 炎 flames 舛 dancing, cf. 舞." According to Guopu, 獜 lìn alludes to having a carapace or scaly body.

- **Líng**. Líng 刢. Guopu describes this animal as similar to a tall goat with thin legs. It is good in the mountain at handling cliffs. Other versions use the character 麢 líng, the antelope. It resembles a tall goat, has curved and sharp horns, and loves to move in difficult mountain terrains. Modern pronunciation: xù.

- **Lǐnghú**. Lǐnghú 領胡. Ox-like animals. It has a red tail and a dewlap on the neck that looks like a dipper. Its name derives from its call. Its consumption prevents mania. Lit. Neck growth. It may be the Gaur (Bos gaurus), 野牛 yěniú.

- **Línglíng**. Línglíng 軨軨. Animal resembling the bull and having tiger stripes. Its call is like an animal groan. Its name derives from its call. Its apparition is a sign of floods in the empire. Ref. 4.2.1.

- **Lóngchí**. Lóngchí 蠪蚔. Animal that resembles pigs and has a horn. Its call is like a howl. Its consumption protects against nightmares. The name lóngchí reminds that of lóngzhí 蠪姪 of SJ 4.2.16. In addition, the character 蚔 chí it may actually be 蛭 zhì or 姪 zhí.

- **Lùshǔ**. Lùshǔ 鹿蜀. Animal resembling a horse. Its head is white, the pattern of its skin like that of a tiger, and its tail is scarlet. Its sound resembles human singing. As pendant waist ornament, it is suitable for the posterity. This name refers to a tiger horse 虎文馬也.

- **Macaque**. Wèi 蜼. A kind of long-tailed monkey belonging to the macaque family. See 5.7.9. Ref. 2.4.19.

- **Mánmán**. Mánmán 蠻蠻. Fabulous beast for which little is known. It a rat body and a soft-shelled turtle head. Its call resembles the dog's bark. See SJ 2.3.2 for a bird of that name. Ref. 2.4.14.

- **Mastiff, Tibetan**. Módà 膜大. According to Hao Yixing, "大 big should be 犬 dog, the *Guangyun* has 犬. The 膜犬 móquǎn, or western mó dog (西膜之犬), is a massive dog with thick fur, ferocious and strong." It is probably the Tibetan mastiff (cángáo 藏獒) also called (xīcáng áoquǎn 西藏獒犬). The western Mó country 西膜, is mentioned in the legendary trip of King Mu (Mùwáng 穆王) in the Occident and Guopu mentions its association with a desert. Asides from that, little is known about it.

- **Mènghuái**. Mènghuái 孟槐. The text describes it as looking like a porcupine and having long fine reddish hair. Its call is like liúliú. It protects against bad luck.

- **Mèngjí**. Mèngjí 孟極. It resembles the leopard, have a spotted forehead and a white body. Its name derives from its call. It loves lying down.

- **Mǐn**. Mǐn [敏牛]. This beast looks like the bull, is greenish and has wide eyes.

- **Monkey, long-tailed**. Wěi 蜼. The wěi is described as a large long-tailed monkey, with a yellow-black fur, and a tail up to 0.33 m. Wangfu comment adds that it has upward nostrils and when it rains it hangs in the trees, using its tail to cover its nostrils. Ref. 5.9.7.

- **Monkey, spider**. Yú 禺. The spider monkey 禺 yú is similar to the rhesus monkey míhóu 獼猴, but bigger. It has red eyes and a long tail. It can be found in great numbers in the Jiāngnán mountain, south of the Yangtze (Guopu) – The míhóu resembles humans, according to the *Bencao Gangmu*. Ref. 1.1.2.

- **Nàfù**. Nàfù 那父. It looks like a bull with a white tail and a call similar to the human voice.

- **Nài**. Nài [隹改能]. Animal that resembles huìshǔ with stripes. Its consumption cures goiter. Also pronounced nuó.

- **Panther**. Fǎn [犬勺]. According to the *Yupian*, it is a leopard or panther 豹. A variant has 豿 zhuó, a wild animal stripped like the leopard or panther.

- **Pí**. Pí 羆. Animals that look like Père David's Deers. Its hindquarter is above the tail. Ref. 3.3.42.

- **Piglet**. Tún 豚. Piglet. Described as 豚 tún, young pig, or in one instance as 逐 zhú, a variant found in SJ 5.7.4.

- **Porcupine**. Huán 貆. Small badger or porcupine. This word is a synonym of porcupine háozhū 豪猪 (*Hystrix*). This animal lives in small groups in the mountains. The distribution of porcupines generally includes Tibet and the area south to the Yangtze River, not beyond N 35° (except for fossil porcupines). The white porcupine was mentioned in SJ 2.1.8. Ref. 3.1.4.

- **Qióngqí**. Qióngqí 窮奇. This beast looks like bulls and having the spines of a hedgehog. Its call is like that of the howl of a dog. It eats humans. According to Guopu, it is said that this creature is like a tiger, has spines like the hedgehog and wings. See also HJ 1.10, 2.7 and 2.10.

- **Qiúyú**. Qiú yú 犰狳. Hare-like animal. It has a bird beak, owl eyes and snake tail. When it sees humans, it pretends to be dead. Its name derives from its call. Its apparition is a sign of locust invasion (in the cultivated fields). The modern translation of this term is armadillo. One must be careful in that armadillos, according to the present knowledge, are native to the Americas only. This has led some authors to the theory of ancient Chinese having visited the American continent.

- **Raccoon dog**. Hé 貉. Raccoon dog (*Nyctereutes procyonoides*), but could also be a badger (狗獾). It looks like a heavy fox, with a relatively short and fluffy tail. Its ears are short and round. Its cheeks are not hairy. Its body is grey brown. Ref. 5.4.2.

- **Ram**. Mǔyáng 牡羊. Lit. a male sheep.

- **Ram, Black**. Lǔ 閭. Often cited with character 麋 mí. Together they could be about black rams and elks (or David's deers); interpreted as one compound character, it is a unicorn lǔmí. See SJ 03.2.3, 05.2.1, 05.8.2, 05.8.4, 05.9.11. According to Guopu, it is the same as 羭 yú black ram. This name refers to the mountain donkey, or donkey-goat. It has one horn. Modern pronunciation: lǘ. Ref. 3.2.3, 5.2.1, 5.8.2, 5.8.4, 5.9.11.

- **Rat, fèi**. Fèishǔ 𪗱鼠. The *Erya* cites 13 types or rats, including this one but its does not describe it. The *Guangyun* mentions that its call resembles that of the barks of a dog.

- **Rhinoceros**. Xī 犀. According to the *Bencao Gangmu*: "This animal resembles the water buffalo. It has a pig head, a big belly, short legs like those of the elephant, and a black color. Three different species are differentiated: the shānxī "mountain rhinoceros", the shuǐxī "river rhinoceros", and the sìxī "common rhinoceros." In addition, there is the hairy rhinoceros. The mountain rhinoceros lives in the mountains and forests and can be obtained in large amount. The river rhinoceros goes in and out of the water and is therefore difficult to catch. It has two horns, a long nasal one and a short frontal one. The river rhinoceros has a carapace skin (zhūjiǎ 珠甲) while the mountain rhinoceros does not. The common rhinoceros, or sand rhinoceros, has one horn on top. It is fine and smooth, grizzled and clearly demarcated. It cannot be used in medicine." Cited in SJ 1.3.2, 2.2.12, 5.8.4, 5.8.9 (white rhinoceros), 5.9.7. See also one-horned bovines.

- **Shāngāo**. Shāngāo 山膏. Its shape is like that of the piglet. It is red like fire and good at cursing at people. The 山膏 shāngāo may allude to the 山都, the shāndōu, a species of baboon or orangutan in the South of China. The History of Tang mentions that the orangutan likes wine and straw sandals. If someone tries to lure it with these two items, as the orangutan realizes it, it will say strong curses at that person. See also the shōjō (猩々 or 猩猩, heavy drinker or orangutan?), a kind of

Japanese sea spirit with red face and hair and a fondness for alcohol. The xīngxīng 猩猩 is mentioned in HJ 13.13.

- **Tiānmǎ**. Tiānmǎ 天馬. Animals resembling white dogs with black head. When it meets humans, it flies away. Its name derives from its call. Celestial horse. This is also the name of an auspicious star.

- **Tiger**. Mǎcháng 馬腸. Tiger. The animal Mǎfù 馬腹 (see SJ 5.2.10) is originally written 馬腸 Mǎcháng. This construction is also found in HJ 11.3 about 女媧之腸 Nǚwā zhī cháng or 女媧之腹 Nǚwā zhī fù. This is about a legendary animal Mǎfù. It has a human head and a tiger body, its call is like that of an infant, and its eats humans.

- **Tōngtōng**. Tōngtōng 狪狪. Animal resembling young pigs with pearls. Its name derives from its call.

- **Wānhú**. Wānhú 婹胡. Animal that looks like Père David's Deers and has fish eyes. Its name derives from its call.

- **Wénlín**. Wénlín 聞獜. It shape is like that of the pig. Its body is yellow, and its head and tail are white. According to Guopu, 獜 (pronounced lín) is also written 䍇 (pronounced líng). Its apparition is a sign of cyclones in the world. Ref. 5.11.48.

- **Wénwén**. Wénwén 文文. Animal that looks like a bee. Its tail is forked and its tongue inside out. It is good at shouting.

- **Xiāo**. Xiāo 囂. Animal that resembles a spider monkey (SJ 2.1.10). It has long arms which are good for throwing. The comment suggests the term 夒 náo which refers, according to the *Shuowen*, to the rhesus monkey. See also HJ 9.32 東海夒牛.

- **Xībiān**. Xībiān 谿邊. Dog-like animal. Its fur protects against evil energies.

- **Xīngxīng**. Xīngxīng 狌狌. A great ape, probably of the orangutan family. According to the *Bencao Gangmu*, "it has both human and monkey features; it has human face and legs, yellow fur that are very long on the head, and a regular face. It sounds like a baby crying or a dog barking."

- **Xīqú**. Xīqú 犀渠. Animals that look like bull but have a blue-green body. Its call resembles that of infants. It eats humans. Now refers to a species of rhinoceros.

- **Yak**. Máoniú 斄牛. Should be understood as 牦牛 máoniú, the yak. It is raised in large quantity to eat its flesh. Its shape resembles that of the buffalo: It has a large body and is very strong. It looks like a bull and has a fur renewing itself by successive shedding at the four seasons. This is the yak 牦牛 máoniú (*Bos grunniens*). Lit. bull with a tail used for banner. There is a "horse with a tail used for banner" in HJ 10.16. The yak's habitat is treeless uplands. The yak-tail banner later became a military symbol (the Mongolian nine yak-tail banner) and religious symbol (as the dhvaja, the victory banner symbolizing the triumph of Buddhism).

- **Yìjí**. Yìjí [犬多]即. Animal resembling the Tibetan mastiff. Its mouth and eyes are red and its tail white. Its apparition is a sign of fire in the locality. The word yì is found in the Yu pian where it is considered a kind of animal.
- **Yǐláng**. Yǐláng [犬也]狼. Fox-like animal. It has a white tail and long ears. Its apparition is a sign of turmoil in the country. According to Wangfu, it is pronounced sìláng.
- **Yín**. Yín [鹿/言]. Animal that looks like a raccoon dog with a human head.
- **Yōnghé**. Yōnghé 雍和. This appears to be a long-tailed monkey. It is an ape-like animal with red eyes, red mouth and yellow body. Its apparition is a sign of terrible events in the country. Ref. 5.11.6.
- **Yōué**. Yōué 幽鴳. It looks like a spider monkey and has a spotted body. It often laughs. When it sees human beings, it lies down. Its name derives from its call. The annotation mentions that the *Taiping Yulan* writes 幽頞 yōué. Modern pronunciation yōuyàn.
- **Yù**. Yù 寓. It resembles rats with bird wings, and its call is like that of the goat. It protects against wars. It appears to be a bat (蝙蝠).
- **Zhì**. Zhì 彘. According to the literal translation, it is one of the names for pig or swine. It is described as having a monkey shape and a tiger shape, four ears, and an oxtail. It has a bark-like sound. It eats humans.
- **Zhūyàn**. Zhūyàn 朱厭. This beast looks like an ape with a hoary had and bare feet. Its apparition is a sign of great rise of troops.
- **Zuóniú**. Zuóniú [牛乍]牛. Mt Xiǎohuá has numerous mountains cows whose weight is up to 500 kg. These cows are called zuóniú (Guopu). This term occurs seven times in the *Shanhai jing*. A variant text has 麋牛 míniú instead.
- **Zúzī**. Zúzī 足訾. It looks like a monkey, has a mane, an oxtail, spotted arms, and horse's hoofs. When it sees human beings, it starts shouting. Its name derives from its call.

Animal hybrids

- **Àoyē**. Àoyē 傲[彳囙]. This beast looks like a bull with a white body and four horns. It has a porcupine-like fur that is like a short rain cape made of reed. It eats humans. The compound character [彳囙] seems to suggest "animal." Some versions also write 傲 ào as [彳敖] ào.
- **Bìbì**. Bìbì 獙獙. Animal resembling a fox with wings. Its call is like that of the swan goose. Its apparition is a sign of major drought in the Empire.
- **Bó**. Bó 駮. Animal, myth. It has the shape of a horse with a white body, a black tail, a single horn, tiger teeth and tiger claws. Its call resembles that of the drum sound. It eats tigers and leopards. It can be used to

push military forces away. It is mentioned in the *Erya* as a horse-like beast with impressive teeth, eating tigers and leopards. See also HJ 3.20.

- **Bómǎ**. Bómǎ [馬字]馬. A kind of unicorn [独角兽]. It has an ox tail, a white body and a single horn. Its call is like a shout. See also SJ 3.1.3.
- **Bóyí**. Bóyí 猼訑. Goat-like animal having nine tails, four ears, and its eyes on the back. As pendant waist ornament, it protects against fear.
- **Chángyòu**. Chángyòu 長右. It looks like a spider monkey with four ears. Its name, deriving from its call. Its apparition in a county is a sign of floods. It appears that it is the same hybrid as the bóyí 猼訑 (see SJ 1.1.8), the goat-like animal with nine tails, four ears and eyes located on its back. See also note on Mt Chángyòu. Ref. 1.2.2.
- **Chuò**. Chuò 连. According to the annotation, this animal looks like a tiger or a rabbit but has deer legs and a blue color. Also written [鹿霝] zhuò.
- **Cóngcóng**. Cóngcóng 從從. Dog-like wish six legs. Its name derives from its call.
- **Dōngdōng**. Dōngdōng [羊東](羊東]. A goat unicorn. It resembles goats and has one horn. It has one eye located behind the ear. Its name derives from its call.
- **Dragon, Flying**. Fēishé 飛蛇. Flying dragon. According to Guopu, "this is the wingless dragon (螣蛇 téngfēi), it rides the fog and flies." Han Feizi states that "in former past, Huangdi joined with the supernatural beings on top of the western Mt Tai, and the winged snake (騰蛇 téngfēi) was tamed. These creatures are mentioned in the ancient works (*Erya*, Xunzi Quanxue …).
- **Ěrshǔ**. Ěrshǔ 耳鼠. It resembles a rat and has a rabbit head and a Père David's Deer body. Its call is like the roar or howl of a dog. If flies by means of its whiskers. Its consumption prevents abdominal distention. In addition, it can be used against all kinds of poisons.
- **Fēi**. Fēi 蜚. Animal that looks like a bull and has a white head. It has one eye and a snake tail. When it goes into water, it dries it up. When it goes into grass, it kills it. Its apparition is a sign of great epidemics. Ref. 4.4.8.
- **Fox with nine tails**. Jiǔ wěi hú 九尾狐. Fox with nine tails. "It sounds like a young child. It can devour a man. Its consumption protects against evil energies." The nine-tails fox is found across Asian culture, from the Chinese Huli jing, the Korean Kumiho and the Japanese Kitsune.
- **Fūzhū**. Fūzhū 夫諸. Animal that looks like a white deer and has four horns. Its apparition is a sign of major floods in the area.
- **Huán**. Huán 羱. Animals that resemble the bull and have three legs. Its name derives from its call. Hao Yixing mentions that the character should be 羱 huán.

- **Huān**. Huān 讙. Fox-like animal. It has one eye and three tails. Its call is as forceful as one hundred sounds. It can be used against bad luck. Also, as a medicine, it protects against jaundice. Huān means cry of joy; noise, bawl. Ref. 2.3.22.
- **Huī**. Huī [馬軍]. Animal that resembles a líng goat, has four horns, a horse tail and rooster's spurs. Its name derives from its call. It is good at twirling and dancing.
- **Juérú**. Juérú 玃如. This beast looks like the deer, has a white tail, the back legs of a horse, the front legs of human, and four horns. Originally written 缠如 biànrú, but corrected in the comments. 玃 jué, a large ape found in Western China.
- **Kuí**. Kuí 夔. Part dragon, part bull and part man, with a single leg (Wells Williams).
- **Lì**. Lì [犭戾] or [犬戾]. Hedgehog-like animal. It is red like cinnabar fire. Its apparition is a sign of major epidemics in the country.
- **Lílì**. Lílì 狸力. It looks like the tún piglet. This animal has cock spurs and a bark-like sound. Its apparition in a county is a sign of major public works. Also called 貍力 lílì.
- **Lóngzhí**. Lóngzhí 蠪姪. Animal resembling a fox and has nine tails and nine heads. It has tiger paws. Its call is like the wail of the newborn. It eats humans.
- **Mǎfù**. Mǎfù 馬腹. Lit. Horse stomach. Animal that has a human face and a tiger body. Its call is like that of infants. It eats humans. The *Shuijing*, Notes on River Miǎn, says: "River Miǎn contains an animal, it looks like a three or four year's old child; it has scales and shell like the animal línglǐ. Its alder head 桤頭 looks like tiger, its extremities are often submerged. This creature has sometimes been compared to the goblin Máhú 麻胡, or the tiger mǎhǔzǐ 馬虎子, both used in tales to intimidate young children. There is also in Northwest China a creature called mǎgāozǐ 馬羔子. However, these comparisons appear erroneous. (See also SJ 5.4.10).
- **Páoxiāo**. Páoxiāo 狍鴞. Goat body, a human face, eyes on its armpits, tiger teeth and human nails. Its call resembles that of an infant. It eats human. The "roe deer owl." This animal was represented on tripods of the Xià dynasty. Ref. SJ 5.2.10
- **Shúhú**. Shúhú 孰湖. It has the body of a horse and wings of a bird, a human face and the tail of a snake. It likes to grasp people. Ref. SJ 2.4.19.
- **Tǔlóu**. Tǔlóu 土螻. This beast looks like a goat and four horns. It eats humans.
- **Water horse**. Shuǐmǎ 水馬. It resembles a horse with spotted legs and an ox tail. Its call resembles the shout. This horse has a black back and streaked legs (*Zhouli*). This term now refers to the dragon-shaped race horse.

- **Yánghuàn**. Yánghuàn [羊患]. This beast looks like a goat, has no mouth and cannot be killed.
- **Yōuyōu**. Yōuyōu 㺔㺔. Animal resembling a horse with sheep eyes, four horns and a bull tail. Its call is like that of the bark of a dog. Its apparition is a sign of deception. Guopu mentions that the *Yupian* writes yōu [上山下攸]. However, according to Guopu, it should be 猫. This comes from 艸 or from 中. Another example is in the HJ 10.29 where 菌狗 comes from [上山下囷]狗.
- **Zháyǔ**. Zháyǔ 窫窳. A bull-like animal. It has a red body, a human face and horse feet. Its call is like that of a small child. It devours humans. According to the *Erya*, this animal resembles a 貙 chú (a tiger-like animal) with tiger claws. The HJ describes the zháyǔ differently (see 10.12 and notes, 10.13, 11.1 and notes, and 11.20), where it has either a dragon head or a human head and a snake body. Modern pronunciation: yàyǔ.
- **Zhēng**. Zhēng 猙. This beast looks like a red leopard with five tails and one horn. Its call is similar to the [noise] of stones hitting one another.
- **Zhūhuái**. Zhūhuái 諸懷. Bull-like animal. It has four horns, human eyes, and pig ears. Its call is like that of the wild goose. It eats humans.
- **Zhūjiān**. Zhūjiān 諸犍. It looks like a leopard with a long tail, a human head, cow ears, and a single eye. It often shouts. When it walks, it holds its tail in its mouth; when it rests, it holds it curled.
- **Zhūrú**. Zhūrú 朱獳. Animal resembling foxes with fish fins. Its name derives from its call. Its apparition is a sign of dread in the country.

Birds

- **Báiyè**. Báiyè 白[夜鳥]. It looks like a pheasants with a mottled head, white wings and yellow feet. Its consumption stops throat pain and can also cure madness.
- **Bird of prey**. Jiù 就. Bird of prey. This is a homophone for 鷲 jiù, the birds of prey such as the condor, vulture, and black eagle. According to the *Guangya*, they belong to the diāo 鵰 category like the hawk, eagle, or falcon (鷹 yīng). Guopu also suggests that 就 jiù is a 鵰 diāo bird. It is a kind of big falcon with a yellow head and red eyes. The feathers of this bird have been used to make arrow plumes.
- **Crane**. Hè 鶴. Crane.
- **Crow**. Wū 烏. Like 鳥 niǎo 'bird', but missing the dot in the head; the eye is invisible because a crow's eye is black like the feathers.
- **Cuckoo**. Shījiū 尸鳩. Also written 鳲鳲 shīshī (turtledove), it is a kind of turtledove 布穀 bùgǔ. It is known for its ability to treat its nestlings as one equally, thus the metaphor of treating without discrimination. It is

also written as "尸鳩之仁", or "benevolence of the cuckoo." The *Erya* mentions the synonyms 鳲鳩 shījiū and 鶻鵃 jíjú.

- **Dānghù**. Dānghù 當扈. Its shape resembles that of pheasants and it flies assisted by its rictal bristles. Its consumption prevents blepharospams. Also called 當戶 dānghù.
- **Duck, Mandarin**. Yuānyang 鴛鴦. Mandarin ducks (*Aix galericulata*).
- **Fān**. Fān 蕃. Unidentified bird. Guopu mentions that some say it is a kind of owl. See also its meaning as the grass sedge. Ref. 3.1.5.
- **Féiyí**. Féiyí 肥遺. This bird looks like quails and have a yellow body and a red beak. Its consumption cures pestilence and may also kill worms. SJ 3.1.22 mentions a snake with the same name féiyí. SJ 2.1.3 mentions a divinity of that name. Ref. 2.1.7.
- **Fènghuáng**. Fènghuáng 鳳皇. This bird looks like the chicken, has five variegated colors and patterns. The patterns on its When feeding, it sings and dances. Its apparition is a sign of peace everywhere under Heaven. While the dragon is the first animal, the phoenix is the first bird. Fènghuáng is said to be made up of the head of a chicken, the neck of a snake, the beak of a swallow, the back of a tortoise and the tail of a fish. Its body symbolizes the six celestial bodies, the five-virtues (head - called "virtue-dé", wings - "justice-yì", back - "ceremony-lǐ", chest - "benevolence-rén", belly - "faith-xìn") and the five fundamental colors (black, white, red, blue and yellow). It is to note that fèng usually refers to the male, and huáng to the female. While not specified here, some texts mention it has three legs. See also *Erya* 17 and Shiji, *Yiwen Leiju* 99, and *Chuxue ji* 5 about this tradition. See also SJ 1.3.13.
- **Fighting bird**. Hé 鶡. Bird known in ancient times for its fighting ability. It would fight to death. According to Hao Yixing, it looks like the pheasant but bigger, and has bulgy blue-green feathers.
- **Fúxī**. Fúxī 凫徯. This bird looks like a rooster and has a human face. Its name derives from its sound. Its apparition indicates the presence of soldiers.
- **Goose, Wild**. Jiànniǎo 駕鳥. It appears to be 駕鵝, the archaic name of wild goose 野鵝. Ref. 5.3.3.
- **Guànguàn**. Guànguàn 灌灌. A bird reputed for its taste. It looks like a kind of turtledove that sounds like men calling. As pendant waist ornament, it protects against confusion.
- **Gǔdiāo**. Gǔdiāo 蠱雕. Appears to be a large vulture with a horn. This bird looks like a vulture and have a horn. It sounds resembles that of babies. It eats humans.
- **Gūxī**. Gūxī 鴣[習鳥]. Bird with the shape of a crow with white spots. Its consumption prevents obscuring of the vision. This seems to be a partridge 鷓鴣 zhègū.
- **Hawk, Sparrow**. Yīngzhān 鷹鸇. Archaic for sparrow hawk.

- **Heron, Night**.   Jiāo 鵁.   Night heron (*Nycticorax prasinosceles* or *Gorsachius*), Black-Crowned Night-Heron or the Chinese Squacco-Heron, also called 鵁鶄 jiāojīng.   It resembles the wild duck but smaller. It has long legs and a short tail.   The SJ describes these birds as gregarious and flying in flocks.   Its feather is like that of the female pheasant.   Its name derives from its call.   Its consumption cures wind diseases.   Hao Yixing, citing the *Yupian* where "the white Nycticorax flies in flocks and has the tail of a hen," think that the text is erroneous and should have tail instead of feather.   See also SJ 1.3.3 for a hybrid bird having the same name.
- **Huángniǎo**.   Huángniǎo 黃鳥.   SJ: birds that look like white-headed owls.   Its name derives from its call.   Its consumption prevents jealousy. This seems to be the Passerine bird or Eurasian Siskin (*Carduelis spinus*) 黃雀 huángquè.   See HJ 2.8, 10.4, 11.31, and 12.1.   It is said that Emperor Wu treated the jealousy of his wife by using the 倉庚 cānggēng, recommended by one of his attendants who referred to the SHJ but confused the Huángniǎo and the cānggēng.   Lit. "yellow bird." .
- **Kingfisher**.   Cuì 翠.   The original text has white pheasants (雉 zhì) and white long-tailed mountain pheasants (翟 dí).   Since there is duplication, and since both Guopu and Hao Yixing suggest 翠 cuì, the kingfisher instead of 翟 dí, I have substituted the terms in the text.
- **Kingfisher-like bird with red beak**.   Mín 六.   Hao Yixing suggests that the character should be [昏鳥] mín.   The [昏鳥] is mentioned in the *Shuowen* and is described in the *Guangyun* as a kind of kingfisher with a red beak, having the property to protect against fire.   Modern pronunciation: liù.
- **Lì**.   Lì 櫟.   This bird looks like the quail, has black patterns and red feathers on its neck.   Its consumption cures hemorrhoids.
- **Língyào**.   Língyào 鴒[要鳥].   Bird looking like pheasants; it has a long tail, its feathers are crimson red, and its beak green.   Its name derives from its call.   As pendant waist ornament, it protects against nightmares.
- **Luò**.   Luò [樂鳥].   This bird resembles the vulture (hawk or eagle) and has black spots and red nape.
- **Luóluo**.   Luóluo 羅羅.   Man-eater bird.   HJ 3.20 uses this name for a tiger-like green animal.   The Hunan tribes used to pronounce tiger luóluo.
- **Magpie**.   Què 鵲.   Magpie.   In the Sanhai jing the word què 鵲 usually refers to a fabulous bird.
- **Myna**.   Qúyù 鴝鵒.   Myna bird.
- **Osprey**.   È 鶚.   Osprey; fish hawk; sea eagle.   This bird looks like a vulture.   It has dark spots, a white head, a red beak and tiger claws.   Its call is like that of the morning swan.   Its apparition is a sign of major military operations.   First avian transformation of Qīnpī.
- **Owl**.   Xiāo 鴞.   It was described in ancient china as a bird eating its own mother once adult.   It was a symbol of superabundant yang and as such

was believed to cause drought. Summer solstice was the Day of the Owl and children born on this day were thought to have a certain natural violence. Such children might even murder their own mother or father. Lei Gong 雷公, the Chinese god of thunder, has the beak, wings and claws of an owl, on the body of a man.

- **Owlet, Striped head**. Liú 鶹. It may be the 鵂鶹 xiūliú, or owl, also known as the Barred owlet (*Glaucidium cuculoides*, Strigidae), 斑頭鵂鶹 bāntóu xiūliú ("striped head owlet"), also called 做橫紋小鴞 héngwén xiǎoxiāo ("horizontal pattern small owl"). (See Strigidae at http://www.cjvlang.com/Birds/strigidae.html).

- **Parrot**. Yīngáng 鸚鴗. According to the annotations, this is the 鸚鵡 yīngwǔ or parrot. This bird looks like the owl, has green feather and a red beak. It has a human tongue and can speak. The tongue of this bird resembles that of small children. The *Shuowen* says that "the yīngáng (or yīngmóu) is a bird that can speak." Several varieties exist, some red, green, white and multicolor. It is confused with the kakatoes. In the south, the green one is eaten. Another version has 鸚[母鸟] or yīngmóu.

- **Pheasant**. Zhì 雉. Pheasant. This is the Chinese ringnecked pheasant 野鸡 yějī, also known as the common pheasant and the true pheasant. The male of the species has a brightly colored red face and wattles, two short "horns" of feathers at the back of the crown, and white ring of feathers around the neck. Ref. 3.4.6.

- **Pheasant, long-tailed**. Dí 翟. Ancient name for the Syrmaticus long-tailed mountain pheasant (长尾雉 chángwěizhì). It is probably the Reeves's Pheasant (*Syrmaticus reevesii*). It is larger than the regular pheasant (up to 210 cm long). The comment suggests it may be the crane (鶴 hè) and Guopu suggests the possibility of the vulture (樂鳥).

- **Pheasant, Mountain**. Shānjī 山雞. Pheasant (*phasianus*), a mountain pheasant. Ref. 2.1.2.

- **Pheasant, red**. Chìbiē 赤鷩. Red pheasant, a mountain pheasant. It has the property to protect against fire. This appears to be either the Golden Pheasant or "Chinese Pheasant" (*Chrysolophus pictus*; 鷩雉 biēzhì, 錦雞 jǐnjī), or a smaller type of it. Guopu pronounces 鷩 as bì. Its throat and belly are dark red, the crest gold, the head yellow and the tail green intermixed with red feathers with delicate and rich nuances. The call of this bird is lovely. The *Erya* says that "among the fourteen species of pheasants is found the pheasant biē." This is probably the one referred to here. Ref. 2.1.4.

- **Pheasant, Reeves's**. Jiāo 鷮. This is the ancient name of the 英文 Reeves's pheasant (*Syrmaticus reevesii*), a long-tailed pheasant. The annotations to the text say that 鷮 jiāo is the 鷮雉 jiāozhì or jiāo pheasant, a kind the ring-necked pheasant and has a relatively long tail.

- **Pheasant, silver**. Báiyóu 白[有鳥]. White pheasant (*Lophura nycthemera*). It goes by several names, including 白鷴, 白翰, 鷴雉. Ref. 3.2.3.
- **Pheasant, silver**. Báihàn 白翰. White pheasant (*Lophura nycthemera*), commonly called báixián silver pheasant. Ref. 2.1.14.
- **Poison-feathered bird**. Zhèn 鴆. Poison-feathered bird. Mythical poisonous bird that eats snakes. Its feathers poison the wine in which they are soaked and there is an expression for "poisoned wine" which is 鴆毒 zhèndú. According to Guopu, "鴆 zhèn is big like a vulture with purple-green feathers, a long neck and a red beak. It eats Pallas pit vipers heads. The male is called 運日 yùnrì and the female 陰諧 yīnxié." According to Hao Yixing, the *Shuowen* mentions that "鴆 zhèn is the poison bird." Its body is poisonous, and it used to be called bird poison. Rosny suggests the secretary bird. Ref. 5.8.4, 5.8.23, 5.9.12, 5.11.9.
- **Qièzhī**. Qièzhī 竊脂. Bird that looks like owls, has a red body and a white head. It can be used to protect against fire.
- **Qīnggēng**. Qīnggēng 青耕. Bird that looks like the magpie. It has a green body and its beak, eyes and tail are white. Its name derives from its call. It is used to protect against epidemics.
- **Qīngniǎo**. Qīngniǎo 青鳥. Messengers of the Queen Mother of the West. Special birds used by her to fetch food. They remain on this mountain isolated from the other birds. See also HJ 7.2.
- **Qūjū**. Qūjū 鸐鸐. Bird that looks like a crow, has a white head, a green body, and yellow legs. Its name, derived from its call, is qūjū. Its consumption prevents hunger and it addresses amnesia.
- **Qúrú**. Qúrú 瞿如. This bird looks like the night heron, has a white head, three legs, and a human face. Its name derives from its call.
- **Shùsī**. Shùsī 數斯. Bird that resembles the sparrow hawk and has human feet. Its consumption cures goiters.
- **Sǔsī**. Sǔsī 竦斯. It looks like a pheasant with a human face. When it sees someone, it starts jumping. Its name derives from its call.
- **Swan goose**. Hóngyàn 鴻鴈. *Anser cygnoides Linnaeus.* It is a rare large and long-necked goose.
- **Swan, morning**. Chénhú 晨鵠. The names è, diāo and chénhú in SJ 2.3.5 refer to birds of the falcon family. It may be a variety of the osprey.
- **Teal**. Líhú 鸑鵊. SJ: It looks like mandarin ducks but have human feet. Its name derives from its call. Its apparition is a sign of major achievements in the country. This is a kind of fabulous teal. This seems to be the pelican (*Pelecanidae*) tíhú 鵜鶘, also known as qiélándiāo 伽蓝鸟, táohé 淘河, and táng 塘. Guopu notes that the pelican 鵜鶘 tíhú has feet that are very similar to human feet.
- **Tōngqú**. Tōngqú [虫鳥]渠. This bird looks like a mountain pheasant or a duck, its feather is ashen and red legs like that of a chicken. It treats chap skins. This bird appears to be the same as the yōngqú 雖渠.

- **Turtledove**. Shījiū 鳲鳩. Cuckoo, turtledove. According to Guopu, 鳲 shī should be 尸 shī. Ref. 3.1.17.
- **Vulture**. Diāo 雕. Raptor or vulture. Ref. 2.3.5.
- **Xiégōu** 絜鉤. Bird resembling a wild duck and having a rat tail. It is experts in climbing trees. Its apparition is a sign of numerous epidemics in the country.
- **Xìngyù** 胜遇. This bird looks like a long-tailed pheasant and is red. It feeds from fishes and its call resembles that of the deer. Its apparition is a sign of floods in the countries. Also called shèngyù.
- **Xíxí** 鰼鰼. It resembles the magpie, have ten wings, and scales at the feathers' extremities. Its call is like that of the magpie. It protects against fire. Its consumption prevents soreness. The xi is the loach (*Cyprinoformes*), a ray-finned fish. The ten wings may refer to ten fins. Ref. 3.1.5.
- **Yǎo** 鴢. Bird like wild ducks but have a blue-green body, bright-red eyes and a red tail. Its consumption brings suitable children.
- **Yīngsháo** 嬰勺. Bird whose name derives from its call. It looks like the magpie, its eyes and beak are red, its body is white, and its tail has the shape of a wine spoon.
- **Zhèn** 鵫. Bird that looks like a pheasant and frequently eats cockroaches. It may be the secretary bird (*Sagittarius serpentarius*). According to Guopu, the 鵫 zhèn of 5.11.9 is not the snake-eating poison-feathered bird 鴆 zhèn seen in SJ 5.8.4, 5.8.23, 5.9.12. See also http://en.wikipedia.org/wiki/Zhenniao. Ref. 5.11.9.
- **Zhǐtú** [鳥只][鳥餘], or [鳥只]鵌. Bird resembling the crow. Its feet are red. It can be used to protect against fire.

Bird hybrids

- **Bànmào** [般/鳥]吒. Resemble crows and have a human face. It flies at night and hides during the day. Its consumption protects against sunstrokes. Also written [般/鳥][冒鳥]. A type of owl.
- **Bēn** [賁鳥]. Bird that resembles the magpie, has a white body, a red tail and six legs. Its name derives from its call. It is easily frightened. The *Guangyun* says that [賁鳥] bēn is similar to the swan 鵠 hú.
- **Bìfāng** 畢方. This bird looks like cranes, with one foot, red spots, green body and white beak. Its name, derived from its call, is bìfāng. Its apparition is a sign of strange fires in the city. See also HJ 1.6 and HJ 6.16.
- **Chǎngfù** 尚付. Rooster-like bird. It has three heads, six eyes, six feet and three wings. Its consumption decreases having to lie down. (尚鳥付鳥 chǎngniǎo fùniǎo).

- **Chī** 鴟. This bird has one head and three bodies. It resembles the luò vulture. Ancient word for sparrow hawk (modern 鷂鷹 yàoyīng).
- **Chúnniǎo** 鶉鳥. These birds manage the one-hundred items of Emperor Di. According to Hao yixing, it may be the phoenix fèng 鳳 (See HJ 2.16, 6.18. 6.19). In addition the Qinjing states that "the red phoenix is called chún 鶉.
- **Dì**. Dìniǎo (or Dàiniǎo) [鳥大]鳥 or [鳥犬]鳥. Birds looking like owls. It has three eyes and it has ears. Its call is like that of the deer (or pig according to the *Yupian*). Its consumption protects from lingering dampness.
- **Jīngwèi** 精衛. Bird that look like a crow, and has a spotted head, a white beak and red feet. Its name derives from its call. A mythical bird trying to fill up the sea with pebbles. The *Guangyun* mentions that this creature has a white head and red beak (SJ: white beak and red feet).
- **Jùn** 駿. The jùn bird looks like a sparrow hawk, with red legs, a straight beak, yellow spots and a white head. Its call is like that of the swan. Its apparition is a sign of great local dryness. Mythological bird cited in the *Huainanzi*, as "in the middle of the sun there is the bird jùn (日中有駿鳥). It may be the three-legged Golden Crow. Second avian transformation of Qīnpī.
- **Lěi** 鸓. This bird looks like the magpie. It is red and black, has two heads and four feet. It protects against fire. The commentary suggests it is a mistake and refers to Hao Yixing term [疊鳥] dié.
- **Luánjī** 鸞雞. Mythological bird for which little is known. The annotators suspect a mistake in the terms.
- **Luánniǎo** 鸞鳥. Auspicious legendary bird belonging to the phoenix category. It is described as looking like a long-tailed pheasant, and having multicolor feathers. Its apparition is a sign of peace in the empire.
- **Mánmán** 蠻蠻. Bird that looks like a wild duck but has a single wing and a single eye. It flies with another one, by complementing one another. Its name is mánmán. Its apparition is a sign of general floods. There may be an allusion to the lover birds (bǐyìniǎo 比翼鳥). See *Erya* on 鶼鶼鳥. See SJ 2.4.14 for an animal with that name. See also HJ 1.3 and HJ 1.4. Ref. 2.3.1.
- **Owl-like bird**. Unnamed in the SJ. It resembles an owl, has a human face, a macaque body, and the tail of a dog. Its name derives from its call. Its apparition is a sign of great drought in the locality.
- **Qīnyuán** 欽原. This bird looks like bees or wasps that are as big as mandarin duck. When it stings animals or birds, it kills them. When it stings trees, it makes them wither.
- **Qíqiāo** 跂雀. Bird that resembles the chicken, has a white head, rat feet and tiger paws. It eats humans. It is also mentioned in the *Chuci* (*Heavenly questions*), where another beast, 跂踵 qíduī, is a synonym to it, and in Liu Zongyuan's Answers to Questions on Heaven.

- **Suānyǔ** 酸與. Bird with the shape of a snake, four wings, six eyes and three feet. Its name derives from its call. Its apparition is a sign of terror in the country.
- **Tuóféi** 橐[上非下巴]. This bird looks like the owl, has a human face and a single foot. It can be seen during winter and it hides during summer. As pendant waist ornament, it [its feathers] removes the fear of thunder.
- **Xiàngshé** 象蛇. Lit. snake-elephant.
- **Xiāo** 囂. A bird that resembles the kuāfù (SJ 3.2.12). It has four wings, one eye, and a dog tail. Its call is like that of the magpie. Its consumption cures intestinal diseases. It is also a method to stop diarrhea.
- **Yīyú** 鴒鵒. Some texts have 鵒 instead of [余鳥]. This bird is hermaphrodite, multicolored with red spots. It resembles a crow, has three heads and six tails and is good at laughing. Used as medicine, it protects from bad dreams and can be used against bad luck. SJ 3.1.3 mentions that its consumption protects against deep-rooted ulcers. Ref. 2.3.22, 3.1.3.
- **Yú** 顒. This bird looks like the owl, has a human face, four eyes, and ears. Its name is derived from its call. Its apparition is a sign of general draught. Hao Yixing mentions that in the *Guangyun* it is the character [禺鳥] yú niǎo. Modern pronunciation: yóng.
- **Yuānchú** 鵷鶵. A phoenix-like bird. Male and female are the same. Guopu suggests that it is the male phoenix fèng 鳳. This bird is also mentioned in *Zhuangzi* 17 - Autumn Floods.
- **Zhū** 鴸. It looks like the sparrow hawk, with human extremities and a quail-like sound. Its apparition in a county is a sign of numerous administrative layoffs. With regard to tales about it, refer to notes HJ 6.7 (讙頭國) and HJ 10.7 (蒼梧山) describing the metamorphosis of the son of Yao into a bird. Also written 鴸鳥 zhūniǎo.
- **Zīshǔ** [此/虫)鼠. Bird resembling chicken covered with rat's hair. Its apparition in a locality is a sign of major draught.

Fishes

- **Anchovy fish**. Tuán yú 鱄魚. A group of fishes. Described as Crucian carps with pig hair, and a piglet-like sound. Its apparition is a sign of general draught. Ref. 1.3.9.
- **Bàng**. Bàng yú [魚丰]魚. It looks like soft-shelled turtles and bleat like goats. According to Guopu, it would be bàng or 蚌, oyster, mussel, or mother-of-pearl. In other words, it is about a mollusk of the freshwater mussel family (Unionidae).
- **Carp**. Lǐ 鯉. Carp. Ref. 4.4.2.

- **Carp, bighead**. Qiū yú [魚差]魚. It seems to be the 鱅魚 yōngyú (*Aristichthys nobilis*, or *Hypophthalmichthys nobilis*), also called variegated carp (花鰱, 胖头鱼, 大头鱼, 黑鰱). Along with the grass, silver, and black carps they are known as the "four famous domesticated fishes." It is also suggested that [魚差] is 鰍 qiū, whose common name is the loach níqiū 泥鰍. According to the *Bencao Gangmu*, the consumption of yōngyú treats wart growth. However, excessive consumption leads to damp-heat and causes skin eruptions and scabies.
- **Carp, Crucian**. Fù 鮒. Crucian carp (*Carassius carassius*). Also called 鮒魚 fùyú and 鯽魚 jìyú. The *Taiping Yulan* uses 無魚 wúyú instead of 鮒魚 fùyú. The breathing of this fish generates bubbles that look like stars. Chinese cuisine uses it commonly, or in luxurious preparations like the congshao jiu (蔥燒鯽魚, Lit. scallion cooked Crucian carp) where, after hours of preparation, the fish is tender enough to consume together with all its bones. It is also used to make soup with tofu as it is believed to benefit women in postpartum periods.
- **Carp, yellow-cheek**. Gǎn yú 儀魚. Yellow-cheek carp (*Elopichthys bambusa*). Some texts use 鱤 gǎn instead of 儀 gǎn. Some commentaries suggest that it is a kind of catfish (mǔnián 母鮎), or rod fish (gānyú 竿鱼), it has a long cylindrical green-yellow body, a big mouth and small eyes, aggressive temper, feeding on various preys. It is sweet, warm and nonpoisonous. It enters the taiyin and yangming, warms the center and harmonizes the stomach. Modern pronunciation: yíyú.
- **Carp-like fish**. Bó yú 薄魚. It looks like huso sturgeons and have a single eye. Its call is like that of someone vomiting. Its apparition is a sign of great drought in the empire.
- **Catfish**. Hù 鱯. Catfish (Mystus pelusius). This fish looks like the stonefish (*Synanceia*) or the sculpin (*Cottus*), but bigger and white. It is slender, ashen-brown, its head is flat, and it has dorsal fins with needle-like spines.
- **Doctor fish**. Yòng yòng zhī yú 鱅鱅之魚. Tench or doctor fish (*Tinca tinca*). It looks like colored cattle. Its call is like that of the pig. It has been suggested that it is the bighead carp (*Aristichthys nobilis*), however I have chosen the term bighead carp for Qiū yú.
- **Eel**. Shàn 媐 or [魚單]. Eel. Guopu: 鱓 shàn, eel (鱓魚 shànyú). In SJ 3.1.14, it is written and suggested by Guopu as the 鱓 shàn, or finless eel 黃鱔 huángshàn (*Monopterus albus*). It is also written [魚旦]. Modern pronunciation dī.
- **Flying fish**. Wényáo yú 文鰩魚. This fish looks like the carp. It has a fish body and bird wings, with dark green streaks, a white head and a red mouth. It continuously goes toward the western sea and travels to the eastern sea. It flies at night. Its call is like that of the luánjī bird. It tastes sweet and sour. Its consumption renders someone crazy. Its apparition

is a sign of great abundance in the world. *Lushi Chunqiu*: "the fishes of River Guān are called yáo."

- **Garra pingi**. Wèi yú 寐魚. Garra pingi fish. This is the 鮇魚 wèiyú which seems to be the Garra pingi (*Discognathus pingi*), a bottom-dwelling fish. It is also called wūbàng 烏棒. However, some commentators have suggested the barbel 嘉魚 jiāyú (*Barbus*) and some translations the char fish (*Salvelinus*). Modern pronunciation: mèiyú.
- **Grouper**. Yì 鮨. Grouper (*Epinephelus septemfasciatus*).
- **Grouper-like fish**. Unnamed in the SJ. It has a fish body and a dog head. Its consumption cures mania. Ref. 3.1.20.
- **Guǒyú**. Guǒ yú 蠃魚. It has fish bodies and bird wings. Its call is like that of the mandarin duck. Its apparition is a sign of floods in villages.
- **Háhá**. Háhá zhī yú 鮯鮯之魚. Fish háhá. Fish that looks like a carp. It has six feet and a bird tail. Its name derives from its call.
- **Háo fish**. Háo yú 豪魚. It resembles sturgeons, and has red mouth and tail and red wings. It is used against white ringworm.
- **Héluó**. Héluó zhī yú 何羅之魚. This fish, as well as the 茈魚 cíyú (SJ 4.4.3) is described as having "one head and ten bodies." Its call resembles the dog's bark. Its consumption cures ulcers. It is feasible that the author's concept of "body" can be interpreted more loosely and includes appendices. In such case, octopus (eight-belt fish, 八帶魚 bādàiyú) and cuttlefish (烏賊 wūzéi) can be viewed as having respectively one head and eight bodies, and one head and ten bodies.
- **Herring, Chinese**. Zī yú 鮆魚. Chinese herring (*Coilia ectenes*). Also called 鱭魚 zīyú, dāoyú 刀魚, or dāojì 刀鮆. This fish has a narrow and thin body and long head. The big ones can reach more than a foot. It abounds in lake Tàihú 太湖.
- **Huái fish**. Huái yú 帥魚. This fish looks like snakes with four legs and feed from fishes. Other texts have (魚骨) huá instead of 帥. It could be a variant of the homophone 䰱魚 huàiyú, which is a four-feet snake that can emit light, eat people, and lead to major drought. See SJ 4.4.6.
- **Kānxǔ** 堪[予予]. Fish, unidentified (Guopu).
- **Lún yú** [魚侖]魚. It looks like a Crucian carp with black spot. Its consumption prevents sleeping.
- **Mandarin fish**. Guì 鱖. Freshwater mandarin fish (*Siniperca chuatsi*). It is also called 鯚花 jìhuā fish and 桂 tǐ fish, and it also known as Chinese perch or mandarin goby. Its body is longer than wide, with a bulging posterior extremity, greenish yellow, irregular black spots and streaks, a large mouth, a protruding lower mandible, small scales, round shape.
- **Needlefish**. Zhēn yú 箴魚. SJ: It looks like the sharpbelly fish, its mouth is armed with a needle. Eating it protects against epidemic diseases. Needlefish. It appears to be the freshwater garfish (*Hyporhamphus sajori* or *ihi*). This fish is present both in rivers and lakes. It can have a small or large size. Its lower jaw has a long beak and it has a silver

white streak. It average length is three to four inches, its spikes are black. Its flesh is white and has a delicate taste. In the northern and eastern seas, a similar fish exists, reaching up to three or four feet.

- **Péipéi** [魚市][魚市]. Unidentified fish whose consumption kills people. Hao Yixing suggests the ray 鯆. On the other hand, Bi Yuan suggests the fish [魚匊] which is the black finless porpoise (*Neophocaena phocaenoides*), 江豚 jiāngtún. The N. phocaenoides asiaeorientalis is a unique freshwater subspecies (best known in the Yangtze river). However, it is not known to have a poisonous flesh.
- **Perch**. Jiāo yú 鮫魚. According to Hao Yixing, the 鮫魚 jiāoyú is now the 沙魚 shāyú sandfish or sand shark. According to other commentators, it is a perch fish. It is described as having a pearl-like skin used to adorn swords (可以飾刀口). Another comment mentions that the jiāo has a fish body, a snake tail, and a skin adorned with pearls. Rosny: These interpretations may be erroneous. The term jiāo often refers to the sea fish sand shark.
- **Rănyí**. Rănyí yú 冉遺魚. Unidentified fish. It has a fish body, a snake head, six legs and eyes like the ears of a horse. Its consumption protects against nightmares. It can be used again evil spells. About this passage, the *Taiping Yulan* says 無遺魚 wúyí yú. See also SJ 3.3.43 for the same problem of identification.
- **Ray-finned fish**. Huá yú 滑魚. Ray-finned fish. This is the *Noemacheilus fasciolatus* or *Schistura fasciolata* (Nichols et Pope) also called 沙钻 and 媒子魚. It has the shape of an eel, with a red back. Its call is like the lute sound. Its consumption cures warts.
- **Rúpí** [上如下魚][魚比] or [如/鱼]魮. Its shape is like that of a decoction pot, its head like that of a bird, it has fins and a fish tail. Its call resembles the sound of a chime stone. It produces pearls.
- **Salmon**. Guī 鮭. Guopu refers to the 鯸鮐: 鯸 zhēng blowfish, and 鮐 tái chub mackerel; tetraodon; globe-fish.
- **Sāo**. Sāo yú [魚蚤]魚. A kind of dace (*Leuciscus*). It looks like of the huso sturgeon. When it is agitated, it is a sign of big battle in the area. Also written 鰠魚.
- **Sea star**. Cí yú 茈魚. The SJ describes it as Crucian carps. It has a single head and ten bodies. Its fragrance is like that of the sea moss ogonori. Its consumption prevents passing gas. See also SJ 3.1.4 for the fish héluó 何羅之魚 with one head and ten bodies. Ref. 4.4.3.
- **Sharpbelly fish**. Yóu or tiáo 鯈. Also written as 鯈 tiáo. The 鯈魚 is 白鰷 or white sharpbelly (*Hemiculter leucisculus*). It has a chicken shape, red feathers, three tails, six feet, and four eyes. Its call resembles that of the magpie. Its consumption removes worries. Modern pronunciation: chóu. The tiáo fish is described as nonpoisonous and sweet in taste. It warms the stomach and, when boiled, its

consumption dispels sorrow and is effective against cold-type pouring diarrhea (冷瀉).

- **Spotted fish**. Wén yú 文魚. Goldfish, carp, or flying fish. The Chǔ Cí (in Hébó (河伯, the Yellow River God)) says "Riding a white turtle he [Hébó] pursues the spotted fishes."
- **Stargazer fish**. Téng yú [馬改魚]魚. SJ: It looks like the mandarin fish and lives in water eddies. It has blue green spots and a red tail. Its consumption prevents furuncles. It can be used against worm abscess. Also written 魚 téngyú, this appears to be the zhānxīng 瞻星 fish or stargazer fish (*Genyagnus Novazelandiae*). It is a stout bluish gray fish with a big flat head; big mouth and small eyes; it usually stays in the bottom of shallow waters; half buried in the muddy sand.
- **Sturgeon**. Zhānwěi 鱣鮪. 鮪 wěi is the ancient term for sturgeon. It appears alone in SJ 5.1.3 and as 鱣鮪 zhānwěi in 4.3.6. If 鱣鮪 refer to two fishes, 鱣 zhān is the huso sturgeon and 鮪 wěi is similar bit has a bigger nose and has no scales. The modern interpretation of 鮪 wěi is generally 鮪魚 wěiyú or tuna. Ref. 4.3.6.
- **Sturgeon, Huso**. Zhān yú 鱣魚. Huso sturgeon (*Huso dauricus*). It is a huge (up to 4.2 m or longer), slow-growing and late-maturing fish with a lower and protractile mouth. Endangered or threatened species. Note that it could also be 鱣魚 shànyú, the eel 鱣魚 zhānyú. See http://www.fishbase.org/Summary/SpeciesSummary.php?ID=4633.
- **Tiáoróng** 儵[魚改虫][虫庸]. Reptile or fish that look like yellow snakes with fish fins. Its movements are accompanied by glistens. Its apparition is a sign of great drought in a locality.
- **Xiànfù** [魚臽]父. This fish is like the Crucian carp; it has a fish head and a swine body. Its consumption prevents vomiting. 臽 [xiàn] is the old form of 陷; A (人 rén) person falling into a 臼 pit, a hole in the ground.
- **Xiūbì zhī yú** 脩辟之魚. Xiūbì fish that has the shape of the mǐn frog, with a white mouth. Its call is like that of the sparrow hawk. Its consumption protects from white ringworms.
- **Zǎo** [魚巢]. Its shape is like that of carps but it has chicken legs. Its consumption protects against warts (SJ). A being consisting of half a fish and half a bird (*Taiping Yulan*, Book 489). It resembles both the chicken and the carp.
- **Zhì yú** [上執下魚]魚. Fish, unidentified.
- **Zhūbiē yú** 珠鱉魚. SJ: This fish looks like lungs. It has eyes and six feet that have pearl-like structures. The taste of its flesh is sour and sweet. Its consumption protects against epidemic diseases. In the *Yulan*, 珠鱉 zhūbiē makes 珠鱉 zhūbiē, the pearl soft-shelled turtle. In the *Lushi Chunqiu* it is the 朱鱉 zhūbiē, vermillion soft-shelled turtle. Hao Yixing says, "珠朱 zhūzhū pearl vermillion, 鱉鱉 biēbiē, biē soft-shelled turtle are really ancient characters. The *Lushi Chunqiu* says that "the name of

the fishes of river Lǐ is 朱鱉 zhūbiē, it has six feet and pearls, and it is beautiful." Hao Yixing: "The sketch of this animal shows four eyes; the *Chuxue ji* section 8 says that "there are lots of 珠鱉 in the sea (ocean), there are like lungs, it has four eyes, six legs and spit pearls." This is in agreement with the sketch. Therefore, it should be considered as "four eyes" and not "eyes".

Fish hybrids

- **Lù** 鯥. The fish called guī 鮭 does not live in water. It has the shape of a bull, with birds' wings and a serpent tail. Its feathers are below its flanks. Its call is that of the liúniú. It dies during the winter and is born in the summer. Its consumption prevents swelling diseases.
- **Hybrid of Mt Tàiqì**. They are flying fishes that resemble the carp. They have a fish body and bird wings, with dark green streaks, a white head and a red mouth. They continuously go toward the western sea and travel to the eastern sea. They fly at night. Their call is like that of the luánjī bird. They taste sweet and sour. Their consumption renders someone crazy. Their apparition is a sign of great abundance in the world. Ref. 2.3.6.

Insects

- **Bee or wasp**. Fēng 蜂. Bees or wasps. The Apoidea superfamily and its two lineages, the Vespidae (wasps, 黃蜂 huángfēng) and the Anthophila (bee, 蜜蜂 mìfēng or simply 蜂 fēng).
- **Cockroach**. Fěi 蜚. Cockroach or gadfly. In the *Erya*, Guopu notes that it is an insect with a plate-like structure on its back, a bedbug (*Cimex lectularius*) 臭虫 chòuchóng. Some commentaries describe it as a small size winged elliptical insect that sends out a foul smell. Ref. 5.11.8.
- **Huángbèi**. Huángbèi 黃貝. Lit. yellow shellfish. According to Guopu, it is a kind of beetle, whose flesh is like that of the tadpole, and yet it has a head, a tail, and ears. See also SJ 5.3.4.
- Insect, stinging. Shìchóng 螫蟲. Stinging insect.
- **Locust**. Zhōnghuáng 螽蝗. According to the *Shuowen*, zhōng, or 螽斯 zhōngsī, katydid, is a kind of locust. Here, this insect is mentioned in terms of invasion of fields.
- **Ringworm, white**. Xuǎn 癬. White ringworm; tinea alba.

Mollusks

- **Conch, Luǒmǔ**. Luǒmǔ 嬴母. According to Guopu it would be the 砳螺 lòngluǒ. 嬴 luǒ is the archaic character for conch (the contemporary meaning being the solitary wasp). There is also a mountain of that name, Mt Luǒmǔ, mentioned in SJ 2.3.10.
- **Snail, purple**. Cíluǒ 茈嬴. Purple snail, maybe the *Pomacea bridgesii* var. "Amethyst" 紫水晶螺. This term in the SJ appears twice and both times seems to be a derivative or degradation of the proper term. In SJ 4.1.12, it is written 茈嬴 cíléi and the second character 嬴 léi should be 嬴 luǒ. In SJ 1.2.13, it is written 芘嬴 zǐluǒ and the first character 芘 zǐ should be 茈 cí (archaic character). The rectified term is therefore 茈嬴 cíluǒ. Ref. 4.1.12, 1.2.13.
- **Bivalve**. Shènyáo 蜃珧. Mother-of-pearl-oyster. If the characters are considered separately, then 蜃 shèn is a large bivalve mollusk. Its shell is oval or slightly triangular, its color and stripes are beautiful (See also http://en.wikipedia.org/wiki/Shen_(clam-monster). 珧 yáo is a small fresh water mussel. Its shell is long and ovoid, its outer surface is dark brown or yellow brown and annular.
- **Snail**. Púléi 僕纍. Also known as 蝸牛 wōniú, it is a mollusk found in marshes and damp places. Ref. 5.3.3.
- **Clam, circular shaped**. Púlú 蒲盧. Mollusk found in marshes and damp places. Note the similarity between the pronunciations of the two mollusks púlú and púléi. Ref. 5.3.3.

Reptiles

- **Chìrú** 赤鱬. It may be the giant salamander, which grows a long tail capable of reaching the trees. See Notes HJ 12.27. It has the body of a fish and the face of a human. Its sounds resemble that of the mandarin duck. Its consumption prevents scabies.
- **Frog, mǐn**. Mǐn 黽. A kind of frog. It looks like the spotted frog, but smaller and has a blue-green skin. Also written [上秋下黽]黽.
- **Guǐ** 蛫. Animal that is like a turtle, its body is white and its head red. It can be used to protect against fire.
- **Lizard, large water**. Tuó 鼉. Large reptile or water lizard. According to Guopu, this animal is similar to the 蜥易 xīyì lizard, the bigger ones reach a length of about 6.5 m., it is covered with scales and its skin is used to cover drums. It may be a monitor lizard (*Varanus*). Today, this term refers to the Chinese alligator.
- **Salamander**. Rén yú 人魚. Salamander, dugong or mermaid. According to Guopu, it is the salamander ní 鯢: it has four limbs and its call is like the sound of a crying infant. It could refer to the 鮎 nián, a kind of catfish or a large carp. The nián is also called □ tí (the sheatfish

catfish, *Parasilurus asotus*). Another suggestion is that it is a synonym of the pangolin fish. See also HJ 2.27. 陵魚 – Notes.

- **Salamander, Giant**. Dì yú [魚帝]魚. Chinese Giant Salamander (*Andrias davidianus*) 大鯢 dàní. The largest salamander in the world, it is considered critically endangered. See also 2.1.8, and 5.7.9.
- Salamander, Zhòuwěi -like. Unnamed in the SJ. Reptile that has long spurs, white legs that are tucked in. Its consumption prevents insanity. It can be used to resist against soldiers.
- **Salamander-like, Giant**. Unnamed in the SJ. It has four legs, and a call like the sound of an infant. Its consumption protects against insanity.
- **Shī yú** 師魚. According to Guopu, it is unidentified but may be the 鯢 ní salamander. See 人魚. There is also a sea fish called 黃條師魚 huángtiáo shīyú (common name 黃尾魚 huángwěi yú), the yellow tail fish (*Seriola quinqueradiata*).
- **Snake, river**. Shé 蛇. Water snakes or river snakes shuǐshé 水蛇, according to Guopu.
- **Snake, singing**. Míngshé 鳴蛇. Singing snake. It looks like ordinary snakes but have four wings. Its call is like the sound of chime stones. Its apparition is a sign of great drought in the locality.
- **Snake, strange**. Guàishé 怪蛇. According to Guopu, this kind of snakes can be found in the Yǒngchāng prefecture. It is hook snakes (鉤蛇 gōushé) reaching up to ten feet in length. Its tail divides into two (岐 qí). It lives in the water. On the riverside by means of its hooks, it captures men, bulls and horses and eats them later one (Guopu).
- **Snake, white water**. Báishé 白蛇. White water snake. The comment of Hao Yixing states that it should be interpreted as 水蛇 shuǐshé or water snake. According to the *Bencao Gangmu*, the water snake is born within the water. It is long like an eel, yellowish-black and with striated nodes. Its bite is not very venomous. See also SJ 3.3.21, 5.12.14.
- **Tadpole**. Huóshī 活師. Tadpole (科斗 kēdǒu). The *Erya* says 活東 huódōng. Could be any of the Anoures (*Rana limnocharis Boie*), the Eastern Golden Frog (*R. Plancyi* (Lataste)), or the Pound frog (*R. Nigromaculata* (Hallowell)). The *Bencao Gangmu* mentions that it is used to dye the hair and whiskers. The eggs improve eyesight. It is also mentioned for clearing heat and removing toxins; especially heat related sores and swellings, mumps, and burns and scalds
- **Tiger flood-dragon**. Hǔjiāo 虎蛟. The jiāo has a snake-like body and four legs. Here, it is described as having a fish-like body, a snake-like tail, a mandarin duck sound. Its consumption prevents swellings and is acceptable for hemorrhoids. According to the annotations to the texts, there should be two wings under the tail.
- **Turtle, good**. Liángguī 良龜. Good turtle.
- **Turtle, Large**. Xiéguī 蠵龜. Large turtle with a variegated striped carapace. This turtle could be the loggerhead turtle (xiéguī 赤蠵龜) if the

marsh is salty. It looks like the seawater hawksbill turtle dàimào 玳瑁 (Eretmochelys imbricata).

- **Xuánguī** 旋龜. River creature that has a bird head and a soft-shelled turtle tail. Its call is like the noise of shattering wood. The xuánguī of SJ 1.1.5 has the tail of a snake.
- **Xuánguī** 旋龜. Rotating turtle. See also SJ 5.6.8 where the xuánguī has a soft-shelled turtle tail.
- **Xuánguī** 玄龜. It resembles turtles but has the head of a bird and the tail of a snake. Its call is like the sound of wood breaking. As pendant waist ornament, it cures deafness. It may also cure callus.

Reptile hybrids

- **Chángshé**. Chángshé 長蛇. The SJ describes it as a snake having pig-like bristles and a call like the drumming of a watchman clapper. It is a long snake said to be more than 30 meters long. It can seize deers and appears like having an animal with it. See also HJ 10.15. Samurai armies use the "long line" formation (chouda or chōda 長蛇の列) in war strategies. Ref. 3.1.16.
- **Dragon, Flood**. Jiāo 蛟. This organism resembles a snake but has four feet, a small head, a thin neck, and a white fleshy growth. The bigger ones can reach a diameter of 10 spans of outstretched arms and its eggs can be as big as one or two hectoliter earthen jars. It can swallow and eat humans. The species with scales is called jiāolóng or crocodile-dragon (蛟龍). The Shiyi ji mentions that Emperor Zhaodi 昭帝, of the Han dynasty (86 B.C.) when going fishing, caught a white crocodile (báijiāo 白蛟). It looked like a snake without scales or carapace, and it has a soft horn and protruding teeth. It was used in a bouillabaisse that was excellent. Its bones were bluish and its flesh purplish (*Sancai tuhui*).
- **Dragons and tortoises**. Lóngguī 龍龜. There is also a dragon tortoise, Lóngguī. It is one of the nine sons of the dragon Long. It has the head of a dragon and the body of tortoise.
- **Féiyí** 肥[虫遺]. Drought divinity. It is a strange snake with one head, two bodies, six long and narrow legs, and four wings. Its apparition is a sign of great drought everywhere. It is seen in 2.1.3 where it is written 肥[虫遺] féiyí and 3.1.21 where it is written 肥遺 féiyí. Guopu mentions that féiyí is similar to the spirit of the river He mentioned in the Guanzi. This spirit is called 蟣 (pronounced qí or guǐ). It has one head and two bodies; it is like a snake and measures over 1.5 m. Its name derives from its call. It can capture fishes and tortoises. SJ 2.1.7 mentions a bird with the same name 肥遺 féiyí. Ref. 2.1.3, 3.1.21.

- **Snake, huà**. Huàshé 化蛇. Reptile that has a human face, a jackal body, bird wings, and the motion of a snake. Its call resembles powerful shouts. Its apparition is a sign of major floods in the locality.
- **Turtle, three-footed**. Sānzúguī 三足龟. Turtle, Three-footed. Its consumption prevents major diseases. It is also pretty good against swellings. The *Erya* in the Fish section says "three-footed turtle, 賁 bì". See also (1) the turtle with three legs and six eyes, and (2) the three-footed soft-shelled turtle (三足鱉 5.11.18).
- **Turtle, three-footed soft-shelled**. Sānzúbiē 三足鱉. Turtle, Three-footed with a forked tail. Its consumption prevents insanity. According to the *Erya*, the three-footed soft-shelled turtle is 能 néng while the three-footed tortoise is 賁 bì. See also 5.7.7.

Unidentified

- **Bóhuáng** 勃皇. Probably animal or bird. Unknown signification (Guopu).
- **Liúniú** 留牛. Unidentified. It may be the 犁牛 líniú (farm-draft cattle) which was described as bull resembling a tiger (Annotation and Guopu). Guopu also comments that (1) 留 liú and 犁 lí sound alike and (2). *Zhuangzi* says that the dogs harnessed to a plow were called niú (cows) (莊子曰：執犁之狗，謂此牛也).
- **Púyí yú** 蒲夷魚. Unidentified. Annotations suggest it to be the rănyí of 2.4.15.
- **Qìsuān**. Unnamed in the SJ. Creature reaching potency after three years. Its consumption addresses epidemic diseases.
- **Reptile, venomous**. Fùchóng 蝮虫. An animal, reptile or insect with a pit like the Pallas pit viper. It could be the archaic characters for a venomous snake. It is described as reaching up to less than a kilogram, is red with ribbon-like streaks. Ref. 1.1.4, 2.1.4.
- **Zhòuwěi** 蝵蛜. Unidentified. 蝵 zhōu was originally 蚅 háo. Hao Yixing noted that 蚅 háo should be 蝵 zhōu (callus), and cited the Guang ya where "狖 yòu, 蜼 yòu." 狖 yòu is a near homophone of 蝵 zhōu (callus). Guopu, in the notes of the *Erya* says that "蜼 yòu is similar to a macaque." Another comment notes that [魚帝] is 鯢 ní salamander, and that 鯢 broken down makes 兒 ér. The Lost Book of Zhou says that "兒 is like a macaque (獼猴 míhóu)." It was then decided to change 蚅 to 蝵.

Flora

Grass

- **Bamboo**. Zhú 竹. Supposed to a short bamboo growing in clumps. This would explain why it is classified as a grass here. Note that modern taxonomy classifies bamboo as a grass. 3.3.13, and others.
- **Bamboo, arrow**. Zhújiàn 竹箭. Appears to be the Common Umbrella Bamboo, or arrow bamboo (*Fargesia spathacea Franch.*). According to Guopu and Kean, jiàn should be understood as 篠 xiǎo, referring to a small bamboo. 2.1.8, and others.
- **Bamboo, arrow-like**. Jiànmèi 箭[上竹下媚]. Guopu mentions a kind of bamboo (上竹下媚)竹 that grows in the Hànzhōng district of the Shaanxi province. The shouts are edible and long and the roots deep. These bamboo shoots grow on barren land. The character jiàn seems to indicate a bamboo specifically used to make arrows. 2.1.7, 5.4.8, 5.12.8.
- **Bamboo, fú**. Fúzhú 扶竹. This is the qióng bamboo (邛竹). The distance between the nodes is relatively large, the center is solid; it can make great walking sticks, and is therefore also called the "old man's bamboo walking staff." 邛 qióng was originally written 卭 qióng. There are several songs and poems building a theme around it, such as 'The Qiong Bamboo Cane' (*Qiong zhu zhang* 邛竹杖) by Xu Zhongxing (徐中行) in the 16th AD. 5.2.3.
- **Bamboo, madake**. Guìzhú 筀竹. According to Hao Yixing, 筀 guì should be 桂 guì. According to the *Qi min yao shu*, this bamboo was reported to grow in the Shixing county (始兴郡), Guangdong province. The mature height of these bamboos reaches about 40 feet. The culms have a diameter of about 2 inches. Note that this is not the toxic guì bamboo mentioned in SJ 5.12.2. 5.12.2, 5.12.4.
- **Bamboo, madake, poisonous**. *Phyllostachys bambusoides*. Guìzhú 桂竹. Also known as Giant Timber Bamboo. The mature height of these bamboos ranges from 40 to 70 feet. The culms have a diameter between 3 and 7 inches. They grow in the Guìyáng suǒ territory (桂陽所), thus the name guì bamboo (桂竹). See also SJ 5.12.4 for the variation 筀竹 guìzhú. The form mentioned in this section is poisonous. Its appearance has not yet been clarified but it appears to be related to the 簨竹 lìzhú, also known as the yellow-gold 筋竹 jīnzhú. These plants have hard pulp, poisonous shoots poisonous and very sharp tips (其利). These shots were used against tigers that would die from the wounds. The barbarians also use this poison when hunting (Hao Yixing). The

poison of these bamboos, whose bark is red, kills people pricked by it (*Guang Qun fangpu*, Book 82). It has been reported that some bamboo species, especially the giant bamboo, containing significant, potentially very toxic, amounts of cyanogenic glycosides in their shoots. Poisonous. 5.12.2.

- **Bamboo, peach-branch**. Táozhī gōuduān 桃枝鉤端. Lit. "peach tree branches, hook drafts". The annotators of the *Shanhai jing* suggest that the gōuduān is a kind of táozhī. The expression táozhī is actually often used in ancient Chinese books where it refers to a "beautiful bamboo species" of which the entire name is 桃枝竹 táozhī zhú, peach branch bamboo. They are used to make mats. The *Erya* defines the peach-branch bamboos as having 4-cuns long knots. 2.1.14.
- **Bamboo, small**. Gǎn 䇗. The *Kangxi zidian* also gives to this name the meaning of arrow feathers. In 4.7.1 this character refers to "arrow stems." 5.11.43.
- **Bamboo, small**. Méi [上竹下媚]. According to Guopu, it is about dwarf bamboos (篠 xiǎo). According to Hao Yixing it is about "dwarf (篠 xiǎo), or arrows (箭 jiàn), see *Erya*. These small slender bamboos also belong to fine bamboos (箘 jùn), making arrows." See also 箭[上竹下媚] jiànmèi. Arrow-like bamboo. See also SJ 5.12.8. 5.11.44.
- **Bamboo, tubular**. Jùn 箘. According to Guopu, "jùn 箘 belongs to the category xiǎo 篠 (dwarf bamboo)." It is small size fine bamboo, used to manufacture arrow shafts. The *Shuowen* suggests 箘簵 jùn lù. See also *Shujing* (chap. *Yugong*). 5.12.8.
- **Bamboo, zhīgōu**. Zhīgōu 枝勾. This appears to a type of táozhī bamboos, with small leave and dense foliage. 5.10.3.
- **Coarse grass**. Jiān 菅. Probably cattail or villous themeda (*themedia forskali*). Their stems can then be used for the manufacturing of mats or coarse fabrics. See also Chen Shouliang and Sylvia Phillips, *Flora of China* 22: 633–637 (http://flora.huh.harvard.edu/china/). 2006. 1.1.11, and others.
- **Cuscuta**. *Cuscuta chinensis*. Túqiū 菟丘. According to Guopu, it is 菟絲 túsī. In other words, it is about the seed of Chinese dodder (*Cuscuta chinensis*), an annual tangled parasitic herbaceous plant, stem soft and delicate, filiform, yellow orange, blossoming in the summer and fall, thin and small flowers, white, fruits flat and round. 5.11.3.
- **Devil grass**. Guǐcǎo 鬼草. The *Taiping Yulan* uses 鬼目 guǐmù instead of 鬼草 guǐcǎo. Its leaves are like those of the sunflower; it has a red stem, and ears like standing rice grains. As a medicine, it protects from sadness. 5.1.11.
- **Dùhéng**. Dùhéng 杜衡. Wild ginger (*Asarum forbesii*). Perennial herbaceous plant, wild and mountainous. Its flowers are small and purple. According to the SJ, it resembles the winter sunflower plant. It smells like míwú. It has the property to render horses tireless when running. Its consumption cures goiter. Medicinal roots. 2.1.15.

- **Jīgǔ**. Unidentified. Jīgǔ 雞穀. They have roots like a chicken egg. Their taste is sweet and sour. Their consumption is beneficial for people. 5.11.8, 5.11.34.
- **Jīgǔ**. Unidentified. Jīgǔ 雞鼓. Herbaceous.
- **Kòutuō**. Unidentified. Kòutuō 寇脫. This plant is described as originating in the south, being slightly over 3 meters tall, similar to the lotus leaf and with its stem containing a white sap. In 5.9.3, the original text has 空奪 kōngduó but it seems that it is actually 寇脫 kòutuō. These two characters, placed immediately after listing trees and herbs, without transition, are difficult to understand as insect or snake slough ([虫空]脫 or 蛻脫 kōngduó) given by some annotations. 5.9.13.
- **Lilac daphne**. Yán 芫. This is probably the Lilac daphne (*Daphne genkwa*) 芫华, also called fish killer (yúdú 魚毒), or fish medicine grass (yàoyúcǎo 藥魚草). It is a deciduous shrub originating from China. All parts are highly toxic. On the other hand, it could be the yánsui 芫荽, coriander (*Coriandrum sativum*) or the Chinese parsley. It is an aromatic annual herb with medicinal flowers. 5.5.2.
- **Nǔchuáng**. Unidentified. Nǔchuáng 女床. It could be the grass 女肠草 nǔchángcǎo. 2.2.8.
- **Qǐ**. Qǐ 杞. 1.2.14.
- **Rush grass**. Lóngxiū 龍脩. This appears to be the Chinese alpine rush (*Eulaliopsis binata*). Rosny identifies it as Common rush (*Juncus effusus*). According to Guopu, it is similar to 莞 wǎn, softstem bulrush (Scirpus tabernaemontani), but thinner, and originates in mountain stone caves, where its stem hangs down. It can be used to weave mats. According to the *Gujin zhu*, "The generations since the Yellow Emperor refined the cinnabar and chiseled the Yànshān 硯山 (in Yunnan), to reach immortality and rid the dragon to sky. The ministers would assist with the lóngxū rush 龍鬚, xū would drip and give birth to the grass, thus the name lóngxū." There is the homophone connection here between lóngxū 龍須 and lóngxū 龍鬚 which occurs in the mythological tales. 5.9.16.
- **Silvergrass, Chinese**. *Miscanthus sinensis*. Mángcǎo 芒草. An herbaceous perennial plant. It is also written 莽草 mǎngcǎo, *Illicium anisatum*, a kind of poisonous shrub (see SJ 5.11.2). With regard to pronunciation of 芒, Guopu suggest wàng and the *Hanyu daci dian* máng. 5.2.7.
- **Water mallow**. Máo 茆. According to Guopu, it should be treated as [上艹下留], which is the 凫葵 fúkuí according to the *Shuowen*. This plant, also called shuǐkuí 水葵 appears to be the banana-plant 荇菜 xìngcài (*Nymphoides peltatum*) or the water shield 莼菜 chúncài (*Brasenia schreberi*). 2.4.1.

- **Zhú**. Unidentified. Zhú [艸下朮]. Found on in the central mountains. 5.9.1.

Moss

- **Fairy Fern**. *Stenoloma chusanum*. Wūjiǔ 烏韭. The literal translation is "dark garlic." It is a parasitic moss, also called Andraea and Common Wedgelet Fern. 2.1.4.

Plants

- **Angelica**. Yào 葯. Leaves of *Dahurian angelica* or 白芷 báizhǐ, root of *Dahurian angelica*. Umbellifer. 2.4.9.
- **Angelica, white**. Xiāo 蘺. Aromatic grass cited in the *Bencao*, *Shuowen* and the *Chuci*. The *Bencao* mentions that it is the white angelica báizhǐ 白芷, cited above. Umbellifer. 2.4.8.
- **Aquatic plant**. Zǎo 藻. It is mentioned in the *Shijing*. According to the *Maoshi mingwu tushuo* (2-711), two species are known both edible in case of famine. They grow in the water and float with the stream. 3.3.47.
- **Aromatic plant**. Zhǐ 苴. A generic term including a large amount of aromatic plants, including various orchids. Modern pronunciation: hāo or chén. 3.3.47.
- **Artemisia**. Xiāo 蕭. Guopu refers to the *Erya* where 蕭 xiāo corresponds to 蒿 hāo, wormwood; artemisia. According to Hao Yixing, the *Erya* says that 蕭 xiāo corresponds to 荻 dí, a kind of reed. 5.6.11.
- **Asparagus**. Zhānjí 蒼棘. According to Guopu and other commentators, this plant is unidentified. Rosny provides the following information: The *Bencao*, cited in the comment of Hao Yixing, states that the plant zhānjí is also named 天冬 tiāndōng (SJ 5.1.13). On the other hand, this name is also written 天門冬 tiānméndōng. This last name is the character for the asparagus. The ancient aspect of this character is certain since the *Erya* states that this plant was called 棘 jí or "thorns" since its leaves, fine like hair, have tiny thorns (See *Guang Qun fangpu*, Book xcviii, p. 13). The *Erya* further mentions several passages of the SHJ speaking of this plant. In SJ 5.5.5 the name 虋冬 méndōng is also given for 門冬 méndōng asparagus, as synonym of 鑪冬 méndōng. 5.1.13.
- **Bá**. Bá 茇. Grass root, dwelling. It is a type of shrub native to east Asia. Also known as daphne genkwa, it can reach a height of four feet, with hermaphrodite flowers that are usually white or yellow. It grows predominantly in the Anhui and Jiangsu provinces. The flower buds are used in herbal remedies. They are gathered in the spring and dried in

the sun, then baked or fried with vinegar. According to the principles of energetic medicine, genkwa has pungent, bitter, warm and slightly toxic properties, and is affiliated with the Lung, Kidney and Large Intestine systems. Its main functions are to transform water, to resolve phlegm, and to stop coughs. Among the conditions genkwa treats are edema (typically with euphorbia kansui root and spurge root), coughs and bronchitis. Genkwa can also be applied to the skin as part of a poultice to treat ringworms and other parasites. It contains the abortifacient diterpene esters yuanhuacine and yuanhuadine. Finally, it is known as a fish-poison plant but modern literature does not explain this function (contrary to 萆薢 bìxiè, the fish-poison yam rhizome). Guopu mentions that some people identify bá as 艾 ài mugwort. Hao Yixing cites (1) the *Erya* where 杬 yuán is the lilac daphne used for poisoning fish, and (2) the *Shuowen* where 杬 identifies with 艸 cǎo (grass) and makes 芫 yuán (Chinese parsley), and therefore doubts the identification of bá with mugwort. Medicinal plant. 5.4.5.

- **Balloon flower**. *Platycodon grandiflorum*. Jiégěng 桔梗. The balloon flower, also known as bellflower or jiegeng, is a heavy bloomer that gets its name from the way each flower bud swells before its starry petals unfold. Medicinal plant whose root saponins are studied in the treatment of immunostimulation, antitumoral effects and antihyperglycemic effects. 2.1.14.

- **Basil, wild**. Sú 蘇. This is the 紫苏 zǐsū, rattlesnake weed or wild basil, or purple perilla (*Perilla frutescens*). 5.4.7.

- **Bush clover**. Dí 荻. Reed, Amur silvergrass (*Miscanthus sacchariflorus*), Pearly Everlasting (*Anaphalis yedoensis*). According to Hao Yixing, this is a mistake and it should be 萩 qiū (scandent hop, tree). 萩 qiū is a kind of wormwood. Its leaves are white; it looks like artemisia but has many branches. Its stems are especially tall and it is about 3.3 meters. In modern dictionaries, 萩 qiū appears to be the bush clover (*lespedeza bicolor*), an upright semi-woody forb (0.9-3 m) with many slender stems and arching branches. Its flowers are rose purple. The Chinese variety, sericea lespedeza 薺萩, has yellowish-white flowers with purple to pink markings and has high tolerance for poor sites. Leaves alternate along the stem and are divided into three smaller leaflets covered with densely flattened hairs. The *Erya* says that "蕭 xiāo (common artemisia); 萩 qiū." Guopu, in his notes on the *Erya* says that it is 蒿 hāo (wormwood). Guopu, in the present editions states that 荻 dí is 蒿 hāo. Guopu on the notes on 荻 also states that 荻 should also be considered as 萩 qiū. 5.7.15.

- **Chrysanthemum**. *Chrysanthemum indicum*. Jú 菊. 菊 jú is generally known as 菊花 júhuā, a medicinal plant. Numerous species (over 100) exist but two major categories were considered in the past: (1) the cultivated type, mum, or 菊花 júhuā, and (2) the wild type or 野菊 yějú (*Chrysanthemum indicum*), also called 苦薏 kǔyì. Medicinal plant. 5.9.1.

- **Gāngcǎo**. Unidentified. Gāngcǎo [上艸下岡]草. It has leaves shaped like those of the sunflower, a red stem, white flowers and fruits like those of the mountain grape plant. Used for stupidity. 5.7.14.

- Gǎo. Gǎo 藁. It may be the 抚芎 fǔxiōng (*Ligusticum sinense*), whose roots system is a thick tuber. 5.3.2.

- **Ginger, wild**. Shǎoxīn 少辛. It appears to be the xìxīn 細辛, the Manchurian wild ginger (*Asarum virginicum*). Purgative and strong sneezing properties. 5.7.13, 5.9.6.

- **Grape, mountain**. Yīngyǔ 蘡薁. Wangfu says that yīngyǔ has a haphazard growth, thin leaves, fruits like small grapes, or it may have been a mistake for 櫻桃 cherry, or maybe 葡萄 grape. According to Hao Yixing, it is the mountain grape. It appears to be a kind of vine, commonly known and wild grape, or a kind of bryony (葡萄 pútao). It flowers in the summer and its fruits are black, and can be used to produce wine, it may be used as medicinal herb. 5.7.10, 5.7.14.

- **Gromwell**. *Lithospermum*. Cícǎo 茈草. According to Wu Ren shen, this is 紫草 zǐcǎo (Lit. purple grass), or gromwell. This name covers several plants, such as the bloodroot, whose roots yield a reddish dye. 2.4.2.

- **Gǔróng**. Gǔróng 菁蓉. Plant whose leaves are like that of the huìlán orchid. Its roots are like that of balloon flower. It has black flowers and no fruits. 2.1.14.

- **Hedge thorn**. Zhǐ mù 枳木. Trifoliate orange; hedge thorn. A representation of it can be found in the *Sancai tuhui*, vol. 84. 2.1.9.

- **Hěn**. Unidentified. Hěn [艸狼]. It looks like the yarrow. It has a fur, blue-green flowers and white fruits. The *Yupian* describes it as "delicate, thin fur, grass name, similar to the yarrow plant, blue-green white flowers" (Hao Yixing). Used for premature death and bowel diseases. 5.7.19.

- **Huácǎo**. Unknown. Huácǎo 華草. Lit. Flowering plant. 3.1.1.

- **Huángguàn**. Unidentified. Huángguàn 黃藋. 2.1.8.

- **Huì orchid**. Huì 蕙. Aromatic plant like the orchid (蘭 lán). Sometimes also called swamp orchid. 2.1.15, 2.2.16, 5.5.14.

- **Jiāo**. Unidentified. Jiāo 艽. Medicinal plant. This may be the large-leaved gentian 秦艽 qínjiāo. Medicinal plant. 5.5.7.

- **Kǔxīn**. Unknown. Kǔxīn 苦辛. This term is commonly used to describe the medicinal quality of taste that is bitter and acrid. The shape of the kǔxīn resembles that of the Chinese catalpa and it has fruits like gourds that taste sweet and sour. Their consumptions protects against fever. 5.6.14.

- **Large tuber plant**. Méndōng 虋冬. These are large tuber medicinal plants: the ophiopogon (麥門冬 màiméndōng) and the wild Chinese asparagus (天門冬 tiānméndōng). According to some opinions, 虋冬

méndōng is now called qiángwēi 薔薇, rambler rose (*Rosa Multiflora*). The flower, fruit, and roots have medicinal properties and the flowers are used in perfumes. Originally written 舮冬 lúdōng. 亹 mén is commonly written as 門 mén. 5.11.35.

- **Lichen, aromatic**. Bìlì 萆荔. Guopu suggest it is a sweet grass. The homophone bìlì (薜荔), a climbing fig, is also mentioned in the *Chuci lisao*. Here, it may refer to a kind of aromatic lichen. 2.1.4.
- **Ligusticum**. Xiōngqióng 芎藭. *Sichuan Ligusticum wallichii*. One of the "fifty" fundamental Chinese medicinal herbs. More commonly known as 川芎 chuān xiōng. Medicinal plant. 3.3.27.
- **Lovage, Chinese**. Gǎobá 槁茇. According to the Shiming, it is one of the names for 槁本 gǎoběn, Chinese lovage or straw weed (*Ligusticum sinense*). 2.1.16.
- **Madder**. *Rubia tinctorum*. Sōu 蒐. 5.3.1, 5.4.3.
- **Madder, qiàn**. *Rubia cordifolia*. Qiàn 蒨. Also written as 茜 qiàn or 茜草 qiàncǎo. It is a climbing species containing alizarin, red pigment, whose concentration is highest in the roots. 5.3.1.
- **Míwú**. Míwú 蘼蕪. Chuanxiong, stem and leaf (*Ligusticum wallichii*), one of the 50 fundamental herbs in Chinese phytotherapy. See also *Bencao Gangmu*, http://baike.baidu.com/view/287523.htm, and http://www.zysj.com.cn/zhongyaocai/yaocai_m/miwu.html. 2.1.9, 2.1.15.
- **Morning glory**. Yáocǎo 瑶草. This plant (see SJ 5.7.3) appears to be the dodder (菟 tú, *Cuscuta sinensis*), of the morning glory family (*Convolvulacea*). It is also identified, with the 荒夫草 huāngfū cǎo "the hungry man's grass" (Guopu), and with the 兔絲 tùsī (see *Kangxi zidian*). It is also written 蘨草 or [上艸下瑤]草. SJ 5.7.10 describes it as thistle-like, with white flowers and fruits black and lustrous like those of the mountain grape plant, and addressing inability to see. 5.7.3.
- **Niúshāng**. Niúshāng 牛傷. LT: Bull's defense. Plant whose leaves are like of the elm, its stem is squared, and it has blue green thorns. Its roots have blue green patterns. Used for fainting and to resist against soldiers. 5.7.7.
- **Onion, Chinese**. Chóu 籌. According to the annotation, it is the Chinese onion (shallot or scallion) 薤 xié (*Allium chinense*). 3.1.8, 5.9.3.
- **Onion, Chinese**. *Allium chinense*. Xié 薤. 3.1.8, 5.9.3.
- **Parasite plant**. Yùmù 寓木. A tree-dweller parasitic plant. According to Guopu, this is a parasitic plant, described as 宛童 wǎntóng in the *Erya*. According to the *Bencao Gangmu*, by specifically putting under this name a mulberry parasite plant that grows in the interstices of the branches and give seeds the size of small beans. It appears that there are two kinds, those with round leaves include the convovulvus; parasitic plants such as mistletoe; *Ribes ambiguum grossulariaceae* (蔦 niǎo), those that have leaves like the ephedra leave is the dodder (女萝 nǚluó).

Although the yùmù grows on trees, they belong to herbaceous plants. This plant has medicinal properties. Note that 寓 yù is a bird (see SJ 3.1.6), and 寓木 could be the yù bird tree. 5.8.14, and others.

- **Patrinia**. Jiān 菅. It appears to be 蕑 jiān, the White Patrinia (*Patrinia villosa*). According to Guopu, this is a coarse grass (*Villous themeda*). Hao Yixing disagrees: "According to the *Shuowen*, jiān is a kind of fragrant grass that originates in mountain forests. According to ideophonetics, it appears to be 蘭 lán, an orchid. 菅 jiān and 蕑 jiān are the same and 蕑 jiān is 蘭 lán, an orchid." While Hao Yixing suggests that the White Patrinia and an orchid are identical, I prefer to keep them separate. 5.1.10.

- **Peony**. Paeonia. Sháoyào 芍藥. Herbaceous perennial plant 0.5-1.5 meters tall. The leaves are compound and deeply lobed and the flowers, often fragrant, range from red to white or yellow blossoming in late spring and early summer. Their roots have medicinal use. 3.3.27.

- **Pepper, red**. Qínjiāo 秦椒. Also called Shaanxi chili pepper. Guopu notes that it is similar to pepper but has thinner leaves. 3.3.10.

- **Píncǎo**. Unidentified. Píncǎo [上艸下賓]草. Other texts have 蘋 pín instead of [上艸下賓]草. They resemble winter sunflowers and taste like onions. Used for fatigue from labors. 2.3.8.

- **Pomelo**. Yòu 櫾. See *Shuowen* and *Erya*. This is the same as 柚 yòu (pomelo). Pomelo 柚子 and tangerine 橘子 are similar. They are thick-skinned and have sour taste. 5.8.2, and others.

- **Potato, mountain**. Chúyú 藷藇. Similar to the Chinese yam 山藥 shānyào. 3.3.10, and others.

- **Proso millet**. Xiāng 香. According to Hao Yixing, this is a strong aromatic herbaceous, like in SH 5.12.2 belonging to the types of White Patrinia, Gracilaria confervoides, peony, and Ligusticum. According to the *Shuowen*, 香 xiāng refers to the proso millet (黍稷 shǔjì, *Panicum miliaceum*) fragrance." 5.11.48.

- **Qìsuān**. Unidentified. Qìsuān 器酸. Unknown plant that reaches medicinal maturity after three years. Epidemic diseases. 3.3.4.

- **Quince**. *Chaenomeles lagenaria*. Mùguā 木瓜. Chinese flowering quince. Now part of Chinese pharmacopeia. 2.4.16.

- **Rice, glutinous**. Tú 稌.

- **Rice, raw unhusked**. Mǐ 米.

- **Rice, sacrificial**. Oriza spiritibus *oblata*, Basile. Xǔ 糈. The *Chuci lisao* also mentions the use of sacrificial porridge.

- **Róng cǎo**. Unidentified. Róng cǎo 榮草. Homophones suggest two plants: (1) 茸草 róngcǎo. *Lindenbergia philippensis*. Perennials, to 1 m tall, stout, erect, straight, much branched, glandular hairy. Dry mountain sides, rocky crevices; 1200-2600 m. Guangdong, Guangxi, Guizhou, Hubei, Hunan, Yunnan; and (2) 蓉草 róngcǎo. Phalaris oryzoides Linnaeus. Perennial, loosely tufted, with slender rhizomes. Wet river banks, marshy places; 400–1100 m. Fujian, Hainan, Heilongjiang, Hunan, Xinjiang. 5.1.15.

- **Runner bean**. Lěi 蔂. According to Guopu, it belongs to the tiger bean (hǔdòu 虎豆) - wild cat bean (lídòu 貍豆) plants, and is called 縢 téng (bind, fasten, cord). The tiger bean, or runner bean (*Phaseolus coccineus*), is a twining vine with pods that becomes black when ripe. It has pricks that resemble tiger paws and the beans in the pods are spotted resembling the tiger body stripes, thus the name. The 虎櫐 now refers to the Chinese wisteria zǐténg 紫藤. 櫐 lěi is a homophone of 蔂 lěi, a trailing plant. 5.11.27.
- **Scallion**. Cōng 蔥. Mountain onion or scallion. See *Erya*. 3.1.10, 3.1.22.
- **Sea moss ogonori**. Míwú 蘪蕪. This term is to be understood as 蘪蕪 míwú, the fragrant sea moss or ogonori (*Gracilaria confervoides*). Its leave resembles that of Chinese Angelica (當歸 dāngguī). Its fragrance is like that of the root of Dahurian angelica (白芷 báizhǐ). 4.4.3.
- **Sedge**. Cyperacea. Fān 蕃. This is the fáncǎo 蘋草, a kind of suōcǎo 莎草 associated with wetlands and eaten by wild geese. Also known as green fān 青蕃. It is known as sedge (*Cyperacea*) and may be the "true" sedge (*Carex*) or grassweed (*Scirpus triangulates*). 2.4.1.
- **Sunflower**. Kuí 葵. Sunflower plant and several species of hibiscus and althea. The mallow family (*malvacea*) is a large family of flowering plants. The single character was used in ancient times to refer mainly to the winter sunflower (冬葵). One member of the malvacea, the marshmallow 藥蜀葵 has medicinal properties but its leaves are pink. 2.1.5, and others.
- **Sùtiáo**. Sùtiáo 夙條. Lit. Precocious branches. It looks like the yarrow plant, has red leaves and a vigorous growth. It is suitable to make arrow stems. 5.7.1.
- **Seaweed, Jūnpú**. Jūnpú 菌蒲. Jūn refers to fungus, bacterium and pú to cattail. This term includes plants like laver (紫菜), agar (石花菜) and kelp (海帶). 4.3.6.
- **Tangerine**. Jú 橘. According to Guopu, 櫡 is similar to a tangerine but bigger, with a thick skin and a sour taste. The original character was 柚 yòu (pomelo). It is also written 桔 jú. The *Bencao Gangmu* mentions that during the fourth month, this tree gives small flowers with a strong smell, then the fruits mature in fall. When rats are buried at the foot of this tree, the fruits become very abundant. This popular belief makes the *Mahaparinirvana Sutra* states that "when the orange trees see rats, their fruits are numerous." 5.8.2, and others.
- **Thistle, mountain**. Atractylodis. Zhú [艹/术]. This is the *Rhizoma Atractylodis*, also known as Shan Ji (Mountain Thistle). Two kinds exist (1) atractylodes lancea (cangzhu, or its former name chizhu, "the red atractylodes") and (2) atractylodes macrocephala (baizhu, the "white

atractylodes"). Both are perennial herbaceous having medicinal roots. While baizhu and cangzhu have some common properties and uses (e.g., Spleen invigorating and diuretic; used in indigestion, diarrhea, and fluid retention), baizhu is a major qi tonic that is now used in counteracting the toxic side effects of chemotherapy and radiotherapy in cancer treatment, while cangzhu is considered a wetness-drying drug, used in treating arthritis and rheumatism as well as the common cold. Both are perennial herbaceous having medicinal roots. While baizhu and cangzhu have some common properties and uses (e.g., Spleen invigorating and diuretic; used in indigestion, diarrhea, and fluid retention), baizhu is a major qi tonic that is now used in counteracting the toxic side effects of chemotherapy and radiotherapy in cancer treatment, while cangzhu is considered a wetness-drying drug, used in treating arthritis and rheumatism as well as the common cold. 5.5.2.

- **Tíngníng**. Tíngníng 葶薴. Also called 苧煢 tīngyíng, or 蒟蒻 jǔruò, its lumpy roots are called 魔芋 móyù. It can produce starch. It resembles the wild basil and has red flowers. It can poison fishes. Also pronounced dīngníng (two sounds according to Guopu). 5.4.7.
- **Tufts of plants**. Tiáo 條. The usual meaning is 'stalk of shrub', or 'trunk of tree'. As an herbaceous plant, this term refers to plants with long and thin branches (i.e., chaste-tree and willow) but remains unidentified as a tree or a herb. Used with other characters, we find the *Stachyrurus himalaicus* tree (通條樹) growing in Xizang, Yunnan and known for its medicinal stems xiao tongcao. SJ 2.1.5, and others.
- **Tuò**. Tuò 籜. Sheaths of bamboo shoots. The SJ describes this plant as plants whose stem resembles that of the sunflower, and whose leaves resemble that of the apricot tree. Their flowers are yellow and their fruits pod-like. They prevent sight loss. 5.1.1.
- **Wútiáo**. Wútiáo 無條. It has round leaves and no stem. Its flowers are red and it has no fruits. See also SJ 2.1.16 for a plant having the same name. Used for goiter. 5.7.4.
- **Wútiáo**. Wútiáo 無條. Plant whose shape is that of the Chinese lovage. Its leaves are like that of the winter sunflower; they are red on the back. See also 5.7.4 for a plant having the same name. It is used to poison rats. 2.1.16.
- **Xūn**. Xūn 薫. Sweet grass that covers both huìcǎo 蕙蘭 and the aromatic grass xūncǎo 薫草. The common name is pèilán 佩蘭 (*Eupatorium fortunei*, also known as fijibakama in Japan). It also refers to the orchid huìlán 蕙蘭 (*Cymbidium faberi*). Since it originates from the Yu lake in the south of línglíng (contemporary Yong prefecture), its fragrance has also been called línglíng fragrance. The red flowers and herbage smell like lavender when crushed. This plant is used medicinally both in China and Japan: it has the property to remove miasma and eliminate worms and insects by fumigation. It is to note that the term also refers to (1) the Coumarouna odorata, a tall tropical South

American tree having pulpy egg-shaped pods of fragrant black almond-shaped seeds (tonka beans) used for flavoring, and (2) the tonka bean itself. 2.1.9.

- **Xúncǎo**. Xúncǎo 荀草. Plant that that resembles the White Patrinia plant. Its stem is squared, its flowers yellow, its fruits red and its root like the gǎo plant. It has the property to bring beauty back. According to Guopu, some people say 苞草 bāocǎo. 5.3.2.
- **Yānsuān**. Unidentified. Yānsuān 焉酸. Its stem is squared, its flowers yellow, its leaves round and triple. According to Hao Yixing and to the *Taiping Yulan*, it was originally written 烏酸 wūsuān. Cures poisoning. 5.7.2.
- **Yarrow**. Shī 蓍. Yarrow (*Achillea millefolium*), also called 蓍草 shīcǎo. This is probably the alpine arrow (锯齿草 jūchǐcǎo also called 蚰蜒草 yóuyáncǎo). According to the *Shuowen*, 蓍 shī belongs to the category of 蒿 hāo, wormwood (artemisia). It is used by seers in the practice of their craft, and has a specific function in the generation of hexagrams in Yijing practice. 5.7.1.
- **Yùpèi**. Unidentified. Yùpèi 育沛. Unknown plant (Guopu). 1.1.2.
- **Zhíchǔ**. Zhíchǔ 植楮. A kind of mulberry. Its leaves resemble that of the sunflower. Its flowers are red and its pod fruits resemble those of the palm tree. 5.1.7.
- **Zhú**. Unidentified. Zhú [上艸下朮]. According to Guopu, this plant is the thistle 薊 jì, which includes any of numerous plants of the family Compositae and especially of the genera *Carduus*, *Cirsium* and *Onopordum* having prickly-edged leaves. 5.9.1.
- **Zhùyú**. Unidentified. Zhùyú 祝餘. It looks like Chinese chives and has blue-green flowers. According to others 桂荼 guìchá (Guopu). Its consumption stops hunger. 1.1.2.

Trees

- **Alder**. Jī 机. This is suggested to be the 槚 qī, the alder tree. 3.1.2, and others.
- **Alder**. Jīmù 機木. This tree resembles the elm tree. Burned, it is used to fertilize fields (Guopu). Yangshen says that it is now the alder. 3.1.1, 5.8.12, 5.11.11.
- **Apricot tree, red**. Unidentified. Niǔmù 杻木. It is about a very dense tree that grows in swamps and blossoms in April. Its leaves are like that of the cherry tree. 杻, chǒu ligustrum sinense. 5.1.1, and others.
- **Apricot-like tree, red**. Shěnniǔ [弓欠]杻. Tree resembling the apricot tree but having a more sinuous trunk. Also written 歀杻. 5.10.9.
- **Arrow tree**. Hù 楛. This is a thorny tree is similar in appearance to the chaste tree or vitex (thorn bush) and crimson stalks like the yarrow plant.

Its wood is good to make arrow shafts. It is mentioned, along with the hazel tree in the *Shijing*: 榛楛濟濟 zhēn hù jǐjǐ, "the hazel trees and the arrow trees grow abundantly" (Daya, ode Han-lu). 2.4.6, 3.1.14.

- **Bǎi tree**. Bǎi 柏. The Song edition and Hao Yixing uses 桓 huán instead of 柏 bǎi. The huán tree has leaves looking like those of the willow tree, its bark is gold and silver, it used to be called 无患子 wúhuànzǐ, bodhi seeds. It can be used to wash clothes and remove dirt. 5.11.11.

- **Báigāo**. Báigāo 白咎. White Blame. It may be 睪蘇 gāosū (Testicle Revive), one of the names of báigāo (Guopu). 1.3.11.

- **Birchleaf tree**. Táng 棠. This character points to the red birchleaf tree (彤棠梨树) or birchleaf pear 杜梨 (*Pyrus betulifolia*), and to the crab apple tree. Its fruits are similar to the pear but smaller. They are edible and taste sweet and slightly sour. 2.2.15.

- **Black thorn**. Méi 梅. According to Guopu, 梅 méi (plum) is similar to the apricot (杏) and has a sour taste. 5.8.13.

- **Camphor tree**. Yùzhāng 豫章. This is a big tree that resembles the catalpa. Its leaves are green winters and summers, it has a 7-years maturation cycle. Another interpretation has that it is the camphor tree, a tall tree having camphor fragrance. 2.2.13.

- **Carambola**. Yángtáo 羊桃. Guopu mentions that it is sometimes called 鬼桃 guǐtáo ghost peach. Also kown as star fruit. Literally, the "goat peach tree." They resemble the common peach tree but have a squared trunk. They can be used to heal skin swellings and ulcers. 5.11.34.

- **Catalpa, Fargesii**. Catalpa Fargesii. Qiū 檽. 檽 refers to the quality "tall and straight" of trees. According to Guopu, this is the 楸 qiū, or catalpa. It seems to be the *catalpa fargesii*, sometimes called Chinese bean tree, a medium-sized, deciduous tree with an open rounded crown that is native to central China. This catalpa is most distinguished by its attractive foliage and spectacular flowers. 5.6.14.

- **Catalpa, yellow**. *Catalpa Kaempferi*. Zǐ 梓. Zǐ 梓 is the classical name that appears to refer to two kinds of catalpas. Today, the term qiū 楸 is used. Zǐ seems to refer to the *Catalpa Kaempferi* (yellow catalpa, or catalpa ovata) while qiū refers to the *Catalpa bungei*. The yellow catalpa is a massive deciduous tree, blossoming in summer time. It has large heart-shaped to three-lobed leaves similar to those of the Tung tree. Its long, cigar or bean-shaped fruit ("Indian beans") are medicinal and treat heat toxicity (热毒 rèdú) and scabies (疥疮 jièchuāng). The *Catalpa bungei* is anthelmintic and stomachic. Its leaf, stem bark and the seeds are all used as dressings for sores, boils. 1.2.14, and others.

- **Cedar palm-like tree**. Zōngnán 棕枏. Zōng refers to hemp palm trees (*Chamaerops*) and nán to an even-grained, yellowish, fine wood used for furniture; cedar. There is no taxonomy for the compound term. 5.6.13.

- **Chaste tree, hemp-leaved**. Mánjū 蔓居之木. Hemp-leaved chaste tree, according Hao Yixing who suggests the "mǔjīng 牡荊 Hemp-leaved chaste tree (*Vitex cannabifolia*) for mánjīng." On the other hand, according to the *Bencao*, mán 曼 is màn 蔓, climbing vines and 曼荊 could then be considered as 蔓荊 mànjīng. This is a kind of shrub growing on water edges and reaching a height slightly above 3 meters. It blossoms in June and gives red and white flowers. It gives fruits in September that have black specks. It looses its leaves in winter. 5.3.4.

- **Cherry tree, wild**. Niǔjiāng 杻橿. This tree resembles the dì 棣, a kind of wild cherry abundant in the Shaanxi province. However, it has finer leaves. It is also called tǔjiāng 土橿 or "earthy jiāng". According to the *Shuowen* it is the tree fāng 枋, used as timber for boats. 2.1.7, and others.

- **Chestnut**. *Castanea*. Lì 栗. The character 栗 alone generally refers to the Japanese Chestnut or *Castanea crenata*. The character bǎnlì 板栗 refers to the Chinese chestnut. 5.8.6.

- **Chinaberry**. Melia azedarach. Jiǎn 揀. This is the 楝 liàn, chinaberry (Melia azedarach). It belongs to the mahogany family, Meliaceae, and is native to southern China. 5.1.2.

- **Chūn**. Chūn 櫄. A large tree resembling the tree of heaven. Some texts have 儿 ér. 5.5.7.

- **Chūn**. Chūn 櫄. According to Hao Yixing, 儿 ér should be understood as 杶 chūn. In other words, it should be 杶树 chūn. This tree resembles the tree of Heaven. Its trunk is used to manufacture carriage shafts. Written 儿 according to the edition. 5.5.7, 5.11.19.

- **Cypress, China**. Jì 稷. Similar to the pine tree, with thorns and a delicate grain (Guopu). A variant text has [木稷-禾] and explains it as the China cypress (水松 shuǐsōng). 2.2.13.

- **Dān tree**. Unidentified. Dānmù 丹木. A legendary tree. Synonym for the mangrove hóngshù 红树. However, the mangrove would provably not grow in the Western mountains. 2.3.4, 2.4.19.

- Diāotáng. Unidentified. Diāo táng 彫棠. The leaves of this tree are like those of the elm but squared. Its fruits are like red beans. Used for ear loss. 5.1.14.

- **Dìwū**. Unidentified. Dìwū 帝屋. Its leaves are shaped like those of the pepper tree, with hooked thorns and red fruits. Used for ominous events. 5.7.11.

- **Dìxiū**. Unidentified. Dìxiū 帝休. Its leaves are like that of the poplar tree. Its branches present [clusters] of five ramifications. It has yellow flowers and black fruits. Used for anger. 5.7.9.

- **Fǔmù**. 榑木. This is the contemporary Fúsāng. See *Lushi Chunqiu*. "On the eastern side Yu arrived to the fǔmù country." 4.03.09.

- **Glossy privet**. *Ligustrum lucidum*. Zhēnmù 楨木. It should be understood as 女楨 nǚzhēn, glossy privet, a hardwood evergreen with medicinal properties. 4.4.8.

- **Guīmù**. Guīmù 櫰木. SJ: "Tree resembling the birchleaf tree with round leaves, and fruits red and big as the quince fruit." Guopu suggests the pronunciation huáimù. Tonic. 2.4.16.
- **Hardwood tree**. Gāngmù 剛木. The character suggests hardwood trees like sandalwood (檀木) or silkworm thorn tree (柘树). 3.1.20.
- **Hawthorn**. Zhā 柤. It looks like a pear tree; its trunk and branches are red; it has clusters (corymbs) of yellow flowers and black fruits. See Notes of HJ 2.16 and HJ 3.19. 5.8.6, and others.
- **Hawthorn tree**. Jū 苴. Tree, unidentified (Guopu). It may be the homophonic jū 柤 hawthorn (Hao Yixing). Some commentaries suggest the pronunciation zhā. 5.11.13.
- **Hazel**. *Corylus*. Zhēn 榛. Its wood is good to make utensils. 2.4.6, 3.1.14.
- **Huángjí**. Huángjí 黃棘. LT: Yellow thorns. 5.7.4.
- **Japanese star anise**. *Illicium Anisatum*. Wàngcǎo 莽草. Highly toxic tree similar to the Chinese star anise. Its toxic seeds were used until recently to kill fish. Branches were offered at graves to ward off wild dogs and other animals. According to Guopu, this is the plant 芒草 mángcǎo, *Miscanthus sinensis* (see SJ 5.2.8). It is also called 鼠莽 shǔmǎng. Modern pronunciation: mǎngcǎo. Topical use in dermatology. 5.11.2.
- **Jiāróng**. Unidentified. Jiāróng 嘉榮. As soon as it appears, it gives an ear, then leaves and flowers come in the middle of the ear. It is more than ten feet high, it has red leaves and red flowers, and although it has flowers it gives no fruits. Used for fear of thunder. 5.7.8.
- **Jìbǎi**. Unidentified. Jìbǎi 蓟柏. It has the shape of the chaste tree. It gives white flowers and red fruits. Used to protect from cold. The *Yupian* states that 鉈 tā is the common thistle 蓟 jì (Hao Yixing). The *Chuxue ji* (Scroll 28) says that 柏 bǎi (cypress) relates to 計柏. Now 計 jì and 鉈 tā sound similar. 5.7.18.
- **Jujube tree**. *Ziziphus zizyphus*. Zǎo 棗. The *Bencao Gangmu* states that the zǎo tree has a red heart and thorns. In the fourth month, small and shiny leaves appear. In the fifth month, small flowers appear; they are white and bordered with green. A species of this tree, xiān zǎo (仙棗), is considered divine. It is also named zhòngsī zǎo (仲思棗). It is said that in the Northern Qí dynasty, an immortal called Zhòngsī obtained this tree, and propagated it, thus its name (see *Bencao Gangmu* – Fruits Section). 2.1.5, 2.3.3, 5.3.3.
- **Kàngmù**. Unidentified. Kàngmù 亢木. Its leaves are shaped like those of the tree of heaven and its fruits are red. Used against evil energies. 5.7.14.
- **Knotty tree**. Jí 棘. The meanings include (1) knotty, thorns; thorny; (2) jujube tree. 3.1.20, 4.3.1, 5.5.14, 5.7.4.

- **Lady Palm**. Zōng 棕. Refers to several species of palm trees, like the Lady Palm (*Rhapis excelsa*). 2.1.4, and others.
- **Laurel**. Guì (Guìmù) 桂 (桂木). Evergreen tree (*Cinnamomum*) of the laurel family. The leaves of the laurel tree resemble those of the loquat (Japanese plum, or *Eriobotrya japonica*); it is about two feet tall and several inches wide. It has a bitter taste and its leaves are white. It is an evergreen. The laurel trees of Mt Zhāoyáo are cited in the *Lushi Chunqiu*. The laurel tree is also found in Japan and Annam. It is a medicinal plant. The *Bencao Gangmu* mentions several species of laurel trees. One of them, the evergreen jūnguì 菌桂, grows on high mountains. Its white flowers open during the third or fourth month, and its fruits appear during the ninth month. Another species, the xiǎoguì (small laurel 小桂), has yellow or white flowers. Its bark is thin and cylindrical like a flute giving it the name of tubular laurel or 筒桂 tǒngguì. The bark of old wood and that of the big branches is firm and cannot be bent. On the other hand the bark of the small branches is flexible and can be wrapped two or three times on itself. The abyss laurel (yuānguì 淵桂) is a variation of the previous one. The one with white flowers is called silver laurel (yínguì 银桂) while the one with yellow flower is called cassiabark tree (jīnguì 金桂). The first ones blossom in the Fall and the second ones in the Spring. There is also a variety with red flowers, the orange osmanthus (dānguì 丹桂). Some blossom throughout the four seasons. They can be used in wine infusions to which they give a specific fragrance. 1.1.2, 2.1.16.
- **Lìmù. Unidentified**. Lìmù [木厲]木. Tree whose fruit resembles the chestnut. Its trunk is squared, its leaves round, the flowers yellow and fury, and the fruit like that of the chinaberry. Also written 栃木. Used for forgetfulness. 5.1.2.
- **Maple, purpleblow**. Jǔ 舉. It appears to be the 櫸柳 jǔliǔ, also written 柜柳, the purpleblow maple. It is a large tree of the willow family. 5.3.2.
- **Mēngmù**. Mēngmù 蒙木. Tree whose leaves are like that of the pagoda tree. It has yellow flowers and no fruits. Used as protection against confusion. 5.7.6.
- **Mígǔ**. Mígǔ 迷穀. Fabulous tree used as talisman. Keep people in the right direction. It has dark veins and splendid flowers. It looks like the paper mulberry tree. 1.1.2.
- **Mulberry, mountain**. Yǎn 檿. Mountain mulberry tree (山桑 shānsāng), according to the commentator. 山桑 now refers to the Bilberry (*Vaccinium myrtillus*). 5.12.13.
- **Mulberry, triple**. Sānsāng 三桑. Also called Sānsāng mulberry. The *Shen Yue ji* refers to it: 八桂暖如画，三桑眇若浮, "the octuple cinnamon tree is warm like a drawing, the triple mulberry is delicate like floats" (*Peiwen Yunfu*, at the word sāng 桑). 3.2.15.

- **Nán**. Nán 枏. Machilus nanmu, a large tree up to 40 m tall or more. It is a tall tree whose leaves resemble those of the mulberry (Guopu. According to the *Bencao Gangmu*, this tree growths in southern areas. Its flowers are red and yellow. Its fruit resembles that of the clove tree: it is green and non-edible. The great Japanese Encyclopedia says that its fruits have the size of a bean and the shape of a pear. 1.2.14.

- **Oak**. Quercus genus. Zuò 柞. It also refer to the *Xylosma congesta* (mēngzǐ 蒙子树), *Quercus mongolicus Fisch* (zǎocì 凿刺树), and the holly (dōngqīng 冬青). It is an evergreen shrub, with early autumn blooms, trunk differing according to gender, small yellow and white flowers, and small spherical black berries. Its timber was used in utensils making and in charcoal. Also written 柞树 zuòshù. 5.5.2.

- **Oak, chestnut, Zhè**. Zhūxǔ 櫧芧. Zhūxǔ or zhū. Chestnut oak, a small chestnut oak (Guopu). The bark can be used to raise silkworms and the leaves can be used for dies. The original text has 藷蕷 zhūxū, mountain potato (see SJ 3.3.10). It can also be written zhū. Since this is not a tree, Guopu states that it should be 櫧芧 zhūxǔ. 5.11.7.

- **Oak, chestnut-leaved**. Zhù 杼. This appears to be a scrub oak tree of the 栎 lì kind: chestnut-leaved oak (*Quercus serrata*). The *Cihai*, the *Hanyu dazi dian*, and the *Hanyu daci dian* pronounce 杼 shù and Guopu 杼 zhù. 5.8.1.

- **Oak, Diāo**. Diāo 椆. Unidentified tree (Guopu). Hao Yixing, citing the Lei Pian, describes it as a cold-resistant tree that does not wither. The modern sense of the character, pronounced chóu, is an oak (*Quercus glauca*). Note that it is always mentioned with the character Zelkowa qū 椐. 5.11.24, 5.11.44, 5.12.3.

- **Oak, Lì**. Lì 櫟. Oak tree or shrub (*Quercus*) of undefined species. There are four main species in China, of which the Diamyo Oak (*Quercus dentata* 柞櫟 zuòlì) predominates in North and West China. 2.4.10.

- **Oak, Mongolian**. *Quercus mongolica*. Zhà 柞. The leaves of this tree are used for food for a kind of silkworm. 5.5.12, and others.

- **Oak, ring-cup**. *Quercus glauca*. Jiāng 橿. 5.1.5, and others.

- **Oak-like tree**. Zhū 櫧. An evergreen tree whose edible fruits resemble those of the Mongolian oak. Its wood resists corrosion and is used in roofing. 5.11.5.

- **Pagoda tree**. Huái 槐. 5.5.2, and others.

- **Palm tree**. Zōngjiāng 棕櫩. This is the zōnglǘ 棕榈, a palm tree (probably the Chinese-coir palm, or helm palm (*Trachycarpus excelsa, Wendl.*)) whose wood is very hard and is used in construction. The following properties are for the closely related *T. fortunei*. They almost certainly also apply to this species. The flowers and the seed are astringent and hemostatic. The root or the fruit is decocted as a contraceptive. The ashes from the silky hairs of the plant are hemostatic.

Mixed with boiling water they are used in the treatment of hemoptysis, nose bleeds, hematemesis, blood in stools, metrorrhagia, gonorrhea and other venereal diseases. 2.4.8, and others.

- **Pàn**. Pànmù 盼木. No known botanical identification for the compound word. It may be the citrus tree (see note 枳 zhǐ). According to the SJ, Its leaves resemble those of the hedge thorn but without its affect and it hosts wood-living insects. 2.1.9.
- **Paper mulberry tree**. *Broussonetia papyrifera*. Gǔ 穀. It appears to be the homophone of 穀 gǔ, the paper mulberry tree. Its bark is used to produce paper. It is also called 楮 chǔ, 構 gòu, gǔshí □□ or chǔtáo □□. Some call it gǔ because its fruits resemble those of the paper mulberry. (Guopu). According to the *Bencao Gangmu*, the gǔ tree is the same as the paper mulberry tree chǔ 楮. It has males and females. The male trees have striated bark and leaves resembling those of the vine but without hooks. Their flowers blossom in the third month and form long spikes like those of the willow; they do not bear fruits. The female trees have a white bark and leaves like those of the males except that they have hooks. They bear fruits resembling those of mountains peaches giving them the name of mulberry peaches". Astringent, diuretic, tonic, vulnerary. The leaf juice is diaphoretic and laxative - it is also used in the treatment of dysentery. It is also poulticed onto various skin disorders, bites etc. The stem bark is haemostatic. The fruit is diuretic, ophthalmic, stimulant, stomachic and tonic. The root is cooked with other foods as a galactagogue. Paper and cotton fabrics were very early on made from the bark of these trees. The paper mulberry is still used in Japan as kozogami 楮紙, a type of washi 和紙. These synonyms and other met in several Chinese dictionaries are not accepted by all scholars. Some consider these various names as pointing to different trees while exhibiting certain resemblance in characters. See *Shuowen* that identifies chǔ and gǔ. 1.1.2, and others.
- **Peach and plum trees**. Táo lǐ 桃李. *Prunus persicia* and *Prunus domestica*. 3.1.11.
- **Pear tree**. *Pyrus*. Lí 梨. Its leaves are like those of the bush clover, and its flowers are red. Used for subcutaneous ulcers. 5.7.15, 5.9.2.
- **Pepper tree**. Jiāo 椒. Guopu describes the pepper tree as a small tree with thick growth, and vegetation sprouting from under. Another comment adds that it is about wild pepper or prickly ash (花椒 huājiāo). The word jiao normally refers to Sichuan pepper (*Xanthoxylum piperitum*). See Katzer's Spice (http://www.uni-graz.at/~katzer/engl/Zant_pip.html). 3.1.6, and others.
- **Phoebe nanmu**. Nán 柟. Phoebe nanmu, variety of evergreen. Another text has 枏 (or 楠 nán). Other pronunciations: dié or zhì. 2.2.12.
- **Poplar-like tree**. Unidentified. No name. This tree is found in the regions of Mt Běihào. It has red flowers and jujube-like fruits but without pit. The taste of this fruit is sweet and sour. 4.4.1.

- **Qǐ**. 芑. According to the SH, "This tree resembles the poplar and has red veins. Its sap is like blood and it has no fruits. The sap of this tree is used to scrub horses." The Li Shan commentary on the *Xi jing fu*, citing this passage, writes qǐ 杞 and says "qǐ is the poplar tree 楊 yáng; it has red fruits." According to Hao Yixing, this is a phonetic loan. Note that this term also refers to millet with white seedlings; edible wild herbs, such as sow-thistle. 4.4.3.

- **Qiáomù**. Unidentified. Qiáomù 喬木. The term qiáomù generally refers to tree having identifiable trunks as opposed to shrubs and bushes. Included as a category in the *Bencao Gangmu* § 35. Lit. "tall tree." 2.1.9.

- **Qiū**. Unidentified. Qiū 楢. One kind of hard wood tree that can be used to manufacture vehicles. This name always appears with 杻 niǔ, the red apricot tree (楢杻 5.9.4, 5.9.15, 5.10.3, 5.11.35; 杻楢 5.9.9, 5.9.12; 楢檀杻 5.11.48). These two characters together may actually refer to one tree. 5.9.4.

- **Regenerating yáo tree**. Yáomù 榣木. This is a big tree. It seems to refer to trees that regenerate and grow where the sun sets, the 若木 ruòmù. The ruòmù are associated with the sun legends. 2.3.7.

- **Salt tree**. Béimù [木備-亻]木. This is a tree from which exudes a salty-like substance in autumn, substance having a good taste. This may be the salt cedar or tamarisk (maybe the *Tamarisk chinensis*). Also written [木+備去掉亻] or 備[人改木]木. 5.6.11.

- **Sandalwood**. Tán 檀. Sandalwood, or hardwood. This term refers to the white sandalwood tree (probably *Santalum album*), the most commonly known source of sandalwood. This tree grows in semi-arid, deciduous dry forests. The *Bencao Gangmu* mentions the yellow sandalwood and the secondary white, blue-green (wingceltis), red, and black ones. Until the end of summer, this tree has no growth. Then, suddenly its leaves develop during the rains. Farmers wait for this moment to draw conclusions on the rains and dryness. This gives the name to this tree, 水檀 shuǐtán or water sandal. 2.2.8, and others.

- **Shātáng**. Unidentified. Shātáng 沙棠. SH, "They resemble crab apple trees. They have yellow flowers and red fruits that taste like plums and have no pits. They resist water." Lit. sand crab apple tree. It seems to be the Julian Hackberry (*Celtis julianae*), whose main name is 棠壳子树 tángkézǐshù, and synonyms are: 沙棠子 shātáng, 沙棠子 shātángzǐ, and coral tree 珊瑚朴 shānhúpǔ. Either they are hardy, or they float and are not submersible. The wood of this tree can be used in boat construction. Used for drowning. 5.5.7.

- **Silkworm thorn tree**. Cudrania tricuspidata. Zhè mù 柘木. Cudrania (*Cudrania tricuspidata*), also known as Chinese Mulberry (not to be confused with the *Morus australis*), and Silkworm Thorn. 3.3.22.

- **Thorn bush**. Jīng 荆. Thorn bush, chaste tree or vitex. It could also be a thorny variety of Chinese wolfberry shrub (*Lycium chinense*) jīngqǐ 荆杞. 1.2.14, 2.1.4, 4.2.6, 5.11.42, 5.12.8, 5.12.10.

- **Thorny oak shrub**. Yùjiāng 棫橿. No known botanical identification for the compound word. Yù is a thorny shrub with yellow flowers and red fruits resembling an ear pendant; a kind of oak. Jiāng is the Japanese blue oak (*Quercus glauca*). 2.1.10.

- **Thorny tree**. Zhǐjí 枳棘. Zhǐjí may allude to two kind of small trees, the hedge thorn (枳木 zhǐmù) and the thorny tree (棘木 jímù). See SJ 2.1.9. 3.1.13, and others.

- **Thorny tree, Zhè**. Zhè 柘. This term indicates a thorny tree or sugarcane. It may also refer to Cudrania triloba, three-bristle cudrania (*Cudrania tricuspidata*), and Chinese mulberry (*Cudrania*). It could also be the 柘树 zhèshù, silk worm thorny tree or 黄桑 huángsāng, the yellow mulberry tree. 3.1.13.

- **Tiānbiān**. Unidentified. Tiānbiān 天楄. Tree whose trunk is squared and resembles that of the winter sunflower. The character 楄 is pronounced biān according to Guopu, and pián according to the *Cihai*, the *Hanyu dazi dian*, and the *Hanyu daci dian*. Used for throat constriction. 5.7.5.

- **Tree of Heaven**. *Ailanthus altissima*. Chū 樗. It is used as an astringent, antispasmodic, anthelmintic, and parasiticide. Fresh stem bark is used to treat diarrhea and dysentery; root bark is used for heat ailments, epilepsy, and asthma. The fruits are used as an emmenagogue and to treat ophthalmic diseases. Leaves are an astringent and used in lotions for seborrhea and scabies. 2.1.8, and others.

- **Tung tree**. Tóng 桐. According to Hao Yixing, this is the Chinese parasol tree (梧桐 wútóng). However, it could also be the Tung tree (yóutóng 油桐), a species of Vernicia in the spurge family (*Vernicia fordii*; syn. *Aleurites fordii Hemsl.*). The oil from the seed is used externally to treat parasitic skin diseases, burns, scalds and wounds. The poisonous oil is said to penetrate the skin and into the muscles, when applied to surgical wounds it will cause inflammation to subside within 4 - 5 days and will leave no scar tissue after suppressing the infection. The plant is emetic, antiphlogistic and vermifuge. Extracts from the fruit are antibacterial. 3.1.6, and others.

- **Varnish**. Qī 漆. Lit. lacquer, this term refers to the 漆树 qīshù, varnish tree or lacquer tree (*Rhus vernicifera*). Originally 桼, qī depicts a 木 (mù) a varnish tree with 人 drops and 水 (shuǐ) fluid flowing. Later 氵 (水 shuǐ) 'water' (liquid) was added. In 2.4.13 it is written 柒木 qīmù and Guopu mentions that 柒 qī should be understood as 漆 qī. 2.4.8, and others. The lacquer is poisonous and kills insects or worms; it has wide actions due to its descending motion and promotion of circulation of blood.

- **Wolfberry shrub**. Jīngqǐ 荆杞. See also thorn bush jīng 荆. In 4.2.6 it is written 荆芑, which according to Guopu, it is a phonetic loan from 荆杞. It appears to be the Chinese Wolfberry shrub (*Lycium chinense*). 2.1.4, 4.2.6.
- **Xiàngzhāng**. Unidentified. Xiàngzhāng 橡章. This could be the 豫章 yùzhāng. See SJ 2.2.12. 5.9.6.
- **Xún**. Unidentified. Xún 栒. 3.3.27, 5.9.6.
- **Yǎn**. Yǎn 棪. According to the *Erya*, it is a shrub. Guopu describe it as looking like the pear-leaved crab-apple (花红 huāhóng or archaic 奈 nài) and having edible red apple-like fruits. 1.1.4.
- **Yūmù**. Unidentified. Yūmù 桙木. The character 桙 is associated with two sounds: (1) yǒu: According to the *Hanyu dazi dian* and the *Hanyu daci dian* and (2) yù according to the *Cihai*, which is the pronunciation adopted by Guopu. 5.7.10.
- **Zelkowa**. Qū 椐. A kind of small tree mentioned in old books. It had swollen articulations and was used to make canes. It is identified with the tree of long life (língshòu mù 灵寿木). Modern dictionaries suggest the Zelkowa acuminata. Modern pronunciation: jū. The trunk of this tree has lots of protuberances used to make walking sticks. 5.10.2, 5.11.24.
- **Zushàn**. Unidentified. Zōushàn 椒樿. Apparently a white-streaked tree with small leaves. 5.9.11.

Unclear

- **Unnamed 1**. It has round leaves, white calyx; red flowers with black veins, and trifoliate orange-like fruits. Its consumption enhances fertility. 3.1.1.
- **Unnamed 2**. It has delicious fruits whose pits are like those of the peaches. The leaves resemble those of the jujube tree, and the flowers are yellow with a red calyx. Their consumption prevents fatigue. 3.1.3.
- **Jiāróng cǎo**. Unidentified. Jiāróng cǎo 嘉榮草. 5.11.47.

Minerals

- **A big protruding rock**. Luò shí 硌石. According to Guopu. Modern pronunciation: gè shí.

- **Agate**. [王雩]琈之玉. [王雩]琈 yǔfú, kind of jade of unknown shape and form (Guopu). The interpretation of the characters remains unknown. This mineral appears frequently in the Western and Central Mountains. The homophone 瑀 yǔ, a stone resembling jade; agate, could be considered, especially since it does not appear anywhere in the SJ.

- **Agate, red**. Fūshí 砆石. This seems to be banded-white red agapes. According to Guopu, "it seems to be a jade-like stone but of inferior quality. It is red and banded white." See also HJ 13.12.

- **Alabaster, white**. Báimín 白禄. However, other versions have □ mín instead of 禄, alabaster. This term also refers to white pebbles.

- **Alabaster, white**. Báimín 白岷. The commentaries suggest that the character 岷 mín has been transposed for □ mín, the purest white alabaster. In the Hao Yixing edition. See SJ 5.8.9.

- **Alum stone**. Nièshí 涅石. Also called alunite, dye black.

- **Amethyst**. Císhí 茈石. 茈石 císhí (SJ 3.1.3) is the original character but Hao Yixing and the original annotation suggest the term □ cí instead of □ cí. The 茈石 císhí, or also 茈菁 cíjīng, is another name for the amethyst (紫水晶 or 水碧) (See also SJ 4.2.8 and 5.6.5).

- **Amethyst**. Shuǐbì 水碧. SJ 4.2.9 (see SJ 3.1.2 for another form). According to Guopu, it is a kind of water jade 水玉 (See SJ 1.1.3).

- **Aragonite**. Wénshí 文石. Streaked or molted stone, agate, aragonite.

- **Azure jade**. Cāngyù 蒼玉. Maybe the aquamarine [jasper] (水蒼玉 shuǐcāng yù) (P).

- **Beautiful stone**. Měishí 美石. Stones of lower grade than jade. See SJ 4.1.10. The qǐshí 啟石 or "opening" stone appears to draw its name for birth legends of Yǔ the Great (大禹) and of his son Qǐ 啟. When Yu was harnessing the large flood, he cut through Huányuán (轘轅) Mountain and would change into a bear. Emperor Yǔ took for wife a woman from Mt Tú (涂山) whose clan name was 攸 Yōu (禹娶涂山氏名攸). Calling upon [his wife] of the clan of Mt Tú, he said "When I desire to be provided food, you will hear the sound of the wěng drum 鼗 and then come." [One time] Yǔ hoped-danced (跳) on a stone, and accidentally hit his drum. [His wife] of the clan of Mt Tú arrived, saw Yǔ manifested as a bear, felt ashamed 慚 and left. She arrived at Mt Sōnggāo (嵩高山), and changed into a stone, yet she was just about to give birth to Qǐ. Yǔ said, "Give me back my son!" The stone cleaved north, opened (qǐ 啟) and gave birth. Additionally, in the *Di wang shi ji* Yǔ's own mother also turned to stone at the time of his birth. See *Huainanzi* (Tian wen commentary), *Hanshu* (武帝紀 Period of Emperor Wǔ) referring to that passage of the *Huainanzi*, and HJ 2.2.

- **Beautiful stone**. Měishí 美石. Stone of lower grade than jade.
- **Blue-green gem**. Qīngbì 青碧. It is difficult to decide exactly what this term qīngbì refers to. Qīng usually refers to the azurite (more commonly referred as biǎnqīng 扁青) and to the greenish-blue of the ocean. Bì seems to be a blue-green stone resembling jade; nephrite; jasper. It is also considered as a green jade stone; some kinds are bluish, and others are greenish, like the deep sea; it is like jadeite and highly prized. Finally, it is also considered as a sort of blue-green jasper. The *Shanhai Jing* uses both qīngbì and bì. To ensure the differentiation, qīngbì is called "blue-green gem" while bì is called "blue-green stone." Qīngbì is also mentioned in the *Hou Hanshu*.
- **Blue-green stone**. Bì 碧. Green jade, jasper.
- **Bó stone**. Bó shí 博石. This stone is used to manufacture chess game pieces. The shore of lake Tàihú 太湖 (between Zhejiang and Jiangsu) is reputed for its beautiful bóshí marble.
- **Chalk**. Bái'è 白垩. Also refers to chalky soil or kaolin. Kaolin is an essential ingredient in the manufacture of china and porcelain and is widely used in the making of paper, rubber, paint, and many other products. Kaolin is named after the hill in China (Gāo Líng 高凌) from which it was mined for centuries. Kaolin as a medicinal component is also known by the name chìshízhī (赤石脂), literally "crimson stone resin."
- **Chime stone**. Qìng shí 磬石. They can be used to produce music (Guopu). The qìng used to be a L-shaped musical stone. 声 shēng was a picture of a chime stone, a musical instrument made with hanging stones. 殳 (shū) 'beat' (a hand holding a mallet) and 石 (shí) 'stone' have been added to clarify the meaning. Now 声 is used as the simple form of 声[聲] shēng 'sound'.
- **Cinnabar** Dānsù 丹粟. One of the many synonyms for cinnabar 朱砂 zhūshā.
- **Copper, red**. Chìtóng 赤銅. The modern term refers to the copper-gold alloy.
- **Dark-green stone**. Bì lù 碧綠. This may be malachite (孔雀石 kǒngquèshí).
- **Dié stone**. Dié shí 叠石. Unknown. It is a stone also found on the ground and in the water. Some texts have 泠石 jīn shí. Dié suggests the meaning of piled up, or stacked, stones.
- **Dragon bone**. Lónggǔ 龍骨. Bird sternum; fossil fragment; keel. The *Bencao Gangmu* defines it as fossil fragment.
- **Echoing stones and black stones**. Chúnyú xuánshí 錞于玄石. The character 錞 chún has several pronunciations and several meanings:

[duì] part of a spear; [duò] cover; [dūn] squat; and [chún] 錞于 ancient musical instrument. In SJ 2.1.19, 3.2.16, 3.3.46 and 4.1.12, the character 錞 is associated with 于 but explained alone. In SJ 1.1.10 SJ 錞 (蹲 dūn or 踆 cūn) means squatting. Finally, 錞 is sometimes considered as an affix whose meaning depends on the context. Chúnyú 錞于 is described as a drum-like instrument used during wars (Guopu), as an archaic musical instrument that stopped being used (Zhou shu), or as an instrument used with drums (*Zhouli*). Xuánshí 玄石 is known today as magnetite. However, its classical description differs from magnet properties. The *Bencao Gangmu* states "that it is found on the southern slopes of mountains where the soil is rich in copper; while magnetite 慈石 is found on the northern slopes where the soil is rich in iron. Although similar in appearance, xuánshí does not attract iron." Guopu's comment about xuánshí is cryptic: Blue-green jade complies with black stone and gives birth to it. It may be that these four words refer to the resonating stone used to make the chúnyú. It could also be that, instead of the enumeration of several mineral stones, it would be interpreted as "the top has lots of green jade produced in the middle of a black stone."

- **Fēng stone**. Fēngshí 封石. Hao Yixing mentions that the notes of the *Bencao* describe the fēng stone 封石 as tasting sweet, being nonpoisonous, and often found in mountains. This rock is found in abundance in the mountains Fúxī (游戲之山), Yīnghóu (嬰侯之山), Fēng (豐山), fú (服山), and Shēngxiōng (聲匈之山).
- **Fossil**. Tiānyīng 天嬰. Unidentified. This shows that at the time of the SHJ, fossils had already been located and used for medicinal properties.
- **Friable stone**. Gǔn Shí 鯀石. Unidentified stone (Guopu). Hao Yixing, referring to the *Shuowen* where 鯀 is described as small, soft, and easy to slice, think that the name 鯀 stems from these attributes. The notes to the text mention that this stone is commonly called 脆石 cuì shí, where 脃 immediately points to 脆 cuì, friable or brittle. In addition, there may be an allusion to Yu the great, since 鯀 Gǔn is the name of his father.
- **Gold**. Jīn 金. This term is commonly translated as "gold", however, in this textual context it may refer to precious metal. Jīn or "gold/metal" is believed to be one of the 'natural forces' that constitute the *wǔ xíng* (五行) or "five phases", an essential philosophical theory upon which much of traditional Chinese medicine was based.
- **Gold, deep-colored**. Chìjīn 赤金. Red metal, most commonly identified as 銅 tóng copper. Hao Yixing doubts the identification made between "red metal" and copper since the Book of the Western Mounts mentions that there are lot of copper (铜 tóng) in the south and lots of red metal (赤 chìjīn) in the north. On the other hand, Guopu, in his annotations to the *Erya*, states that pure gold is red metal (鏐即紫磨金).

- **Gold, yellow**. Huángjīn 黃金. Guopu: Today, gold like chaff intermingled in sand be isolated from the river of the Yǒngchāng 永昌 department. Shizhi: gold of prime quality springs from the fresh water.

- **Graphite**. Shíniè 石涅. Several suggestions exist: (1) 石墨 shímò, graphite. (2) 煤 méi, coil. (3) 礬石 fánshí, alum. It was used as a black dye, and to blacken eyebrows. See *Dan qian xu lu* section 石涅, *Bencao Gangmu*, section stones. See also SJ 5.9.1 and 5.9.11.

- **Grindstones and sharpening whetstones**. Dǐlì 砥礪. Guopu: 磨石 móshí, polishing or sharpening stones. Theses characters refer to two kinds of grinding stones. The thin one is dǐ and the coarse one lì. Used together they refer in a general sense to sharpening or polishing stones. However, they may also refer to two-sided whetstones that provide both fast-cutting surface and higher-grit surface, such as the whetstone coticule.

- **Hematite**. Zhě 赭. Also called red ochre. See *Bencao Gangmu* (§ 8 - Metals). See also red ochre.

- **Jade**. Yù 玉. While yú has been translated here as jade, in early Chinese texts it refers to precious stones. It was used in death burials to preserver the corpse, and jade elixir was believed to confer immortality while excess consumption would lead to fevers.

- **Jade exudate**. Yùgāo 玉膏. It appears to be an elixir. Guopu, citing the Hetu yuban, says that "on top of Mountain Shàoshì, there is a white jade exudate; one dose immediately brings immortality."

- **Jade, beautiful**. Měiyù 美玉.

- **Jade, black**. Xuányù 玄玉.

- **Jade, fine**. Yú 瑜. Luster of gems; a beautiful stone like Jasper. According to Guopu, it means beautiful jade (měiyú). It is also the root for the term yoga 瑜伽 yújiā.

- **Jade, green**. Yáobì 瑤碧. The stone bì 碧 is often confused with jade yù 玉. It also refers to green jasper. The text may refer to jade that is azure in color, green jasper, or to emeralds.

- **Jade, jǐn**. Jǐnyú 瑾瑜. A fine piece of jade.

- **Jade, lower grade**. Xuányù 璇玉.

- **Jade, striated**. Zǎoyù 藻玉. Multicolor striated. "Multicolor jade spreads white, cinnabar flaws flow red." Xiaoze.

- **Jade, thriving**. Yùróng 玉榮. Also called 玉華 yùhuá or Jade Flowers.

- **Jade, water**. Shuǐyù 水玉. Also known as water essence (做水精 zuòshuǐjīng). Today, it seems to refer to cryolite (水晶石 shuǐjīngshí). It is a jade-like stone that glistens like water. It is also mentioned in the *Liexian zhuan* where "Chìsōngzǐ was the yǔshī 雨师 (master of rain) in the time of Shénnóng 神农. He ate shuǐyù 水玉, and taught the Shénnóng how to do so. He could enter into fire and burn himself."

Water jade also used to be the name for quartz 石英. It also used to be called rock crystal, or shuǐjīng 水晶, jīngshí 晶石, and shuǐjīngshí 水晶石.

- **Jade, white**. Báiyù 白玉. Probably creamy white nephrite.
- **Jade, yān**. Yānyù 珚玉. Unidentified (Guopu). The *Shuijing* (section 'Gu river') mentions this mineral as [王困]玉 jùnyù. The *Taiping Yulan* (Yingsongben, section 62) describes jùnyù as 齊玉 or 奇殞切.
- **Jade, yīngduǎn**. Yīngduǎn 嬰短. Unidentified mineral. See SJ 2.1.10.
- **Jade, yīngyuán**. Yīngyuán 嬰垣. Unidentified jade. The comment refers to SJ 2.3.21.
- **Jadeite**. Shíyù 石玉. If the characters need to be read separately, then it is about "lots of rocks and jade.".
- **Jiān rock**. Jiān shí 瑊石. This is a stone of lower grade than jade.
- **Lapis-lazuli**. Qīngshí 青石. The blue stone.
- **Lěi stone**. Lěi Shí 礨石. Unidentified stone. The character 礨 lěi could be considered as a misconstruction of 壘 lěi, a big pile, as in a boulder.
- **Líng stone**. Língshí 泠石. Mineral, unidentified (Guopu). Hao Yixing suggests that it is the mineral 叠石 diéshí (see SJ 2.4.8). 泠 means cool and clear.
- **Lodestone**. Cí shí 磁石. Hao Yixing mentions that this stone can be used to attract iron. Guanzi also mentions that "as soon as there is loadstone on top of a mountain, there certainly is copper on its base." In the *Shuijing* (§ 19, notice on the river Wei), it is said that the Afang Palace had a front gate made entirely of lodestones. Barbarians called to the court hid their helmets and swords under their armpits. When they arrived to the door, they abruptly were attracted by the magnet and thrown one against the other, causing them great fear and making them think that the Emperor was a God.
- **Loess**. È 堊. Chalk, white earth. The SHJ describes several types of soil, white 堊, yellow 黄堊 (loess), and variegated (see SJ 5.1.4).
- **Loess**. Huángè 黄堊. Lit. yellow soil. This is a synonym for loess (黄土 huángtǔ), a yellow sandy soil typical of North China.
- **Lúdān**. Lúdān 櫨丹. Unidentified. Lú includes the character 卢 lú. According to some, 卢 renders the idea of black color. 卢丹 lúshì would then be 黑丹沙 hēidān shā, some kind of black mineral (黑色矿物).
- **Mí stone**. Míshí 麋石. Unidentified. Hao Yixing suggests that it may be the stone 畫眉石 huàméi shí, or eyebrow blackening stone, like the various mica minerals (雲母 yúnmǔ). The character 眉 méi is an archaic form for 麋 mí. This explanation is doubtfully.
- **Mineral**. Guīshí 邽石. This term should be rectified and written 封石 fēngshí. (See SJ 5.10.2). It might have been a medicinal drug, of sweet taste, and non-toxic.

- **Jade, míyù**. Míyù 麋玉. Mineral, unidentified. Hao Yixing suspects that 麋 mí may derive phonetically from 瑂 méi, which is a jade-like stone according to the *Shuowen*.
- **Multicolor rock**. Cǎishí 采石. The word cǎi, which normally means "variegated color", also renders the idea of multiple colors (wǔcǎi 五彩 the "five colors"). It also means "bright, adorned." Guopu mentions that this rock would include colors yellow (orpiment, or cíhuáng 雌黄), empty green (kōngqīng 空青), and dark green (bìlǜ 空青). Finally it means mine. The compound term cǎishí could actually mean mine stone.
- **Ochre, red**. Dānhuò 丹膉. Red stone, good cinnabar.
- **Ochre, red**. Měizhě 美赭. Also called beautiful ocher, měizhě appears to be a high-quality iron ore used in the path for weapon blades, among other iron smelting works.
- **Ochre, red**. Zhě 赭. Here, Guopu suggests that it refers to 赤土 chìtǔ, barren land, land made barren by severe drought. See also hematite.
- **Pearl-like stone**. Lánggān 琅玕. According to the *Bencao*, the lánggān is found in Mt Kūnlún and in the northwestern mountains. It is a precious gem shaped like coral and blue. When it is produced in the bottom of the sea, it is called coral (shānhú). Produced within mountains, it is called lánggān. Note that 青琅玕 means malachite.
- **Purple stone**. Císhí 茈石. Originally written as 茈 cí (water chestnut).
- **Realgar**. Xiónghuáng 雄黄. This expression refers to the arsenic sulfide mineral realgar. However, it is possible that the term may have included both realgar and orpiment. Main ores are found in Hunan. According to the *Bencao Gangmu*, it is used for the treatment of internal heat, and to kill worms and insects.
- **Red silver**. Chìyín 赤銀. Also called an ore of silver, of a ruby-red or reddish black color, it includes proustite, or light red silver, and pyrargyrite, or dark red silver.
- **Ruǎn stone**. Ruǎnshí 礝石. Hao Yixing suggests it is 湷 which, according to the *Shuowen*, is a mineral having a quality lower than that of jade. The *Yupian* suggests it is a gem 瓀 (瓀石). The stone 湷石 is white like ice and half of it is red. These stones are drawn today from Mt Yen-men. It could be a white and red quartz.
- **Sandstone**. Shāshí 沙石. This term refers to sandstone or rock.
- **Sediment**. Liúshā 流沙. Drift or shifting sand; quicksand; sediment.
- **Sounding stone**. Míng Shí 鳴石. It looks like blue-green jade stone. When hit, it resonates loudly and the sound propagates at long distance. It is part of a class of musical instruments (乐器 yuèqì) like chime stones (磬石 qìngshí) of the western Mts.
- **Stone of lower quality than jade**. Bàngshí 廄[麦改夆]石. Unidentified stone (Guopu). Also written [广夆]石. The *Shuowen* describes it as a stone of lower quality than the jade. It could be that the word bàng is simply a stone or a pebble.

- **Strange stone**. Guàishí 怪石. A jade-like stone. The literal translation of guàishí is "rocks of grotesque shapes."
- **Suān stone**. Suānshí 痠石. Mineral, unidentified.
- **Thorn stone**. Zhēnshí 箴石. Stone needle used as a medical instrument for specific therapeutic purpose. Grinding and polishing this stone provide an excellent sharp piercing tool used to treat abscess, subcutaneous ulcers and pustules and to drain pus and blood. The *Huangdi Neijing Suwen* (§ 24) mentions the therapeutic use of stone needles coming from the East. These stones were called 砭石 biān shí. They later on became 箴石 zhēn shí and the term 鍼 zhēn was finally used to indicate the metallic acupuncture needle.
- **Tin**. Xī 錫. As for gold, silver, copper, tin has to be understood in the SH as an unrefined material, an ore.
- **Tú stone**. Túshí 涂石. According to Guopu, this seems to be the gàn stone (see SJ 5.4.1).
- **Ultramarine**, or azure blue. Qīnghuò 青腹. A kind of mineral thought of as the marine blue or ultramarine (shíqīng 石青). The original version has 鋪 pū instead of 腹 huò but this has been corrected by Guopu.
- **Wash stone**. Xǐshí 洗石. Guopu suggest it is a stone used to clean the body by rubbing. Hao Yixing suggests that the term referring to rubbing qiǎng 磢 used by Guopu is actually 爽瓦 which is congruent with the entry filth tile stone 垢瓦石 in the *Shuowen*. The *Yiwen Leiju*, section 5, suggests it is a marvelous stone: "On the border of the well kuàng that belonged to king Yǒngkāng, there was a wash stone. At that time one could see a red steam-fog. Later, two people from the northern tribes, who were residing close to the well, asked to purchase it. The price was exorbitant. The one called Fùsūn saw two yellow birds fighting on these stones. He ran and was able to reach them. The birds immediately changed into gold. These tribal people did not know how to purchase such pricy stones but finally succeeded. [However] they broke one. Inside, there was an emptiness representing the location of the two birds.".
- **Whetstone**. Dǐ 砥.
- **Whetstone, black**. Xuánsù 玄[石蕭]. Also called dark whetstone (磨刀石).
- **White metal**. Báijīn 白金. Most commonly identified as 銀 yín silver (see *Shuowen* and *Erya*). Hao Yixing also doubts the identity between white metal and silver and thinks that they are two different metals. The *Shuowen* mentions that white metal (báijīn) should be understood as wù 鋈 while red metal would be zǐmójīn 紫磨金 (赤金者紫磨金类). On the other hand, the *Sancai tuhui* states that (a) báijīnyín and wù are synonyms, and that copper is the red metal (赤金) as well as hóng tóng 紅銅 (red copper). As for the *Bencao Gangmu*, it mentions three types of copper: red 赤, white 白 and green 青 (銅有赤白青三種). Finally, to make

things more complex, the *Baozang lun* mentions 17 types of silver, among which four are genuine silver (眞銀). Since the SHJ uses both báijīn 白金 and yín 銀 (see SJ 2.1.13), the translation "white metal" is used for báijīn 白金.

- **Yīng stone**. Yīng shí 嬰石. According to Guopu, it is a kind of veined and multicolor stone looking like jade as the 燕石 yàn shí.
- **Yù stone**. Yù 礜. Arsenic mineral.

Geography

Abyss 淵

- **Qīnglíng**. 清泠之淵. 5.11.6. This abyss is mentioned in *Zhuangzi's Miscellaneous Records* (讓王). Shùn offered his empire to his friend, the Northerner Wúzé. The Northerner Wúzé then said, 'How strange! You resided in the middle of ditches in the field and then within the gates of Yao. This was not enough. Now you wish to inundate me with your humiliating conduct. I am ashamed to be exposed to this." Then, he threw himself in the qīnglíng abyss."
- **Yān**. [虫焉]淵. 2.3.1.

Basin

- **Yī and Luò**. 伊洛. 5.6.1

Forests 林

- **Dānlín**. 丹林. 3.3.19
- **Fánzhǒng**. 墦冢. 5.6.10
- **Mǎngfú**. 莽浮之林. 5.12.5. Forest of Mǎngfú.
- **Táolín**. 桃林. 2.6.13. Peach tree Forest, in Sanmenxia, Henan. (1) Guopu says about Táolín, Hongnong 宏農 Hú county, Wénxiāng county, south of valley center. It abounds in wild horses, mountain goats and mountain bulls. (2) It appears to be the forest Dèng 鄧林 made by the staff of Kuāfù after his death. See HJ 3.9 about Kuāfù. (3) Táolín is now located in the Shaanxi province, to the east of Tóngguān 潼關 (Tong Pass, between Henan and Shaanxi) and in the Henan province, Lingbao prefecture, west. The Shu 書 (*Zhou Book*, Military Excellence) mentions that "[King Wu of the Zhou] then promoted culture over military activities, returned the horses to the east of Mt Huà, and the graze cattle to the wilderness of Táolín."

Islet

- **Tián**. 墠渚. 5.3.2. An islet in the middle of a river is called zhǔ (Guopu). In addition, the etymology of tián reflects an artificial sacrificial tumulus.

Lakes

- **Hūshǎo**. 虖勺. 1.2.8.
- **Jùqū**. 具區. 1.2.7. It is a big lake located in the southwest of the Wú 吳 province of Jiangsu. It is called Zhènzé 震澤 in the *Shujing*.
- **Xīhǎi**. 西海. Several lakes in the western part of China, including Lake Qinghai (Blue Lake, 青海), and even sometimes the lake Baikal.

Marshes 澤

- **Cháng**. 長澤. 3.3.4. Marsh Cháng.
- **Chí**. 泜澤. 3.3.29. Marsh Chí.
- **Dà**. 大澤. 2.3.7. This is the place where Hòujì 后稷 metamorphosed or where he was buried. See also HJ 6.5.
- **È**. 闕之澤. 1.2.13.
- **Fānzé**. 蕃澤. 2.3.16. Luxuriant
- **Gāo**. 皋澤. 3.3.31. Eminent
- **Gāo**. 皋澤. 4.4.5. Marsh Gāo
- **Hǎi zé**. 海澤. 3.3.25. Ocean Marshes. This also means the "northwest side."
- **Hú**. 湖澤. 4.2.17. Marsh Hú or Lakes and Marches, the Great Unclear if the two characters should be used together. See also 沙澤 shāzé.
- **Huáng**. 黃澤. 3.3.14.
- **Jì**. 稷澤. 2.3.4. The name of this marsh comes from that of Hòujì 后稷.
- **Jíyì**. 即翼. 1.1.9. See Note about Mt Yuányì 猨翼山 SJ 1.1.4.
- **Lì**. 櫟澤. 3.1.14.
- **Língyáng**. 陵羊之澤. 2.4.15. Marsh of the Hill-sheep.
- **Mǐn**. 湣澤. 4.2.1. Marsh Mǐn refers to the contemporary Jù yě Marsh 鉅野澤, which with the building of the Yùnhé (運河) or "Great Canal" during the Yuán dynasty (元朝, A. D. 1279-1368) resulted in the present-day formation of Lake Shǔ shān (蜀山湖) in southwestern Shandōng.
- **Qióng**. 邛澤. 3.2.11.
- **Shā**. 沙澤. 4.2.14. Marsh Shā (shāzé). Unclear if the two characters should be used together. See also 沙澤 Húzé.
- **Shēn**. 深澤. 4.3.7. Deep Marsh.
- **Tài zé**. 泰澤. 3.1.19. March Tài.
- **Tài zé**. 泰澤. 3.3.8. Great
- **Tài zé**. 泰澤. 3.3.8. This march is 100 square lis.
- **Yáoyao**. 瑤[去王]之澤. 2.3.1.
- **Yìn**. 印澤. 3.2.9. The character 邛 qióng is missing. It should be 印邛澤, which is congruent with the swamp described in 3.2.11.
- **Yōu**. 泑澤. 2.3.3.

- **Yú**. 余澤. 4.2.5.
- **Yúrú**. 餘如之澤. 4.4.6. March Yúrú
- **Zé**. 澤. 4.1.7. Marsh

Mounds 丘

- **Bóshòu**. 搏獸之丘. 2.3.1. The comment to the text mentions that several editions use the character 山 mountain instead of 丘 mound. Guopu mentions that 搏 bó should be 簿 bù.
- **Huò**. 霍山. 5.1.12. Now in Shanxi province, Huo county. Southeast.
- **Kūnlún**. 昆侖之丘. 2.3.8. See HJ 6.6, 6.12.
- **Qīngqiū**. 青丘. 1.1.9. The Green Mound. See also the Green Mound Countries in HJ 9.7 and HJ 14.15.
- **Xuānyuán**. 軒轅之丘. 2.3.12. This mound was the capital of Emperor Huangdi who took for spouse Léizǔ 嫘祖, a woman from Xīlíng 西陵. This is why this mountain was named Mt Xuānyuán since it is the name of this Emperor prior to being called Huangdi.

Mountain Ranges 山岭

- **Bèi** (Beishan). 蒼山. 5.3. 在河南省巩县北. or 苿山 Mt Fù (Fushan)
- **Bó**. 薄山. 5.5. The first central mountain range.
- **Jǐ**. 濟山. 5.2.
- **Jīng**. 荊山. 5.11. Eleventh mountain range of the central mountains.
- **Jīng**. 荊山. 5.8. Eight central mountain range.
- **Lí**. 釐山. 4.4. This name refers to (1) the fourth central mountain range, and (2) its third mountain (see SJ 5.4.3). Located in Henan province, west of Song county.
- **Mín**. 岷山. 5.9. Ninth central mountain range. It extends from the southern part of Gansu province to the northwest of Sichuan province. It roughly presents a north-south orientation, and covers approximately 500 km. Its highest peak is in Sichuan and is 5588 m above sea. It is famous in the works of Yu the Great and references to it are found in most classics. The *Shujing* (chap. *Yugong* 禹貢), says that it was cultivated at that time together with Mt Bō 嶓. The Mínshān mountain range formed the northwest limit of Liangzhou, one of the nine provinces of Emperor Yu.

Mountains 山

- **Ào**. 奧山. 5.11.45.

- **Aóan**. 敖岸. 5.3.1.
- **Bàfù**. 罷父之山. 2.4.3.
- **Báibiān**. 白邊之山. 5.4.6.
- **Báimǎ**. 白馬山. SJ 3.3.32. Four contemporary mountains have this name, in four different provinces. White horse.
- **Báishā**. 白沙山. 3.2.5.
- **Báishí**. 白石之山. 5.6.6. Now in the Henan province, Xin'an county, within the borders. White Stones Mount.
- **Báiyū**. 白於之山. 2.4.10.
- **Bànshí**. 半石之山. 5.7.8. Today in the Henan province, Yanshi county 偃师 Southwest.
- **Bào**. 暴山. 5.12.8. The compilation *Jiaoliao fu* referring to this passage, say Mt jǐng 景山.
- **Bēi**. 卑山. 5.11.27.
- **Běidān**. 北單之山. 3.1.22.
- **Běihào**. 北號. 4.4.1.
- **Běixáo**. 北囂之山. 3.2.11.
- **Běixiān**. 北鮮之山. 3.1.24.
- **Běiyuè**. 北嶽之山. 3.1.20.
- **Bēnwén**. 賁聞之山. 3.3.7.
- **Bì**. 畢山. 5.11.20.
- **Bì**. 碧山. 4.2.13.
- **Biānchūn**. 邊春之山. 3.1.10. Synonyms: Mt chōng 春, Mt zhōng 鍾.
- **Bǐng**. 丙山. 5.10.9.
- **Bǐng**. 丙山. 5.12.4.
- **Bǐng**. 柄山. 5.4.5.
- **Bó**. 薄山. 5.1.1. This mountain is one of the 11 names of a medium-size mountain range called Mt Léishǒu 雷首山 (the other names being 中条 Zhōngtiáo, 历 Lì, 首阳 Shǒuyáng, 蒲 Pú, 襄 Xiāng, 甘枣 Gānzǎo, 猪 Zhū, 狗头 Gǒutóu, and 吴 Yú). Under the name of Mt Xiāng, it was located in Puban county (which was in Hedong prefecture, west of present-day Yongji in Shanxi province).
- **Bóqí**. 勃齊之山. 4.1.4. 齊 qí is the modern character for 涂 tú found in some texts. This may be Mt Xīn fǔ (新甫山) in Shāndōng
- **Bōzhǒng**. 嶓冢之山. 2.1.14. Located in Gansu province, Tiānshuǐ prefecture.
- **Bùzhōu**. 不周之山. 2.3.3. The term 不周 comes several times both in names and in the annotations. Mt Bùzhōu is one of the pillars that hold up the sky. Gònggōng 共工 butted it and the world tilted, all rivers ran to the east and stars began to move. Nǚwā 女娲 patched the pillar but it was never fully corrected. This explains that sun, moon, and stars move towards the northwest, and that rivers in China flow southeast into the

Pacific Ocean. It is said that this name comes from the way this mountain looks, with a breach in it thus making it look unsatisfactory in the landscape. There is also a wind of that name coming from there.

- **Cáoxī**. 曹夕之山. 4.2.2.
- **Chái**. 犲柟. 4.1.9. Wolves' Mountain. The original text has 柟山, which is corrected by Hao Yixing.
- **Cháisāng**. 柴桑之山. 5.12.14.
- **Chángliú**. 長留之山. 2.3.14. See also the *Taiping Yulan*, chapter 29 - section 388.
- **Chángshā**. 長沙之山. 2.3.2.
- **Chángshí**. 長石之山. 5.6.9. Now in the Henan province, Xin'an county.
- **Chángyòu**. 長右山. 1.2.2. It is cited in the Song rhyming dictionary (*Guǎngyùn* 廣韻).
- **Chángzhēng**. 常烝之山. 5.6.12. In Henan Province, Shan County. Synonyms: 幹山 Mt Gàn (*Shuijing* – River Hé).
- **Chányuán**. 擅爰之山. 1.1.7.
- **Chāo**. 超山. 5.5.6.
- **Cháogē**. 朝歌之山. 5.11.2.
- **Chéng**. 成山. 1.2.8.
- **Chénghóu**. 成侯之山. 5.5.7.
- **Chóngwěi**. 虫尾之山. 3.3.14.
- **Chóngwú**. 崇吾之山. 2.3.1. See also Shiji, section fēngshàn (封禪).
- **Chǒuyáng**. 丑陽之山. 5.11.44.
- **Chǒuyáng**. 杻阳山. 1.1.5.
- **Chǔ**. 楮山. 5.10.6. Synonyms: Mt Zhǔzhōu 渚州之山 (Guopu),.
- **Chúnyú** Wúféng. 錞于毋逢之山. 3.3.46. In SJ 3.3.47 it is referred to as 無逢之山 Mt Wúféng. The characters 無 wú and 舟 zhōu used to have the same pronunciation.
- **Cóng**. 從山. 5.11.18.
- **Cōnglóng**. 蔥聾山. 5.1.4. Wild Goats Mountain.
- **Cōnglóng**. 蔥聾山. 5.5.4. See also Mt Cōnglóng (5.1.4).
- **Cuì**. 翠山. 2.1.18.
- **Dàcì**. 大次之山. 2.2.10.
- **Dàguī**. 大騩之山. 5.11.40.
- **Dàguī**. 大騩之山. 5.7.19. Now in the Henan province, Xinmi district.
- **Dài**. 帶山. 3.1.3.
- **Dàkǔ**. 大紮之山. 5.7.7. The *Taiping Yulan* (§ 931) and other texts say Mt Dàkǔ (大苦). Now located in the Henan province, within the borders of Dengfeng county and may be the modern Mt Dàxióng (大熊山).
- **Dānhú**. 單狐之山. 3.1.1.
- **Dānxué**. 丹穴之山. 1.3.3.
- **Dānxūn**. 丹熏之山. 3.1.8.

- **Dānzhāng**. 單張之山. 3.1.12.
- **Dǎoguò**. 禱過之山. 1.3.2.
- **Dàshí**. 時之山. 2.1.13.
- **Dàshú**. 大孰之山. 5.11.26.
- **Dàxián**. 大咸之山. 3.1.16. The *Taiping Yulan* (§ 383) calls this mountain Mt Dàtóng 大同之山 with regard to the snake chángshé.
- **Dàyáo**. 大堯之山. 5.8.12.
- **Dàzhī**. 大支之山. 5.11.37.
- **Dì**. 柢山. 1.1.6.
- **Dī**. 隄山. 3.1.25.
- **Dìdōu**. 帝都之山. 3.3.45.
- **Dìqūn**. 帝囷之山. 5.11.3. The *Guangyun* says 箘 qūn instead of 囷 qūn (Hao Yixing).
- **Dōngshǐ**. 東始之山. 4.4.3.
- **Dòngtíng**. 洞庭之山. 5.12.7.
- **Dòngtíng**. 洞庭山. 5.12.1. Twelfth mountain range of the central mountains.
- **Dú**. 獨山. 4.1.10.
- **Dǔ**. 堵山. 5.10.10. May allude to 楮山 Mt Chǔ (5.10.6).
- **Dǔ**. 堵山. 5.7.5.
- **Dǔ and Yù**. 堵山, 玉山. 5.11.49. This could be about Mt Yù 楮山 (SJ 5.10.6) and Mts Yù 玉山 mentioned above (SJ 5.18.19 and 5.9.12) because these two mountains are not included in Section 11. However, it is rather difficult to assess since the present part of the *Shanhai jing* has gone through severe alterations. (See SJ 5.10.9).
- **Dùfù**. 杜父之山. 4.2.7.
- **Dūnhóng**. 敦薨之山. 3.1.17.
- **Dūntí**. 敦題之山. 3.2.16.
- **Dūntóu**. 敦頭之山. 3.2.9.
- **Dūnyǔ**. 敦與山. 3.3.29. Located in Héběi province, within the borders of Linchéng county, Xingtái city.
- **Dúsū**. 獨蘇之山. 5.2.8.
- **Ěrshì**. 爾是之山. 3.2.6.
- **Fājiū**. 發鳩之山. 3.3.22. It is located in Shanxi, 25 km west of Zhangzi County town. Synonyms: Mt Fābāo 發苞山, Mt Lùgǔ 鹿谷山, and Mt Lián 廉山, on account of its richness.
- **Fànggāo**. 放皋之山. 5.7.6. According to Guopu, 放 fang could be 效 xiào, and it is sometimes written 牧 mù. It is believed to be located in the Henan province, Yichuan county south, 鳴皋山 Mt Mínggāo.
- **Fánkuì**. 繁繢之山. 5.10.3.
- **Fāntiáo**. 番條之山. 4.1.5.
- **Fāshì**. 發視之山. 5.2.2.

- **Fāshuǎng**. 發爽之山. 1.3.4.
- **Fāwán**. 發丸之山. 3.3.9.
- **Fēi**. 非山. 1.3.6.
- **Fēng**. 豐山. 5.11.33. See the previous Mt Fēng (SJ 5.11.6). These mountains may overlap at their feet but are not the same.
- **Fēng**. 豐山. 5.11.6.
- **Fēngbó**. 風伯之山. 5.12.5. The *Chuxue ji* (Scroll 28), referring to this section, says 鳳伯之山. The characters 風 (S 风) fēng and 鳳 (S 凤) fèng used to be inverted.
- **Fēngyǔ**. 風雨之山. 5.9.11. The Mountain of Winds and Rains.
- **Fú**. 服山. 5.11.46.
- **Fú**. 浮山. 2.1.9. Location: Shaanxi province, south of líntóng xiàn. .
- **Fù**. 傅山. 5.6.10.
- **Fūfū**. 夫夫之山. 5.12.6. Or 大夫之山 Mt Dàifu.
- **Fúlí**. 梟麗之山. 4.2.16.
- **Fúxī**. 浮戲之山. 5.7.13. Now located in the Henan province, Xinmi city (old Mi county), northwest. Fúxī 浮戏 immediately suggests the legendary Fúxī 伏羲. The *Zhuangzi* (Scroll 6: Da zong shi) uses "伏戏" Fúxī.
- **Fúyāng**. 符惕之山. 2.3.17.
- **Fúyú**. 符禺之山. 2.1.5.
- **Fúyù**. 浮玉山. 1.2.7. Located in Zhèjiāng province, Húzhōu prefecture. This is the Golden Mountain (Jīnshān 金山). Under the reign of Emperor Xuanzong 玄宗, of the Tang dynasty (713-756 A.D.), the name of Mt Fúyù, was changed in that of Jīnshān, because of the gold present in the vicinity of the river. According to the Daqing yitongzhi, Mt Fúyù is in the middle of the Jade Lake Yùhú 玉湖 (now called 碧浪湖), seven li from the south of the Húzhōu prefecture. There is a big rock similar to accumulated waves that cannot be crossed by water. This gives the name of this mountain: Heaven eye, Tiānmù shān 天目山. Lit. Floating jade.
- **Fùzhōu**. 復州之山. 5.10.5.
- **Fúzhū**. 扶豬之山. 5.4.2.
- **Gān**. 乾山. 3.3.41.
- **Gāng**. 剛山. 2.4.13.
- **Gānnmèi**. 乾昧. 4.1.1. In Shāndōng Province, north of of Mt Sǔzhǔ.
- **Gānzǎo**. 甘棗山. 5.1.1. See note on Mt Bó. Also known as Mt Léishǒu 雷首山.
- **Gǎodī**. 縞羝之山. 5.6.2.
- **Gāoliáng**. 高梁之山. 5.9.5.
- **Gāoqián**. 高前之山. 5.11.16.
- **Gāoshān**. 高山. 2.2.4.

- **Gāoshì**. 高是之山. 3.3.37.
- **Gāoshì**. 高氏之山. 4.1.7.
- **Gāotú**. 皋塗之山. 2.1.16.
- **Gé**. 葛山. 5.9.15.
- **Gé**. 鬲山. 5.9.7.
- **Gé**, Extremity. 葛山之尾. 4.2.4.
- **Gé**, Head. 葛山之首. 4.2.5.
- **Gěng**. 耿山. 4.2.8.
- **Gǒuchuáng**. 苟床. 5.5.1. Also called Mt Gǒulín 苟林山. This is the name used in later sections and in other texts.
- **Gōumí**. 勾檷之山. 5.9.10.
- **Gōushì**. 緱氏之山. 4.2.14. Synonym: Mt Xiáshì 俠氏之山 (Guopu).
- **Gōuwú**. 鉤吾之山. 3.2.10.
- **Gǔ**. 榖山. 5.6.7. Now in the Henan province, Mianchi county. Mt Paper Mulberries.
- **Guǎncén**. 管涔山. 3.2.1. It is located in Shanxi province, Ningwu County, northeast.
- **Guāng**. 光山. 5.8.8.
- **Guàntí**. 潘侯之山 灌題之山. 3.1.13.
- **Guànxiāng**. 灌湘之山. 1.3.8. Synonym: 灌湖 Mt Guànhú (Guopu).
- **Gǔchéng**. 榖城山. 5.6.1. Now in the Henan province, Luoyang prefecture, northwest.
- **Gǔdèng**. 鼓鐙之山. 5.1.15.
- **Gūér**. 姑兒之山. 4.1.6.
- **Gūféng**. 姑逢之山. 4.2.15.
- **Gūguàn**. 姑灌之山. 3.2.13.
- **Guī**. 厜山. 5.6.3. Now in Henan province, Luoyang prefecture. Synonyms: 魏山 Mt Wèi, it is now called 谷口山 Mt Gǔkǒu.
- **Guī**. 邽山. 2.4.17.
- **Guī**. 騩山. 2.1.19.
- **Guī**. 騩山. 2.3.19.
- **Guī**. 騩山. 5.3.3. Now located in Henan province, west of Luoyang. Guopu suggests the pronunciation wēi but the *Ciyuan*, the *Cihai*, *Hanyu dazi dian*, and the *Hanyu daci dian* suggest guī. This mountain is also known as 魏山 Mt Wēi. It may also be written 厜山 Mt Guī. Now known as 谷口山 Mt Gǔkǒu.
- **Guī**. 騩山. 5.9.14.
- **Guī**. 龜山. 5.12.3.
- **Guìjī**. 會稽山. 1.2.9. Huìjī is the name of an ancient province that included the contemporary territory of Zhèjiāng 浙江, the north of Fújiàn 福建 and the south of Jiāngnán 江南. Mt Huìjī was located in the south of Wú 吳 kingdom and in the northern part of the Yuè 越 kingdom (below

30° North latitude). Guopu: "Today, it is located in the south of the Huìjī 會稽 prefecture, district of Shānyīn 山陰. On top, there is the tomb of Yǔ the Great (13th century B.C.) and a well."

- **Guó**. 號山. 3.1.6. The name of this mountain is unsure. Citing this passage, the *Chu xue ji* and the *Taiping Yulan* both write hào shān 號山. The *Erya* writes [豸虎]山, but this last character is only a variant of 號 (Hao Yixing). The apposite [豸虎] occurs many times in the commentaries of the SJ and HJ.
- **Guó**, **Extremity**. 號山之尾. 3.1.7. Extremity of Mt Guó (Guóshān zhī wěi)
- **Guǒmǔ**. 贏母. 2.3.10.
- **Gǔwěi**. 蠱尾之山. 5.5.13.
- **Gūyáo**. 姑媱之山. 5.7.3.
- **Gūyè**. 姑射山. 4.2.10. This name also appears in HJ 7.24, HJ 7.25.
- **Gūyè**, **Northern**. 北姑射之山. 4.2.11.
- **Gūyè**, **Southern**. 南姑射之山. 4.2.12.
- **Gǔzhōng**. 鼓鍾之山. 5.7.2.
- **Háo**. 豪山. 5.2.3.
- **Hào**. 號山. 2.4.8.
- **Hé**. 和山. 5.3.5.
- **Hégǔ**. 合谷之山. 5.1.13.
- **Héng**. 衡山. 5.11.32. Located in Hengyang city, Hunan county. For Guopu, it is the southern Héng of the Five Sacred Mountains. Synonyms: Mt Gǒulǒu (岣嶁山). See HJ 13.23.
- **Héng**. 衡山. 5.8.15. Located in Henan.
- **Huá**. 華山. 2.1.1. The first western It seems to be the modern Qinling complex. The Huá mounts form one of the five famous groups called wǔyuè 五嶽, considered sacred in ancient China. They were supposedly located at the four cardinal points. The northern one, héng 恒山, is located in the northeastern Shanxi province. The western one, huá 華山, described here is in Shaanxi province, east from Xi'an city. The southern one, héng 衡山, is located in the center of the Hunan province, Hengyang city. Finally the eastern one, tài 泰山, is in the center of Shāndōng province. Under the Zhou, the Central Mt Sōng 嵩山 was added, on the right bank of the Yellow River, in the Henan province.
- **Huái**. 槐山. 5.5.9. 槐 was considered as [禾鬼], which ought to be 稷 (harvest god). Mt Jì 稷山 is located in Jishan county, Yuncheng, Shanxi. Hòujì seeded all kinds of grains on this mountain, thus the name. See SJ 2.3.7 and HJ 6.5.
- **Huáijiāng**. 槐江之山. 2.3.7.
- **Huán**. 洹山. 3.2.15.
- **Huān**. 灌山. 5.8.20. The *Taiping Yulan* says 濯山 Mt Zhuó.

- **Huáng**. 黃山. 2.1.17.
- **Huángrén**. 皇人之山. 2.2.14.
- **Huānjǔ**. 讙舉之山. 5.4.9.
- **Húguàn**. 湖灌之山. 3.2.14.
- **Huīzhū**. 煇諸. 5.2.1.
- **Húnxī**. 渾夕之山. 3.1.21.
- **Húqí**. 狐岐之山. 3.2.4.
- **Húshè**. 胡射之山. 4.3.5.
- **Hǔshǒu**. 虎首之山. 5.11.24.
- **Hūshuò**. 虖勺之山. 1.2.14.
- **Hǔwěi**. 虎尾之山. 5.10.2.
- **Jǐ**. 几山. 5.11.48.
- **Jī**. 基山. 1.1.8.
- **Jī**. 雞山. 1.3.9.
- **Jī**. 雞山. 5.11.15.
- **Jiǎchāo**. 賈超之山. 5.9.16.
- **Jiān**. 菱山. 5.2.7.
- **Jiān**. 葴山. 5.11.22.
- **Jiǎng**. 講山. 5.7.11.
- **Jiāngfú**. 江浮之山. 5.12.11.
- **Jiānggǔ**. 橿谷山. 5.1.9. Guopu suggests that it may also be called 檀谷 Mt Tángǔ.
- **Jiāo**. 教山. 3.3.9.
- **Jiāo**. 驕山. 5.8.3.
- **Jiéshí**. 碣石之山. 3.3.43. It is located on the seashore, in the Chānglí county (Héběi province) to the east of modern Luan River. It is an important historical mountain due to its geographical location in coastal areas of northern China in ancient times and by being part of the ancient culture. In the Spring & Autumn and the Warring States Period, Mt Jiéshí was known as the "Immortal Mountain 仙山." According to the historical records, China's first emperors Qín Shǐhuáng 秦始皇 and Hànwǔ 漢武 visited this mountain to seek the Immortal(s). Emperor Wèiwǔ Cáocāo 魏武 曹操 and the first emperor of the Táng Dynasty Lǐ Shìmín 李世民 also traveled here. This mountain was made famous for its inclusion in several poems, including 浪淘沙北戴河 *Làngtáoshā Běidàihé* (Běidàihé, to the Melody of Làngtáoshā (Ripples Sifting Sand)) by Mao Zedong and 觀滄海 *Looking at the Ocean* (from MT Jiéshí) by Cáocāo.
- **Jígōng**. 即公之山. 5.12.9. Located in Henan Province, it is the watershed between Yangtze and Huái Rivers, located in a transitional belt among northern subtropical zone and southern temperate zone and providing a superb breeding ground for plants and animals.

- **Jígǔ**. 即谷之山. 5.11.14.
- **Jīhào**. 雞號之山. 3.3.46. It is located in the northern sea. The *Yupian* uses the term 號之山 only.
- **Jǐng**. 景山. 3.3.10. A mountain of this name exists in the central section).
- **Jǐng**. 景山. 3.3.25. Located in Héběi province, Hándān county, southwest.
- **Jīng**. 京山. 3.3.13.
- **Jǐng**. 景山. 5.8.1. Li Daoyuan in the *Shuijing Zhu* (Section 32) states that "River Jǔ 沮水 goes out of Wènyáng prefecture Jǔyáng county northwest Mt Jǐng 景山, that is the head of Mt Jīng 荊山, where rosy clouds rise, high and respectful stratus." "Mt Jǐng 荊山 is now at about 100 li east of Mt Jǐng 景山, at the boundaries of Xīnchéngyí town (新城沵)." In the *Taiping Yulan* (Section 49), Mt Jǐng 景山 is on the upper part of Luo county southwest 200 li, east where it joints Mt Jīng 荊山, where the source of River Jǔ 沮水 is located. The mountain whose name is Mt Yànfú 雁浮山, at the head of Mt Jīng 荊山 is called Mt Jǐng 景山, wild goose circle the air from south to north return everywhere, and the natives therefore call this mountain Mt Yàn 雁山 (Wild Goose Mt) or Mt Yànfú 雁浮山 (Soaring Wild Goose Mt)." In the *Dushi Fangyu Jiyao* (Scroll 79), it is stated that "Mt Jǐng 景山 is in the county (that is Yúnyáng prefecture, Fang county) southwest 200 li. Li Daoyan is mistaken, namely the *Yugong* states 'the head of Mt Jīng 荊山 is called Mt Yàn 雁山, also known as Mt Yànfú 雁浮山. The SHJ states that the head of Mt Jīng 荊山 is called Mt Jǐng 景山. The Taiping Huanyu Ji states that "at Fánglíng 房陵 there are 35 brooks, 34 mountains, this is where Mt Jǐng 景山 rises."
- **Jīng** (II). 荊山. 5.8.2.
- **Jīnggǔ**. 涇谷之山. 2.4.12.
- **Jǐnlǐ**. 堇理之山. 5.11.12.
- **Jīnxīng**. 金星之山. 5.1.7. Golden Star. Modern term for Venus.
- **Jīshí**. 積石之山. 2.3.13. See also HJ 3.11 for the relationship of this mountain and Yu the Great.
- **Jīwěi**. 箕尾之山. 5.4.4.
- **Jīwěi**. 箕尾山. 1.1.10. Constellations Sagittarius and Scorpio.
- **Jǔ**. 柜山. 1.2.1.
- **Jū**. 崌山. 5.9.4.
- **Jǔrù**. 沮洳之山. 3.3.20.
- **Jùyú**. 句餘山. 1.2.6.
- **Kōngsāng**. 空桑之山. 3.3.33, 4.2.1. Kōngsāng 空桑 (SJ 3.3.33 or SJ 4.2.1) is a place name associated with Shāndōng and Confucius. It is also the name of a 瑟 sè zither and a mountain good for making both qín

琴 and sè. Guopu says: "the zither-like instruments come from this mountain, see *Zhouli*." The *Huainanzi* (Fundamental Norm) says: "Shun, to inspire the laborers during the works against the Flood, used thin kōngsāng (hollow mulberry)." Gao Youzhu says: "Kōngsāng, this is a geographical name located in 魯 Lǔ." The exact location of Kōngsāng 空桑 (SJ 4.2.1) is unknown, however, it may be in the vicinity of the present-day Mount Dà tiān 大天山 on the eastern peninsula of Shāndōng (Schiffeler).

- **Kǔ**. 苦山. 5.7.4.
- **Kuāfù**. 夸父之山. 5.6.13. It was situated in today's Henan province, Lingbao county, southeast. Mt Kuāfù is supposed to have been created from the body of Kuāfù after his death. Kuāfù was the leader of the Kuāfù clan (夸父族) residing on top of the mountain called Chéngdū Zàitiān (成都载天山), in northern China. Kuāfù loved the sun and hated the darkness and so decided that he would catch the sun and fix it in the sky for ever. He died in the process. He always carried with him a staff 杖 made from the wood of the peach tree. When he died this stick became the forest Dèng 鄧林 (according to HJ 3.9), or the forest Táo 桃林 (according to HJ 3.9 - Note 6), both in Mt Kuāfù. Synonyms: 秦山 Mt Qín.
- **Kuáng**. 狂山. 3.2.7.
- **Kūnlún**. 昆侖. 2.3.7.
- **Kūnwú**. 昆吾之山. 5.2.6. It is well-known for its copper red like fire and used to make blade and work jade (Guopu). Its features led to a sword called the "magical sword of Kūnwú." It is also the name of a person (HJ 10.22.).
- **Lái**. 崍山. 5.9.3. Could be 邛崍 Mt Qiónglái, located in Sichuan.
- **Lái**. 莱山. 2.2.17. Contemporary name of Laishan district of Yantai city 煙台市|烟台市, Shāndōng.
- **Láo**. 勞山. 2.4.2.
- **Lěi**. 蠚山. 4.1.2. Mount Lei is located in Shāndōng province, however, its precise location remains unidentified.
- **Lèmǎ**. 樂馬之山. 5.11.21.
- **Lèyóu**. 樂游之山. 2.3.9,
- **Lí**. 釐山. 5.4.3. Third mountain of the fourth central mountain range, also called Mt Lí.
- **Lì**. 歷山. 5.5.10. According to Hao Yixing, this is Mt Lǐ'ér 歷兒. The *Shuijing* states that in the south of Hedong prefecture there is Mt Li. Shun used to plough there.
- **Lì'ér**. 歷兒山. 5.1.2. Also called Mt Lì in Shanxi province. The *Shuijing* says "in the south of Hedong prefecture (today Yongji) is found Mt Lì. This is the place plowed by Emperor Shùn." The *Shujing* also mentions that Mt Pú 蒲山 is also called Mt Lì.

- **Liángqú**. 梁渠之山. 3.2.12.
- **Liángyú**. 良餘之山. 5.5.12.
- **Líng**. 靈山. 5.8.13.
- **Lìngqiū**. 令丘之山. 1.3.10.
- **Lìshí**. 歷石之山. 5.11.42. The character 歷 lì could be 磨 mò according to Guopu.
- **Lóng**. 龍山. 5.8.14. Dragon Mount.
- **Lónghóu**. 龍侯之山. 3.3.2.
- **Lóngshǒu**. 龍首之山. 2.2.6. Dragon Head.
- **Lóuzhuō**. 婁涿之山. 5.6.5. Now in Henan province, Xin'an county, south.
- **Lù**. 陸山. 3.3.38.
- **Lùguì**. 陸[危邑]之山. 5.8.7. [危邑] or 陒 guì.
- **Lún**. 倫山. 3.3.42.
- **Lún**. 綸山. 5.8.6.
- **Lúnzhě**. 侖者之山. 1.3.11.
- **Lúqí**. 盧其之山. 4.2.9.
- **Lùtái**. 鹿臺之山. 2.2.7.
- **Lùtí**. 鹿蹄山. 5.4.1. Located in Henan province, southeast of Yiyang county.
- **Lùwú**. 鹿吳之山. 1.2.16.
- **Mǎchéng**. 馬成之山. 3.3.3.
- **Mánlián**. 蔓聯之山. 3.1.11.
- **Mánqú**. 蔓渠之山. 5.2.9. Now in the Henan province, Luanchuan county, West.
- **Máo**. 旄山. 1.3.5.
- **Máo**. 旄山. 4.4.2.
- **Měi**. 美山. 5.8.11. The Beautiful Mount.
- **Mèngmén**. 孟門之山. 3.3.11.
- **Mèngzǐ**. 孟子之山. 4.3.6.
- **Mì**. 密山. 5.6.8. Now in the Henan province, Xin'an county south.
- **Mì**. 峚山. 2.3.4.
- **Mín**. 岷山. 5.9.2. Synonyms: Mt Wèn 汶山.
- **Mǐn**. 敏山. 5.7.18.
- **Mò**. 末山. 5.7.16.
- **Mǔ**. 牡山. 5.4.8.
- **Mǔyú**. 踇隅之山. 4.3.8. The *Yupian* and *Guangyun* write 踇偶 Mǔyú (Guopu).
- **Nán**. 南山. 2.1.12.
- **Nányú**. 南禺之山. 1.3.13.
- **Ní**. 鯢山. 5.11.29.
- **Niǎo**. 鳥山. 2.4.5.

- **Niǎoshǔ Tóngxué**. 鳥鼠同穴之山. 2.4.18. Lit. "The grotto where birds and rats are gathered." Guopu mentions about it that in the Longxi Yangshou county southwest mountains, there are birds and rats in the same grotto, the birds are called kàn 鵌 and the rats tú 鼵. Tú is like a short-tailed domestic mouse, and kàn is similar to a swallow but yellow. The grotto, several feet deep, has the rats and the birds coexisting, with the rats in the center and the birds at the periphery.
- **Niǎowēi**. 鳥危之山. 2.2.8.
- **Niúshǒu**. 牛首之山. 5.1.11. Zhejiang province or Jiangsu province?
- **Nǚchuáng**. 女床之山. 2.2.5.
- **Nǚjǐ**. 女几之山. 5.8.4.
- **Nǚjǐ**. 女几山. 5.9.1. 几 jǐ has two other homophones: 紀 and 伎.
- **Nǚzhēng**. 女烝之山. 4.4.4.
- **Pānhóu**. 潘侯山. 3.1.14.
- **Péngpí**. 彭毗之山. 3.3.15. Also written 彭[肉比]之山.
- **Pí**. 皮山. 5.11.8.
- **Piānyù**. 篇遇山. 5.12.1.
- **Píchā**. 羆差之山. 3.1.23.
- **Píng**. 平山. 3.3.12.
- **Píngféng**. 平逢之山. 5.6.1. Now in Henan province, Luoyang prefecture, north, northeast of Mt Máng 邙山. Synonyms: Mt Tàipíng 太平山, Mt Jiá 郏山.
- Púgōu. 僕勾之山. 1.2.11.
- Qí. 岐山. 4.3.2.
- Qí. 岐山. 5.8.9.
- Qí. 岐山. 5.9.9.
- Qí. 沂山. 3.3.39.
- **Qián**. 前山. 5.11.5.
- **Qián**. 鈐山. 2.2.1.
- **Qiánlái**. 錢來之山. 2.1.1.
- **Qiáomíng**. 譙明山. 3.1.4.
- **Qīn**. 欽山. 4.4.5.
- **Qíngǔ**. 琴鼓之山. 5.8.23.
- **Qīngyào**. 青要之山. 5.3.2. Now located in Henan province, west of Luoyang.
- **Qiú**. 求山. 5.11.43.
- **Qiū**. 丘山. 1.2.17. It also refers to the "wild country."
- **Qiúrú**. 求如之山. 3.1.2.
- **Qīwú**. 漆吳之山. 1.2.17.
- **Qǐzhǒng**. 跂踵之山. 4.3.7.
- **Quèquè**. 鵲山. 1.1.1. Also written [昔隹]山. The *Sancai tuhui* mentions a spirit of Mt Què: This is about the same mountain.

- **Qúfù**. 瞿父山. 1.2.5.
- **Qūwú**. 區吳之山. 1.2.15.
- **Qūwú**. 區吳之山. 5.11.38.
- **Qúzhū**. 渠豬之山. 5.1.3.
- **Ráo**. 饒山. 3.3.40.
- **Rénjǔ**. 仁舉之山. 5.8.21.
- **Róngyú**. 榮余之山. 5.12.15.
- **Ruò**. 若山. 5.8.17. Guopu suggests that 若 may also be 前.
- **Sānwēi**. 三危之山. 2.3.18.
- **Shàn**. 剗山. 4.4.7.
- **Shàngshēn**. 上申之山. 2.4.6.
- **Shǎo**. 少山. 3.3.23. It seems to be located in Jiangsu province, in the western part of Wuxi city.
- **Shàoshì**. 少室之山. 5.7.9. This is not Shǎoshì. Within the high mountain Sōng (Henan, 1,440 m.), the western mountain peak is Shàoshì. The eastern mountain peak is called Tàishì. The two peaks are separated by a distance of 15 li. Today it is in the Henan province, Dengfeng county 偃师 northwest.
- **Shǎoxián**. 少咸之山. 3.1.18.
- **Shǎoxíng**. 少陘之山. 5.7.14.
- **Shǎoyáng**. 少陽之山. 3.2.2.
- **Shé**. 蛇山. 5.9.6. Snake Mountain.
- **Shēn**. 申山. 2.4.4.
- **Shēng**. 升山. 5.5.14.
- **Shēngxiōng**. 聲匈之山. 5.11.39.
- **Shénqūn**. 神囷之山. 3.3.21.
- **Shēnshǒu**. 申首之山. 2.4.11. According to the annotation, the term 申 shēn should be 由 yóu.
- **Shí**. 時山. 2.1.11.
- **Shí**. 石山. 3.3.35. Rocky Mountain.
- **Shí**. 石山. 5.8.16. Rocky Mountain.
- **Shì**. 視山. 5.11.4.
- **Shī**. 尸山. 5.5.11. Maybe 戶山 Mt Hù.
- **Shícuì**. 石脆之山. 2.1.6. There is also a river called Cuì 脆.
- **Shīhú**. 尸胡之山. 4.3.1.
- **Shīměi**. 師每之山. 5.8.22.
- **Shízhě**. 石者之山. 3.1.9.
- **Shǒu**. 首山. 5.5.2.
- **Shǒuyáng**. 首陽之山. 5.10.1. It is also called 首山 Mt Shǒu in 5.10.10 (Hao Yixing).
- **Shùlì**. 數歷之山. 2.2.3.
- **Sōng**. 松山. 3.3.28.

- **Sōngguǒ**. 松果之山. 2.1.2.
- **Sǔzhǔ**. 楸孟[矛改朱]之山. This mountain is located in Shāndōng Province. It may be the present Mt Shímén 石門山. 4.1.1.
- **Tài**. 太山. 4.4.8.
- **Tài**. 太山. 5.7.15. According to Wangfu, this mountain is located at 鄭 Zhèng and is not the eastern mountain Tài 太.
- **Tài**. 泰山. 4.1.11. This is the eastern sacred Mt Tai (Taishan), once called Mt Dàizōng 岱宗. It lies in Tai'an county in the middle of the Shāndōng Province, encompassing an area of 426 square kilometers.
- **Tàihàng** (head Guī). 太行之山. 3.3.1.
- **Tàihuá**. 太華之山. 2.1.3. This corresponds to the contemporary Huá Mountain (see Huá 2.1.1). Guopu: "On the top, there are mingxing jade maidens (明星玉女) that hold the jade syrup. The one who obtains this essence immediately becomes an Immortal. The journey is perilous, remote and full of obstacles. It is constantly surrounded by divine fogs and clouds.
- **Tàimào**. 泰冒. 2.2.2.
- **Tàiqì**. 泰器之山. 2.3.6.
- **Tàishì**. 泰室之山. 5.7.10. According to Guopu, it is located in the middle of the sacred mountain Sōnggāo and is now located west in the Yángchéng county. Mt Sōnggāo 嵩高 is located in the Henan province, Dengfeng county, North.
- **Tàitóu**. 泰頭之山. 3.3.17.
- **Tàiwēi**. 泰威之山. 5.1.8.
- **Tàixì**. 泰戲. 3.3.34. It is located in Shānxī province, Fánshì county, northeast of the mountain range of Mt Héng 恒山. Synonyms: Mt Wǔfū 武夫山, Mt Shùfū 戍夫山, and Mt Gūfù 泒阜山.
- **Tángtíng**. 堂庭山. 1.1.3.
- **Tiān**. 天山. 2.3.20. Located in Xinjiang.
- **Tiānchí**. 天池之山. 3.3.5. Mt Heavenly pound. See also Acupuncture point MH01.
- **Tiāndì**. 天帝之山. 2.1.15.
- **Tiānyú**. 天虞之山. 1.3.1.
- **Tiáogǔ**. 條谷之山. 5.5.5.
- **Tíshǒu**. 題首山. 3.3.26.
- **Tóng**. 銅山. 5.8.10. The Copper Mount.
- **Tóngróng**. 童戎之山. 3.3.36.
- **Tùchuáng**. 兔床之山. 5.11.7.
- **Tuó**. 橐山. 5.6.11. Now in Henan province, Shan county, west.
- **Tuōhù**. 脫扈之山. 5.1.6.
- **Wángwū**. 王屋之山. 3.3.8. Located in Henan Province, Jiyuan City. It is one of the nine most famous ancient mountains and the top one of the

ten Taoist sacred mountains in China. Together with Mt Tàihàng 太行山 (SJ 3.3.1), it is known for being removed by the Foolish Old Man in the story of *Liezi*. The Heavenly Peak, the main one of this mountain was were Huangdi set up a temple to offer celestial sacrifices. This mountain is also known as the birthplace of Taoism, and was described as the "natural storehouse for Chinese medicinal herbs" by Sun Simiao.

- **Wéilóng**. 維龍之山. 3.3.31.
- **Wén**. 文山. 5.9.17. Mt Wén does not figure in the list of mountains cited previously. Hao Yixing therefore suggests 岷山 Mt Mín instead (See § 5.9.1) instead. This Mt is moreover mentioned as Mt Wén in the narration of the trip in occident of King Mu Wang 穆王, fifth sovereign of the Zhou dynasty, 984 B.C.
- **Wō**. 湲山. 5.1.5. Or [水委]山 Mt Wō.
- **Wúgāo**. 無皋之山. 4.3.9.
- **Wúlín**. 吴林之山. 5.1.10. Also called Mt Yú 吴山, Mt Yú 虞山, Slope Yú 吴坂, Slope Diānlíng 颠[车令]坂. In addition, it is one of the names of Mt Bó (see Mt Bó SJ 5.1.1). The *Hanyu daci dian* pronounces it yú, while the *Ciyuan* and the *Cihai* pronounce wú. Now it is within Yuguo territory. It is said that in the Shang Dynasty, Fù Shuo 傅说 once hid here. The *Xu Hanshu* (Junguo zhi 郡国志) states that "Dayang county is Mt Yú (吴山), on top of it there is the city of Yú (虞城). The Tang writer Zhang Xiaobiao (章孝标) in his "*Provincial Examination of the steed yowl*" said "Their strength exhausted on Yu's high mountains' slopes, they neigh in the bitter north wind sounds." In the former Shu 蜀, Wei Zhuang 韦庄 in his work "和郑拾遗秋日感事" said, "in the slopes of Yu the legendary horse qíjì 骐骥 neigh, in Mt Qi the phoenix Fenghuang gathered." Yuguo is now located in the Shanxi province, Pinglu county.
- **Xī**. 錫山. 3.3.24. It seems to be located in Jiāngsū province, Wúxī county.
- **Xián**. 咸山. 3.3.4.
- **Xiān**. 鮮山. 5.11.35.
- **Xiān**. 鮮山. 5.2.4.
- **Xiāng**. [歹羊]山. 4.3.1.
- **Xiányīn**. 咸陰山. 1.2.12.
- **Xiànyōng**. 縣雍之山. 3.2.3.
- **Xiànzhuó**. 縣斸山. 5.5.3. 縣 is also pronounced xuán, and 斸 zhú (some texts have [属 刂] instead).
- **Xiǎocì**. 小次之山. 2.2.9.
- **Xiǎohóu**. 小侯之山. 3.3.16.
- **Xiǎohuá**. 小華之山. 2.1.4. The Shuǐ jīng zhù says: "To the south-west of Tàihuá Shān is found Xiǎohuá Shān.".
- **Xiǎoxián**. 小咸之山. 3.1.15.
- **Xīhuáng**. 西皇之山. 2.2.16.

- **Xióng**. 熊山. 5.9.13. Bears Mountain.
- **Xióng'ěr**. 熊耳. 5.4.7. This mountain range is an important scenic area located in the western part of Henan province. It consists in two mountains peaks, thus the name "ears" of the bear. It runs in the northeast-southwest direction. It rises in the west in the Lushi county, goes east to north unbroken to Yichuan 伊川 where it breaks and goes east. In the south it connects with the mountain system Fúniú 伏牛山 and in the north it is adjacent with Mt Xiáo 崤山. It is high and tall in the northeast and flattens as it goes to the southwest. Its highest peak is Mt Quánbǎo 全宝山 (2094 kilometers) in the Luoning county southwest.
- **Xiù**. 繡山. 3.3.27.
- **Xiūyú**. 休與. 5.7.1. According to Guopu, 與 yú should be considered 興 yú. This mountain is located in Henan province, Lingbao prefecture west of Wénxiāng.
- **Xuān**. 宣山. 5.11.31.
- **Xuánhù**. 玄扈山. 5.4.10. This is probably Mt Huānjǔ 讙舉之山 (5.4.9). Now located in Shaanxi province, west of Luonan county and south of the river Luo. This is where Huangdi was transmitted the map of the phoenix Fèng 鳳.
- **Xuānyuán**. 軒轅之山. 3.3.18.
- **Xún**. 洵山. 1.2.13. The Mountains of savages.
- **Xūnwú**. 薰吳之山. 2.2.11.
- **Xúnzhuàng**. 枸狀之山. It may be Mount Lǔ (魯山) in Shāndōng.4.1.3.
- **Yǎ**. 雅山. 5.11.30.
- **Yàn**. 燕山. 3.3.39. Swallow Mountain. Note that this mountain is under the chapter of Mt Yí. It does not have its own chapter as the summery of this chapter states that there are 46 mountains and not 47.
- **Yáng**. 陽山. 3.3.6.
- **Yáng**. 陽山. 5.2.5.
- **Yángdì**. 陽帝之山. 5.12.13.
- **Yánghuá**. 陽華之山. 5.6.14. It is in the south side of Mt Huá, thus the name Mt Yanghua. Now, in the southeast of Mt Huá.
- **Yángjiā**. 陽夾之山. 1.3.7.
- **Yángxū**. 陽虛之山. 5.5.15.
- **Yànmén**. 鴈門之山. 3.3.44. Now in Shanxi province, northeast from the Daizhou department called in the past Yànmén 鴈門. See HJ 6.3. Its name comes from the gooses going through the gate-like structure of this mountain. There is also a Yànmén river (see SJ 3.1.18).
- **Yānzī**. 崦嵫之山. 2.4.19. Located in Gansu. Legendary western region where the sun sets. The bottom of this mountain is filled with water. Within this water surface is found the 虞淵 yúyuān. It is cited in the *Chuci lisao*.
- **Yáo**. 堯山. 5.12.10.

- **Yǎo**. 杳山. 5.11.47.
- **Yáobì**. 瑤碧之山. 5.11.9. The *Yiwen Leiju* (Scroll 89) says 搖 yáo instead of 瑤 yáo.
- **Yáoguāng**. 堯光之山. 1.2.3.
- **Yèlì**. 謁戾之山. 3.3.19. Now located in Shanxi, within the system of the Tàiyuè Mt 太岳山.
- **Yí**. 夷山. 1.2.10.
- **Yì**. 役山. 5.7.17.
- **Yǐdì**. 倚帝之山. 5.11.28.
- **Yìgāo**. 嶧皋之山. 4.2.3.
- **Yīkū**. 依軲之山. 5.11.13.
- **Yīn**. 陰山. 2.4.1. Located in Mongolia.
- **Yīn**. 陰山. 2.3.16. Located in present Mongolia.
- **Yīn**. 陰山. 5.1.14. Synonyms: 險山 Mt xiǎn (according to Guopu).
- **Yīng**. 嬰山. 5.11.23.
- **Yīng**. 英山. 2.1.7.
- **Yīngdī**. 英鞮之山. 2.4.15.
- **Yīnghóu**. 嬰侯之山. 5.11.25.
- **Yīngliáng**. 嬰梁之山. 5.7.12. Now located in the Henan province, with the borders of Gongyi city.
- **Yīngzhēn**. 嬰[石璽]之山. 5.11.19.
- **Yísū**. 宜蘇之山. 5.3.4. Now called 蘇山 Mt Sū. Now located in Henan province.
- **Yìwàng**. 翼望. 2.3.22.
- **Yìwàng**. 翼望山. 5.11.1.
- **Yízhū**. 宜諸之山. 5.8.5.
- **Yǒngshí**. 勇石之山. 5.10.4.
- **Yǒu**. 泑山. 2.3.21.
- **Yōudū**. 幽都之山. 13.28 HJ. Located in "Mountains within the Seas".
- **Yóuxì**. 游戲之山. 5.11.17.
- **Yòuyuán**. 又原之山. 5.10.7.
- **Yú**. 盂山. 2.4.9.
- **Yù**. 嫗山. 5.11.34.
- **Yù**. 玉山. 2.3.11.
- **Yù**. 玉山. 5.8.19. The Jade Mountain. See also SJ 2.3.11 for the Western Jade Mt.
- **Yù**. 玉山. 5.9.12.
- **Yǔ**. 羽山. 1.2.4.
- **Yú'é**. 餘莪之山. 4.2.6.
- **Yuányì**. 猨翼山. 1.1.4. The first sentence is found in the *Chuxue ji* scroll 27 but has the term 稷 jì instead of 猨 yuán (Hao Yixing). The

Yiqie jing yinyi scroll 93 has the term 即 jí instead of 猨 yuán. This last name is congruent with the name of the river mentioned in 1.1.9.

- **Yúcì**. 豰次之山. 2.1.10.
- **Yuè**. 嶽. 5.6.14. There is a mountain with this name in SJ 4.1.8. In addition, if yuè is taken as reference to the Five Sacred Mountains, the sentence 嶽在其中 may allude to the central one, which is 嵩山 Mt Sōng in Henan. Rosny suggest Mt Huà (see SJ 2.1.1).
- **Yuè**. 嶽山. 4.1.8.
- **Yuèchóng**. 嶽崇之山. 2.3.3.
- **Yùfǎ**. 嶽法之山. 3.1.19.
- **Yúgǎo**. 禺稿之山. 1.3.12.
- **Yún**. 雲山. 5.12.2.
- **Yúyáng**. 隅陽之山. 5.9.8.
- **Zhāng**. 章山. 5.11.36. According to Guopu, it may be Mt Tóng (童山). According to Hao Yixing, referring to the notes of the *Shuijing*, it should be Mt Gāo (皋山).
- **Zhāngé**. 章莪之山. 2.3.15.
- **Zhānzhū**. 瞻諸之山. 5.6.4. Now in Henan province, Xin'an county, south.
- **Zhāogē**. 朝歌山. 5.5.8. A mountain of this name is now called Mt Lǎozhài 老寨山, located in Laiyang county, Yantai, Shāndōng. However, Zhāogē was the capital of Shang Dynasty, and later capital of State of Wei (衛國). It is located in current Qi County, Hebi, Henan.
- **Zhāoyáo**. 招搖之山. 1.1.2. Mt Què and Mt Zhāoyáo are two names of the same mountain 是一山而二名. The Shuyi ji says: "Mt Zhāoyáo is also called Què". (Rèn chén 任臣).
- **Zhè**. 柘山. 3.3.30.
- **Zhēn**. [石壐]山. 4.2.17.
- **Zhēnlíng**. 真陵之山. 5.12.12.
- **Zhì**. 巍山. 5.8.18.
- **Zhìdiāo**. 袟[上卜竹下周]之山. 5.11.11.
- **Zhìgāng**. 至剛. 2.4.14. Or Extremity of 剛山 Mt Gāng.
- **Zhīlí**. 支離之山. 5.11.10. Commentaries based on Hao Yixing suggest 攻離之山 Mt Gōnglí.
- **Zhìyáng**. 厎陽之山. 2.2.12.
- **Zhōng**. 鍾山. 2.3.5.
- **Zhōngfù**. 中父之山. 4.3.4.
- **Zhōnghuáng**. 中皇之山. 2.2.15.
- **Zhǒngjiù**. 踵臼之山. 5.11.41.
- **Zhōngqū**. 中曲之山. 2.4.16.
- **Zhòngshòu**. 眾獸之山. 2.2.13.

- **Zhǒngsuì**. 冢遂. 2.3.1. This is the name of a mountain according to Guopu.
- **Zhú**. 竹山. 2.1.8. Location: Shaanxi province, 40 li southeast of the Wèinan xian district. See its drawing in the *Jingdian tu du Shanhai jing.* "Bamboo mountain."
- **Zhú**. 竹山. 4.1.12. It may be Mount Fèng huáng (鳳凰山) located in Shāndōng.
- **Zhūcì**. 諸次之山. 2.4.7.
- **Zhūgōu**. 諸鉤之山. 4.3.3.
- **Zhuō**. 涿山. 5.10.8.
- **Zhuōguāng**. 涿光之山. 3.1.5.
- **Zhūpí**. 諸毗. Mentioned in. See also SJ 1.2.1.
- **Zhūpí**. 諸毗之山. 2.3.3. The southern Mt Jǔ 柜山 (SJ 1.2.1) faces a Zhūpí 諸毗 in the north.
- **Zhūpí and Chángyòu**. 諸毗 長右. 1.2.1. Adjacent mountains (Guopu). Zhūpí is also the name of a river. The *Guangyun* citing the *Shanhai jing* writes 長舌 Chángshé instead of 長右 Chángyòu.
- **Zhūyú**. 諸餘之山. 3.2.8.
- **Zǐtóng**. 子桐之山. 4.4.6.

Rivers 水

- **[qù shuǐ]**. 淲水. Mt Yí. 1.2.10. According to Guopu, "others say river pèi, or pèishuǐ 淲水." See SJ 1.2.9.
- **Ào**. 奥水. Mt Ào. 5.11.45.
- **Bān**. 般水. Mt Qí. 3.3.39. 般 bān pronounced pán.
- **Bēi**. 陂水. Mt Lóuzhuō. 5.6.5.
- **Biān**. 邊水. Mt Pānhóu. 3.1.14.
- **Bìhú**. 芘湖. 3.1.3. Chinese mallow.
- **Bìyáng**. 碧陽. Mt Mèngzǐ. 4.3.6.
- **Bó**. 薄水. Mt Chóngwěi. 3.3.14.
- **Cāngtǐ**. 蒼體之水. Mt Máo. 4.4.2.
- **Cén**. 涔水. Mt Běixáo. 3.2.11.
- **Cén**. 涔水. 4.2.9.
- **Chàn**. 浪水. Guopu states the pronunciation of 浪 as Yín.
- **Chǎngtiě**. 敞鐵之水. Mt Wéilóng. 3.3.31.
- **Chéng**. 承水. Mt Tài. 5.7.15.
- **Chì**. 赤水. Mt Kūnlún. 2.3.8. Going through SJ 1.2.1, 2.1.17, 2.2.8, 2.2.14, 2.3.8. Red river.
- **Chu**. 楚水. Mt Shùlì. 2.2.3.

- **Chuáng**. 牀水.
- **Cǐ**. 泚水. Mt Shízhě. 3.1.9. There are three rivers with this name (SJ 2.3.2, 3.1.9, and 4.4.3).
- **Cǐ**. 泚水. Mt Dōngshǐ. 4.4.3.
- **Cóng**. 從水. Mt Cóng. 5.11.18.
- **Dàijiāng**. 大江. More commonly known as the Yangtze river 长江. See 江 Jiāng.
- **Dān**. 丹水. Mt Dānxué. 1.3.3. "Red River".
- **Dān**. 丹水. Mt Nán. 2.1.12. Ancient variant for Red River 丹江. See Baidu (http://baike.baidu.com/view/580549.htm).
- **Dān**. 丹水. Mt Zhú. 2.1.8.
- **Dān**. 丹水. Mt Mì. 2.3.4.
- **Dān**. 丹水. Mt Chóngwěi. 3.3.14.
- **Dānlín**. 丹林之水. Forest Dānlín. 3.3.19. River of the Red Forest.
- **Dǐ**. 泜水. Mt Dūnyǔ. 3.3.29. Modern pronunciation: chí.
- **Dī**. 隄水. Mt Dī. 3.1.25.
- **Dìqūn**. 帝囷之水. Mt Dìqūn. 5.11.3.
- **Dìyuàn**. 帝苑之水. Mt Bì. 5.11.20.
- **Duān**. 端水. Mt Hào. 2.4.8.
- **Dūn**. 敦水. Mt Shǎoxián. 3.1.18.
- **Dūnhōng**. 敦薨之水. Mt Dūnhōng. 3.1.17.
- **Ěr**. 洱水. Mt Bàfù. 2.4.3.
- **Fàn**. 汎水. Mt Fāshuǎng. 1.3.4.
- **Fàn**. 氾水.
- **Fāng**. 汸水. Mt Jīwěi. 1.1.10.
- **Féi**. 肥水. Mt Wéilóng. 3.3.31. See SJ 3.3.15.
- **Féi**. 肥水.
- **Fén**. 汾水. Mt Guǎncén. 3.2.1. After rising in the Guǎncén Mountains in northwestern Shanxi, it flows southeast to Taiyuan and then southwest through the central valley of Shanxi to join the Huang near Hejin. Its total length is about 340 mi (550 km).
- **Fēng**. 漨水. Mt Dānhú. 3.1.1.
- **Fú**. 浮水. 3.2.7.
- **Fǔ**. 滏水. Mt Shénqūn. 3.3.21. River in Héběi Province.
- **Fúháo**. 浮濠之水. Mt Xióng'ěr. 5.4.7.
- **Fúyú**. 符禺之水. Mt Fúyú. 2.1.5.
- **Gān**. 甘水. Mt Lùtí. 5.4.1. There is actually in the southwest of the Henan province, a river called Gān. It pours into the Luò.
- **Gāng**. 剛水. Mt Gāng. 2.4.13.
- **Gāng**. 杠水. Mt Biānchūn. 3.1.10.
- **Gāo**. 高水. Mt Jīng. 3.3.13.

- **Gāo**. 皋水. Mt Zhāng. 5.11.36. Some texts have the variant 皋水 gāo shuǐ, which is congruent with Hao Yixing's note on Mt Gāo (皋山).
- **Gāotú**. 皋涂水. Mt Tóngróng. 3.3.36.
- **Gé**. 鬲水. It seems to be the 鬲津 géjīn, the Ge river, cited in the *Cihai*. It is a river originating in Héběi Province and flowing into Shāndōng Province. It is associated with the nine rivers of the Yellow river.
- **Gòng**. 共水. Mt Tàitóu. 3.3.17.
- **Gòng**. 共水. Mt Bó. 5.1.1.
- **Gòng**. 共水. Mt Chángshí. 5.6.9.
- **Gōu**. 鉤水. Mt Tài. 4.4.8.
- **Gǔ**. 榖水. Mt Fù. 5.6.10. Today, the river Gǔ emerges from the northeast of the Guyang valley (Xiangfan prefecture, Hubei province) and pours into the Luò. Is it the Han river 漢水? .
- **Gǔ**. 榖水. Now written 谷水, it is also called 涧河 Jiànhé. It originates in Henan, Mianchi county northwest of Mt Mǎtóu 马头山, flows southeast and meet the river Miǎn 渑水, flows east through Xin'an county towards Luoyang prefecture west then goes southeast and pours into the river Luo.
- **Guài**. 怪水. Mt Chǒuyáng. 1.1.5.
- **Guàn**. 灌水. Mt Shícuì. 2.1.6. According to the *Shuijing* Zhu, this river would be the river xiǎochì 小赤. See also note on river 濩 huò in SJ 2.1.2.
- **Guān**. 觀水. Mt Tàiqì. 2.3.6. *Lushi Chunqiu*: "River Guān is found in the remote western regions."
- **Gūér**. 姑兒之水. Mt Gūér. 4.1.6.
- **Guǐ**. 溈水. Mt Yízhū. 5.8.5. Today, this river emerges from the east of Mt Wéi 溈山, flows through the Huàróng xiàn district (華容縣), and pours into the 江 Jiāng. Pronunciation: wéi (*Xiandai Hanyu Cidian*, *Hanyu dazi dian*, and *Hanyu daci dian*), guǐ (Guopu).
- **Guó**. 虢水. Mt Fúzhū. 5.4.2. Now located in the Henan province, within the borders of Lushi county. In Lushi county, half a li northeast, there is a Mt Guó.
- **Hàn**. 漢水. Mt Bōzhǒng. 2.1.14. The Hàn river is a the longest Yangtze tributary (1532 km). Also called Hanjiang, it was historically referred to as Hànshuǐ. It rises in the Mǐcāng 米仓 Mountains in the extreme southwestern part of Shaanxi province. Its upper stream is known successively as the Yùdài 玉带, the Yàng 漾, and, below Miǎnxiàn 沔县, the Miǎn. It becomes the Hàn river at Hànzhōng, and flows eastward at the foot of the Qin (Qinling) Mountains. The *Shanhai jing* gives Bōzhǒng as the source of the Hàn river. This was later rectified.
- **Hàn**. 漢水. 2.4.18. The longest Yangtze tributary.
- **Háo**. 豪水. Mt Mì. 5.6.8.
- **Hé**. 河水. Mt Kūnlún. 2.3.8.

- **Hé**. 合水. Mt Bànshí. 5.7.8.
- **Hé**. 河. The original text has hé only. This was a synonym for the Yellow River (like 河水 and the present 黄河). The river changed courses many times and to add precision here, we will call it "Yellow River". Mentioned in 2.2.2.
- **Hēi**. 黑水. Mt Jī. 1.3.9. Black river.
- **Hēi**. 黑水. Mt Kūnlún. 2.3.8. Black river.
- **Hú**. 湖水. Mt Lěi. 4.1.2.
- **Hú**. 湖水. Mt Kuāfù. 5.6.13. Ancient river name. Now in the Henan province, Lingbao prefecture, western part of Wénxiāng 阌乡 (in the past called Hú county 湖, in the Sui dynasty Wénxiāng county, and in 1954 merged with Lingbao county.
- **Huá**. 滑水. Mt Qiúrú. 3.1.2.
- **Huái**. 槐水. Mt Dūnyǔ. 3.3.29. The Pagoda River.
- **Huáizé**. 滚澤. Mt Yùfǎ. 3.1.19.
- **Huán**. 環水. Mt Tài. 4.1.11.
- **Huán**. 洹水. This river, now called Ānyáng hé 安阳河, is in the Henan province. Guopu suggests the pronunciation wán. Mentioned in 3.3.21.
- **Huáng**. 皇水. Mt Huángrén. 2.2.14.
- **Huáng**. 黃水. Mt Shénqūn. 3.3.21.
- **Huáng**. 黃水. The Yellow River.
- **Huángsuān**. 黃酸之水. Mt Shēng. 5.5.14.
- **Húguàn**. 湖灌之水. Mt Húguàn. 3.2.14.
- **Huì**. 惠水. Mt Báishí. 5.6.6.
- **Huò**. 濩水. Mt Sōngguǒ. 2.1.2. Guopu mentions that the *Shuijing* Zhu calls this river Guàn shuǐ 灌水. According to the *Shanhai jing* the Guàn shuǐ originates from Mt Shícuì (See SJ 2.1.6, and Gayou zhu's note about Guàn shuǐ 觀水 in SJ 2.3.6).
- **Huòhuò**. 濩濩水. Mt Shí. 3.3.35.
- **Hūtuó**. 虖沱. Mt Shí. 3.3.35. 虖 hū is written as 沲 chí in the Wukian's Transcript of the SHJ. This river is located in Shanxi province Xīn prefecture.
- **Jǐ**. 濟水. Mt Zhīlí. 5.11.10. Commentaries based on Hao Yixing suggest 泲水 Yù.
- **Jǐ**. 濟水. 5.11.1.
- **Jī**. 激水. Mt Zhú. 4.1.12. It may be the lake Dōngpíng (東平湖) located in Shāndōng
- **Jiā**. 夾水. Mt Báiyū. 2.4.10.
- **Jiàn**. 澗水. Mt Báishí. 5.6.6. This river originates from the south of Xin'an county.
- **Jiǎn**. 減水. Mt Fāntiáo. 4.1.5.

- **Jiǎn**. 减水. Mt Qí. 5.9.9. Hao Yixing mentions that Liu zhao in the *Junguo zhi*, citing this passage, writes 城水 chéng shuǐ instead of 减水 jiǎn shuǐ and that ancient texts sometimes have 堿 jiǎn instead of 减 jiǎn.
- **Jiān**. 蒹水. Mt Jiān. 5.2.7.
- **Jiāng**. [姜阝]水. Mt Lù. 3.3.38. Guopu suggests 郯水 Tán.
- **Jiāng**. 江水. Mt Mín. 5.9.2.
- **Jiāng**. 江水. Mt Lái. 5.9.3.
- **Jiāng**. 江水. Mt Jū. 5.9.4.
- **Jiāng**. 江. According to Guopu, in another text, this character is replaced by hǎi 海 the sea. Mentioned in 4.1.11.
- **Jiāng**. 江. The terms 江 jiān or 江水 jiānshuǐ were commonly used alone. They would mostly refer to the Yangtze river 长江. However the names of mountains and rivers in ancient texts, as well as the movements of rivers across time render these names sometimes unreliable and this could also apply to the Yangtze river. Today, these terms 江 jiān and 江水 jiānshuǐ systematically refer to the Yangtze river 长江. The translation uses this assumption throughout the text, to differentiate from regular waterways 江水.
- **Jiànghán**. 匠韓. Mt Guàntí. 3.1.13.
- **Jiāo**. 教水. Mt Jiāo. 3.3.9.
- **Jiāoshāng**. 交觴之水. Mt Guī. 5.6.3. According to the *Shuijing*, notes on the Luo, it is 交觸之水 jiāochù zhī.
- **Jígū**. [糸昔]姑之水. According to Guopu, [纟昔] sounds like jí. The *Ciyuan, Cihai, Hanyu daci dian* do not mention this character. For the *Hanyu dazi dian*, it sounds like zuó but the *Shanhai jing* is not mentioned.
- **Jíhuò**. 集獲. 2.1.16.
- **Jìn**. 晉. Mt Xiànyōng. 3.2.3. In ancient Shanxi, the State of Tang was renamed by Ji Xie to the State of Jin (晉國), after the Jin Shui (晉水) river that flowed through his domain.
- **Jǐng**. 景水. Mt Jǐng. 3.3.25.
- **Jīng**. 涇水. Mt Gāoshān. 2.2.4.
- **Jīng**. 涇水. Mt Jīnggǔ. 2.4.12. Guopu states that the water course of this river is unknown. A river of this name is mentioned in SJ 2.2.4.
- **Jīrǔ**. 激女水. 4.2.3. The *Erya* and the *Yupian* both say 激汝 jīrǔ instead of 激女.
- **Jíyú**. 即魚之水. Mt Fāshì. 5.2.2.
- **Jū**. 雎水. Mt Jǐng. 5.8.1.
- **Jué**. 渼水. 1.2.9.
- **Jué**. 潏水. 5.1.11.
- **Juéjué**. 决决之水. Mt Lónghóu. 3.3.2. Guopu, citing the *Taiping Yulan* (938), mentions that 决决 juéjué should be 决 jué.

- **Kǎn** (or Jiàn). 濫水. Mt Niǎoshǔ Tóngxué. 2.4.18. Flooding river.
- **Kōngsāng**. 空桑之水. Mt Kōngsāng. 3.3.33.
- **Kòu**. 滱水. Mt Gāoshì. 3.3.37.
- **Kuáng**. 狂水. Mt Kuáng. 3.2.7.
- **Kuáng**. 狂水. Mt Dàkǔ. 5.7.7.
- **Kuàng**. 貺水. Mt Jīng. 5.11.1.
- **Láirú**. 來需. Mt Bànshí. 5.7.8. The *Shuijing Zhu* (Scroll 15 - River Yī 伊水) says that "the river Láirú originates at Mt Bànshí."
- **Láo**. 勞水. Mt Niúshǒu. 5.1.11.
- **Láo**. 勞之水. 4.4.8.
- **Lì**. 櫟水. Mt Dānzhāng. 3.1.12.
- **Lǐ**. 澧水. Mt Gé. 4.2.5.
- **Lǐ**. 澧水. Mt Yǎ. 5.11.30.
- **Lǐ**. 澧 (澧水). A river in Hunan province, one of the Yangtze River's four largest tributaries in the province. 5.12.7
- **Liètú**. 列塗. 1.2.10.
- **Lìguó**. 歷虢之水. Mt Ráo. 3.3.40.
- **Lìjī**. 丽[鹿旨]. Mt Què. 1.1.2.
- **Lìjù**. 歷聚之水. Mt Zhè. 3.3.30.
- **Liú**. 留水. Mt Yáng. 3.3.6.
- **Lóngyú**. 龍餘之水. Mt Gǔwěi. 5.5.13.
- **Lóu**. 漊水. 3.3.34. 漊 lóu is written as 婁 lóu in the Wukian's Transcript of the SHJ.
- **Lù**. 鹿水. Mt Qūwú. 1.2.15.
- **Lún**. 倫水. Mt Lún. 3.3.42.
- **Lún**. 淪水. Mt Xuān. 5.11.31.
- **Luò**. 洛水. Mt Báiyū. 2.4.10.
- **Luò**. 洛水. Mt Zhìgāng. 2.4.14.
- **Luò**. 濼水. Mt Yuè. 4.1.8.
- **Luò**. 雒水. Mt Huānjǔ. 5.4.9. Ancient name of the Luò Hé 洛河 The Luò Hé rises in the southeast flank of Huashan in Shaanxi province and flows east into Henan province, where it eventually joins the Yellow River at the city of Gongyi.
- **Luò**. 洛水. Mt Mín. 5.9.1.
- **Luò**. 洛. This river is a tributary of the Yellow River. It rises in the southeast flank of Huashan in Shaanxi province and flows east into Henan province, where it joins the Yellow River at the city of Gongyi. While not a major river, it flows through an area of great archeological significance in the early history of China.
- **Luò**. 洛. 5.2.9. River in Henan and Shaanxi provinces.
- **Luò**. 洛水. 2.1.8.
- **Lǔyè**. 漊液水. 3.3.36.

- **Máo**. 旄水. Mt Dūntóu. 3.2.10.
- **Mén**. 門水. Mt Yánghuá. 5.6.14.
- **Méng**. 濛水. Mt Guī. 2.4.17. Misty river.
- **Miǎn**. 沔. 2.1.10, 4.1.10. Head of the Hàn River located in the southwest of the Shaanxi province.
- **Míng**. 明水. Mt Fànggāo. 5.7.6.
- **Míngzhāng**. 明漳之水. Mt Xiǎohóu. 3.3.16.
- **Mò**. 末水. Mt Mò. 5.7.16.
- **Mòtú**. 末塗水. Mt Dú. 4.1.10.
- **Mùmǎ**. 木馬之水. Mt Báimǎ. 3.3.32. It may be the contemporary Nánběi Hé 南北河. Lit. "River of the Vaulting Horse."
- **Ní**. 鯢水. Mt Ní. 5.11.29.
- **Niǎn**. [氵聯]水. Mt Wángwū. 3.3.8.
- **Niǎowēi**. 鳥危之水. Mt Niǎowēi. 2.2.8.
- **Niúshǒu**. 牛首水. Mt Xī. 3.3.24. Bull Head. This river is now called 西河 xī hé (Western River), or zhǔqìn shuǐ 渚沁水. It is located in the Western part of Hándān county, Héběi province.
- **Oū**. 歐水. 3.3.21.
- **Pàn**. 盼水. Mt Huáng. 2.1.17.
- **Pāng**. 滂水. Mt Hūshuò. 1.2.14.
- **Péng**. 彭水. Mt Dài. 3.1.3.
- **Péng**. 彭水. 3.3.29.
- **Píng**. 平水. Mt Píng. 3.3.12.
- **Púhōng**. 蒲[蔑鳥]之水. Mt Gé. 5.9.7. [蔑鳥] hōng is written 鸛 hōng is some versions.
- **Qí**. 瀑水. Mt Jǔrù. 3.3.20.
- **Qī**. 漆. Mt Yúcì. 2.1.10. Today the river Qī springs from this mountain Qí 岐 (Guopu).
- **Qī**. 淒水. Mt Guī. 2.1.19.
- **Qiàn**. 涔水. Mt Dàshí. 2.1.13. No clear description. A river 涔水 is the major water supplier of the Lǐ county in Hunan.
- **Qiáo**. 譙水. Mt Qiáomíng. 3.1.4.
- **Qiáo**. 潐水. Mt Chángzhēng. 5.6.12. Guopu, the *Hanyu dazi dian*, and the *Hanyu daci dian* say qiáo, the *Ciyuan* says jiào, and the *Cihai* has no entry.
- **Qìn**. 沁水. Mt Yèlì. 3.3.19.
- **Qìn**. 瀙水. Mt Jiān. 5.11.22. The original character is 視 shì but Guopu suggests 瀙水 Qìn. River Qìn is now on the southern slope.
- **Qìn**. 瀙水. 5.11.22, probably. The original text has 視水 River Shì. The correction here follows the suggestion of the annotation: According to Wangfu, 視水 should be 瀙水 River Qìn, now in the Nanyang prefecture, Henan Province. Guopu mentions that the Qìn river is now south of the

southern slope. According to Hao Yixing, 視 should be 瀙. The *Shuijing* states that the river Qìn (瀙) is in the northwest, the river Shā (殺) emerges in the southwest of Mt Dàshú (大孰之山), flows northwest and pours into the Qìn (瀙).

- **Qìnán**. 器難. Mt Shǎoxíng. 5.7.14. Guopu suggests that 器 could be 嚻 xiāo.
- **Qīng**. 清水. Mt Dàshí. 2.1.13. It could be related to Qīngshuǐ county in Tiānshuǐ 天水, Gānsù 甘肅 province.
- **Qīnglíng**. 清泠水. When Gēngfù appears, river Qīnglíng become red and lightening occurs. Alluded to in 5.11.6.
- **Qīngzhāng**. 清漳水. Mt Shǎo. 3.3.23. The pure river of Zhāng. One of the major rivers of Shanxi province. It originates in the 昔阳 Xīyáng county (晋中 Jìnzhōng).
- **Qiú**. 求水. Mt Qiú. 5.11.43.
- **Qiūshí**. 丘時之水. Mt Huáijiāng. 2.3.7.
- **Qū**. 區水. Mt Shēn. 2.4.4.
- **Qǔtán**. 娶檀之水. Mentioned in 4.1.12.
- **Qúzhū**. 渠豬水. Mt Qúzhū. 5.1.3. It flows in the Young-Luò district.
- **Rǔ**. 辱水. Mt Niǎo. 2.4.5. See also *Shuijing* 3 (He river).
- **Rǔ**. 乳水. Mt Liángyú. 5.5.12. The Milk river.
- **Rǔ**. 汝水.
- **Ruò**. 弱水. Mt Láo. 2.4.2. This river was known for its swallow course and was called "weak" because it is not even capable to carry the wisp of straw. See also *Shujing - Yugong*, HJ 5.12, 5.13, 6.16, *Hou Hanshu*, *Hanshu*, *Shiji*, and *Zizhi Tongjian*.
- **Sé**. 薔水. Mt Gāotú. 2.1.16.
- **Shā**. 沙水. Mt Lúqí. 4.2.9.
- **Shā**. 殺水. Mt Dàshú. 5.11.26.
- **Sháo**. 勺水. Mt Guìjì. 1.2.9.
- **Shǎo**. 少水. Mt Yīn. 5.1.14.
- **Shǎo**. 少水. Mt Zhànzhu. 5.6.4.
- **Shēn**. 申水. Mt Shēnshǒu. 2.4.11.
- **Shéng**. 繩水. Mt Jiéshí. 3.3.43. Also see SJ 3.3.5.
- **Shéng**. 澠水. Mt Tiānchí. 3.3.5. Ancient river in modern Shāndōng province.
- **Shèng**. 勝水. Mt Húqí. 3.2.4.
- **Shēng**. 生水. Mt Yú. 2.4.9.
- **Shí**. 食水. Mt Sǔzhǔ. The present-day name of this river is the Zī River (缁河) and it is located in Shāndōng. 4.1.1.
- **Shí**. 食水. Mt Běihào. 4.4.1.
- **Shī**. 師水. Mt Qín. 4.4.5.
- **Shī**. 尸水. Mt Shī. 5.5.11.

- **Shī**. 尸水. (see SJ 5.5.11).
- **Shígāo**. 石膏水. Mt Nǚzhēng. 4.4.4.
- **Shuǎng**. 爽水. Mt Gǔ. 5.6.7.
- **Sì**. 汜水. Mt Fúxī. 5.7.13. It originates in the Henan province, Gong county, southeast. In the north it flows into the Xingyang area, Sishui town, west. In the north it pours into the Yellow River.
- **Suān**. 酸水. Mt Shǎoyáng. 3.2.2.
- **Suǒ**. 潨水. Mt Dūnyǔ. 3.3.29.
- **Tài**. 太水. Mt Tài. 5.7.15.
- **Tàilù**. 泰陸. Mt Dǎoguò. 1.3.2. "Peaceful land." Mentioned in 3.3.29.
- **Táng**. 棠水. Mentioned in 3.1.8.
- **Tāng**. 湯水. Mt Shàngshēn. 2.4.6. Hot Springs River.
- **Tāng**. 湯水. Mentioned in 2.1.14.
- **Táo**. 桃水. Mt Lèyóu. 2.3.9. The peach river.
- **Tāodiāo**. 滔雕之水. Mt Bǐng. 5.4.5.
- **Tiáo**. 苕水. Mt Fúyù. 1.2.7.
- **Tiáo**. 苕水. Mt Lóngshǒu. 2.2.6. It was stated above that River Tiáo originates in Mt Fúyù (SJ 1.2.7).
- **Tiáo**. 苕水. Mt Yānzī. 2.4.19. Also written 若水 ruò. According to Guopu, citing Yu the Great (The waterways of the Wei River basin emerge from Yānzī Mountain) and supported by the *Chuci lisao*, Tiáo shuǐ and the Wěi are one and the same.
- **Tiáojiān**. 條菅水. Mt Xián. 3.3.4.
- **Tú**. 塗水. Mt Gāotú. 2.1.16.
- **Tuān**. 湍水. Mt Jīng. 5.11.1. Swift River. According to Guopu, it should be pronounced zhuān. Usually, the character 湍 is pronounced tuān.
- **Tuó**. 橐水. Mt Tuó. 5.6.11.
- **Túwú**. 涂吾之水. Guopu mentions that during the second year of the Yuan shou period of the Han (B.C. 127), horses emerged from this river. Mentioned in SJ 3.1.24.
- **Wèi**. 渭水. Mt Niǎoshǔ Tóngxué. 2.4.18. It flows east and pouring into the waters of the Yellow River. River of the Shaanxi province. It is the largest tributary of the Yellow River.
- **Wèi**. 渭. Mentioned in 2.1.10.
- **Wěi**. 鮪水. Mt Báishā. 3.2.5.
- **Wěi**. 洧水. Mt Xiù. 3.3.27. This small river still exists and is located in the Henan province.
- **Wǔ**. 潕水. Mt Cháogē. 5.11.2. A river now located in the Henan province.
- **Xiān**. 鮮水. Mt Běixiān, Northern. 3.1.24.
- **Xiān**. 鮮水. Mt Xiān. 5.2.4.

- **Xiāng**. 湘. 5.12.7. Originating from Haiyang Mountain (海陽山) in Lingui of Guangxi, the Xiāng is the largest river in Hunan and one of the largest tributaries of Yangtze River. It is 856-km long and 670-km of it is in Hunan.
- **Xiànyì**. 憲翼. 1.1.5.
- **Xiānyú**. 鮮于水. Mt Shí. 3.3.35.
- **Xiāo**. 囂水. Mt Bōzhǒng, Western. 2.1.14.
- **Xiāo**. 囂水. Mt Húnxī, Northern. 3.1.21.
- **Xiāo**. 囂水. Mt Zhuōguāng, Northern. 3.1.5.
- **Xiāo**. 瀟. 5.12.7. This river is both deep and clear. It flows into the Xiāng near Changsha.
- **Xiè**. [水射]水. Mt Zhānzhū. 5.6.4. Located in Henan province, Luoyang prefecture, west, Xin'an county south. It may also be written 灖水 and the *Shuijing*, notes on the Luo, writes 谢水.
- **Xiū**. 脩水. Mt Liángqú. 3.2.12.
- **Xiū**. 休水. Mt Shàoshì. 5.7.9.
- **Xú**. 洵水. Mt Xún. 1.2.13.
- **Xú**. 徐之水. Mt Yúyáng. 5.9.8.
- **Xuánhù**. 玄扈水. Mt Xuánhù. 5.4.9. Now located in the Shaanxi province, west of Luonan county. It originates in Mt Xuánhù and pours into the Luo. It is also known as the Luo confluence. This is where Cāngjié saw the turtle shell inscriptions (the ling gui fu shu) that led to the Chinese characters.
- **Xuānyú**. 宣余之水. Mt Fēngyǔ. 5.9.11.
- **Xún**. 洵水. Mt Xuānyuán. 2.3.12.
- **Xūn**. 熏水. Mt Dānxūn. 3.1.8.
- **Yàn**. 燕水. Mt Yàn. 3.3.39.
- **Yáng**. 洋. Mt Kūnlún. 2.3.8.
- **Yáng**. 陽水. Mt Sōng. 3.3.28.
- **Yáng**. 陽水. Mt Yáng. 5.2.5.
- **Yáng**. 楊水. Mt Yánghuá. 5.6.14.
- **Yànmén**. 鴈門之水. The river of the "Door of wild ducks." Mentioned in SJ 3.1.18.
- **Yànrǎn**. 厭染之水. Mt Fù. 5.6.10.
- **Yènǚ**. 液女水. Mt Tàixì. 3.3.34.
- **Yì**. 役水. Mt Yì. 5.7.17. Some write 侵 qīn instead of 役 (Guopu). The original annotation states that 役 should be 沒 méi.
- **Yī**. 伊水. Mt Guó. 3.1.6.
- **Yī**. 伊水. Mt Mánqú. 5.2.9.
- **Yī**. 伊水.
- **Yìgāo**. 嶧皋之水. Mt Yìgāo. 4.2.3.
- **Yīn**. 陰水. Mt Yīn. 2.4.1.

- **Yīn**. [石垔]水. Mt Yánghuá. 5.6.14. 4.2.17
- **Yīng**. 英水. Mt Qīngqiū. 1.1.9.
- **Yīng**. 英水. Mt Jǔ. 1.2.1. See 1.1.9
- **Yīng**. 英水. Mt Tiān. 2.3.20.
- **Yīnghóu**. 嬰侯之水. forest Dānlín. 3.3.19.
- **Yōngyōng**. 潚潚之水. Mt Yísū. 5.3.4. Now in Henan province, Song county west. In the Northern Wei dynasty, Li Daoyuan in the *Shuijing Shu* (Yi river) says that "this river emerges from Lùhún county (陆浑 old appellation now Song county northeast thirty li) of the southwest Wangmu gully (王母涧). On top of Mt Jiànběi (涧北山), there is the ancestral temple of Wangmu. Its death gave name to the small stream, in the east it flows into the river Yi, also called river yōngyōng."
- **Yōngyōng**. 潚潚之水. Mt Lí. 5.4.3. See SJ 5.3.4.
- **Yōu**. 泑水. Unknown. Mentioned in 2.3.2. This river has black waters (Guopu). In addition, there is the river yōu (SJ 2.3.1, 2.3.7, 3.1.1) and the marsh yōu (SJ 3.1.10, 3.1.13, 3.1.17).
- **Yú**. 禹水. Mt Yīng. 2.1.7.
- **Yú**. 魚水. Mt Guó, Extremity. 3.1.7. The Fish river.
- **Yú**. 餘水. Mt Liángyú. 5.5.12.
- **Yù**. 浴水. Mt Tàimào. 2.2.2.
- **Yù**. 浴水. Mt Chúnyú Wúféng. 3.3.46. According to Guopu, it is the Black River (hēishuǐ 黑水).
- **Yù**. 郁水. Mt Huān. 5.8.20.
- **Yù**. 淯. Mentioned in 1.1.10. Sometimes written 育. Ancient name of the river 白河 báihé in the Henan province.
- **Yuán**. 原水. Mt Gōushì. 4.2.14.
- **Yuán**. 沅. 5.12.7.
- **Yuān**. 涴水. Mt Yīngdī. 2.4.15.
- **Yúsuí**. 俞隨之水. Mt Guī. 5.6.3.
- **Zǎolín**. 蚤林之水. Mt Péngpí. 3.3.15. Lit. Herb paris.
- **Záyú**. 雜余之水. Mt Yú'é. 4.2.6.
- **Zégèng**. 澤更. Mt Lùwú. 1.2.16.
- **Zégèng**. 澤更. Mt Lùwú. 1.2.16.
- **Zhǎn**. 展水.
- **Zhān**. 瞻水. Mt Lóuzhuō. 5.6.5.
- **Zhāng**. 漳水. Mt Fājiū. 3.3.22. The *Shuowen* calls this river 涷水 Dòng. River located in Henan.
- **Zhāng**. 漳水. Mt Jīng. 5.8.2.
- **Zhěn**. 畛水. Mt Qīngyào. 5.3.2.
- **Zhènghuí**. 正回之水. Mt Guī. 5.3.3.
- **Zhǐ**. [氵只]水. Mt Xúnzhuàng. Tributary of the Shí River 食水. 4.1.3.
- **Zhú**. 逐. Mt Shí. 2.1.11. Guopu suggest it could be 遂 suì.

- **Zhú**. 竹水. Mt Zhú. 2.1.8. The "bamboo river".
- **Zhū**. 諸資. Mentioned in 2.1.16.
- **Zhūcì**. 諸次之水. Mt Zhūcì. 2.4.7.
- **Zhūhuái**. 諸懷之水. Mt Běiyuè. 3.1.20.
- **Zhuō**. [外門內豕]. Mt Chéng. 1.2.8. The character 豕 has been changed to 豕 in the Buddhist Canon Zangjing 藏經本.
- **Zhuóyù**. 濁浴. Mt Yīn. 2.3.16.
- **Zhuózhāng**. 濁漳水. Mentioned in 3.3.23. The muddy river of Zhāng.
- **Zhūpí**. 諸毗. Mt Zhūpí, Western. This term could also be understood as "the adjacent waterways." See SJ 2.3.7. Mentioned in 3.1.2.
- **Zhūshéng**. 諸繩之水. Mt Gāoshì. 4.1.7.
- **Zhūyú**. 諸餘之水. Mt Zhūyú. 3.2.9.
- **Zǐ**. 泚水. Mt Chángshā. 2.3.2. (modern pronunciation: cǐ)
- **Zī**. 滋水. Mt Gāoshì. 3.3.37. According to the *Shuowen*, this river, also known as river Zī 滋水, emerges from Mt Niúyǐn 牛飲 in the Báixíng 白陘 valley and then merges with river Hūtuó.
- **Zī**. 菑水. Mt Chángzhēng. 5.6.12.
- **Zǐtóng**. 子桐之水. Mt Zǐtóng. 4.4.6.
- **Zuǒ**. 佐水. Mt Nányú. 1.3.13.

Seas 海

- **Bóhǎi**. 渤海. Mentioned in 1.3.3. The sea between Liaodong and Shāndōng peninsulas. Ancient designation of the Zhílì golf 直隸 and of a region bordering this golf, under the Han dynasty and before.
- **Hǎi**. 海. Mentioned in 2.4.19.
- **Yáng**. 洋水. Ocean river, or ocean waters. Mentioned in 2.4.17.
- **Yòuhǎi**. 幼海. 4.3.9. Sea Yòu. In other words 少海 shǎohǎi. The *Huainanzi* says, in the east is found a big bank called shǎohǎi.
- **Běihǎi**. 北海. The Northern Sea. Cited in 4.4.1.

Spring 池

- **Hū** (hūchí). 虖池. Spring Hū. Written as 虖沱 hūtuó in SJ 3.3.32 to 3.3.37 but 沱 may be 池.

Valleys 谷

- **Gòng**. 共谷. 5.6.9.
- **Guàn**. 藋谷. 5.6.3. According to the *Shuowen*, 藋 guàn is also the writing of 萑 huán. There may be an identity between 藋谷 and 萑谷.
- **Jī**. 机谷. 5.5.2. Elm Valley
- **Shé**. 蛇谷. Snake valley.
- **Tāng**. 湯谷. Valley Tāng. This name is also found in HJ 4.10 and HJ 9.24.
- **Xiāogǔ**. 梟谷. 5.1.8. Valley Xiāo. Lit. Owls Valley.
- **Yùyí**. 育遺. 1.3.5. Guopu: maybe 隧 suì.
- **Zhōng**. 中谷. 1.3.10. Central valley.

Wells 井

- **Tiānjǐng**. 天井. 5.11.4. Heavenly Well. Also, acupuncture point (SJ10).

Winds 風

- **Tiáofēng**. 條風. 1.3.10. "Wind going through the twigs." It refers to the Northeastern wind dōngběifēng 東北風 (Guopu). It may be the diàofēng 调风 or the róngfēng 融风, gentle northeastern breezes.
- **Kǎifēng**. 凱风. 1.3.5. A southern wind. It is described in the *Shijing*, Odes of Bei 邶风 and Odes of Guo 国风.

Unclassified

- **Chǒutú**. 醜塗. 2.3.8. A river or mountain name. As a mountain, it is the mountain located in the extreme south. See also HJ 10.21 "There is a mountain called xiǔtú, the river Qīng "ends" there." That is this mountain.
- **Dàyú**. 大杅. 2.3.8. A river or mountain name.
- **Fàntiān**. 氾天. 2.3.8. A river or mountain name. As a mountain, "there is Fàntiān mountain; the river Chì is exhausted [there]." HJ 10.2.
- **Fǔmù**. 榑木. 4.3.9. This is the contemporary Fúsāng. See *Lushi Chunqiu*. "On the eastern side Yu arrived to the fǔmù country." Mentioned in 4.3.9.
- **Jǔwú**. 沮吳. 4.2.1. Geographical structure. This appears to be the Miào Island 廟島, which is north, not east of Mt Kōngsāng (See Schiffeler).

- **Liúhuáng**. 流黃. 1.2.1. It consists of the countries of Fēngshì 酆氏 and Xīnshì 辛氏 (See also Within the Four seas – Western Section, and Within the Four Seas).
- **Shālíng**. 沙陵. 4.2.1. Geographical structure. This appears to be the Tuō zǐ kào shā sandbar 拖子靠沙 in the Huáng Hǎi 黃海 or "Yellow Sea" off the eastern coast of Jiāngsū Province 江蘇省 (See Schiffeler).
- **Wúdá**. 無達. 2.3.8. A river or mountain name.
- **Yànmén**. 鴈門. 3.2.12. Geographical structure. Lit. "Wild gooses gate".
- **Yíng**. 滎. 5.11.2. Probably a river. The annotation of HJ 2.3 (Western Wastelands) mentions a river of this name originating from Mt Bùtíng (不庭之山 see HJ 2.3).
- **Zhūpí**. 諸毗. 1.2.7. Geographical structure. Guopu says it is a river name. However see SJ 1.2.1.
- **Zhūpí**. 諸毗. 1.2.1. Name for a river or a mountain: SJ 3.1.2 mentions a river and SJ 2.3.7 mentions a mountain (same ambiguity in SJ 1.2.7).

The Problem of Distances

The following table highlights some interesting inconsistencies when summing the distances mentioned in the SHJ. It is to my knowledge the first time these inconsistencies are been mentioned as even the original comments to the text do not mention them.

	Book	Distance Mentioned in SHJ (Column A)	Computed Distance (Column B)	Total Mentioned in SHJ	Total Computed from Sections (From Column A)	Total Computed (From Column B)
South	1.1.	2950	2690			
South	1.2.	7200	7210			
South	1.3.	6530	5730			
				16380	16680	15630
West	2.1.	2957	2817			
West	2.2.	4140	4570			
West	2.3.	6744	6640			
West	2.4.	3680	3585			
				17517	17521	17612
North	3.1.	5490	5680			
North	3.2.	5690	5240			
North	3.3.	12350	12440			
				23230	23530	23360
East	4.1.	3600	3500			
East	4.2.	6640	6640			
East	4.3.	6900	6400			
East	4.4.	1720	1700			
				18860	18860	18240
Center	5.1.	6670	937			
Center	5.2.	1670	1770			
Center	5.3.	440	80			
Center	5.4.	1670	1670			
Center	5.5.	2982	2982			
Center	5.6.	790	802			
Center	5.7.	1184	1056			
Center	5.8.	2890	3080			
Center	5.9.	3500	3650			
Center	5.10.	267	310			
Center	5.11.	3732	4415			
Center	5.12.	2800	1849			
				21371	28595	22601
			Grand Total:	64056	105186	97443

References

- *A Chinese Bestiary. Strange creatures from the Guideways through Mountains and Seas.* U. of California Press. Berkeley and Los Angeles, California. 2002. Strassberg, Richard E.
- *Baozang lun* 寶藏論. The Treasure of Buddha's Law.
- *Beitang shuchao* 北堂書鈔. Comp. by Yu Shinan 虞世南 (558–638; courtesy name Boshi 伯施).
- *Bencao pin hui jingyao.* 本草品汇精要. Collected Essentials of Species of Materia Medica. 1505. Comp. Liu Wentai 劉文泰.
- *Bencao Gangmu* 本草綱目. Materia Medica, a dictionary of Chinese herbs, written by Li Shi Zhen (1518-1593).
- *Chan-Hai-King. Antique géographie chinoise.* Tome Premier. J. Maisonneuve, Paris. 1891. de Rosny, Léon.
- *Chinese Kama Sutra.* Innovations & Information. 2007. Eric Serejski.
- *Chu xue ji* 初学记. Encyclopedia comp. under Xu Jian 徐坚 (659-729).
- *Chuci* 楚辭. Songs of Chu. Anthology of Chinese poems by Qu Yuan and Song Yu from the Warring States period and subsequent imitators of their poetic style. Consisting of fifty-eight short poems and six long poems, Chu Ci is the second oldest collection of Chinese poems in record. The poems Sorrows (Lisao 離騷) and Heavenly questions (Tianwen 天問) have references to the SHJ.
- *Chuxue ji* 初學記. Notes for Beginners.
- *Cihai* 辭海. Sea of Words. Comprehensive dictionary that remains a popular dictionary and has been frequently revised (1936). Shu Xincheng.
- *Ciyuan* 辭源. Sources of Words. Shanghai: Commercial Press. 1915. Rev. ed. 1939. Lu Erkui.
- *Conception of Terrestrial Organization in the Shan Hai Jing.* In: Bulletin de l'Ecole française d'Extreme-Orient. 1995. 82, pp. 57-110. Dorofeeva-Lichtmann, Vera.
- *Dan qian xu lu* 丹铅续录. Yang Shen 杨慎 (CE 1488-1559).
- *Di wang shi ji* 帝王世紀. Record of the Lives of Emperors and Kings. Book in one folio compiled by 皇甫謐 Huangfu Mi (215 - 282).
- *Dushi Fangyu Jiyao* 读史方輿纪要. Essence of Historical Geography or Essentials of Geography for Reading History. Book written by the Qing Dynasty geographer Gu Zuyu (顾祖禹, 1631-1692 or 1624-1680), between 1630 and 1660.
- *Erya* 爾雅. Oldest extant Chinese dictionary or Chinese encyclopedia dating from about 3rd century BC.

- *Flora of China Project.*   http://flora.huh.harvard.edu/china/.   Harvard University Herbaria.
- *Guan cang hai* 觀滄海. Looking at the Ocean (from MT Jiéshí). Cáocāo 曹操.
- *Guang Qun fangpu* 廣群芳譜. Enlarged Thesaurus of Botany 1718. Wang Hao 汪灝.
- *Guangya* 廣雅/广雅. The Expanded [Er]ya. An early 3rd century CE Chinese dictionary, edited by Zhang Yi 張揖 during the Three Kingdoms period. It was later called the Boya 博雅 (Bóyǎ; "Broadened [Er]ya") owing to naming taboo on Yang Guang (楊廣), which was the birth name of Emperor Yang of Sui.
- *Guangyun* 廣韻. Extensive Rimes. Dictionary - Chinese rimes.
- *Guanzi* 管子. [Writings of] Master Guan. Encyclopedic compilation of Chinese philosophical materials named after the 7th century BCE philosopher Guan Zhong. Edited by Liu Xiang circa 26 BCE.
- *Gujin zhu* 古今注. Note Old and New. Cui Bao 崔豹, ca. 300 CE.
- *Hanshu* 漢書. Book of Han. Dictionary. Classic Chinese historical writing covering the history of the Western Han Dynasty (206 BCE-9 CE). It is also sometimes called Qian Hanshu (前漢書, "Book of the Former Han") in order to distinguish it from the Hou Hanshu ("Book of the Later Han"), which covers the Eastern Han Dynasty..
- *Hanyu daci dian* 漢語大詞典/汉语大词典. Comprehensive Chinese Word Dictionary.
- *Hanyu dazi dian* 漢語大字典/汉语大字典. Comprehensive Chinese Character Dictionary.
- *Hou Hanshu* 後漢書. History of the Later Han. Dictionary.
- *Huainanzi* 淮南子. The Masters/Philosophers of Huainan. 2nd century BCE Chinese philosophical classic from the Han dynasty.
- *Huangdi Neijing Suwen* 黃帝內經. The Inner Canon of Huangdi or Yellow Emperor's Inner Canon.
- *Jiaoliao fu* 鷦鷯賦. Rhapsody on the Wren. 1st or 2nd century BCE. Zhang Hua (232-300).
- *Jingdian tu du shanhai jing* 经典图读山海经.
- *Junguo zhi* 郡國志. Junguo Administrative geography. Liu Zhao 劉昭.
- *Kangxi zidian* 康熙字典. Kangxi Dictionary.
- *Langtaosha Beidaihe* 浪淘沙·北戴河. Beidaihe, to the Melody of Langtaosha (Ripples Sifting Sand). Poem. Mao Zedong.
- *Liexian zhuan* 列仙傳. Biographies of Immortals. Liu Xiang 劉向 (attributed to).
- *Liezi* 列子.
- *Lushi Chunqiu* 呂氏春秋. Mister Lü's Spring and Autumn [Annals]. Dictionary. Encyclopedia compiled around 239 BCE under the Qin Dynasty Lü Buwei.

- *Mahaparinirvana Sutra.* One of the three great masterpieces of Mahayana Buddhism. The Nirvana Sutra (Chinese: Nièpán Jīng (涅槃經).
- *Maoshi mingwu tushuo* 毛詩名物圖說. Histoire naturelle du Livre canonique des Poésies.
- *Mu tianzi zhuan* 穆天子传. The travels of Mu, the Son of Heaven. Work of Xian Qin Dynasty, including six volumes recording Zhou Mu Wang's travels, unearthed during the second year of Emperor Jing Wu's reign (281 A.D). Guo Pu 郭璞.
- *Peiwen Yunfu* 佩文韻府. Dictionary - James Legge calls it the "Kangxi Thesaurus", not to be confused with the Kangxi dictionary.
- *Qi min yao shu* 齊民要術. Main techniques for the welfare of the people. The book is believed to have been completed in the second year of Wu Ding of Eastern Wei, C.E. 544, while another account gives the completion between C.E. 533 and 544. Jia Sixie.
- *Qiong zhu zhang* 邛竹杖. The Qiong Bamboo Cane. 16th AD. Xu Zhongxing 徐中行.
- *Ruan Ji Qin Si Fu* 阮籍 清思赋. Rhapsody on Pure Thinking.
- *Sancai tuhui* 三才圖會. Illustrations of the Three Powers, Illustrated Sino-Japanese Encyclopedia.
- *Sanhuang benji* 三皇本纪. History of the Three Emperors, Chapter of *Shǐjì* by Sima Zhen.
- *Shanhai jing* 山海經.
- *Shen Yue ji* 沈约集.
- *Shengshi qiji changming* 省试骐骥长鸣. Provincial Examination of the steed yowl. Zhang Xiaobiao 章孝标 (791-873).
- *Shiji* 史記. Sima Qian.
- *Shijing* 詩經. Book of Odes.
- *Shu Yi Ji* 述異記. Extraordinary stories. Commonly ascribed to Liang Ren Fang 梁任昉 (460-508).
- *Shuijing Zhu* 水經注. Notes on the Book of Rivers or Comments of the Water Classic. Li Daoyuan (Northern Wei).
- *Shuijing* 水經. Waterways Classic.
- *Shujing* 書經.
- *Shuowen* (Jiezi) 說文 (abbreviation of 說文解字注). Dictionary.
- *Taiping Yulan* 太平御覽. Imperial Readings of the Taiping Era.
- *The Classic of Mountains and Seas.* Penguin. 1999. Anne Birrell.
- *The Nine Songs. A Study of Shamanism in Ancient China.* City Lights. 1973. Arthur Waley.
- *The Songs of the South. An Ancient Chinese Anthology of Poems by Qu Yuan and Other Poets.* Penguin. 1985. David Hawkes.
- *Xi jing fu* 西京賦. Western Metropolis Rhapsody.
- *Xiandai Hanyu Cidian* 现代汉语词典. Contemporary Chinese Dictionary.

- *Xu Hanshu* 续汉书. Continued History of the Han.
- *Yiqie jing yinyi.* 切經音義.
- *Yiwen Leiju* 藝文類聚. Collection of Literature Arranged by Categories. Could be Rosny's Piwen Yunfu.
- *Yiwu zhi* 異物志. History of Extraordinary Things.
- *Yupian* 玉篇. Dictionary. Circa 543 CE. Gu Yewang (顧野王; 519-581), editor.
- *Zhouli* 周禮/周礼.
- *Zhuangzi* 莊子.
- *Zizhi Tongjian* 資治通鑒. Comprehensive Mirror to Aid in Government. Reference work in Chinese historiography, published in 1084.
- Chén Yìguāng. *Setting the term「epidemic illness 疫疾」in the traditional Chinese medicine canons - Collecting and Indexing.* J Chin Med 15(1): 39-46, 2004

www.ingramcontent.com/pod-product-compliance
Lightning Source LLC
Chambersburg PA
CBHW022016120726
47902CB00012B/314